BRINDY POLARIS

BRINDY POLARIS

A Novel of the American West
1866–1972

By Kerry McCan

MEDIO PRESS
Box 146
106 1/2 South Main Street
Victoria, Texas 77902

A map that illustrates the route of the cattle drive depicted in this novel appears on Page 98. The author also extends his grateful acknowledgement to Dian Malouf, who provided the cover photograph, and to Hillary Napier, who designed the cover.

ISBN 0-9652404-0-1

*Dedicated to my nephew, George R. Cannon, Jr.,
who first read and edited this book. He was lost to
lightning in the spring of 1992.*

Author's Notes

Taking place between 1866 and 1872, *BRINDY POLARIS* is a story about driving wild cattle from South Texas to market at the Kansas railheads. The story culminates in an 1,800-mile drive of 5,000 head to stock Montana ranches.

The principal characters are associated with the cattle trade and most of them are treated from a commercial and financial aspect, not a romantic one.

Brindy Polaris is a longhorn cow that leads the drive to Montana. She is anthropomorphic.

There is in the story a mix of historical characters, among them Abel H. "Shanghai" Pierce, the Indians Gall, Wash-a-kie, and others. Historically and geographically correct to the best of my knowledge, the book portrays the nineteenth-century cattle trade as it really developed. Although it lasted only 20 years (1865—1885), profits from that period funded almost all the large ranches in latter-day Texas.

The book's love story, while germane, is secondary to the central theme: the growth and settlement of the trans-Mississippi west; the fur trade, homesteading, and Indian wars of pacification.

Organized in four parts, Part I defines John Dunigan. Part II, "The Deal," describes preparations for driving 5,000 head of cattle to Montana. Part III covers that drive. Part IV is "The Epilogue."

Throughout his life, John Dunigan tries to control his circumstances as much as he can, so he isn't carried along by events and can protect himself and his family fortunes. He is seldom surprised, which is very much in keeping with his character.

The settings are divided among Dunigan's home in Refugio and the area variously called the wild horse desert, the Nueces strip, the Brasada, and South Texas, that part of the state between the Nueces and Rio Grande rivers, whose control was the rationale for the Mexican War of 1846—48. Other locales: the Chisholm Trail, the Western Trail, the Mormon Trail, and their conclusions at Abilene, Newton, and Dodge City, Kansas, and Fort Fetterman, Wyoming. The larger area is the Great Plains of the central United States, from northern Mexico to Canada, and from St. Louis and Kansas City to Denver.

The characters are as historically accurate as I could draw them. I knew some of them as a boy, and listened to tales of the old cattle drives, some of them admittedly second and third hand. I hope the story conveys a true picture of that turbulent time.

—*Kerry McCan*
Victoria, Texas
Spring 1994

PART I

Dunigan

Chapter 1

The New Orleans mail packet had been tied to the Galveston wharf for an hour before a smiling John Dunigan finally appeared on deck, his back slightly bowed from the burden of his clothes, saddle, arms and other assortments. He had good reason to be mightily pleased with himself. Not only had Dunigan's herds brought over $80,000 at Abilene, Kansas, he had been almost as successful on the river boat from Kansas City to New Orleans, simply by staying out of a crooked poker game in the boat's saloon. There had been no game on the packet.

Dunigan gestured at a young deckhand. "Hey there, sonny, would you be giving me a hand with this gear?" As soon as he told the boy to move his necessaries to the pier and into a hired carriage, Dunigan's long stride carried him down the gangplank and into the shipping office.

"Any messages or mail for John Dunigan?" he asked the clerk, who pulled a letter and a telegram from the D slot in the pigeonhole rack behind him. Quickly, Dunigan slit the wire envelope and unfolded the message confirming receipt by his St. Louis bank of the cattle proceeds from Kansas. The last item was the balance after his loan was liquidated.

The letter, from Calvin Block in San Antonio, looked more interesting. Tucking the envelope into his shirt pocket, Dunigan thanked the clerk, then stepped out into the warm, muggy September sunlight and strode rapidly along the pier toward his carriage.

Flipping a silver coin to the boy who had loaded his baggage, Dunigan told the driver which hotel he wanted and the rig moved off.

In his room, Dunigan opened the letter. Calvin Block was one of the early trail bosses, but Dunigan had not seen much of him since Block had become more of a trader and broker. The man made all kinds of deals: cattle, to be sure, but land, finance—anything potentially profitable that crossed his path— even a little politicking.

> *Friend John,*
>
> *I have a proposition that you may be interested in. It involves taking cows to Montana to stock a ranch for some Englishman. They have plenty of money and will pay generously.*
>
> *If you are interested in this venture, meet me in San Antonio on the 25th day of September. I will be at the Menger Hotel on Alamo Plaza.*
>
> *Your friend,*
> *Calvin Block*

Rereading the letter, Dunigan pondered it for a bit. If Block was involved, there would certainly be money to be made. He knew the man that well at least. But driving cows all the way to Montana from Texas? A substantial chore, indeed.

At least the date was no problem—Dunigan was leaving for St. Mary's the following afternoon and that boat would deliver him in Refugio by the twelfth. He'd have plenty of time to check on things at his place on the Aransas River and still reach San Antonio for the meeting with Block.

Chapter 2

According to the standards of the time, John Dunigan did not consider himself unusual. He was born Sean Dunigan in 1835 in County Cork near Fermoy, to an Irish peasant family farming a small plot on the estate of the Earl of Spey Marnock. When Sean was six, after his father had died of a fever, the boy, his mother and two older sisters were evicted from the farm and went to live in the village of Fermoy.

With scant work there and even less money, after two years the family decided Sean would go to Texas, joining his uncle in the Power Colony at Refugio. Arriving at Indianola in 1843, the little boy had traveled the forty or so miles overland to meet his uncle at his family farm on the Aransas River. Sean had felt right at home, because all the Power colonists were Irish and so were the adjacent McMullen and McGloin colonies.

Rebellious by instinct and experience, the Irish immigrants had supported enthusiastically the Texian revolt, only a few having serious reservations about splitting from a Catholic nation to join the predominantly Protestant independence movement.

Aloysius Dunigan, Sean's uncle, harbored little religious bias. Oh, he went to mass if his wife Jane persuaded him to, but he was more concerned with the natural perils threatening his cotton farm and his horses and cattle than any threat to his own mortal soul. Which suited just fine kindred spirit Sean.

The boy loved the wild South Texas coastal prairie, learning quickly to hunt, and supplying much of the meat for his aunt's table. Hunting and trapping also kept a few coins in his pockets, the surplus he sent off to his family in Fermoy. There was never a lot, because there wasn't much ready cash in the fledgling Republic of Texas.

After Texas was annexed by treaty to the United States in 1845, Sean Dunigan became an American, celebrating his citizenship by changing his first name to John. He announced his new identity in the town saloon the night annexation was proclaimed. "Now that we are all Americans, I shall no longer be Sean Dunigan. As befits my new status as an American, from now on I shall be known to one and all as John Dunigan, American citizen!"

He raised his glass high to a chorus of whooping celebrants shouting his new name and toasting him and their new country. Otherwise, Dunigan's life was largely unaffected by that momentous event, except cash became more common in Texas with the advent of the Mexican-American War the following year. The passage of hungry federal troops through the area meant John's uncle could supply them with beef and horses.

John was able to send a bit more money home to Ireland because Aloysius had paid him some wages during the war. While not exactly booming, South Texas became more prosperous and began to attract settlers and investors. Dunigan made some money rounding up wild cattle, plentiful in the land west and south of the Aransas River, selling them to a tannery and abattoir in nearby Rockport.

In 1855, at twenty, he had saved enough to buy a small place of his own over toward San Patricio, across the Aransas from his uncle's farm. Dunigan kept right on gathering, taming, and selling horses and cattle. A born trader and swapper, he prospered in those years. By the time the Civil War erupted in 1860, he had acquired more acreage and a substantial herd.

Never a slave owner and preoccupied with operating and expanding his own holdings, Dunigan wasn't much interested in the war between the states. Nominally a Unionist, he wasn't too enthusiastic about either side and had little patience with firebrands of either persuasion.

One night in Refugio, Dunigan passed a recruitment rally outside one of the saloons. James Collins, a prosperous cotton and cattle operator called him.

"John! Will you come with us to fight the Yankees? We need all you strong young men to repel the blackguards."

"Does that 'we' mean you're going to war, too, Mister Collins?" Dunigan said with only the slightest hint of a twinkle.

Collins's broad grin was erased by a scowl, then his features eased into deep chagrin. "Alas, John, I've been told I'm too old to bear arms." He perked up a bit. "But I am supplying the company with uniforms and arms." Collins stepped back quickly when Dunigan drew his Colt revolver from his waistband.

Smiling, Dunigan reversed the pistol and handed it grip first to Collins. "Then here's my contribution, too, Mister Collins. You be sure to see it is well used."

As Dunigan strolled away, he left a somewhat flabbergasted Collins standing on the board sidewalk holding the Colt, his jaw sagging against his shirt collar.

After Texas seceded and joined the Confederacy, Dunigan stayed out of the army, preferring to tend to his business. However, when federal troops were withdrawn from the Confederacy and the western frontier, Indian raids beyond the Brazos and Mexican banditry below the Nueces became a problem in the state.

In 1857, Dunigan served in the Nueces Strip in a Ranging Company, which had driven the bandidos back beyond the Rio Grande. After war came, he was called up again in 1862, because he was known to the Rangers and there were few fighting men left in Texas.

Once again, in 1864, John was enlisted by the Rangers, this time on a West Texas patrol against marauding Comanches and Kiowas. Dunigan liked the country beyond the Brazos and thought about moving there once the Indian menace was re-moved. By nature and inclination a businessman, Dunigan resented slightly the time he had to spend away from his ranch to campaign with the Rangers. Even so, he tolerated his role as a civic duty. A keen tracker, he was valuable to the ranging companies, but too committed to his own interests ever to be more than a part-timer.

During the 1864 expedition, Dunigan and four other Rangers were on the right flank defending against a Comanche charge, when twenty or so Indians broke the Ranger line. Dunigan, Dick Wharton, Jim Scott, "Tish" Bell and Zack Fenton were forced apart from the main Ranger body by the Comanche onslaught.

Spotting a buffalo wallow about 30 yards to his left, Dunigan hollered to the others, "Follow me, boys! Come on back here and we'll fight on foot."

The five quickly rode to the mud hole, dismounted and

pulled their horses onto the ground as a rampart. Almost at once, as the Comanches charged, the quintet laid down withering fire from the two repeating pistols each man carried. Quickly, Dunigan realized they had better establish some fire discipline or they'd be out of cartridges well before they ran out of Indians.

After another foray, Dick Wharton was dead with an arrow in his throat and Tish took one in his right thigh.

Dunigan took over. "Tish, you handle reloading and the rest of us, we'll do all the firing. Zack, you and Jim give Tish your gun with the least bullets in it and keep the other. I think we can keep 'em off us if we conserve shells."

Tish's fingers were a blur as he shoved cartridges into the revolvers and flipped the loaded weapons to his mates. The three shooters fended off five more Indian assaults, stacking up seventeen dead Comanches in front of the wallow. Finally, one brave avoided the fire and got close enough to skewer Zack to the ground with his lance. Before he could withdraw, Tish blew the Indian off his horse.

Just then, the main body, having defeated most of the Comanches, arrived to drive off the braves attacking the wallow. "'Bout time you all stopped drinking coffee long enough to give us a hand here," Dunigan hollered to the troop leader when he passed at a gallop. "We were just about out of cartridges."

"Jim, are you all right?" he asked Scott.

"Few scratches is all, John, thanks to you and Tish."

"Well, slide on over here, then, and let's get that arrow out of Tish's leg, before he turns this mud hole into a blood hole." By the time the troop returned with fresh horses to replace the animals that had formed their "fort," Tish was ready to ride, the arrow out and his leg bandaged.

When the three survivors chose not to take scalps from their foe, the other Rangers decided they wouldn't either, figuring they hadn't the right.

*　*　*　*　*

After Appomattox, Texans expected federal troops to come back and continue their frontier protection efforts. They came back all right, but most were stationed in East Texas, mainly to enforce the strict edicts of postwar reconstruction.

These jack-leg troops were little interested in protecting a former rebellious state from the depredations of either Indians or Mexican bandidos. Too often, it was hard to tell which of the marauders stole more from the Texans—men in blue or indigenous redskins and border hoppers.

While the old South had been totally impoverished by battle and economic disaster, Texas was slightly better off because considerably less of the state's capital had been invested in human beings. Besides, the native longhorn cattle, untended while the men were off to the war for four years, were plentiful enough to save Texas from the worst effects of reconstruction.

Dunigan's last stint with the Rangers came in spring 1866, against some troublesome Comanches in northwest Texas. In the absence of federal troops, the Indians had become bolder. The Ranger troop had no official standing and was clandestine, because any armed body of Texans was discouraged by federal authorities.

The Rangers dealt the Comanches a very bloody nose in a skirmish along the Pease River. That night Dunigan decided his fighting days were over. Back in Austin, Sergeant John Dunigan made it clear to Ranger headquarters that he had campaigned for the last time. Reluctantly, the Ranger staff accepted his resignation.

At six-three and a hundred and eighty pounds, John Dunigan was imposing—strong, with broad shoulders, long arms and legs. On a horse, he resembled a centaur.

With his jet black hair and brown-black eyes, his almost swarthy complexion, Dunigan was a typical black Irishman. Doubtless, he had descended from some vagrant Moorish survivor of the Spanish Armada, who had somehow washed ashore upon the verdant slopes of Ireland.

Even after his years in Texas, Dunigan still retained a faint lilt of Irish brogue. The other holdover from his Gaelic past was a visceral Celtic belief in himself, which sometimes made him appear almost regally arrogant. Whether it did nor not, Dunigan was utterly confident he could ride, shoot, fight, and think better than anyone else and believed those qualities were a gift from the Almighty or some similar deity. That confidence was tempered by a strong sense of reality, so Dunigan was well aware of his limitations, too. Whenever he failed at anything, he was always sure it was because he hadn't worked or wanted hard enough.

Like many Celts, and especially Irishmen, John Dunigan devoutly detested the English, particularly those nonresident Sassenach families with Irish estates. More often than not, they treated their human Irish tenants far worse than the livestock they owned. Dunigan blamed his family's landlord, the Earl of Spey Marnock, for his own father's death and for his family's consequent poverty.

"Bloody Sassenachs" were anathema to John Dunigan and would remain so for the rest of his life.

Chapter 3

By fall 1866, a few Texas cattlemen had made successful drives to Baxter Springs, Kansas, and gotten good prices. The more Dunigan heard about the drives, the more they intrigued him. The following spring he vowed he would find some way to participate.

Some weeks later, Dunigan joined a cow hunt on the lower Nueces and his share earned him two hundred steers. The hunt was promoted by Tom Cameron, a drover from Gonzales, who intended to drive four herds north the following spring. Cameron had fronted supplies for the hunt so he could acquire most of the captured cattle to fill out his drive herds.

When Cameron offered to buy Dunigan's steers for seven dollars, a premium price, the Irishman's reply surprised the trader.

"Mister Cameron, I'd like to suggest a different deal altogether." Dunigan paused and considered Cameron for a moment.

The drover was tall, graying, and thickening a bit around the middle like most men entering their fifties. A shrewd but fair cowman who treated his hands and his horses with consideration, Cameron had a good reputation in the area and he'd been quite successful as a drover.

"What is it you want, Dunigan? Did I not make you a fair enough offer?" The older man tucked his thumbs into his belt and squinted suspiciously.

"That you did, Mister Cameron, but I want to go up the trail with one of your herds. I have two hundred more steers at home, and I propose to put them together with these and travel with you to Kansas and sell them there. I will supply my own horses and just be one of your hands.

"All I ask is that you feed me on the trail. My steers would be handled and sold just like yours. I expect you have seen enough of me by now to realize I am a fair hand. I know how to follow orders and I don't cause trouble. Compared with your other hands, all I want to do is get my cattle sold at Kansas prices. Besides, these Nueces steers could use a little taming before spring, and I expect to accomplish that this winter."

Cameron stroked his jaw with a weather-beaten hand while he considered Dunigan's proposal. Such arrangements were common and the drover knew he'd be getting a top hand. If what he had heard about Dunigan's Ranger exploits was true, he'd have an experienced scout, too. And at no extra expense. All he'd be out would be the profit he'd make on Dunigan's steers.

Cameron realized he'd be putting a competitor into business for the future, but he likely couldn't keep the Irishman out anyway.

"All right, Dunigan, I'll do it. The herd will make up at my place on the Guadalupe outside of Gonzales the fifteenth of March. Be there on time with your four hundred head. I'll not wait for you." Cameron held out his hand to seal the compact.

Shaking it, Dunigan fixed his brown-black eyes on the older man's. "I'll be there, Mister Cameron, don't ye worry. And I'll bring everything I'll be needing."

*   *   *   *   *

That winter, Dunigan broke and trained three young horses before taming and breaking his steers to trail. On a trip to Gonzales, he learned Cameron branded his animals with a long L, so on it went, next to Dunigan's lazy D.

The cattle wintered over well, actually adding flesh in the mild South Texas climate. Dunigan spent some of that time mending his traps, tack, and arms. He decided to bring his Henry rifle and a Navy Colt, both in .44 caliber, thereby reducing his ammunition burden. All of his gear was sound, but well used.

Dunigan replaced all the strings on his saddle, but the other repairs were minor—like patching a few leaks in his black slicker. He also braided two new rawhide ropes, two horsehair cinches and three bridles. In the fall, he'd made a new pair of shotgun leggins that became well broken in that winter.

By mid-February, Dunigan figured he was well fixed to travel up the trail and was excited by the prospect. He was right antsy by the time March 1 rolled around and the time came to drive his own cattle out of the river bottom where they had wintered.

On March 10, Dunigan's Uncle Aloysius, his son Ben, and Jimmy Lomax, their hand, arrived to help drive the herd to Gonzales. Late on the thirteenth, they reached Cameron's place on the Guadalupe and threw their stock in with the main bunch. Dunigan turned in his horses to Cameron's remuda and tossed his warbag in the wagon.

After visiting with Cameron, the elder Dunigan and his companions headed back to Refugio, and John moved into Cameron's bunkhouse to wait for the drive.

At daylight on the fifteenth of March, 1867, the first Cameron herd moved up the trail for Kansas. As trail boss and overall foreman of the herd, Pete Smollett did all the hiring and firing, issuing all orders, subject only to suggestions from Cameron, who would soon have three other herds on the trail. Cameron's chief duty was marketing the cattle once they got to Kansas.

Pete Smollett was capable, completely loyal to Cameron and apparently without much ambition to be on his own. Averse to risk, he was an ideal employee. Raised on a Georgia plantation, Pete was assistant overseer when the war broke out in '61. He'd served four years in the Confederate cavalry before drifting over to Texas after Appomattox.

For two years he had worked for Cameron, a fellow CSA veteran. Pete was as good with men as he was with stock.

Besides Dunigan, the rest of the hands included ten riders, a remuda of fifty horses supervised by a young Mexican wrangler, and a wagon driven by Jeremiah Bass, a former slave and a fine camp cook.

The 2,463 steers in the herd ran the first five miles before milling and sulling, so the crew drove them until dark, then put them onto the bedground with night riders to guard them.

The next day was a little better, except the cattle didn't run as far, but they had a long mill. Finally, during the third day, the animals began to line out and by the end of the fifth were pretty well trail broke.

From then on, the herd made about fifteen miles a day and everything went well all the way to the Colorado River crossing. The weather was fair and the grub was good. The well-marked and often-used ford was no problem for the men or their charges.

The crew was getting along well and the steers were moving steadily and calmly, gaining strength and flesh as they waded through the fresh spring grass, green as Dunigan remembered his Emerald Isle homeland. That year in central Texas, colors abounded. Following a dry mild winter and early spring rains, bright bluebonnets and pink-orange Indian blankets painted the hillsides.

Most days, Dunigan rode ahead scouting waterholes and bed-grounds, trying to spot any signs of Indians or cow thieves so he could give early alarm. Breaking trail, he got the first unspoiled look at the countryside dressed in its fresh spring clothes, sighing at such beauty. Just when they were making good time for the Brazos crossing the fickle Texas weather intervened. All of a sudden the wind shifted strong out of the north and a fine drizzle was driven straight into their faces. That wretched pattern persisted for three days, then the rain came down even heavier. Thankfully, the temperature went up, but everyone and everything was soaked.

Without dry bedground the steers became tired and edgy. So did the drovers. Slogging through deep mud, as the animals passed their hooves cut a deep scar in the land.

Dunigan was spared most of the worst slogging because he was out front scouting. Finding water was no longer a problem—it was everywhere. But dry bedgrounds were scarce. He wasn't spared the soggy food and cold coffee, either. Under those conditions, not even Jeremiah Bass could manage decent grub.

When Pete complained, Jeremiah said, "Mist' Pete, ain' noway I can be puttin' out good grub less'n I can keep it under cover. Lemme mosey on ahead a ways and set up camp under a tarp. At least the grub'll be dry when you all gets there."

Chuckling at Jeremiah's grand dry food strategy, Pete quickly agreed and for the next few days the food situation was much improved.

After a week in the murky stuff, Pete Smollett took Dunigan

aside. "John, ride on ahead to the Brazos and see if it's even crossable. If not, try and find some good grazing for us so we can hold the cattle till the river drops."

Dunigan left at once, grabbing some supplies so he could camp out. Three days later, he reached the Brazos, finding it in full flood and about 600 yards across at the ford. The third day of his scout had been a more pleasant ride through warm spring sunshine. The next day, he located a suitable pasture about five miles upriver. Turning back toward the herd, he recalled patrolling the area during his Ranger service.

Two days south of the river, he met the herd. Although the spring sun had been shining for three days, there were still muddy spots along the trail, but things were generally a lot dryer.

When Dunigan told Pete what he'd found along the Brazos, the drover just grinned and shrugged. "Hell, John, I about had it figured we'd have to spend a few days waiting for the Bloody Brazos to find its banks again. 'Sides, we can all use a couple days' rest. Even the steers."

The sun continued to beam down and everyone's spirits glowed right along with it.

When the herd reached the pasture Dunigan had found, the animals were allowed to spread out and graze. Too tired to eat, many of the steers dropped where they stood. The hands were almost as weary, but took a few moments to stretch their damp clothes across every available tree limb and bush around the pasture. Before long, the whole area resembled a gypsy camp, reminding Dunigan of the itinerants whose caravans sometimes stopped at his village in Ireland.

After checking the water level at the ford, Pete announced they'd rest for at least a week. The respite gave everyone a chance to repair the ravages of the wet spell. On the fourth day, a brisk spring norther blew in and cooled things down.

At that point, Pete called a meeting and declared they would be following a new trail north of the Brazos. Instead of western Missouri, their new destination was "end of the track" in Kansas in a town called Abilene. An Indian trader named Jess Chisholm had marked a trail through the Indian territory to Abilene and early reports were favorable about both the new route and the Kansas cattle market.

Abilene was about 150 miles north of the territories and some 350 miles west of the Mississippi, just east of the middle of

Kansas. In the early settlement days before the war, the area was part of the battleground called "Bloody Kansas," scene of some of the fiercest conflicts between proslavery and abolition factions.

Only last year had the railroad finally been extended to Abilene, during the first spate of construction beyond the Missouri River. Now the cattle drives were taking advantage of the shorter distance. Besides its other virtues, Abilene was also far enough west to be beyond the range of Missouri raiders left over from the war.

After Pete's announcement, the hands exchanged comments about the new plans. Some were not too thrilled about going to Kansas. Harvey Langer, a usually taciturn Missourian admitted he been in Kansas during the war while riding with Quantrill. "Shoot, boys, I can hardly recollect the places I went, they're so small. More like wide spots in the road."

Although most of the others were Confederate vets, too, they weren't happy to hear about Langer's service experience. They generally considered Quantrill's Raiders little better than bloodthirsty outlaws, not soldiers. Then too, because of its recent history, Kansas was almost a metaphor for what had gone wrong in the war.

"Kansas jes' ain't much to mah likin'," drawled Joe Suggs, who like Eli Brown was a Mississippi veteran of the Army of Northern Virginia. "'Bout all they grow up there is sunflowers and sonofabitches, startin' with that rascal John Brown and includin' ever'body born there since."

"You tell 'em Joe," Eli put in.

Once Kansas had been put to rest as a topic, talk soon turned to the Indian Territories. No one seemed to know much about them, except for Noah Kanes, who was from northwest Arkansas. "Boys," he said, "ah bin through there a few times huntin' and sech before I jined up with Braxton Bragg's corps in '62.

"The country's got mostly the leftovers of ol' Andy Jackson's Injuns what he moved there from back east. But they's also some right mean folks whose ancestors were river pirates back in Mississippi. They pretty much got the territory to themselves, 'ceptin' for the Injuns."

The steers were well rested, so the hands figured they'd be excitable when they hit the crossing. The river was high enough that the wagon had to be floated across. It would go first, which meant a cold camp for a couple of days. The following day, after serving an early supper, Jeremiah drove down to the crossing and the crew helped him across at dawn.

After that, they all loped back to the herd, gathered them and left for the ford, where the steers began swimming about two in the afternoon.

The Brazos was still flowing rapidly, but the crossing, though perilous, was going very well until Henry Bemis's horse was hooked in the belly by a swimming steer and was upset in mid-river.

Dunigan saw the incident from the north bank. He spun his horse downstream and kicked him into a gallop, all the while keeping his eye on the stream, waiting for Bemis to surface. Dunigan rode three miles downstream, but Bemis never appeared.

Just as John got back to the crossing, Smollett rode up. "Did you spot Henry Bemis, John?"

Dunigan shook his head. "Nope. I saw him and his horse both go under in midstream, but the only sign of Henry was this." Dunigan waved the soggy Stetson he'd plucked off a downriver snag.

After supper, Pete led a brief prayer service from the Bible he kept in his saddlebag. But it was Henry's old war buddy Shad Milam who spoke his friend's epitaph. "Ol' Henry never could have no luck."

As soon as the herd was underway next morning, Pete took two pack horses to replenish supplies in Waco, only a few miles south of the crossing. He'd pick up some fresh flour and beans to replace the soaked food ruined by the spring rains, wire Tom Cameron a progress report, and tell about Bemis's death.

Next day, Pete caught up with them and the drive continued on toward Fort Worth and Denton. With their early start, they were well ahead of most other herds and by midApril were crossing the Trinity at Fort Worth.

The grass was green and the herd was moving steadily but quietly, putting on flesh as they strolled toward Kansas. May first would see them across a placid Red River and into Indian territory.

Entering Indian lands, Dunigan worked well ahead of the herd, because there were also renegade whites abroad. Most of the Indians were peaceful enough, but some bands charged herds a fee for crossing tribal lands. They accepted cattle and were usually satisfied with a couple or three weak animals that would likely not have survived anyway.

The outlaws were another case. They weren't at all interested in only a few steers, they wanted all of them and weren't too picky about how they got their thieving hands on them. Fortunately, most of the crooks were plying their devious trade farther east, because many of the herds were still headed for Missouri.

Ten days into the territory, Dunigan crossed a trail of shod horses about 15 miles northeast of the herd. Cautiously, he followed the track, eventually discovering a camp where seven rough-looking men were seated around a wood fire. From their gestures toward where the herd was passing, Dunigan deduced their intentions.

Easing toward his horse, Dunigan raced back to the herd.

He and Pete decided an ounce of prevention was preferable to jeopardizing the cattle or the men. Dunigan led five of the crew back to the outlaw camp, where the Cameron bunch attacked about 2:00 A.M. Three of the hands ran off the outlaw horses to the southeast, while Dunigan and the two others galloped through the camp firing pistols, raising hell and creating confusion and consternation.

In seconds, the foray was over and the six cowmen were on their way back to the herd, leaving behind seven startled and marooned outlaws. The only casualty of the night: Nick Mc-Curry's horse caught a stray bullet in its hindquarters.

The wound wasn't deep enough nor serious enough to cause the horse much pain, in fact wasn't discovered till the men were unsaddling at camp.

The level in Jeremiah's overnight coffee pot was lowered considerably while the raiders reviewed their intrepid assault and compared notes.

Nick was the first to point the finger at John.

"Dagnabit, Dunigan," Nick complained, "I surely do wish you'd be more careful with your firearms. That beast I was riding tonight was my best horse. It's gonna be a whole week before he's worth a damn."

"I'm surprised at you, Nick," Dunigan retorted. "If you were so all-fired fond of that animal, how come you didn't lean back a ways and take that bullet in your own hip pocket? Why you might have been a hero tonight, 'stead of just another walkin' cowhand."

Early next morning, they tied down Nick's horse and pried

out the bullet with a pocket knife. They packed the wound with moss and seared the incision with a red-hot knife blade.

For the next few days, Dunigan scouted alertly along the east flank, but found no further signs of the crooks, so he reported to Pete that they were likely safe from the outlaws.

Before the first of June, the herd had crossed the Canadian and Cimarron and was approaching the Arkansas crossing. There, one steer was lost to quicksand and two others had to be roped out of a bog. One of them, bailing out of that mud fightin' mad, hooked a horse in the belly and spilled the poor animal's guts. No one knew enough to help the animal, so he was shot.

As soon as they left the territories, a rider was dispatched to post a letter to Cameron in Kansas City, informing him they expected to arrive in Abilene around the twentieth of June. Meantime, the grass was lush and untrampled by other herds, so the steers moved slowly along, fattening nicely on the waving sea of green. They would reach market in excellent condition.

They were well west of settlements, and few grangers had ventured forth to watch, but there was a chance of Kansas border raiders, so Dunigan stayed on the lookout, scouting well ahead. Not a sign proved to be dangerous.

By June seventeenth, the herd was well spread out, grazing belly deep in a small valley south of Abilene. The crew established a good camp along a clear creek that ran north into the Kansas River, slightly downstream from where it was formed by the confluence of the Solomon, Smoky Hill, and Saline rivers.

From that pasture, they would await the arrival of Tom Cameron, who would handle the sale. Arriving promptly at mid-morning on the twentieth, he reported an active and generous market. The sale would begin as soon as Cameron got back to Abilene. He ordered the crew not to move the herd until he returned, because two other herds had already reached Abilene from East Texas. But those herds had been driven hard and were in poor condition.

Next morning, Cameron left for Abilene, returning three days later with a man the hands presumed was a buyer. Most of June 24, the visitor and Cameron rode through the herd. That evening, accompanied by Pete Smollett, the buyer and Cameron rode back to Abilene to trade on the cattle.

Late on the twenty-sixth, Pete returned. "Boys, the herd is sold! We got twenty-one fifty a head! I took a look at the pens and they're all right, so we should be done by three o'clock tomorrow." They all cheered and waved their hats.

As dawn cracked the eastern horizon, the steers were on the move into Abilene, arriving at the railroad loading pens by 11:00 A.M. Once they were penned, Dunigan, Pete, and the buyer counted them, agreeing upon 2,439. Tom Cameron and Nick McCurry tallied Dunigan's steers, coming up 417, which pleased Dunigan, because he knew he'd left the Aransas with only 415 and one had been lost on the trail.

Obviously, Cameron had lost his original tally and Dunigan was not about to enlighten him. The contract price was $21.50 a head in gold, so Dunigan had $8,965.50 coming to him, more money in one lump than he had ever seen in his life, let alone possessed. While they finished loading the steers amidst the huffing and chuffing of the locomotive, Dunigan was almost floating on air.

Noticing the silly smile on his lips, Nick McCurry hollered at Dunigan as the last few steers were being loaded. "Hey, John, whatcha gonna do with all that gold? Maybe if I stick close to you for the next few days some of it'll rub off on me. What do you say?"

Dunigan realized Nick was funning him, but decided to play the scene straight anyway. "Sure, Nick, stick around. Maybe we'll ride out and sell my horses to the army. Want to come along?"

"You bet. I shore don't have any better plans."

Well after five o'clock, the Long L outfit finally departed the Abilene pens, its job complete. But a few loose ends remained: the remuda was sold to a local horse trader for resale mostly to stockmen. Much to the liveryman's regret, Dunigan's animals were held out of the sale. They had considerably more breeding and training than Cameron's.

Dunigan had already decided to sell his string to the Fort Riley cavalry post a few miles north of town. After Dunigan and Cameron had completed their business, the Irishman said, "Mister Cameron, I do believe I'll ride on back to Texas after I sell my horses."

"Listen, Dunigan, why don't you go back with Pete and Jesse with the wagon? I believe Nicholas McCurry will be accompanying them, as well. Seems the rest of the boys are planning to stay here to visit the elephant for a few days after I pay them. Hmmph!" Cameron's bushy eyebrows came together in an obvious scowl of disdain. "Of course, they'll have nothing to show for their hard work by the time they get home, but I suppose that's their business."

Cameron's suggestion sounded good to Dunigan, so he talked to Pete and made arrangements for the trail boss to wait a day or two so Dunigan and Nick could visit Fort Riley and sell John's horses to the army. They found an eager buyer; the post wrangler was willing to pay $80 each for five of the mounts, but John held out his favorite blood bay for the trip home.

As they were about to leave, a fussy Yankee major appeared and inquired about Dunigan's bay. "I say, my good man, that is a splendid animal. I simply must have it for my personal mount. What would you say to $150?"

Dunigan glanced levelly at the man in blue and shook his head once.

Instantly, the major came back. "$160!"

Dunigan shook his head again, this time gathering his papers and getting ready to depart.

"$185! Not a cent more!"

"Major, you just bought yourself a horse," Dunigan said, shaking hands to seal the deal.

When he realized he'd just disposed of the vehicle that would take him back to Texas, Dunigan quickly reacquired one of the other horses. Still, he had picked up over $500 for his mounts and was well pleased.

Back in Abilene, he and Nick had supper at the best hotel and were soon back at the wagon for a good rest before leaving next morning for Texas and home.

Chapter 4

T he long trip home was uneventful. Other than crossing rivers on bridges where they were available, they took the same route they'd followed north. With only four mouths to feed, Jeremiah outdid himself with the chuck and they all put on an extra pound or two.

Dunigan had come to respect Nicholas McCurry. The oldest hand on the drive, he was a lot like John. Nearing the half century mark, Nick stayed mostly to himself and was always an independent cuss. At six feet and a hundred sixty pounds, Nick's life in the saddle had kept him buggy whip lean and wiry.

A superb horseman, Nick had first come to Texas with the cavalry during the Mexican War and there he had taken his discharge. His ancestors had arrived in Kentucky through the Cumberland Gap with Daniel Boone's first colonists. Hill people, they had tilled the thin Appalachian soil and eked out some kind of living, but when war broke out in the '40s, Nick had recognized his ticket out of that hard life and enlisted.

Nick knew horseflesh and had a fine reputation in Texas as a trader until the Civil War erupted, but he'd never made more than a subsistence living at it. He served along the border with Rip Ford and Santos Benavides and after the war had worked mainly for wages, cowboying and riding rough strings.

Only that spring had he hired on with Cameron. Although Nick was very nearly Dunigan's alter ego, unlike John, his harsher existence had blunted the edge of a once-keen optimism. Where Dunigan was confident he still had a lot to look forward to, Nick treated the big Irishman as if he were an overly ambitious nephew. Both men shared their affection for and knowledge of superior horses.

Pete Smollett was a different case. Forty, stocky, a talented cowman and able trail boss, Pete was a veteran of Hood's Texas Brigade and the Army of Northern Virginia. He recognized Dunigan as a kindred spirit, but as something of a rival, too. Pete respected John for his ability and his judgment, but envied Dunigan's ownership of the cattle sold in Kansas.

Dunigan sensed Pete's feelings, but there wasn't a spiteful bone in the trail boss's muscular frame, so they got along fine on the trip home.

Making steady time, they spent a month getting back to the Aransas, and Dunigan took every opportunity to persuade Nick McCurry to join his outfit, because John meant to drive his own herd to Kansas the following year.

They had just crossed the Colorado and were riding together a hundred yards or so from the wagon when John made his strongest pitch.

"All right, Nick, this is the deal: there's plenty of wild cattle left in South Texas and we'll be trailing them for many a year to come. You know the kind of horses I have and I'd like you to handle that part of the operation yourself. I'll also cut you in for a share in the steers we sell, too. What do you say?"

"John, I've only seen a few of your horses, but what I saw, I liked. Your plan to start your own cattle operation sounds mighty fine to me, too. You've got yourself a wrangler." Extending his hand toward Dunigan, Nick leaned out of the saddle and John grasped the hand of friendship and partnership.

Nick McCurry was an almost perfect companion for Dunigan, matching John's ambition with his own seasoned equanimity, John's fierce optimism with Nick's own brand of alert skepticism.

*　*　*　*　*

The new partners moved out to the place west of the Aransas that John called his ranch and began breaking the seven colts that were ready to train.

"Damn, John," Nick said one evening while they were forcing themselves to eat a poorly prepared supper, "we should've brought ol' Jeremiah along. You're a terrible bean burner and I'm worse. We better get us a cook or we'll both waste away to nothin'."

"You're right, Nick, but before we do, we've got to plan things out. The way things stand, I'll have no more than two hundred head ready for the trail next spring and free cattle in this area are becoming scarce. There are plenty of them west of here, but we can't drive them to the ranch for winter because I haven't enough grass to support them until spring."

"I don't see the problem, John. All I see is the solution. Let's go west, gather the cattle and look after them there. But first, for the good Lord's sake, let's get a cook!" Laughing, Dunigan raised both hands in surrender to his epicurean wrangler.

Late in August, the two men left to scout the trans-Nueces country. South and west of that river was ample grass for grazing cattle and animals that could easily be captured and driven to market in Kansas. However, the inhabitants of that region had a reputation for ignoring ownership of other people's assets so it was dangerous not only to stay there, but to own anything at all that might tempt a thief.

Sometimes called The Wild Horse Desert, sometimes La Brasada, title to the region below the Nueces had been disputed by Mexico until the Treaty of Guadalupe-Hidalgo in 1848, which ended the Mexican War and established once and for all American title to it.

Nearly unpopulated and naturally inhospitable country, the only inhabitants were transient American or Mexican bandits and the only law came out the end of a gun barrel. During the Republic, Texas had neither the population nor the resources to establish a presence, but the area was ceded nonetheless under the terms of Santa Anna's surrender. Twenty-five years later, any Americans laying claim to any part of the raw land were well advised to protect themselves.

As soon as they crossed the Nueces, Nick and John immediately spotted herds of cattle and wild horses that belonged to no one so were ripe for capture. A week later, they happened upon an abandoned station that had once been a resting stop on the stage line between Laredo and San Antonio, when Texas was still part of Mexico.

A long one-story adobe, the station had a kitchen, main room and five smaller ones suitable for bunkrooms. Located on a creek that ran north into the Nueces, the station even had remnants of corrals and some sheds. This would be their headquarters and they decided to move in at once.

Nick went off to Laredo to hire some laborers to build pens and fences and fix the place up some, but he was more determined to find a capable cook.

Meanwhile, Dunigan returned to the Aransas for horses, utensils, equipment, and tools.

Nick's quest was successful. He could have hired five hundred good men just by offering to feed them. The cook he hired was Pablo Mendoza, who had a wife and five kids, but who knew how to cook goat so it could be savored. Of the seven other hands, three had been lancers with Maximilian, forced into Texas by his defeat. Nick figured they'd need a few fighters to fend off bandidos.

Nick brought his crew back to the station in a wagon he bought in Laredo. The men's first task was to build jacales (huts) for themselves. While they were busy cutting brush and thatch, Nick rode out on his horse to scout the area around the station.

There seemed to be plenty of cattle hiding out in the bush not far from the station. Suddenly, he spotted a young doe, and drew his rifle and shot it for camp meat. Draping the animal across the back of his saddle, Nick offered it to Pablo when he got back to camp.

"Ah, muy bueno, señor! Carne fresco (fresh meat)!" Quickly dressing out the deer, Pablo proceeded to prepare a delicious roast venison super.

Three days later, Dunigan appeared in another wagon laden with tools, with ten colts tethered behind it. Seated next to John was the greenest looking kid Nick had ever seen.

"Where in the world did you find that young 'un, John?"

Dunigan roared with laughter, waving his arm toward the boy. "Better find him a towel, Nick, 'cause this lad is still damp from crossing the ocean. Meet Michael O'Grady of Connaught."

"I've got a towel, but we've already got one Irishman in the outfit, John. This one'll put us over the limit."

Poor Michael swiveled his head from one to the other of these giant men, uncertain whether to laugh or consider leaving.

Dunigan eased his uncertainty with a crisp order. "Turn the team loose in the corral, Michael, unload these tools in the shed, then wash up and come inside for supper."

Michael grabbed up the reins and expertly guided the horse toward the corral.

"Big news here, John," Nick declared, grinning broadly. "We

got us a damned fine cook! His name's Pablo Mendoza." Nick patted his middle as he pronounced Pablo's name in a flawless Tex-Mex accent.

Characteristically, silence mostly reigned later when Nick, John and Michael sat down in the station dining room to a meal of venison stew, spicy beans, rice, tortillas, and coffee. As they were finishing with another cup of coffee, Nick turned to Michael O'Grady.

"Son, how long you been here in Texas?"

"I arrived seven weeks past, sorr, to St. Marys. Mister Dunigan was kind enough to take me on. Me own cousin, Henry Fogerty, already had plenty of help on his farm."

Nick had to concentrate to fathom Michael's thick brogue, but he got most of it. "And what is it you can do, young Michael? Have you any particular skills we might use?"

"Well, sorr, in Connaught I was working in a racing stable, but I am always willing to learn more. Like many a farm lad, I can do many tasks, carpenter and sech. And I once overheard the Lord say to the overseer that I was a gifted farrier."

Nick turned to his partner. "Has he got a saddle?"

Dunigan nodded. "I let him have one of my old ones from the place." John sipped his coffee before changing the subject.

"Tell me Nick, what did you find in Mexico?"

"Seven men, as you've already seen. Mostly peons, but three rode with Maximilian, so they can fight, which could be helpful. I put them to work building the pens we discussed out of the mesquite hereabouts. They all appear to be willing and competent workers and I think the three lancers may be vaqueros, as well. They'll be handy once we start the cow hunts."

Nick led the way outside so he could show John the progress that had already been made. "The boys are cutting mesquite for the corrals out there and over there," Nick said, pointing south, then east. "Removing the brush will give us decent fields of fire if we ever have to defend the place."

They continued to walk and talk, while Nick explained the tasks he had set for the men.

"Before you got back, John, I did some scouting and there are plenty of unmarked cattle around here. Most are bulls and after they're cut, they'll make fine steers. I noticed a good many barren older cows, too. Some of them can make the drive."

Before they turned in, they decided Michael would work with the colts while the Mexicans finished work on the station. The two partners would explore the countryside and scout for cattle.

The next day only two miles from the old station, Dunigan found an arroyo where cattle had been watering, an ideal location for a trap corral. Nick found a similar setup, but it was a good four-and-a-half miles away. In all, they found five possible trap locations, but most of them were quite a distance from headquarters.

Both men, edgy about the presence of rustlers, had watched carefully for any signs, but hadn't seen any. They were reassured by the lack of other human activity, but precautions were never relaxed around headquarters.

In a few days Michael had gentled the colts so some of them were ready to be ridden, which pleased John and Nick because their regular mounts needed a rest. From now on, they'd do their exploring on green horses.

The pens and corrals around headquarters were almost complete, so Nick took three of the men out to the spot he had found to begin work on a catch pen.

"Here's the way we do this," Nick told the men in Spanish, as he sketched a diagram in the dusty soil with a stick. "We build these long wings by weaving cut branches into the trees along here." Nick stabbed his stick into the dirt.

He went on to describe a typical brush country cow trap, designed to entice the unsuspecting wild cattle into a large corral with a water hole, then into a smaller pen without water just beyond the first one.

August and September were still blazing hot in the Nueces country, so it was too hot to capture cows, but cooler days and nights would be coming soon enough.

The more Dunigan thought on it, the less he liked the idea of overwintering the cattle at the station. After supper one evening, he turned to his partner. "Nick, there are just too many outlaws out here and no law at all. Besides, the grazing is poor at best. The longer we stay here, the likelier it is some cow thieves will discover our place and drive off the cows. What do you think?"

"I agree. This whole area is no-man's land and we're only trespassers. For sure someone will try to get our cattle if we stay. Couldn't we rent some pasture closer to civilization? We'd all be a whole lot safer."

Dunigan clapped his hands on his thighs and leaned back in his chair. "That's settled then. I'll leave in the morning."

At dawn, Dunigan set off to find some pasturage around Refugio and Goliad. He also planned to bring back some more men and young horses.

Back at the station, work was progressing well. The headquarters corrals were finished and the second trapping corral was almost done. Nick took his lead worker to the third location where they would build and issued instructions how and when to construct it.

He let the three lancers try out the green horses and the men proved to be good horsemen with some experience handling stock. The three, Abel Castro, Manuel Menchaca, and Juan Redondo were unmarried and in their late twenties, except for Castro, who was 34. None of them spoke much English, but they all understood some. Nick had been fluent in Spanish since his days on the border with Benavides, so communicating with them was no problem.

Out scouting next day, Nick spotted a band of wild horses about ten miles from headquarters. Determined to catch them because they'd need plenty of horses for the cow hunt, he rode back to the station and spoke to the three vaqueros and Michael. Nick decided to corral them at headquarters.

The five men saddled up and set out, riding in a long line, but within sight of one another while they hunted for the horses. In the lead, Nick spotted the horses first. Numbering between sixty and seventy, they were pretty well bunched when Nick started them. He'd already told the other men what to do.

The mustangs were about ten miles southwest of headquarters, and the riders were strung out east to west. Nick got the band going directly east. His riders loped easily eastward parallel to the mustangs' line of flight. As the wild horses came abreast of each rider, he bore in on them, gradually turning the mustangs in a circle that went north and then west. When a rider was outdistanced by the pack, he cut north at an easy pace to be in position when the horses came back around.

All five riders arrived around the mustangs about a mile and a half southeast of the headquarters corrals, having galloped about six miles each to the mustangs' fifteen. When the wild horses reached the wing pen prepared for them, they were locked in the corrals before they knew they were caught, secured in a large pen with no water and only sparse grass.

It was almost dark when the men finished their work, so they turned their worn-out mounts into the water pens for the night.

Some of the mustangs had peeled off from the main bunch during the run and escaped, but Nick figured they'd penned almost sixty. The five hands were well satisfied that evening as they consumed one of Pablo's tasty meals, recounting their experience with much laughter and good humor.

Nick decided to leave the mustangs alone for three days before breaking them, weakening them a bit to make them more tractable. They'd use water and hay as rewards for good horse behavior.

In the morning, Nick sent Michael and the three vaqueros to the Nueces bottom to cut grass for hay to add to the growing supply at the station. Two days later, Nick had tubs of water carried to the holding pens so the mustangs wouldn't die, but he kept a close watch on their intake so they wouldn't regain too much strength. After all, wild desert horses could survive on little water.

That evening, Dunigan was back with two new men, including Jim Daniels, an Arkansawyer about thirty who had been wounded and invalided out of the Confederate army in 1864. He had made a full recovery and was able to pursue his career as a cowhand. The other man was Pete Roussel, a younger cowboy who had been with the Cameron herd that spring, where Nick and John had met him.

Born in Louisiana, Pete was a quiet, smart hand who minded his own business and did his work efficiently and well. Dunigan had bumped into the pair in Goliad and offered them work until trail time. Likely, they'd be going up the trail with Dunigan's herd in the spring.

As the three men rode up, Dunigan noticed the dust over the corral and went over to see what was causing it. He wheeled back over to Nick. "Where'd you find the broomtails?"

"Southwest of here. I reckon we've got about 35 or 40 possibles in there. I'm mighty glad you brought some fresh hands, because I thought we'd start them in the morning. They've been here three days, so maybe they've calmed down enough for us to break tomorrow. The boys have been plaiting halters every night and we've got right smart of them already."

After watering and haying their horses, Dunigan and the new arrivals unsaddled their mounts and turned them in with the remuda. By then, supper was ready, so all eight hands sat down to eat. Pablo's meals were getting better and better because he'd had time to gather wild peppers, herbs, and other edibles from the vicinity to supplement the dry staples that made up their usual fare. After the other men went into the station to sleep, Dunigan and Nick stayed to drink coffee and compare notes.

"I've ordered a wagonload of lumber, Nick, so we can build some sheds and such. It should arrive in Goliad the day after tomorrow. I noticed some of those horses are still studs, so we'll have to cut them and we'll need some pine oil and carbolic acid. We'll need a brand, too. What about Dee Gee [DG] for the trail? Okay with you?"

When Nick nodded, Dunigan continued. "Let's talk some business as well, Nick. You know I'm putting up all the money we're using and you're drawing a salary. Even so, I want you to have ten percent of the profit off this deal and that makes you a partner. We'll settle up after the cattle are sold in Abilene. That suit you?"

"It does. In fact, it's right generous of you, John, and I thank you. You know you don't have to worry about me doing what needs to be done, but it's nice to have something to put aside for my old age."

Dunigan snorted. "Old age, my backside," he grunted, stomping off to bed.

At dawn, after telling Michael O'Grady to harness a team to the wagon, Dunigan detailed Jim Daniels to accompany Michael to Goliad for lumber. He gave Jim a list of supplies to pick up, cautioning the pair to take care coming and going because he wanted their location kept secret as long as possible. Pablo presented a list of groceries, to which Dunigan added molasses. Some of the other men needed a few things, too, and they gave Daniels some money. The two wagoneers finally got away about eight o'clock.

As they left, Dunigan saddled a horse. "I'm going to take a look at the trap corrals, Nick. How far do you think they've gotten with them?"

"They should be working on the last one by now, John. You know, the one due west of here?"

"I think I remember. I'll check them all, though. I'll be back tonight. Oh yeah, good luck with your rough string. Makes me kind of glad I've got something else to do. I'm not looking for any bruises, and besides, I'm not too fond of doing that rough stuff to horses. Any horses." Waving, he trotted off.

Nick assembled the four vaqueros, the horsehair halters and several ropes and off they went to the corrals. Nick's horse was already saddled in the corral and he mounted.

"Abel," he asked, "sabe usted la mangana?"

"Si, Jefe. Lo puedo." ("Sure, boss. I can do it.") Abel Castro was a man of few words.

Adjacent to the mustang corral were three smaller pens, each with a stout oak snubbing post in the center, to which they would tie the haltered horses.

Nick assigned Abel to forefoot, Manuel to hold the horse's head and Juan to place the halters. Pete Roussel would help hold them and Nick would tie up their hind feet, then hold them with his horse. He went into the pen for the first one and was challenged at once by a mean-looking stallion with his teeth bared. Nick just made it back to the small pen, the stud right on his heels.

"Be sure you catch that son of a bitch," he hollered at Abel as he passed him. Castro neatly flipped his rope around the stud's front hooves, tripping him and slamming the horse hard into the ground. Before the slack could go out of Abel's rope, Manuel, Pete and Juan were on the animal and Nick's rope was on his hind legs, immobilizing the mustang while Juan slipped the halter over the beast's head.

Once the halter was secure, everyone but Nick tied the lead rope to the snubbing post. Nick played his own rope to keep the horse from getting at the men on foot. Snubbed tightly to the post, the stud screeched and plunged at the end of the rope, but could go nowhere. Nick eased his own rope off the hind legs and they left the pen to get the next animal.

The second horse reacted pretty much the same, but was a mare, so Nick was able to cut her out of the corral. Abel laid out a perfect mangana and she was soon tied to the post in the middle pen. When the third horse was snubbed tight, they turned their attention back to the stallion.

He was lathered and still screeching with his teeth bared, so they went into the station to eat dinner. When they came back, the stud was calmed, but still white eyed whenever a human approached. He definitely wasn't ready to work. Abel Castro shrugged and said once the stud lost his huevos he'd be more manageable. No one argued with that.

The mare in the middle pen had given up and was standing with the snub rope slack. After snubbing her tight and releasing her several times, she was even quieter, so Nick wrapped the lead rope around his saddle horn and led her around the pen a few times. Once she was following easily, they led her into another pen with hay and water and turned her loose.

Another slightly older mare was snubbed in the middle pen while the hands repeated their act with the third horse. That day, they turned out seven horses to hay and water, each with a halter on. But the mean stud just wouldn't give up.

The second morning, they untied him and while Nick was leading him around the pen, he craned his neck and bit Nick on the leg. Nick just shrugged, slipped off the halter and put the stud back in with the wild bunch. At least the stallion didn't try to fight any more.

On the second day, back after his tour of the traps, Dunigan helped out, too. When Michael and Jim returned the fourth day with the lumber, the rough breaking went even more quickly.

After five days, Nick had forty horses in halters. All that was left of the original bunch were older mares, most of which were in foal, and the mean stud, so Nick turned them all loose to roam the range again.

Three weeks later, the forty horses were workable, except for a mare that looked pregnant. She was branded and turned loose to find the band.

The Mexicans working the traps came back to pronounce them complete and immediately got busy with the lumber, finishing sheds and some small cottages.

More than sixty mounts were now available, so that evening at supper, Dunigan declared the time had come to hunt some cows. Cheers erupted from the vaqueros, who truly enjoyed nothing more than thrashing through the brush after loose cattle. To a man, they detested foot work.

Chapter 5

Dunigan put out the word in San Patricio, Beeville, Goliad, and Refugio that he was organizing a cow hunt on October 27. Seventeen men showed up at San Patricio to take part.

Dunigan thought it best to set out the ground rules first. "Boys, this cow hunt is not going to be much different from others. There are seventeen of you, and eight of us, plus I am feeding you at my camp, with a house to sleep in. We have prepared five corrals to pen into, and you will have access to my remuda, plus your horses will be fed corn with mine. For these extras, I figure a fifty-fifty split ought to be right, and I'll buy any and all steers you want to sell out of your share for seven dollars a head. Any questions?"

There was some low talking, but finally one spoke up. "Sounds all right with me, Mister Dunigan, any of you others object?" No one did so they rode off to the old stage station to drop off extra horses and bed for the night.

Two northers had already blown in that fall, so it was about 48 degrees when they all arose at 3:00 A.M. Pablo's wife cooked bacon and biscuits for breakfast because he had moved to the first trap corral with the chuck wagon to have dinner ready on time. Each man took along some extra food from the kitchen to have a bite for later on in the morning.

Horses were saddled, a few crow-hopping because they felt good in the cool morning air, then the riders set out, riding generally south. The crew worked like a purse seine, throwing cattle north toward the pen, the riders spread wide at first, then closing tighter until they were below the wings of the pen. The wings, though impenetratable, looked like the brush in the country, so the cattle did not know they were trapped.

Once they were inside the wings, the riders closed with a whooping rush, and pushed them into the pen, where the animals were trapped before they knew it. Three sweeps were made that first morning, yielding about 850 cattle. At nooning, the riders changed horses, ate lunch at the wagon, and prepared for the afternoon work, which was branding and castrating the bulls suited to become steers.

Steers were roped by the horns and neck, dragged into the smaller pen, where another rider roped the steers' hind legs. The steer was stretched out, thrown and tied down, then branded with a hot iron from a wood fire. All got the DG because all the outside riders wanted to sell. The same procedure was used on bulls, except that while a bull was being branded, he was also castrated with a sharp pocket knife.

When that was over, a few men wanted to brand some cows to take home, so each roped those he wanted, and their own brand was put on. A running tally was kept on all head, and at the end of the day 512 of all types had been branded. The unwanted cattle were let go as seed stock; most of the men feeling this way of doing things would go on forever. However they did brand and castrate the bull yearlings and other bulls not big enough or old enough to go up the trail, turning them out with the others to go free. Supper was eaten at the trap corrals before they headed back to headquarters to sleep.

The next morning the outfit worked the second trap corral. They made three sweeps in the morning, gathering about 550 head altogether. They followed the same procedure and ended up with about 284 cattle for the trail herd. The third day was the same except for working sweeps to the third trap corral farther to the west. This effort yielded 744 head out of over a thousand, totaling 1,540 branded and trapped cattle.

Dunigan figured that it was time to move some of the cattle to headquarters for water and hay, so they picked up the 512 head from the first corral. Four of the bulls had died from bleeding; a fifth was too weak to be moved and was shot and butchered for camp meat. Dunigan ordered his three carpenters to skin the dead ones for their hides.

Off water and grass for three days, the first bunch was weak enough not to cause much trouble, although two ran off and had to be roped and tied to mesquite trees. But the main herd arrived quickly at headquarters and was penned in the water lot, with hay thrown to them from the growing haystack harvested from the river flats. Those men then took two burros back to the steers tied to trees, yoked a burro to each and turned them loose. The burros would show up at the headquarters sometime that afternoon with the errant steers. The smaller herd was moved from the second pen that afternoon, the fall weather having become cool enough to handle cattle throughout the day. Another major benefit of the cool weather was suppression of screw worms. One of the steers was found infected, but he was roped and treated at headquarters.

Another week passed before all the traps had been worked and the steers brought in to headquarters. The final count was 1,792, not counting 167 cows the other men wanted, and 40 fresh hides were stacked by the old stage station. The haystack was dwindling but could last about a week more. By then everyone would be gone back to the Aransas and San Antonio river country. For the most part, that time was spent getting the cattle used to men, who went through them at least three times each day, checking for infections and illness. There were assorted bumps and bruises afflicting both men and horses and these were tended to, as well as repairs to tack and equipment.

By November 10, the outfit was ready to move the cattle east to winter pasture. Dunigan had been careful moving to and from the old stage station, taking a different route each time, so as not to leave a well-marked trail outlaws might follow. He intended to use the same location in succeeding years and did not want it to become known. He cautioned the cowboys about talking about it and they understood his reasons.

Everything not nailed down was loaded into one wagon that also carried the hides, to be driven by Michael O'Grady to the tannery at Rockport. Pablo Mendoza and his family rode the chuckwagon, following the herd. The race was on. The steers ran for about two miles before they were contained, but then settled down and were remarkably well behaved the rest of the way. It took three days to get them back home, where the cows were cut out and the steers turned loose to winter. Michael was back home by then with $120 of hide money, and Dunigan settled up with his cow hunters in gold. He would have to buy a few more steers to bring his total to about 2,500, which he had determined to be the size of his trail herd, but that could be taken care of during the winter. Before they left Dunigan asked if any of them wanted to go up the trail with the herd in the spring. Six volunteered and Dunigan told them to be at his ranch on March 1 next year.

He had had no social contact in a long time, so Dunigan rode into Refugio that afternoon. He wanted to find out what was going on. The saloon was the news center of town and as he was dry he went there first.

Trading gossip and rumors about prices and newcomers occupied about three drinks, while Dunigan heard everything about what was going on in the area. He was about to leave when three men entered the saloon, one of whom was Tom Cameron.

"John, I'm glad to see you. I came down to ask you if you would go north with me again in the spring, and you can take your own cattle as you did last spring."

"Mister Cameron, I am going to take my own herd to Abilene in the spring, so I won't be available to go with you."

"Well, branching out into trail driving is becoming popular, and I certainly think you are capable of doing it—I wish you luck, but I am sorry you won't be with my herds."

Pete Smollett was one of the men with Cameron, and the other was introduced as Joe Carter. The four of them had a few drinks and passed a pleasant time, mainly reminiscing about times past. They visited until almost dark and parted, Cameron, Smollett, and Carter going to their rooms, and Dunigan heading back to his ranch for supper.

Dunigan rousted out the hands the next day to start the more mundane preparations for the trail. There would be a chuckwagon and one to carry bedding, traps, and whatever else anyone was taking. Both vehicles to be repaired and maintained, axles greased and harnesses repaired. Michael had brought four tanned hides from Rockport when he sold the green hides. He had traded some of those for the tanned leather on Dunigan's orders and sold the rest. Naturally, the cow hunters had an interest in all the hides, but it was merely a peccadillo, and that didn't bother Dunigan.

The hides were useful for saddle repair, and both Manuel Mendoza and Pete Roussel made themselves new pairs of leggins. Abel Castro kept himself busy plaiting ropes, reins, halters, and such from rawhide and horsehair. All hands took their turns seeing after the cattle, and throwing them back on the home range. Dunigan had eight or ten young horses to be trained and everyone except Jim Daniels picked one to break. Because of his war wound Daniels did not break horses, but did all other work. No one begrudged him his exception.

The winter of 1867 was wet and cold, freezing four times and staying below freezing for three days in February, which was hard on the cattle, and by spring they were well gaunted.

While training the young horses, Dunigan had delayed finding and buying the additional 500 steers he needed, but now he got on with it. Leaving Pete Roussel in charge, he and McCurry set out to hunt up more steers, taking young Michael O'Grady with them. In Refugio, they heard of a man down toward Salt Creek who was supposed to have some steers to sell. They rode down and inquired about cattle for sale and were directed to a man named Maille. He was at a ramshackle house near the mouth of the creek.

A small man, aged by sun, wind and work, and resembling most a big monkey, Maille was one of the original Power colonists. He had Ireland written all over him. "Maille's the name," he said, "can I do somep'n for ye?"

"I'm told you have some steers for sale. I might be interested," Dunigan said.

"And who would you be, sir?"

"John Dunigan, from up on the Aransas."

"I've heard of ye, and who be yer friends?"

"Nicholas McCurry and Michael O'Grady are their names, and they are with me."

"I've heard of you, Mister Dunigan, and I knew your uncle when we first came here with Colonel Power."

"I'll tell my Uncle Aloysius I met you when I see him, but my business is to buy steers, and I'll like to be about it."

"Well, lad, you've come to the right man, for I have six hundred of the finest in Texas, and so filled I am with the milk of compassion, that I will sell them to you for nearly nothin'."

"Sounds fine to me, but may I have a look at these paragons of bovine beauty?" Dunigan said, competing with Maille's blarney.

"Wait a minute for me to saddle my horse and we'll have a wee peek at my little beauties," Maille said, heading for his barn.

The four men rode out to look at the steers, determining they were indeed acceptable: four and five years old in adequate condition and quite uniform in appearance for longhorns. Back at Maille's house, after they were served coffee by an aging black woman, the trading commenced.

Dunigan began. "I'll give you six dollars now, or six fifty in March." Dunigan knew that was below market, but Maille appeared to be making a case for a premium, so he started low.

"Tis the sun has made you daft, boy, these bovine roses are worth at least eight right now."

The haggling picked up in earnest then, for Dunigan wanted the cattle and Maille knew it. After two hours and much coffee, the trade was struck for seven dollars a head to be paid off at delivery in March. Dunigan put up two dollars each with five due upon delivery. Maille's count of 573 was accepted, to be confirmed at pick up.

Maille broke out a bottle to seal the trade, then told them stories of the early days of Power's Colony as he was one of the original settlers from Ireland and a friend of Dunigan's and O'Grady's kin. After arrangements were made for some of Dunigan's hands to help Maille drive the steers to the main herd in March, the cowmen made their way back to the Aransas, arriving for a late supper of venison and beans heated up by Pablo.

Chapter 6

By March 1 the outfit had assembled all the supplies it would need to get under way. The chuckwagon was built and stocked with staples: rice, beans, flour, and a supply of tasso, dried beef held in reserve for when a fresh beef was not available for slaughter. There were several sides of bacon in the chuckwagon, too. The other wagon was ready to take on bedrolls, war bags, and possibles. The men's rifles and ammunition would also be carried in the camp wagon, to be retrieved if serious fighting became likely. Rifles, even in saddle scabbards, were a hindrance to a trailhand, and each carried at least one sidearm, so they were never without protection. Three eight-mule teams were provided for each wagon, added to the remuda of almost a hundred saddle horses.

Just before dinner, four of the cow hunters arrived who had signed on to go up the trail: Lon Castle from San Marcos, 19, the only one of the early arrivals who was not a Confederate veteran; Billy Parmalee, a Georgian of 24; and from Tennessee, George Harris, 25, and Lem Bracken, 27, the oldest. The two others would drift in well before supper.

Lon Castle was not one of the original Nueces cow hunters. A farm boy, sent away from the family by his stepfather, he was pretty green, but Dunigan took him on as he seemed to be strong and willing. George Harris was one of the best, a good tracker and capable with horses and cattle, he would likely be named a segundo.

Present to start work was a crew of sixteen, including Pablo Mendoza the cook, Dunigan, and a Mexican lad, 15, Chito Guerrico, whom Dunigan had found at San Patricio in the winter. Predictably, Dunigan designated Michael O'Grady, to his great disappointment, to stay at the ranch to care for the stock, and to begin gentling the young horses, which he accomplished with a skill only the Irish seemed to possess. Michael wanted badly to take part in the great adventure, but he adored John Dunigan more, and accepted his disappointment as the price of his youth and inexperience. He would have help at the ranch if he needed it from two of Pablo's sons who were big enough to do chores. Pablo's family was staying at the ranch, too.

Nick was named caporal, and Pete Roussel, segundo. As trail boss, Dunigan would spend most of his time scouting trail, as would George Harris, an excellent tracker. When not busy with the remuda horses, Chito Guerrico would help Pablo cook. The rest of the cowboys would handle the herd, with Nick in nominal charge and Roussel taking over when Nick was away. Being experienced hands, every man knew his job, so there was no confusion about what was to be done and by whom.

Next morning after breakfast each man selected five horses, the regular hands choosing their usual horses first, then the new men selected theirs one at a time. All the horses belonged to Dunigan and bore his brand, but by tradition a cowboy's work horse was his, to do with pretty much as he would provided he remained an employee in good standing with the brand. No one else was ever allowed to ride a mount belonging to another hand without his permission.

Michael O'Grady cut out the greenest horses to remain at the ranch for more training. The rest would provide replacements when horses became lame or jaded. Each man topped off his own mounts. Some were inclined to crow hop a bit, but no harm was done to anyone, although Billy Parmalee was thrown by one of his mounts, to everyone's delight. It was expected that at least one mount would throw a rider and the others were happy they weren't unlucky.

That night at supper, Dunigan announced they would start gathering the steers back at the ranch, beginning early in the morning.

At 3:30, the outfit left headquarters, rode eight miles in the dark, then spread out along the Aransas River and rode beside it driving the steers before them. By 11:00 they had over 800 gathered, which they drove to the pens at headquarters, arriving for a late dinner at 2:00 in the afternoon. After that, a smaller sweep was made that yielded 250 more steers that were added to the 800 in a large water trap where they would be held until the herd started up the trail.

The next morning sweeps were made along the San Antonio River and 800 more steers were added to the growing herd. Only 150 strays were unaccounted for and Dunigan was sure they would be caught in the next few days.

Dunigan sent McCurry with Daniels, Harris, and Abel Castro to Salt Creek to help bring in Maille's steers. They would be gone three days. Meanwhile, the rest of the outfit scoured the range and came up with 143 head, only eight or ten short of two thousand.

Maille's steers arrived the next day, adding 536 more. Dunigan paid him the five dollars a head he owed with a draft on his account with Jim McFaddin, and the herd was complete at 2,525 head. That night final preparations were completed for leaving at daybreak the next morning.

Dunigan was excited. This was really his first chance at real money. He had figured his costs as close as possible, settling on $4.86 a head as his cost. A dollar a head would likely see them through to Abilene so he figured he could count on selling them in Kansas at a considerable profit. Marketing this herd could make Dunigan a big auger.

They would follow generally the same route as last year with Tom Cameron and Dunigan planned to drive from the Aransas to the Guadalupe, crossing at Gonzales. His only worry was that his steers were thin, requiring a slower drive that could miss the early market. But that would depend on available grass along the trail.

At daylight, March 10, 1868, Dunigan's steers were counted out of his trap. Three men counted and at 2,530 there was a disagreement of only one head out of all three counts. Abel Castro led, with Pete Roussel and George Harris flanking him on the points. The rest of the outfit took their places around the herd, the youngest and least experienced consigned to drag, where they would be eating dust all the way to Kansas. Abel pointed the herd north to cross the San Antonio River south of Goliad, the Guadalupe at Gonzales, the Colorado east of Austin, and the Brazos near Waco. After that, the herd would be on the main trace of the Chisholm, which they would follow to Abilene.

It would be three months of mostly boredom, long days and short nights, too little sleep, rain, wind, sun, and dust. There would be moments of elation and excitement, almost all of them dangerous: swimming across rivers, stampedes, raids by Indians and renegade whites, varmints, and forced drives to scarce waterings.

The long-legged steers were going well, but Dunigan was still worried about the herd's lack of flesh. He hoped they could pick up enough along the trail to be more salable but knew that was a long shot. More likely he would have to stop somewhere in Indian territories to fleshen them. Although now he was staying close, most days he would be absent scouting. If the steers had not picked up flesh before they crossed the Red, he would have to find range to fatten them before reaching Abilene.

The herd was well strung out and moving. Dunigan glanced back to see Pablo coming up with the chuckwagon, with Lon Castle driving the baggage wagon, and after them the remuda under Chito Guerrico. The herd wouldn't reach the San Antonio tonight, but would probably camp just below it, to cross the first thing next day.

Nicholas McCurry wanted to get started right, so he was on the move all day, checking with all hands, so they'd have no mistake about how he wanted them to handle the cattle. The steers had been guided well enough in the not-too-distant past and seemed to know what was expected.

Nick wore out three horses making his rounds that day, but ended up satisfied with progress. He was concerned about the herd's gauntness, but hoped the trail would help. Spring had better come fast, though, because the grass here was still sere, with not much green showing. It had not been too cold until recently, but the new shoots should be abundant soon.

At nooning, the men rode in to change horses and to grab a quick bite. Dunigan did not think it was necessary to stop and feed a big meal at noon, so the outfit ate biscuits and bacon, and then on the fly.

About 3:00 P.M. Dunigan rode ahead to locate a good camp close to the river crossing, signaling Pablo to move ahead of the cattle, so he would have camp ready before the herd arrived at the bedground. Dunigan found a live oak mott about a half mile from the river and told Pablo to set up there. The herd passed about 5:00 P.M., watered at the river and was thrown out on the bedground before sunset.

Night guard was detailed, the first watch staying with the cattle while the rest of the outfit went into camp. Night horses were saddled before supper because Chito had the remuda in a rope corral by the time the men got in.

Four visitors showed up—a storekeeper and three cattlemen who came out from Goliad to visit and eat a free dinner. The visitors brought some whiskey, but few of the outfit had more than one drink. Old stories were retold and before 10:00 the visitors were gone and all but the night hawks on duty were rolled up in their beds.

Next morning the outfit was in motion at first light and by 9:00 A.M. the herd was moving along past the river crossing at a good clip. Dunigan's herd was making good time because the steers' lack of flesh was an advantage: they were thin but strong, thus able to travel quickly. By the time the herd crossed the Guadalupe at Gonzales, the steers were well trail broken, and no trouble to drive.

At Gonzales Dunigan stopped to visit Tom Cameron and saw that his herds wouldn't start for another week, so the DG outfit was well ahead along the trail to Kansas. Cameron's steers had wintered worse than Dunigan's, actually being a bit weak, and Dunigan figured they might stay out on their home range longer than a week to gain strength for the drive. Dunigan's outfit should be able to stay well ahead of the herds just starting north, but he kept the herd at a lively pace to gain as much of a cushion as he could. The herd was moving so well he saw no reason to wait.

The herd settled into a real ground-eating pace and was across the Brazos in under two weeks. The cattle moved into the north breeze with surprising speed. Because the weather was still cool, the grass hadn't begun growing along the trail. The animals were growing leaner, not weaker, so Dunigan saw no reason to slow them down, although it was becoming clear they would have to stop somewhere later to fleshen them.

Twice they had come upon small groups of unbranded steers and Dunigan threw them into his herd, driving them four or five days with the herd before stopping to brand. He wanted to get them well off their home range before claiming them with his brand in case their owner, if they had one, could look at the herd. All of the steers were earmarked, but not branded, so were fair game for any passing herd. Everyone knew the rules and prudent owners branded their cattle as early as possible.

Nothing untoward occurred, although the carpetbagger state police stopped and rode through the herd just south of Fort Worth. They quarreled about the fresh brands, but there was no proof of theft. Dunigan cut out three spindly steers, which was what they wanted anyway, and the march continued.

By May 5, the herd was resting in a pleasant prairie south of the Red River. Some warm rains had finally fallen and grass was growing, so they held the herd for a week to add strength and flesh. Dunigan felt he could afford to because he figured he was at least ten days ahead of any other herds going to Abilene. His steers were content to rest and graze, and they obviously put on some meat on the fresh green grass. The rains had mostly run off or soaked in, so the Red was normal and easy to cross.

While the herd waited, Dunigan rode into Fort Worth to find out the news. He hung around the hotel and stockyards and listened to the men talk. Most of what he heard was about the hard winter that was delaying north-bound herds. He kept his mouth shut about his own herd, but heard it mentioned a time or two, as it had been spotted by passersby, but Dunigan and his DG was new to most of the natives and all the talk was speculation. He did hear about some good grass land controlled by the friendly Osage Indians in the territory just east of the trail. Dunigan decided to try to graze his cattle there for three or four weeks if he could.

The day after he returned to the herd it crossed the Red into the Indian Territory. The bedding got wet when the baggage wagon lost a wheel in the boggy crossing and had to be dragged out of the river by riders. Luckily, the errant wheel was captured before it could float off, so little time was lost. It took less than a day to trim the axle and reset the wheel and the outfit was back in motion on May 12.

Two days later, taking George Harris, Dunigan left the herd to see about grazing his steers on the Indian lands. Harris spoke a little Cherokee so maybe they could communicate with the Osage, Cherokee being used widely by all eastern Indians. Dunigan left orders with Nick to trend the herd eastward until he could determine what he might do with the Indians, and if he hadn't returned in a week to stop the herd and wait for him. He and Harris took an extra riding horse and a pack horse for supplies, setting out northeast to locate the Osage and their grass. Three days later, Dunigan and Harris found them. After smoking pipes, powwowing and eating dog meat for two more days, Dunigan agreed to pay twenty steers and three horses for pasturage. That was about how many he had picked up along the trail and he would use a few cripples to fill out the fee. He could well afford the three ponies as he had plenty, and at least seven of those weren't even being ridden. He planned to give the chief a paint pony so prized by the Indians as a present to insure his cooperation.

He and the chief got on famously as Dunigan had brought two bottles of whiskey for the powwow. The Indians had a few cattle of their own, but not near enough to overgraze the sea of grass they owned. Dunigan would feed his cattle there for a month, foreseeing little trouble since he was now such a big pal of the Osage chief.

Dunigan told Harris to go back and guide the herd into the Indian land, where it would be grazed south of the Cimarron and north of the deep fork of the Canadian. The herd should have crossed the Canadian by the time Harris got to it, and four more days should see them onto the range. He told George to pick up some more whiskey if he could, as the chief seemed right fond of it. Harris grinned and said he thought he could, then rode off to find the herd.

Dunigan realized he had somewhat misjudged the old chief; he was not only fond of whiskey, he positively loved it. That night he finished off what Dunigan had brought with him and almost set fire to his hogan. Dunigan spent as much time as possible scouting the range he intended to graze. He found the grass tall and green, with plentiful water in the Cimarron and in several creeks that crisscrossed the prairie.

Three days later Lon Castle rode into the Osage village saying the herd was three miles south and coming on. Dunigan got the chief and four of his men to ride with him to meet the cattle and they met them just as the herd was entering the range.

The first thing Dunigan did was have Chito bring up the pinto he wanted to present to the chief. The old man was clearly pleased and immediately mounted, laughing and turning the pony. Then Dunigan cut out two steers for the Indians' first payment. Taking them, the chief and his cohorts set out for the village, the chief running his pinto, grinning from ear to ear. Before he left he invited the cowboys to join the feast the Osage would have that night off the two steers. The Osage chief, called Black Deer by most white men because he had an unpronounceable Indian name, was a man in his early sixties, rotund and cheerful. He was a "peace" as opposed to "war" chief, and had been the leader when the Osage were moved from the east. He commanded affection and an amount of respect from his tribe and got along with everybody, which was what he did best, being a brilliant politician.

Dunigan had talked to him seriously about an ongoing grazing deal, and the chief liked the idea and wanted to do it, but knew he would have some trouble with the Indian Bureau, because they wanted to control every aspect of the Indians' existence. But Dunigan felt he had found the chief's touchstone with the whiskey and hoped he could build a lasting relationship, both commercial and social. Even so, Dunigan knew he had to be careful.

I hope, he thought to himself, *I don't have to get tangled up with those Indian agents, because they are like cockroaches. It's not that they eat so much but what they get into and mess up.*

Under Dunigan's direction, the crew set about scattering the steers over the range, setting up patrols to keep them from straying or being stolen. Dunigan had found a small box canyon to corral his horse herd feeling so many horses might tempt the Indians, horse stealing being second nature to them, so he sent the remuda there along with the wagons, to set up camp. George Harris informed Dunigan he had secured a barrel of fair whiskey and Dunigan told him to keep it hidden and to fill bottles from it because of the chief's prodigious thirst. They would ration him some, giving him just enough to keep him jolly.

About dark, Dunigan and seven others rode to the village to attend the feast. The Indians had slaughtered the two steers and had them roasting. Dunigan took along one bottle of whiskey, which delighted the chief. They had a fine paranda that night, the Indians singing and dancing to celebrate fresh meat. The hands did not participate much in anything but the eating, and were careful about their behavior. They were especially warned to ride shy of any Indian girls that might make eyes at them.

Dunigan wanted to use this free time to scout out the range for possible future grazing in later years, if this deal with the Osage worked out all right, and he would be absent much of the time. The steers were pretty well settled on their new range with only a half dozen hands needed to keep them there, plus Chito Guerrico to watch the horses. The camp was taking on a more permanent appearance as several men had built brush arbors for protection against the elements, and Pablo had set up a table and benches to serve meals. Pete Roussel and six men were left to tend the horses and cattle. Dunigan, Nick McCurry, and George Harris each led parties of three or four men—few Indians having volunteered to go along to scout against raiders. Dunigan went northwest, Nick northeast, and Harris southeast. One of the herd hands was to scan the western sector each day, but east was thought to be the danger area, so it was watched more intently. He also cautioned the herd crew to keep a good watch on the horses.

The scouts rode out next morning, each with a pack horse for supplies and each group arranging to send word to the other if danger appeared so as to congregate back at the herd for defense. Dunigan instructed each group to make a general scan of its sector, to watch for old campsites that might be used again by raiders, to investigate new signs in case word was already out that a herd was in the Osage, and generally to familiarize themselves with each sector to learn where to look on later patrols.

With those warnings in mind, the patrols parted to carry out their assignments. Dunigan moved generally north and west and found the countryside similar to the Osage range. A few campsites were found, but most appeared to be related to Pawnee hunting parties, although two looked as if they may have sheltered jayhawker gangs. Those noted, Dunigan swung west to check for traffic from Abilene-bound trail herds.

There they encountered a herd belonging to "Shanghai" Pierce from Matagorda County. Dunigan's group accepted their hospitality for the night and exchanged news of the trail. Pierce's herd had been early on the trail, too, and had received news from Pierce at Red River that there was no hurry. Their herd was lean but gaining and there was a chance they would stop to fatten south of Abilene. Word was, most of the traffic was about two weeks behind and that the Abilene market was strong, so maybe they wouldn't stop but go directly on to Abilene to sell. After that stop, Dunigan proceeded westerly crossing a few Indian trails that appeared to be heading west to the buffalo grounds. As Indians preferred buffalo meat to beef, that reassured him.

After four days, they met back at camp and reported nothing unusual. Harris said he saw what looked to be Tonkawa tracks to the southeast, but they were headed away from the herd. Each bunch had found some old sign of rustler camps, but nothing recent and there had been no unrest among the cattle. Everyone arrived back just in time for supper, so the intelligence was exchanged over beef, beans, and coffee.

Pete supplied the news that the chief had demanded whiskey and someone to help him drink it every night, so the barrel was being well used. Only the chief had yet to figure out the bottle trick and did not know about refilling from the barrel, but the toll on the herd hands was awesome. Abel Castro had had a bit of a donnybrook over an Indian girl, but that had been straightened out, the chief deciding boys would be boys, or however that translated into Osage.

Dunigan was determined not to get caught unaware, so after a day in camp doing necessaries and eating Pablo's cooking rather than their own, the scouts rode out again. This time soon after they left camp they split into pairs and scouted a bit farther. Four days later they were back with little to report except for Harris, who had met a herd bound for Abilene, reporting that their steers were in poor condition and at least forty had been left behind. He hadn't seen any of them, although he had gone south a ways looking.

"Tonks got them, most likely," he shrugged.

On his return Dunigan inspected the herd and was pleased at its condition. They had added tallow enough that ribs and hip bones were no longer prominent. He estimated they might be able to move on in about two weeks. Dunigan had seen some evidence of rainfall in the northern sector and felt by moving slowly the herd might improve even more on the way to Abilene. Two days later saw them on the scout again, separating again into pairs. That would be the last scout because they would be moving the herd on to Abilene after they returned.

About thirty miles out from the Indian village, George Harris's group crossed a fresh trail of about ten shod horses, heavily laden but traveling slow, headed toward the Indian village. Harris dispatched his partner to Nick's group to tell them it looked like raiders and to head back to the herd to alert everyone. Harris then followed the trail the rest of that afternoon until he saw their dust cloud. He slowed so as not to alert them, but continued to follow until he saw their campfire. Carefully, he scouted the camp, counting nine very hard cases indeed. George moved back to his horse and set sail for the herd, arriving at noon the next day, his horse completely worn.

Harris had estimated it would take the raiders all that day to get close to the herd before they would be in position to attack that night.

Pete Roussel talked to the old chief about the impending raid, and the chief volunteered his two best scouts to keep surveillance on the party and sent them off eastward.

About midafternoon, the other two scouting parties showed up, so the outfit was back at full strength, plus the old chief and seven braves who also wanted a share in the fight.

Dunigan was torn between defending the herd where they were or attacking the raiders before they could attack.

The outlaws had numbers but they would be reacting, instead of having the initiative. Also there was the village: some of the Indian women and children might be hurt in a night foray. Dunigan decided to attack first and ask questions later, even though he had no proof the party was on its way to steal his cattle. There could be many reasons for the men to be traveling as they were, even heavily armed, and Harris had been unable to get close enough to identify any of them. However, there was little doubt that these men intended to steal the herd and that everyone, including the Indians, was in peril.

Dunigan, Harris, Roussel, and Nick McCurry held a council of war, deciding that since there was some doubt the men were rustlers at all, they would surround their camp, disarm them and drive away their horses. The attack would come after midnight.

About 5:00, the Indian scouts returned reporting the raiders were about five miles away, camped behind a hill to the east. That cinched it for Dunigan. This bunch had evil intentions toward his cattle. After dinner, arms were cleaned and checked, horses saddled, and Dunigan, ten of his trail hands, and four Indians were ready to move out at 8:00 o'clock.

Dunigan's final instructions reminded everyone to remove spurs and other noisemakers, to keep their approach silent. His plan was to come over the hill in a V toward the campfire, with himself and Roussel in the center, both armed with shot guns. The next two men on either side had big Sharps .50's; Nick McCurry and George Harris anchored each end of the line with the Indians and the other hands interspersed. Everyone was cautioned not to look at the campfire, for it would blind them in the night. Dunigan told them not to shoot until it became necessary, but if it did to shoot to kill. The Indian scouts had reported the enemy horses were on a picket line so there was no worry about splitting off to cover any horse guards.

A little after 8:00 the party set out riding to within 400 yards of the outlaw camp before dismounting, leaving two men to hold on to the horses. At the foot of the masking hill they formed into a V and marched within 30 yards of the campfire. The outlaws were seemingly unconcerned with security—they were all cleaning weapons and drinking coffee around the campfire.

Dunigan spoke. "You are surrounded. Do not move until you are told. Throw your weapons toward the fire."

The outlaws were completely surprised and not one of them moved. Dunigan counted nine, so they had them all sacked up. "Raise your hands over your heads and stand up. No sudden movements or you're dead."

All began to comply, but one man whirled, drawing a pistol from his waistband, and Dunigan shot him, knocking him back into the fire. No sound came from the body, so he was evidently dead on impact as his clothes were starting to burn. The eight survivors were moved together, searched and their hands and feet tied. The DG crew found assorted boot and belly guns, knives and even a set of brass knuckles, plus the rifles and pistols they first saw. Dunigan detailed two men to saddle the outlaw horses, drive them southeast about ten miles, then run them off. These same two would check the captives at the campfire on their way back to the herd.

Dire threats to life and limb and protestations of innocence were forthcoming from the captives. Dunigan responded. "I will remember your faces, and if I ever see any of you again, I will shoot you on sight, so ride clear of any DG outfit."

Dunigan had all their boots removed and sacked up with their weapons and these he would keep with his outfit. No money or valuables were taken and the captives were warned to go southeast to pick up their horses, then to keep on going, as they would be watched for a while.

The DG party then mounted up and rode off, Nick McCurry and the two Indian scouts being detailed to watch until daybreak to make sure the outlaws didn't try for the herd or the village. Their only possible weapon was a spade left so the dead outlaw could be buried. Dunigan and his bunch were in their bedrolls by 11:00.

Chapter 7

Security was tight that night around the herd and village but everyone was present at breakfast, Nick reporting in a little late because he had stayed to spy on the outlaws. He said they had gotten loose about 2:00 A.M. and set out at daybreak for their horses.

The crew started throwing the herd together and was ready to move by 11:00 A.M. Dunigan cut out thirteen steers, mostly lame, and two horses, which they owed the Osages, and threw in the outlaws' boots, guns, knives, and ammunition. He also left two bottles of whiskey for the chief. Their account settled, the outfit pointed the herd for Abilene and moved out across the Cimarron. Everyone was glad to be on the move again; even the drag raiders were elated. Recent rains meant there was very little dust and the fleshy cattle moved out smartly. They seemed happy to be moving north again, too.

Dunigan figured to reach Abilene within a month, maybe less, with the herd eating its way at over fifteen miles a day. Ten days saw them in Tonkawa country, where passage cost two footsore, but fleshy steers. Having crossed the Arkansas River without incident, Dunigan was optimistic about the rest of the drive.

As they bedded the herd after crossing into Kansas, Nick rode up to Dunigan. "Things are going too good, John. Something is bound to happen."

"Nothing is going to happen, Nick, don't worry. If you are really uneasy, why don't you scout for the next few days?"

"Thanks, I will. I just don't believe we'll get by as easy as we have. Besides, maybe I can find some real boogers for us to worry about," Nick laughed.

With Nick out scouting for wooly boogers, Dunigan rode off to see what was going on in Abilene. It took four days, but he was pleased with what he found. Most of early arrivals were thin, and steers in good condition were bringing premium prices. Many ranchers were in the market, taking the thin cattle to pasture on prime grass in the Flint Hills. Very few fleshy cattle had arrived and the market was strong, so Dunigan decided he might as well sell his herd upon arrival.

After contacting several brokers, Dunigan traded with a Kansas City broker at $23 a head, the price depending on the cattle being as good as Dunigan had described them. That done, Dunigan decided to sample some of Abilene town, visiting several bars and noting things were fairly wild, with fights and shootings almost every night. He also relieved the pressure on his brain with a couple of saloon ladies, whom he enjoyed immensely. He could see how the young drovers were being separated from their wages by the town and vowed to keep his crew from impoverishing themselves.

After three days in Abilene, Dunigan went back to the herd. Arriving after a three-day ride, he was happy to find all going well. The herd was still moving smartly, gaining weight. Nick was unable to find any hoodoos, but was still out looking. Fair enough, Dunigan thought, it can't hurt to be vigilant.

Seven days later, the commission broker rode out to inspect the herd, to make sure its condition justified his offering price. Satisfied, he stayed for supper, then rode back to Abilene that night, the herd being close to town. Dunigan told the broker to arrange for the pens by eight the next morning. The outfit would load the steers before noon, as there was plenty of rolling stock available.

Next day, Dunigan's men brought the herd in and had it penned before eight. They began loading steers right away and were finished by noon. Dunigan invited everyone to the dinner Pablo had prepared near the pens. All of the trainmen plus the Abilene pens workforce attended, and Pablo did himself proud with some fresh groceries he had picked up in Abilene that morning. The final head count, carefully tallied by the buyer and Dunigan jointly as the cattle were loaded on the train, was 2,563 steers, a total of $58,949, more money than Dunigan had ever seen in his life. Dunigan requested and received $5,000 in cash for immediate expenses, and had the rest deposited with Daniel Sullivan of Indianola, Texas.

After the tally was confirmed, everyone adjourned to the chuckwagon where a barrel of beer brought from a local saloon was tapped. Several rounds later, Pablo announced dinner was ready and most everyone got a plate and ate. A few, particularly the hands, did not want to leave the beer, but finally everyone was fed and fed well. After dinner, Dunigan gathered his hands.

"Boys", said Dunigan, "you all know I spent some time in this town before you got here. I know you are all anxious to have some fun, but I have something to warn you about."

"Abilene is a wide open town and quite a few young blades from Texas have been killed here. You each have about $150 coming in wages and I don't want to see you waste all of it here, so I have an offer. If you will all leave with me in three days for Texas, I will provide you with horses and food for the trip, and I will give you fifty dollars in cash now, and will deposit a hundred dollars for you whenever you want me to. Fifty dollars ought to buy you enough whiskey and women in three days to satisfy yourselves, then you will have a free trip home and a hundred dollars when you get there."

Dunigan stopped to let his offer sink in and there was considerable discussion about his proposition. In the end, all but three men took it, and August 5 was set for departure.

Dunigan continued. "I want to ask all of you to leave your guns here at the wagon until we leave. The marshal here is awful tough. Print Olives' bunch has just delivered a herd, and although they are from the San Gabriel River country, they are a gun outfit. There is considerable danger here and if you don't have a gun, most of it can be avoided. I beg you, don't wear a gun. Most of this town is waiting to rob or kill you. Don't give them the excuse."

Most of the hands were impressed by the boss's thinking and agreed to leave their guns at the wagon. The older ones wondered why Dunigan was so concerned about their safety. Pete and Nick knew why. He wanted to start hunting cows soon after he got home, and he liked this outfit he had trained to work the Dunigan way. Even two of the three who were not going back to Texas with them left their guns at the wagon, saying they would see them off on the fifth. They drew their wages and went off to town, mainly to get washed and barbered before night. Dunigan did not leave the wagon that night, thinking he might set a good example, but Pablo was the only one who stayed and even he went into town for about two hours.

Next day, the men going back to Texas selected two horses apiece, and Dunigan cut out seven of the best to sell at Fort Riley. He and Nick took them over and were told by the quartermaster they could probably sell them all, if the rest had the quality of the ones they had with them. There was quite a bit of Indian activity on the plains and the cavalry needed horses. Dunigan left the seven and they went back for the others. He sold thirty-four to the cavalry for $115 each, and sold two more to the Abilene livery for $40 a head. That taken care of, he helped Pablo sort out and load up for the trip back starting at dawn the next day.

But they did not leave the environs of Abilene until almost 10:00 A.M. The hands had had a real bang-up time on their night in town and their hangovers were acute. Even Nick felt none too pert, and there was considerable moaning and vomiting and treatment of cuts and bruises before everyone was saddled up to leave. Fortunately, no one got involved in any mortal disagreements, so they were all still in one piece, although a few were not too sure their heads were still with them. Chito Guerrico had been called a greaser by one of the saloon bullies, and Lon Castle proceeded to pound the man into the floor, and Nick McCurry had a mouthing with someone, but all in all it could have been called a quiet night on the town.

Dunigan made as much time as possible that day, wanting to get as far away from Abilene as possible so no one would be tempted to return. They covered about thirty miles and ate nothing until supper, which was ready about 8:30 that night. Although there were some wistful thoughts about 'Mary and Peggy Sue,' the men were too tired to do anything but roll up in their blankets.

Next morning everyone was up and saddled at dawn, feeling much better and the trip from then on was swift, aside from a rough crossing for the chuckwagon over the Red River. The wagon tongue broke, but nothing else bad occurred and the whole bunch was back on the Aransas by midSeptember. Much fuss was made on their return by Pablo's family and by Michael O'Grady, and tears of joy were shed by the stay-at-homes upon seeing their travelers. The joyous reunion continued that night and through the next day, and didn't end until Dunigan began talking about the upcoming cow hunt.

Chapter 8

Preparations for the cow hunt began in earnest. Hands were selecting horses, repairing tack, and gathering supplies. Nick and Dunigan rode over to the old stage station to see if anything needed doing. A few repairs were in order, but most everything was still intact and looked unused. Dunigan hoped it was still unknown to the bandits of the border.

They returned to the Aransas, covering their trail as before and watching carefully. When they got back, almost all the preparations for the move were done. Michael O'Grady had broken ten new horses, and each had been claimed, except one he had broken especially for Dunigan: a beautiful blood bay with long, clean legs, and a perfect star on his forehead. Dunigan named him Texas for the star and was grateful to Michael. All the men were a little envious of Dunigan, not only for the horse, but for Michael's obvious devotion. Such loyalty was rare in Texas during Reconstruction and was highly valued. Right then, Dunigan decided to let Michael go up the trail next time.

The next week, Dunigan led the party out to the old stage station. In all, there were ten men and Pablo and his family. They took two wagons and two pack horses loaded with supplies so they would not have to make any side trips for replenishment, reducing the danger of discovery by bandits. Dunigan did not intend to stay at the camp, because he felt the wild cattle population had shrunk considerably, so he figured he would need to buy some. He did stay for two weeks while they captured sixty horses, and realized that indeed, there were fewer wild cattle below the Nueces, but they were still numerous.

Many of the steers and bulls had been captured and taken,

but there were more out there. Quite a few people seemed to have taken up cow hunting while Dunigan was on the trail to Kansas, boding ill for the costs of trail drivers. Now, most cattle would likely have to be bought from ranchers and hunters.

No more free steers, Dunigan thought, thanking his stars he had enough gold to buy what he needed. There were good summer rains and that fall, too, so the wild cattle were in decent shape. If the winter were mild, maybe Dunigan's herd could go straight through to Abilene.

After two weeks at the old stage station, Dunigan was satisfied everything was going well, so he saddled up Texas, his new bay pony, and set out to find some steers to buy. Instead of going back to his ranch, Dunigan headed toward Oakville and Beeville. From there he went to Karnes City and found quite a few. Most of them had been captured out of the Nueces strip that summer and were in bunches of 50 to 300. Since he had no cash with him, he contracted to pay on delivery in sixty days, paying from six to nine dollars a head. When he left Karnes City, Dunigan had bought 650 head, picking up 200 more from Goliad to Victoria, but he bought those for less from farmers and townsfolk, because they were mostly out of milk cows.

Stopping in Victoria for a few days to rest his horse and himself, he rode to Indianola to visit his banker, Danny Sullivan, arranging payment for the cattle he had bought. Dunigan spent the night on the coast, and next morning set out to see old man Maille at Salt Creek to fill out his herd. He had a lively visit with the crusty Irishman, and arranged for spring delivery of 600 steers at eight dollars. Arriving on the Aransas after six weeks, Dunigan had bought 1,485 steers at an average price of $7.18. He thought he had done well, but his cost had escalated over last year.

By the time he got home the weather had turned cool and very pleasant. The first thing he did was write letters to everyone from whom he had bought steers telling them when he would arrive to take delivery. He was eager to get back to Nick and the outfit to see how many steers they had caught. He was sure that they would have plenty, but was still worried about rustlers. The three men who had stayed behind in Abilene had arrived at the ranch broke but in one piece, without too many new scars. Dunigan was glad to see them and they told him all the gossip from Kansas, and of the narrow scrapes they had had.

"You sure were right, boss. We all nearly got shot up. Them

Olive hands had a fight with them sunflower sons of bitches, and we were caught in between," Billy Parmalee related.

"And their marshal? He knocks me out and puts me all night in the calabozo," Abel Castro said.

"Well, we're going back to the stage station in the morning to see how things are going and to help bring back the steers. If they're not ready, I have bought a bunch up around Beeville and Goliad and we'll need to bring them home."

Dunigan, Billy Parmalee, Abel Castro, and Lem Bracken rode out the next day for the Nueces, arriving after an overnight camp. Nick greeted them warmly, telling Dunigan they were nearly through, with only one more bunch to bring in from the trap corrals making 1,097 steers and 62 horses.

Over supper, George Harris said he had seen some distant dust trails to the south and southwest late that afternoon. He had not had time to check them out, but would in the morning.

Dunigan was worried that they might be hit that night so he spread all his men around the corrals and set watches for the night. He rode rounds at dark and reassured himself all the men were in place, protected, and alert. He unrolled his own blankets next to the main corral gate with his shotgun by his side.

The outlaws hit at midnight with little advance warning. Pete Roussel shot one man off his horse when they were within fifty yards of the corrals and with Pete's first shot, all hell broke loose. About twenty horsemen, half Anglo and half Mexican came charging in from all directions, firing toward the corrals. The fight lasted over a half hour and it was a very near thing that they were finally driven off. Dunigan himself killed three as they charged up to open the gate. Pablo and Abel Castro did a great deal of damage from their position atop the roof of the old station, as did George Harris and Billy Parmalee, at the back gate of the pens. Parmalee was the only casualty, taking a bullet through the leg, but he would recover. At dawn they counted ten dead outlaws and a trail of another being dragged off by a frightened pony. Seven horses with empty saddles were standing at the pens. Harris was off at daylight back-trailing the outlaws, returning in time for dinner to report he had trailed them about fifteen miles south before they stopped to lick their wounds.

"Looks like three or four were hit, and I sent them on their way with a few shots from my old Sharps. Got another one, too. Leastwise he didn't move from where he hit the ground. Last I saw them, they were moving south, going too fast for me to catch up. I don't think they'll be back. There were only about three left with their skins whole."

Dunigan had crowded the cattle in the inner pens for the night, and they didn't break out during the shooting, probably because they were too weak and tired. One horse was killed by a stray bullet, but the outlaws' horses and saddles more than made up for that. Billy's wound was not serious, but was painful, so he would have to go back in the wagon. By the time Nick got in with the last of the steers, everything was packed up.

They were ready to move out in the morning, but Dunigan set a watch that night. Not that he expected any trouble after the beating they gave the outlaws, but the DG's whereabouts were known and would soon be wider known. Dunigan wanted to leave as soon as possible; it was no longer safe here.

Three days later they turned the steers loose on the Aransas. There was good grass because it hadn't been frosted back yet, so the cattle settled down quickly and began filling up.

By then, it was nearly time to collect the purchased steers—the first delivery was in four days at Oakville. Dunigan had made arrangements with Sullivan to forward funds to Refugio and Beeville so he could pay gold for the cattle.

He took ten men. The first herd of 150 steers was south of Oakville and ran all the way to Beeville, so the outfit had to backtrack to get the next bunch of 75 only 10 miles from the first. The cattle stampeded from ranch to ranch all the way to Victoria; they lost three horses.

From Victoria back to Refugio the steers were tuckered out from so much running and moved along pretty well. It was four days to Dunigan's rented pastures on the San Antonio River. Pete Roussel and two others saw to the cattle and Dunigan and the rest went to the ranch. He was worn out from running cattle over three counties. They had branded the steers as they were received, so everything was ready for next spring's drive except for Maille's Salt Creek steers, last-minute repairs, and packing. When Nick had left to brand the Salt Creek steers, all the other cattle were in place and the crew ready.

Dunigan had nothing to do so he went off to Corpus Christi to find out what was going on in the rest of the world, stopping off at Rockport to sell some hides.

Chapter 9

Planning a three-day visit in Corpus Christi, Dunigan took a boardinghouse room before going downtown to find a cafe for his evening meal. He was uneasy because he realized he was becoming a man of substance. He owned over two thousand acres of land on the Aransas River and had hard cash in the bank, a far cry from the immigrant Irish lad who lived with relatives and ran errands for pocket money. He was not sure he was comfortable with his new prosperity, because he still enjoyed more the company of working cowhands than any other class. He was uneasy about moving into the moneyed class, having to worry about taxes, politics, a home, and a family.

Dunigan had always taken his pleasures where he found them, mostly with whores and in saloons and at horse races and other sporting endeavors. He was not at all sure he wanted to become respectable. But he was growing older and a desire for gaining permanence in a new generation was rising within him. He had been infected with the normal ambitions that all men succumb to eventually.

The next two days Dunigan spent seeking out other men of substance in coffeehouses and hotels, banks and business houses, to see if he really wanted to change his ways.

As luck would have it, Dunigan met a Mister Augustus Thrall of Thrall and Company, a prosperous merchant and customs broker, who had been involved in the cotton trade with Mexico during the late war. The men exchanged memories of that enterprise, and agreed to meet over drinks late that afternoon in one of the city's better saloons to get acquainted.

Talking mostly about his own business, Augustus Thrall had little good to say about anything else. Portly and loud, his opinions were overheard by everyone in the saloon. Dunigan worried about trouble, because some of Thrall's views were not universally popular, such as his support of the state police of Governor Edmund J. Davis. The police administered and enforced the reconstruction laws that were choking Texas. Many of the state police were negroes, ex-slaves, and in a state only four years past negro slavery, that didn't set too well with white Texans, although even they agreed law and order were necessary. The state police were mostly busy in East Texas and didn't often get as far west as the coastal bend. Dunigan had no desire to get into a brawl so he made his excuses to leave, but then Thrall asked him to dinner at his home the following night. Dunigan accepted the invitation readily and left, returning to his boardinghouse for supper and an early sleep.

Next morning, Dunigan walked downtown to buy some clothes more befitting his status as a man of substance. He found a tailor, ordered two suits and bought a nice ready-made suit, too. Then he located a bootmaker and ordered two new pair with tooled leather tops as well as a pair of shoes. He also bought some shirts and a new 5X Stetson before deciding he had enough. On his way back to his lodgings, he passed a hardware store displaying firearms. Inside he saw a strange looking rifle he had not seen before: a Winchester repeater with a brass frame with a lever that worked the action to reload. The rifle was nicely balanced and Dunigan liked its feel, so he bought two, one for Nick. The store also had some nice pistols, but since his own was fairly new, Dunigan decided to halt his profligacy and arrived at his room just in time for dinner.

The plain fare of the boardinghouse, pot roast, rice and green beans suited Dunigan just right, and set him to worrying again about his new image. He enjoyed this kind of food and would much rather have it than all the delicacies that abounded in the Corpus Christi restaurants he visited. There was nothing in his makeup to incline him toward the levelers or even to populism, the new movement just beginning up north. Dunigan wanted to be rich, but was uncomfortable becoming a nabob. His whole experience militated against such goings on, and he was just more comfortable with cowhands and commonfolks than bankers and merchants.

He spent the following day preparing for his social debut. He had his best suit cleaned and made sure his shirt was freshly laundered and that his boots shone. He hired a carriage to take him to Thrall's house and to wait for him. At six the carriage and driver arrived and drove him to the address Thrall had given him, arriving on time. The house was on the bluff over-looking the bay and was large and imposing, with lots of ginger-bread on the galleries surrounding the house on all sides. It was set back from the street on a generous lot. With some trepi-dation, Dunigan approached and rang the doorbell. The door was opened by a handsome, white-haired negro in livery.

"Mister Dunigan?"

"That is my name. I take it this is Mister Thrall's residence."

"Yessuh, it is. The family is waiting for you in the parlor."

Dunigan was shown into a small room crowded with furni-ture, and where Thrall, his wife, and a young woman Dunigan took to be a daughter Thrall had mentioned were waiting. She was a pretty woman, but a bit long in the tooth to be single. Dunigan figured she was about twenty-five. Mrs. Thrall was a plump lady, trussed to the eyes and sweating, although it was chilly at that time of the year, even in Corpus Christi. Dunigan was seated and offered a glass of sherry, which he took, watching all the while and noticing it was sipped, rather than drunk, and did likewise. Small talk ensued, as the Thrall ladies were quite garrulous and they asked him all about trail driving and the cat-tle business. They also asked in a roundabout way about his background. He spoke of his childhood in Ireland and his uncle in Refugio and his past history.

There was a noticeable cooling in the atmosphere during these revelations, particularly from the older Thralls. But the young lady just gushed on and on. The houseman appeared with more sherry, and when Dunigan accepted gratefully, Mrs. Thrall pursed her lips. In a while they moved to the dining room for dinner, which was oysters, roast chicken and trimmings, with ice cream for dessert.

As Dunigan ate he contrasted the meal with his boarding-house supper and in his mind the Thralls' effort came in second. The conversation continued along the same lines: Dunigan's early history, then his trail drives. The elder Thrall's pursed their lips tighter and tighter, but Miss Thrall, Augusta (never Gussie) just oohed and aahed. Dunigan was increasingly uncom-fortable, even sweating in the cool room. He managed to turn the conversation to Thrall's history because Dunigan wanted to know more about him.

Thrall liked talking about himself and once launched, was unstoppable.

"I first came to Texas as a supply contract agent for the army; my family's company in Waterbury, Connecticut, was the supplier of harness, saddlery and leather goods to the army, and we did a good business. I followed the army south as far as Fort Brown, and returning home in 1847, as most of the supplies were being shipped direct to Vera Cruz from New Haven. In 1854, I returned to Corpus Christi, having decided the opportunities here were enormous. I was selling our family products here until 1860, when I returned home to Waterbury because of the onset of the war. When the war broke out, I again became a contract agent to the army, working mainly in Washington.

"The war was good for our business and we prospered, but after Appomattox my older brother came home from the army and took over the company, my father having passed away just as the war ended. I had made many contacts in Washington and was able to secure an appointment in civil administration in San Augustine and I worked there until two years ago, but I had not forgotten Corpus Christi, having done what I could to bring Texas back into the union, and ease the plight of the poor negroes in East Texas. I resigned and came back to Corpus, going into the hardware business, as well as selling our family leather products here. I have done rather well as you can see, and moved my family here in 1868."

When Thrall spread his arms to encompass the house and grounds, Mrs. Thrall smiled smugly and Augusta looked on admiringly.

So he is a proper carpetbagger and proud of it. Ain't that a kick in the ass, Dunigan groused to himself.

They adjourned to the parlor and Thrall had brandy and cigars brought in. Having gained the floor over dinner, Thrall was reluctant to relinquish it and went on about the glories of the union victory. He spoke at length about his older brother, who he obviously did not care for. But as he had lost an arm at Gettysburg, he was a hero of the Republic and so praised by Thrall. The women had left them for a time, but once the cigars and brandy were consumed they returned to the parlor.

Dunigan had had a difficult time with the silverware at dinner, but had watched and copied the Thralls, so he made no major gaffes. He felt much better now that all of it was over, so he turned his attention to Miss Thrall. She was indeed a pretty woman. Auburn hair and black eyes accentuated a fairly voluptuous figure, which caused stirrings in Dunigan's loins. These stirrings were not accompanied by any appreciation for her mind and character, for he had already appraised her frivolous, but she did have a definite aura of sensuality.

Dunigan had no experience on the wife-hunting trail, so he had not heard the old adage of the daughter resembling the mother in twenty years, and he had paid scant attention to Mrs. Thrall, but later would recall much more.

Dunigan was on the verge of saying goodnight and leaving when the elder Thralls stood up and announced they were retiring but suggested Dunigan and Augusta stay and enjoy the night air. The host and hostess promptly went upstairs. Mrs. Thrall asked Augusta if she needed anything as she was going to let the servants off. The daughter shook her head and smiled warmly as she poured Dunigan another brandy.

"Would you like to get a wrap and take the night air before I leave, Miss Augusta?"

"Yes, that would be pleasant," she said, widening her smile.

She got a shawl and they went out on the gallery on the west side where there was some cane furniture. He seated her in a chair and took a seat on a settee, the only other piece of furniture there. The night was pleasant and Dunigan relaxed. He had felt warm in the parlor, mainly from nervousness, but the brandy had calmed him and the fresh, cool night air helped even more.

Dunigan finished his brandy and sensed a movement. Lowering his glass, he was astounded to find Augusta's lips only inches from his. They kissed and her tongue forced its way into his mouth. Seldom had any girl been that quick with him and he was even more startled when she unbuttoned his trousers and grasped his member. Things became lively indeed, and soon the settee was rocking to the urgent motions of lovemaking. Dunigan almost felt as if he had been raped, but he enjoyed every moment. Twenty minutes after they left the parlor, he was saying goodnight, his teeth well cleaned by Augusta's agile tongue. He found his carriage parked discreetly around the corner. He was soon fast asleep in his boardinghouse.

Dunigan sent small gifts to Mrs. Thrall and Augusta, enclosing a promise to write to the latter, packed his traps and left for the ranch. It had been an eye-opening trip for him and he was still in a daze as he traveled north. His entry to polite society had left him awash in a sea of confusion. One thing he did know, however, was that Augusta was not whom he wanted to sire a family with, even though she was a lot of fun. He would return to Corpus Christi in about a month to pick up his new suits and boots and planned to have another round with her then.

Chapter 10

The weather was a bit colder than usual, but the rains came on time and Dunigan's steers wintered over quite well. He picked up his new clothes in Corpus Christi and when he visited Augusta Thrall, if anything, she was more ardent. Maille's steers from Salt Creek were delivered and the herd headed for Kansas on the 12th of March, 1869.

The drive to Red River was boring and uneventful, but the herd hit rain north of Waco for three days. After the Brazos crossing the herd was stampeded by a nearby lightning strike. It was a fifteen-mile run and they lost twenty-three animals. Their only other losses were the twelve they gave the Osage tribe they had pastured with the year before. In Abilene, the herd brought $22.25 per head. By that time the trail was pretty nearly clear of rustlers because every passing herd had had a crack at them, so the outlaws were looking for easier pickings in other places.

Trail herding had become more boring than anything else and less of an adventure. The routine of cow hunting in the summer and trail herding in the spring had began to pall on Dunigan, but it was a business like any other and the profits were still good. So good Dunigan decided he would send two herds the following year, if he could find enough steers.

That decision made, Dunigan hurried back to Texas to put together his herd and to start hunting cattle in South Texas, hoping to get his catch together before the wild cattle were picked over. He led his crew back right after the herd was delivered and took his horses back as well, because he would need them for the second drive.

On the way back, he told his crew about the two-herds plan

for next spring, designating Nick McCurry and Pete Roussel as trail bosses for each. That picked up everyone's spirits and Nick and Pete entered into a good-natured rivalry that would last until next summer when the cattle were delivered in Abilene. Both men were thinking how to put their outfits together, what men they could hire and how Dunigan would split up the existing crew and equipment.

Dunigan was concerned only that they did it right, but in the back of his mind he realized too much competition between them would be bad. Right now he wanted only to get below the Nueces to start capturing cattle. He hoped the rivalry would stay at a competitive level and not result in animosity. He told Nick his 10 percent interest would only hold for his own herd and not Pete's, which Nick thought was fair.

The outfit arrived in Refugio on July 5th and was back on Salado Creek by August 1st. They found most of the installation intact, but some things had been deliberately destroyed, Dunigan reasoned, by the outlaw band they had shot up so badly the year before. They had probably done it out of spite, otherwise, if they knew about the place, why discourage Dunigan from using it again? Dunigan knew more stringent security measures would have to be adopted, but except for that, they would proceed as before.

Delegating George Harris and Pete Roussel to permanent scouting, Dunigan began to organize the cow hunt. The crew had repaired the outlaws' vandalism so they could devote their energies to capturing steers. Because they had fresh horses and plenty of hands they ranged farther west and south and spotted many, many cattle that did not appear to have been hunted.

Dunigan sent Nick McCurry to Laredo to pick up some wet-backs to build catchpens in the areas where they had spotted the bigger bunches. Because the area with the most cattle was sixty miles south and seventy-five west of the stage station on Salado Creek, Dunigan built his pens a bit bigger so he could hold the steers longer. He also had to jury-rig some water for the pens.

One of his wetbacks knew where there was some bamboo for piping close to Laredo and knew how to fix it, so that was accomplished, too. Even by working a larger and more distant area, Dunigan figured he should come out with more cattle. Since it was only August 10th, Dunigan took two more weeks strengthening his old trap corrals and enlarging the pens at the stage station, plus cutting grass for the penned steers so they would have enough feed to handle the larger herd. At the end of August, the temperature was cool enough to start capturing cattle and there had been some rain, too, putting their water in good shape.

After three weeks, they had assembled some 2,700 head, mostly from the farther areas. Dunigan decided to take them back home, figuring to come back, for there were still plenty of cattle to be caught. Dunigan was uneasy because the fresh grass had brought the cattle along in good shape. He thought they might have trouble getting all of them back to the ranch on the Aransas.

He was right. When they turned them out, the cattle ran for over fifteen miles and by the time they got them stopped and gathered, he was short five hundred. He figured to pick up most of them in subsequent sweeps when they returned below the Nueces. The cattle, their run over, settled quickly into a ground-eating walk, reaching the home ranch in two days. The crew took time and care in putting them out along the river, then were back on the Salado in a week, having left Michael O'Grady and Manuel Menchaca to line-ride the new steers to keep them on the home range.

Chapter 11

Crossing the Salado, coming up on the old stage station, Dunigan sensed something unusual. Harris and Roussel had stayed behind to keep scouting and the footmen from Mexico were there putting up more hay and caring for the horses. As they rode up, Pete and George walked out of the old building and waved.

"Come on in, dinner's ready," yelled Pete.

"Got some news," said George Harris, "some good and some bad." He grinned evilly.

"Uh oh," Dunigan said. "I knew it was too good to last."

They dismounted, unsaddling their mounts and turning them in with the horses in the pens. Dunigan thought he saw some strange horses in the bunch. They all walked over to the station for dinner. There was plenty, as Pablo had been expecting them.

"Good news first, boss?" George asked, as soon as they were seated.

"Yeah, George and then the bad."

"Well boss, we got ten more good horses. Ran across them a week ago, penned them, and just kept these. Turned about forty-five back and brought these here. That is the good news. The bad news is that we have a bandit captured. We got him yesterday after tracking him up from the south. He probably came from around Mier or Camargo, across the river. I don't know what to do with him. He's tied to a tree outside. Maybe Abel or Juan Redondo can get something out of him."

"Abel, Juan, vaya hablar con el. Necessitamos informacion de su lugar y quien es su jefe."

"Si, patron, lo hago," said Abel, economical as ever with his words.

Castro and Redondo left and Nick got up to follow them.

"I think that guy is a Cortinista, and they were pretty rough with any Maximillianos they captured. I think I better go along to see we don't lose him too soon."

"Yeah, Nick, we need to know if word about what we're doing has got back across the river and if anyone is coming behind him."

"Okay, John, I'll try to keep him alive." McCurry walked out toward the Mexican captive.

For the next hour, Dunigan heard a few thumps and bumps and some squalls of discomfort, but nothing serious. Nick came back to the station and reported no progress.

Dunigan and Nick watched the interrogation through the open door. Castro took out a large knife, and there were a few more yelps, but evidently no information, for they were still at work. Castro spoke to Juan and he walked off toward the corral. He caught a horse and saddled him and walked back to where the bandit was tied.

Dunigan felt it was time to get involved. He and Nick got up and walked over to the tree. The Mexican did not look too much the worse for wear.

"Dice algo, Abel?" Dunigan asked.

"No, patron, pero yo se es Cortinista, bandido y asesino, y el va hablar prontito." (No, boss, but this Cortinista killer will talk, and soon.) With that Abel cut loose the bandit's hands, knocked him to the ground and rearranged the ropes that held his feet to the base of the tree. Juan had mounted the horse and he tossed his rope to Castro. Castro put the loop around the captive's neck. The bandit's eyes were like saucers when he saw Redondo tie the rope fast to his saddlehorn and take up the slack.

Castro bent down and spoke to the terrified bandit. "Oye, hijo de la chinagada, es importante que hablas ahora, antes que quitamos su cabeza, porqué no podría hablar sin cabeza." (Listen to me, you son of a bitch, talk to me right now, before we take your head off, because you won't be able to without a head!)

Castro signaled Juan, who nudged his horse as far as the slack in the rope allowed. The bandit became extremely voluble, talking so fast Dunigan could not follow, but Castro was listening intently. The rope had not been slacked, but when the man stopped talking and swallowed, Juan eased up his horse, as the bandit's face was getting almost black.

Several of the Mexican hands had gathered around and Castro told them to get the man up. They did, but with difficulty as he was limp with terror and there was no starch left in him. He was shaking and had soiled himself.

Castro turned to Dunigan. "He told me everything. They are coming across the river tonight and will attack tomorrow night. There will be about thirty of them, coming through Roma and San Ysidro. The survivors of last year's raid will be with them so they will know to try something different this time."

Dunigan grinned. "How come you speak such good English now, Abel?"

"Quien sabe, patron?" He walked off.

"Wait a bit, Castro, I got a question."

"Digame?" Tell me.

"Do you know that trail?"

"Si, patron, es un sendero bien marcado. Pasa por San Ysidro y va por Cotulla, y otro sendero viene aqui como quince millas." (Sure, boss, it's well marked. Goes through San Ysidro and passes Cotulla, where the other trail reaches us after about 15 miles.)

"Could they reach that branch before tomorrow afternoon?"

"No, patron, no pueden. Dispenseme porqué necesito limpear este maricon." (Not a chance, boss. If you'll excuse me, I'll go clean up this sissy.)

"No es necessario, Castro. Llevaremos al rama del sendero, y dejamos su cuerpo alla. Ojala que regresaran todos los bandidos a Mexico." (Don't bother, Castro. We'll dump his body where the trail forks. One look it his corpse and the rest of his gang will high-tail it for Mexico.)

"Nick, get everyone ready. If they don't turn back to Mexico, we'll ambush them along the trail here. Pete should know a good place."

"I sure do, boss. About six miles from here the trail widens suddenly around a curve so you're in it before you know it. It is really a great ambush."

Pete was enthusiastic about the place, almost bloodthirsty, Dunigan thought. They set out with their prisoner, who although tied, was given a wide berth because of his aroma. Dunigan left Pablo and four others at the station in case they missed the gang. In about two hours they arrived at the place

Pete had recommended.

Dunigan was impressed. It was a perfect spot and the ambushees were in a clear depression before they knew it and the ambushers had clear fields of fire from the high ground. Dunigan left Nick with nine men at the ambush and continued on with Castro, Redondo, and George Harris to the junction with the trail from San Ysidro.

They arrived with about an hour of daylight left. Dunigan found a tall mesquite beside the trail, threw his rope over a high limb and tied it to a lower limb. He motioned Castro to bring up the terrified bandit. Dunigan put the loop over his head, then quirted his mount out from under him. The man's neck broke at once.

Then Dunigan rode out to see if the scene was set properly. It was perfect. When the bandits rode into the junction, the first thing they would see was their hanged compadre. If that didn't stop them, then came the ambush.

The men gathered up the bandit's horse and set out for the ambush. George Harris and Abel Castro dropped off to find a spot to watch from when the bandits found their compadre. If they came on, Harris and Castro would follow, to catch any fleeing survivors. The two of them moved off the sendero, finding a good place to camp and wait. It would be the following afternoon before the outlaws could get to the junction and they made sure to get upwind.

When he and Juan Redondo got back to the ambush, Dunigan was pleased with the arrangements. If the bandits came, it was likely none would escape, but he wouldn't enjoy it. He had had enough with hanging the outlaw.

Since they were well up the trail they lit a fire and made coffee and fried some bacon. They could have fires and food until noon tomorrow, but after that they could expect the bandits to be around.

Harris and Castro did not have that luxury. Their promixity to the trail dictated a dry and cold camp and extreme vigilance. They first saw the dust cloud about 9:00 A.M., and fifteen minutes later the outlaw band rode into the junction. The display of the hanged bandit was effective. By now, the body was still and putrefying, so it exercised a terrifying fascination for the outlaw band.

They all slid to a halt and gazed at the apparition for several minutes before anyone spoke. One bandit dismounted and threw up while another approached for positive identification, then ensued a discussion for about twenty minutes, everyone yelling and pointing fingers and going around in circles. About half way through this uproar the bandit who had vomited mounted his horse and rode south. Harris and Castro were close enough to hear allegations about "Rinches," but finally the whole band became silent, turned, and rode back the way they had come, not bothering to cut down and bury the unfortunate rustler. Harris backtrailed them for about a mile to make sure of their intentions, then returned. He and Castro rode back to the ambush site, approaching gingerly to forestall any mistakes in identity, arriving about 2:00 A.M.

Everyone was much relieved that the bandits had chosen the better part of valor and all rode back to Salado Creek, mostly in silence. Even Pablo's excellent supper did not dispel the somber atmosphere that night, but tomorrow's dawn would bring relief. There were no jolly cowboy songs that night. George Harris and Abel Castro took up the role of being called "Rinches."

"Mira," Harris said, "the great ranger's band defeats the Cortinista bandidos."

Castro added his curse. "I wish I was a 'rinche' for I would cut the nuts out of those maricones. I would make them squeal like piggies."

*Rinches—Mexican pronunciation of "rangers," who in their forays to the Rio Grande and below had earned bloody reputations for shooting first and asking questions later. Even to this day Rinches invoke fear and loathing on both sides of the Rio Grande.

Chapter 12

The next day was spent repairing equipment and choosing and spreading out the horses Pete and Harris had brought in. Preparations were completed for the cow hunt starting in the morning. The following three weeks produced close to 2,500 steers, which were driven to the San Antonio River country Dunigan had arranged for earlier. It was familiar ground, as he had pastured steers there for two years running, and his cattle had always wintered well. The steers were turned out by November 1, and he left Pete, Lem Bracken, Lon Castle, and Juan Redondo to watch them and ride the line. Dunigan promised to send over a cook as soon as he could find one, and the four cowmen settled into two frame houses in the middle of the range.

The rest of the year was spent securing stock and equipment for two crews instead of the one Dunigan was used to. He bought a couple of wagons and cooking utensils for a chuckwagon and ran across two negroes in Refugio that he hired. One, Adam Johnson, said he had been a camp cook for an East Texas outfit, but the other man was no cook. He was tall, straight and dignified, a man in the Old South who would have been labeled an 'uppity nigger.' Dunigan was fascinated by him, having never met a black man who was so stand-offish. Abner Cottrell said he had a lot of experience breeding and handling mules. Dunigan did not really know what he would do with Abner, but hired him anyway. He was going to need several teams of mules, because they would need twice as much of everything for the coming year.

Abner Cottrell was born on a cotton plantation in 1841, the

son of a slave couple. When he was sixteen, the plantation changed hands and the new overseer's attitude toward the slaves hardened considerably. Floggings and beatings became commonplace, slave schooling was ended, and it wasn't long before young Abner was tied up and flogged. That violence changed Abner overnight from a happy teenager to a silent, sullen man who did his work but nothing more.

In 1859, he escaped to Arkansas, heading for Kansas, but was captured and returned. This time, Abner was flogged almost to death and could not work for several months. By the time he recovered, the war had broken out, so he escaped again, heading once more toward Kansas. He was picked up and put in a forced labor battalion digging defenses in Arkansas, from which he again escaped and went west into Indian territory, still trying to reach free territory.

Working his way north, Abner hooked up with a wagon train on the Santa Fe Trail as a mule skinner and made two round trips. Traffic on the Santa Fe fell off considerably because of the war and in 1863, the freighters sold him out to slave catchers who took Abner to Texas, where he was a slave on a cotton farm when the war ended.

Set adrift at that point, Abner began sharecropping in East Texas, but after two crop failures was cut loose again. He scratched out a living for two years, breaking and training mules for various farms in East and Central Texas until he arrived in Refugio, where he met John Dunigan.

Abner Cottrell had become a keen judge of men's characters and in Dunigan he saw a man who would treat him as a man, nothing more but nothing less. Abner did not give loyalty easily nor quickly, but he would give it to a man who, in his estimation, earned it. He thought Dunigan might be such a man, so he hooked up with him, not really sure yet where that would take him.

Abner had picked up all the tricks negroes had to know to survive in the postwar South, but cared little for them, preferring to provide honest work for wages. He saw in John Dunigan a man who might want the same thing.

Dunigan thought he ought to tell old man Maille at Salt Creek that he wasn't going to buy any of his steers this year, so he and Michael O'Grady rode down to visit. The old man was the same as ever and very hospitable, so Michael and Dunigan spent the night and talked to Maille for most of it. The result was that Dunigan agreed to take Maille's steers to Abilene and sell them for him, collecting a fee. Dunigan liked the old man and Maille reciprocated. He was especially fond of Michael. Maille didn't have but five hundred steers that year and Dunigan figured those few would not overly burden him. Maille already had Dunigan's trail brand and said he would brand his animals and deliver them to the herd in the spring.

When Dunigan mentioned he was in the market for horses and mules, Maille said he had the best. They looked at some of his stock and Dunigan told him he would send Michael and Abner Cottrell down the next week to pick out what he would need. When Maille agreed, Michael and Dunigan went home.

As soon as they got back, Dunigan sent for Cottrell.

"Mister Cottrell, you have seen our mules, what more do we need for three wagons all the way to Abilene?"

"Mistah Dunigan, yo' mules is all wore out. You is got to have five new teams, but we can use one of the old teams fo' light work."

"I'll tell you what, Mister Cottrell, there is a Mister Maille down on Salt Creek who has lots of mules and horses on his place. Next week, I want you and Michael to go down there and pick out the mules we'll need and about eight or ten horses, too. I want you to help Michael with the horses and the trading, if you would, please. Think you can take care of it for me?"

The black man showed a bright set of teeth and grinned widely. "Yessuh, Mister Dunigan. I'll take care of that for you, though I don't think young Michael O'Grady needs a whole lot of help on the horses, particularly pickin. Doan you worry, I'se done lots of mule tradin' in my time."

Dunigan hoped that was not brag, as he was running low on money and hoped Abner would pick young mules and break them to work himself, as he had said he had in the past. Dunigan was a bit uneasy about trusting the negro with these tasks, but was relying on his own estimation of the man's worth and did not think Cottrell would let him down.

Michael O'Grady was proud to be sent to buy horses, and chattered on about ranches in the area that had good horses for sale cheap.

"Hold on, boy," Dunigan warned. "We don't need but eight or ten more and I want them to be real good, so pick and choose careful. Besides, the more you get the more you're going to have to break and train this winter."

Pete Roussel rode in the next evening for supper and he and Dunigan and McCurry sat down to plan the drive and divvy up hands, horses and equipment. Nicholas was to take out the first herd and Pete would follow the next day, staying more or less within a day's drive for mutual protection. Nick would have Pablo Mendoza as cook and Pete would have Adam Johnson. Nick selected Lem Bracken as segundo and Pete wanted Abel Castro.

Dunigan let them select the other men they wanted, but reserved George Harris and Lon Castle to work with him as scouts. They would provide scouting for both herds and he would also keep Abner Cottrell with him to drive a wagon, as they might be out of range of both camps from time to time. Strong vigilance had served Dunigan well in the past and he would depend on it to sustain him in the future.

Each herd would only need about twelve men total, because they wouldn't need scouts. Both Nick and Pete were authorized to fill out their crews on their own. Dunigan told Pete to take a wagon over to Adam, so he could fix it up with a chuckbox. Dunigan's wagon would carry extra tools and supplies both outfits could draw on. Dunigan announced that horse and mule selection would take place in February and that Michael O'Grady would wrangle for Pete, and Chito Guerrico would wrangle for Nick. Both would stay at the home place with the horses that were chosen.

Pete left the next morning with his new wagon, his worn-out team, and a few supplies—and Abel Castro. His crew would dribble over to him as he needed them, but most of the hands would winter with Nick and Dunigan on the Aransas. The details were pretty much set for the drive; the only real work left to do was horse and mule breaking and that hadn't started yet.

Abner and Michael went down to Salt Creek and secured five teams of mules and ten saddle horses from Maille. The mules weren't really teams as only four of them had been trained to harness, but working together, the two men had them broke to harness in about six weeks. The saddle horses were all broken out and green trained by the other hands who had wintered on the Aransas. In February, all the hands got together and there was a big choosing and trading. Dunigan represented the half-dozen hands who were wintering at other places and after three days everyone had his string sorted out. There were over a hundred horses to be sorted out and that took a while.

At the end of February, all the hands had made it in so the cattle were gathered and the herds were headed out by March 10. The two herds were about a day's drive apart and would stay that way all the way to the Osage. The only real problem encountered was at the Brazos, where they had to wait five days to cross and then the crossing was a swim, even after five days. Dunigan used men from Pete's herd to help Nick across, and vice versa. Three steers were drowned during the crossing, and two were maimed or killed during stampedes between the San Antonio and Guadalupe rivers before the herd became trail broke. Dunigan sent the wagons on a fifty-mile detour to cross at the bridge at Waco. That caused a hungry night in Pete's camp, but no lasting harm.

The cattle were moving fine, being well broke, almost like saddle horses. Dunigan, George Harris, and Lon Castle were combing the country to the east and north, as that was the presumed danger area. However, occasional sweeps were made to the west to guard against raiding Kiowas and Comanches, but none were spotted. No rustlers were encountered on the drive, either, mainly because trail drivers had been very aggressive toward them and had even put posses along the trail on a cooperative basis, so life was unhealthy for rustlers along the Chisholm.

As always, Dunigan's herds were early on the trail, so there was good grass along the way and his steers were fleshening well. So far as the scouts could determine, there were only two small herds ahead of them, one of about eight hundred and the other twelve hundred. The herds were getting close to Osage country, and although the cattle were in good shape there was a substantial number that could use more flesh. Dunigan sent Harris and Castle to each herd with orders to bring Pete and Nick, along with four fresh horses, a pack horse, and two pinto ponies that could be used for gifts to the Osage chief. Dunigan's camp was over twenty miles north of the lead herd.

When the trail bosses and extra horses arrived two days later, they all had a big powwow. Dunigan discussed his plan with them and after minor objections, they all agreed. What he proposed to do was to cut the thinner steers out of both herds, combine the fatter cattle into one herd, and have Pete Roussel and his crew take the better one on to Abilene. The thinner cattle Nick's crew would hold on the Osage for a month or so until they fattened, then bring them on to Abilene. Dunigan would make the arrangements with the Indians and would be able to satisfy them with enough steers for pasturage. Some swapping of drovers was decided on, to lessen any possibility of trouble with the Indians.

After the meeting, Dunigan and Abner Cottrell set off north to the Osage.

The Indians were glad to see their old friends and Dunigan gave the chief the two calico ponies before he told him of his desire to graze his herd on the Indian lands. Everything was settled amicably and Dunigan was ready to go on to Abilene. There was a slight hitch. The Osages had never seen a negro and made a great to-do over Abner, including some of the women. Cottrell was delighted at being the center of attention, but Dunigan felt they better get away before some mulatto Indians were spawned.

Setting out north for Abilene, they encountered the two trail herds that were ahead of the Dunigan drives. They had supper and passed the night with each one and Dunigan caught up on the news. Both herds were from East Texas, one from Montgomery County and the other from Lee. Most of the conversation was about carpetbaggers and the administration of Governor Davis, and the drovers glared somewhat malevolently at Abner Cottrell. However, both crews had negro hands, so nothing came of their hostility.

After thanking the crew for their hospitality, the two men pushed on north, Dunigan noting that the steers in both herds were not fleshy, so they shouldn't affect the price his herds would command.

A week later, he and Abner arrived in Abilene. The town was fairly quiet as no cattle had arrived at the railroad yet, but buyers were already there, although not in profusion. They found a place to stay and Dunigan devoted the next few days to gathering market news.

He found the market strong, mainly because a good corn crop was in the offing across the Mississippi, so there would be increased demand for steers to feed and that would put pressure on the buyers of cattle for slaughter. Some Texas cattlemen were there, too, having come ahead of herds they had put on the trail earlier and most were optimistic about prices, having seen good cornfields on their journeys.

The man who had bought Dunigan's steers in past years was not there, but was due in a few days later so Dunigan was in no hurry to price his herds. He exchanged information with the other Texas men about conditions at home and along the trail and some were worried that there might be too many cattle for the market to absorb. Dunigan wasn't concerned about that because his herd would be the first slaughter cattle to arrive. Even though it was a big herd it should sell high.

Dunigan and Cottrell rode over to Fort Riley to see about selling the herd's horses. The army market was a bit uncertain, because the cavalry had just about made up its losses from Red Cloud's war. However, now that peace with the Sioux was in effect, the whites were again penetrating Sioux country, and the military was becoming more active in trying to keep them out and keep the peace.

They found the same quartermaster, who was eager to secure the Dunigan mounts, as they had proved to be good cavalry horses. Dunigan informed him about numbers and arrival dates, and they made a tentative trade that pleased the officer. He even said he would come to Abilene to pick them up. Dunigan and Abner rode on back to Abilene to await the arrival of Pete's herd in about two weeks.

Chapter 13

Dunigan and Cottrell rode into Abilene the next day and went by the railroad pens just to take a look. There were cattle being off-loaded when they rode up and there were lots of onlookers. There, walking leisurely down the ramp from the railroad car, was something neither Dunigan nor Abner had seen before. Compared to the longhorns they were accustomed to these cattle were broad and blocky. Uniformly red-bodied with white faces and underbodies and a white cape on their necks, their horns drooped down and were short, as were their legs.

Dunigan had heard of these cattle called Herefords and had read of them, but had never seen any. He had seen the Durham cattle that had been imported to Northeast Texas but not these. There were perhaps eight or ten carloads of them, maybe two hundred in all, and they were all pretty much alike. He liked them better than the Durhams he had seen, as they appeared to be longer legged and thriftier, but the possibility of their surviving in the thorns and heat of South Texas seemed tenuous at best. They watched them for a long time and it was Abner who broke the silence.

"Think them longhorn critters of ours would fall in love with them dwarfs, Mistah Dunigan?"

"I dunno, Abner, but if they did, I don't think even their calves could walk far enough to find water."

A dapper little man who was looking through the fence at the bulls looked up at Dunigan. "Mister, I don't know who you are, but you are gazing at the future of the cattle business. I am Joshua Spinks and I am the owner of all that magnificent livestock. I put them together out of Tennessee and Illinois, and they will make the grade anywhere, even Texas."

"Mister Spinks, I ain't even sure they can make it to Texas, let alone live there. Even if they got there they wouldn't last a week among our longhorns. Them that wasn't killed outright would be whipped out of the country," Dunigan answered.

Spinks snorted. "I will arrange, if you like, a confrontation between one of my bulls and one of your longhorn bulls and it will show you that you are wrong. You see, the Hereford, being shorter, can get under the taller animal and be able to handle him."

Dunigan had to admit the point, at least to himself. He had seen shorter bulls whip taller ones.

"I don't have any bulls in my herd, Mister Spinks, but I can probably find one. By the way, I am John Dunigan from Refugio, Texas, and I will try to find a suitable champion for your Hereford. Where can I find you later, Mister Spinks?" Dunigan asked.

"I am staying at the Drovers Cottage and I will stand ready with my bull until you find a longhorn."

Dunigan asked the Texas men if there were any bulls in the incoming herds and found it would be nearly a month before any would be in from the trail. He dispatched Abner to find a suitable bull, if any, at the ranches in the area, with the authority to buy or pay reasonable fees. Dunigan did not think he would find a suitable bull unless a Texas herd arrived early, but the bull fight would generate a lot of interest and perhaps some spirited betting. He intended to bet on the Hereford, and spent much of the time trying to find out how the Herefords performed locally. There were a few who had imported them around Abilene, mostly farmers and not range men, but their comments were generally favorable.

Six days later, Abner rode into Abilene with a wagon following. Driving the wagon, in which a monstrous longhorn bull was encaged, was Jake Klever, a rancher from west of Ellsworth, where the bull had been found. Klever, the bull's owner, was a crusty old rancher, originally from the Sulphur River country of northeast Texas, who had been ranching in Kansas for three years. He was proud of his longhorn, and stated that his bull could beat any bull, especially a dwarf from Tennessee. He was prepared to back him. The bull was big, with wide upstanding sharp horns, and Klever bragged his bull had already killed four others on the range and had whipped off many others.

The bull was off-loaded at the railroad pens and ran around hooking at posts and rails, but the pens were well made, and he didn't do much damage. He gazed over two pens away, and saw the Herefords and immediately issued a challenge and tried to get to them, but couldn't.

Abner dismounted and related the tale. "Mistah John, I went plumb west of Ellsworth to find that bull. He is a sho nuff he-bull, and is an experienced fighter. I know because we tried to drive him at first, but he just fought us. Mister Klever rigged up that cage on his wagon then and we roped and loaded him. That warn't no easy job, neither."

Dunigan chuckled, as he could see that Abner's clothes were torn some and he was favoring his right leg. It must have been a mighty fight to get that bull in a wagon, but here he was and the fight would take place. Abner and Dunigan went off to tell Spinks of the bull's arrival and met him on the way to the pens to see his antagonist.

"Mister Spinks, I would like to delay this fight until my herd arrives, as my hands would like to see it, but I don't think we can do it because if that bull has a week or more to work on those pens, he will destroy them and get away. I am not a principal in this matter, like Jake Klever, the bull's owner who is here for the fight, willing to back his bull. He is ready for it to start, so why don't you and he get together and make the arrangements?"

"I am like you, Mister Dunigan. I would like to delay it, too, but I need to sell my bulls and I don't think I can do much business until this fight is over," Spinks replied. "I will get with Mister Klever and make the arrangements."

"How much do you want for your bulls now, Mister Spinks?" Dunigan asked.

Spinks was so surprised at Dunigan's query he did not answer for a moment. "I will sell these bulls for $250 apiece, Dunigan. You can pick any bull for that price."

"I will give you $150 a head for the whole bunch, one-half now, and one-half after the fight, cash money, and I will even take your fighter if he survives."

"Dunigan, what are you trying to do? You got up this fight, and now you are trying to buy the opposition. I just don't understand it."

"Do you want to sell or not? I have made an offer and I want an answer," Dunigan answered coolly.

Spinks was hesitant, but finally said, "I'll take $220 and all up front in cash."

"I will pay $175 on the same basis as before with the stipulation that nothing is said about it until after the fight," Dunigan continued.

"No," Spinks said with finality.

"Fine, but if you change your mind you know where to find me." Dunigan and Abner walked off from the perplexed little man.

When they had moved out of earshot, Abner said, "Mistah John, I'm telling you, that longhorn is going to kill that Hereford bull, and it will be all over Texas in a week. How come you want to buy them squatty bulls?"

"Abner, I ain't so sure the longhorn will win. Even if he does, the Herefords and such are going to replace the longhorn anyway. He's too rough and stringy, and he won't always have to walk to market. Railroads will come to Texas some day and the conditions will get tamer in Texas, too. My hope is that we will be able to drive these home without losing them all."

That afternoon the announcement was made that the fight would take place at eleven the next morning. Markets were forgotten and all the talk was about the great bull fight. Betting was favoring the longhorn at three and four to one. To maintain his anonymity, Dunigan got hold of Jim Blaylock, the man who had bought his steers in past years, to place $200 on the Hereford bull for him. Blaylock got his bets down at four to one. There was hooraw all night long in the saloons, but Dunigan retired to his room early, expecting a call.

Sure enough, there was a knock on his door about 8:30. Opening it revealed Spinks, who greeted him and sat down.

It was Dunigan who spoke first. "Spinks, you've done this before, haven't you? I saw one of your bulls had some scars on him from fighting and I'll wager he has been in the same sort of fight before."

"You're right, but never against such an animal as Jake Klever brought in. My bull is good, but he's never been up against such a beast," Spinks admitted. "I have done it in Arkansas and Missouri in the past and had success, so I decided to try Abilene, but I am scared of this bull you found, so I have come to let you have my bulls, if we can come to an agreement."

Dunigan voiced his misgivings about being able to drive the Herefords all the way to Texas and about the dangers of Texas fever to imported cattle, and so on. Spinks argued the opposite tack, but in the end they traded. Dunigan bought 240 bulls at $182 per head; Spinks wanting to keep his fighter to be able to stage the fight elsewhere, but if he didn't win, that wouldn't matter.

Dunigan did not have $36,764 in his pocket, as Spinks well knew, but offered a draft on Daniel Sullivan that night for half, or half in gold the next morning and the other half after the fight. Spinks agreed to take all the money in gold, shook hands on it and they parted.

When Spinks was gone, Dunigan went down to Blaylock's room to arrange for the money. He had already priced his first herd to Blaylock at $25 a steer, which was only slightly over the market, but Dunigan figured he could sell the steers very close to that figure. The herd was due in Abilene inside a week, so the money shouldn't bother Blaylock, as all their dealings in the past had been amicable.

When he answered Dunigan's knocks, Blaylock invited him in.

"Jim, I know you're going to buy my steers and I need some money in advance. I want $37,000 in gold the first thing in the morning, advanced against the delivery of my steers. Can you do it, or do I have to deal with someone else?" he asked.

Blaylock looked surprised for a time, then a look of grinning comprehension creased his features. "What did you do, John, buy those Hereford bulls?"

"Yes, and I want you to keep quiet about that if you will. Can you get me the money?"

"Sure, I'll have it right after the bank opens in the morning. You can give me an IOU or a mortgage on the herd, if you like."

"That's fine, Jim, whatever you need, I'll sign. Will you bring the money back here for me, as I don't want to be seen paying Spinks until it's all over with. We can go out day after tomorrow to see the herd, if you like. Should be within a day's ride."

"That'll be fine, John. Can you lend me a horse? Yours are a lot better than what they have at the livery."

"Sure, and I won't even charge you for it, if I get my price."

The big day of the great Abilene bull fight dawned gray and cloudy. Rain began around 8:30, really only a drizzle, but it drizzled all day long. By 10:30, a crowd had gathered around the shipping pens where the fight was to start at eleven. Earlier in the hotel, Dunigan had paid Spinks the half price down and watched Spinks as he selected his fighter. The Hereford chosen was an older bull, with a few scars on his flanks and sides. Its forward-set horns were down sloped with a wicked looking inward curve to their sharp tips.

The spectators, clad in slickers or carrying umbrellas, were still betting as Spinks caught the bull and brought him into the empty pen that was to serve as the arena.

Betting was furious for about five minutes and then subsided, as it was time for the fight to start. The odds on the Hereford had shortened because of the slick footing, but the final bets were at three to one. Klever did not try to lead his bull into the pen, as he was upset at being penned up by himself for two days, so he opened the gate and got out of the way, closing it behind the longhorn.

Chapter 14

The two bulls were facing each other glaring and bellowing, and each advanced on the other until they met in the middle of the arena. The bulls slammed together, neither giving an inch, the uptilted horns on the longhorn not coming into contact, whereas the Hereford's horns, being lower set, were hitting the longhorn's neck, but not seriously. After wrestling for an advantage and finding none, both bulls backed away and started circling one another, each looking for an opening.

The longhorn charged, but the Hereford met him head on and stopped him, and the Hereford, having leverage from under, began to twist his head, his horns goring the longhorn in the neck. Pushing and shoving from both bulls continued and the Hereford worked his head down gradually under the longhorn's, then hooked him in the brisket.

The big bull roared and disengaged himself, bleeding from his brisket, not a mortal wound but a painful one. He backed away from the Hereford until he was clear, and he stopped as though regrouping. Dunigan saw some blood on the Hereford from a small cut on the top of his neck, but it was clear the longhorn's brisket wound was the more serious.

The two bulls commenced to circle each other again, trying to gain advantage. They were sidling toward each other when the longhorn charged, seeking to get to the Hereford's side. The Hereford swapped ends and met him head on and low, twisting his horns as he did. This move, combined with the longhorn's momentum, threw him aside and the longhorn slid on the slippery ground and fell. The Hereford was on him, sinking his horns in the longhorn's exposed belly, ripping him open and scattering guts and blood.

The longhorn delivered a powerful kick to the antagonist's head, which backed the Hereford away, but the fight was over. The longhorn tried, but could not rise, and the Hereford was ready to do more damage. One of the spectators drew his pistol and shot the longhorn in the brain, mercifully killing it.

Spinks got the Hereford out of the pen and in with the others. One of the yard workers brought in a team and sled to haul the dead bull to an abattoir. The great Abilene bull fight was over and the winners, Dunigan among them, collected their winnings. The losers drowned their sorrow in the saloons.

Dunigan paid Spinks the balance of the money, got a bill of sale, and set about finding Abner, who had located a pasture for the bull herd about five miles west. Dunigan, Abner, and Jim Blaylock took the bulls away that afternoon as Dunigan wanted them out of sight. He felt they would bring much more in Texas than in Kansas and didn't want to be tempted into selling them.

The three left before daylight next morning and met the herd in time for supper. The outfit was regaled mightily on the subject of the bull fight, and tales were told until late. Everyone turned in and the next day Jim Blaylock inspected the herd on its way into Abilene. Much talk between Blaylock and Dunigan finally led to a price of $24.40 per head and Blaylock rode off to arrange transportation and payment.

Dunigan stayed with the herd on into Abilene, using the time to instruct Pete on the handling of the Hereford bulls. Dunigan was very meticulous about his instructions. He told Pete to use whatever hands wanted to go back and to take his time, staying well west of the trail because the bulls were not yet immune to Texas fever. Although Dunigan knew Pete would lose some, he wanted to hold down the fever losses.

He also told Pete not to sell any until he got to Texas, and then to price them at $700, not taking less than $500. Pete should arrive back at Refugio with no fewer than a hundred head. Dunigan was adamant in telling Pete not to try to make time, because the bulls could not cover the ground as fast as longhorns and would be sorefooted at first. He said he did not expect Pete back in Refugio until some time in September.

The herd was delivered, as were the horses bound for the army. Dunigan told the quartermaster sergeant to expect more in about a month and that McCurry would be contacting him.

Pete's crew would not be leaving for a couple more days, as they were seeing the elephant and hooting at the owls. Dunigan made arrangements with Blaylock to see the other herd. Dunigan and Blaylock took almost two weeks to reach McCurry's herd, which was then five days on the road from the Osage country. They were surprised by the condition of the cattle. They were very fleshy, almost fat. Of course, Dunigan had not seen the cattle after they were cut, but he was surprised they were in such prime condition already. Blaylock said they were the best steers Dunigan had ever had. The market had grown stronger as more herds arrived at Abilene, and as a consequence, the second herd sold for $25.50 per head.

Nick was instructed to dispose of his extra horses and to make his way back to Texas with those who wanted to go back on the same basis as years before.

After Blaylock and Dunigan agreed on payment arrangements, Dunigan announced he was not riding back to Texas, but going by rail to St. Louis, then by steamboat down the Mississippi to New Orleans, and on to Indianola, Texas. Everyone was envious of his trip and Blaylock gave him the names of people, cattle dealers, and bankers that Dunigan might contact in St. Louis and Kansas City.

Dunigan thanked him and Blaylock rode back toward Abilene to bid on some new herds. Before leaving, Blaylock also told Dunigan another railroad was building and might have reached Wichita. If not, he could probably find end of track and catch the train northeast of there.

Nick's herd was eased onto the bedground that night and the night watch set up. Supper was ready when they rode into camp and the crew got their food and settled down to eat. Dunigan thought the time was right, so he related the tale of the Great Abilene Bull Fight, telling the whole story.

He told Nick he could probably catch up to Pete and the bulls on his return to Texas. Everybody wanted to know every detail, which Dunigan let them have, and it was discussed until past the second night watch.

Then the first watch wanted to hear, too, so he went through it all again. This was really the first news any of them had had since they left Texas, and every hand probed for the tiniest detail. They also wanted to know about Dunigan's trip home and speculated on the fun he would have in St. Louis and New Orleans. It was almost midnight before they let Dunigan turn in.

Chapter 15

Dunigan reached Wichita at noon the next day, but found no sign of the railroad. He rode to a saloon and went in to eat dinner, asking about the railroad. He was told it might be at Newton, north about a day's ride, thirty miles or so, but they expected it to reach Wichita next summer or fall. The right-of-way was already purchased and surveyed.

After eating, Dunigan rode out and found the right-of-way, and started along it. He was in no hurry, so he rode leisurely and spent the night sleeping on the surveyed ground. He rode on in the morning, arriving at Newton by 10:00 A.M. Still no railroad, but the townspeople told him it was less than five miles north of town. When he arrived at end of track, he was told he could catch the work train for Topeka at 2:30 that afternoon. He thanked them and told them he would be back.

In Newton, he ate dinner and went to the town livery, where he sold his horse and arranged with the liveryman to take him to end of track. There, he found the construction superintendent and questioned him in detail about plans. He found they intended to reach Wichita in late spring or early fall. But Newton would be ready to send freight by spring, and someone was already contracting to build stock pens. This cheered Dunigan, who figured to drive cattle to Newton for sale. He caught the work train, changing twice before arriving in Kansas City before sundown in good time to get a hotel room.

Kansas City was a spritely town and Dunigan wandered around downtown visiting several saloons and eating houses. Wearing his new clothes from Corpus Christi so he looked like a tourist or a businessman, he got acquainted in several bars and had conversations with men who seemed well informed. The impression he got was of a very lively town trying to become a major center for cattle, agricultural products, and distribution.

Several people mentioned slaughterhouses being built, with some already in operation. His train to St. Louis did not leave until noon, so he thought he would visit that part of town next morning. Dunigan met some agreeable companions during the evening, merchants and commission brokers and such, and he listened as they talked about the facilities planned for the city. About 11:00 P.M., he joined a group going to Baghdad House, and they walked five or six blocks to a large three-story, well-lit, well-cared-for house on the outskirts of the commercial district.

Walking through the door, Dunigan realized he was in a high-class brothel. In the main room that housed a bar were about fifteen scantily clad young women, plus one older woman, who was tending bar. From her dress and air of authority, she was obviously the madam, and Dunigan made a note not to cross her, as she was never far from a Colt's pistol, either on the bar or in a sash around her waist, although she seemed pleasant.

The air in the place was almost genteel, as the whores' behavior was fairly quiet and demure, except for one blonde who was laughing raucously as she sucked on a red-faced man's earlobe. That she was violating the code of conduct for the Baghdad whores was evident in the glaring eyes of the madam. Everything else that night was well within prescribed rules of decorum. The blonde was put to bed after her session with the red-faced man, and everyone else stayed on their good behavior.

Dunigan preferred it that way and his own session with a coy redhead, although lengthy, was in no way frantic. Throughout the evening, Dunigan fraternized most with the madam, whose name was Joan Salter. He learned she had plied her trade successively in Louisville, Akron, Indianapolis, and Rock Island before reaching Kansas City. They talked of horses, the lady having been raised in the Kentucky horse country, and generally he passed a pleasant evening, drinking little.

Early next morning, Dunigan caught a cab to the riverfront district and saw the new and still in construction slaughterhouses and the allied new industries being built in the district. He was impressed by the slaughter capacity being generated in the bustling city and could see it would be a power in the meat business. He met some of the people involved and felt a kinship with their optimism.

Chapter 16

Dunigan caught the noon train to St. Louis, arriving before dark in time to check into a hotel. He ate dinner and went to bed early to be fresh for calls on some of the people Blaylock wanted him to see. After breakfast, he made arrangements at the hotel desk for a stateroom on the *Crescent Queen* to New Orleans the following night. Then he walked around to visit some of the people Jim Blaylock had suggested. They were mostly bankers and brokers and they all had the same enthusiasm for business he had seen in Kansas City, except they were older and better established.

Dunigan asked polite questions and received polite answers, but generally did not find out much of interest. One banker he met he liked very much and they got on well. Gerard Alton ran the Bank of St. Louis. Originally from Kentucky, he had volunteered for the Confederate army and been a cavalry officer with the Army of Northern Virginia. He was captured in 1863, and sent to a prison out west. There he had become a galvanized Yankee, serving in a federal unit keeping peace among the Utes, Navajos, and Apaches. It beat rotting in jail and Alton was kept busy. Not that he hadn't seen enough action in Virginia, but he was active and gained considerable knowledge of the west and of the western tribes. A practical man, Alton knew about freighting and mining and other activities west of the Mississippi.

Dunigan liked him and decided he would do business with him. Alton opened an account for him and Dunigan sent a wire to Blaylock asking him to deposit his cattle proceeds with the Bank of St. Louis. Arrangements to forward needed monies to Texas were made and Dunigan was satisfied they would work.

Alton asked Dunigan to have dinner with him and his wife that evening. Dunigan accepted, meeting them at eight in a downtown restaurant. Genevieve Alton was a pretty, outgoing and pleasant woman, and Dunigan liked her immediately as he had her husband. She was about Dunigan's age and her husband but a few years older, and they all got along famously, while enjoying a fine meal with wine and the best service.

Alton had chosen the eating place well and Dunigan was impressed. Mrs. Alton wanted to invite him to dine at their home with their friends the next night, but as he was leaving he reluctantly refused. He left the delightful couple before midnight and made his way back to his hotel. He had not had such a good time for many years and vowed to spend more time in St. Louis.

The next day, Dunigan confirmed his reservation with the steamboat office and inquired about connections to the Texas coast. He was informed that a mail packet was sailing for Corpus Christi the afternoon he arrived in New Orleans and the office people assured him he could catch it. Inquiring of the next boat to Indianola or Corpus Christi after that, he was told that it would be at least a week, so he decided to skip a New Orleans visit this trip.

Dunigan went by Gerard Alton's bank, as they had made plans to eat lunch that day. They went down the street to a pleasant restaurant and shared a good meal. Dunigan discussed his plans for his cattle year with Alton and the banker advised him to ship the cattle into Kansas City and sell them there, because many slaughterhouses were already in operation or under construction and competition would be lively for cattle as there was good demand back east for beef.

Dunigan absorbed all that and asked about the possibility of selling his cattle under a contract to, say, Jim Blaylock, on a bought-to-arrive basis.

Alton thought that might work and agreed to consult with Blaylock. He felt he could handle the payment arrangements for Dunigan and it could be a good deal for all three.

Dunigan left full of ideas and walked down the street, window shopping. He bought some clothes, went back to his hotel, packed, and went to the riverfront to board the *Crescent Queen*.

There were only twelve cabins on the little steamboat and Dunigan had his pick, as he was almost three hours early for departure. He stored his luggage, and as an ex-mariner, went exploring. Not too much of interest on the boat, as the cargo was mostly cotton and hides, but he looked it all over. The craft was clean and trim and all the brass shone like glass. He met the captain, who ran down the cargo and itinerary for him, then Dunigan retired to his cabin.

The boat left on time, about 8:00 P.M., with stops scheduled at Cairo, Memphis, Vicksburg, Natchez, and Baton Rouge. Dinner was served underway and he shared a table with a cotton broker from Memphis and a drummer from Chicago. They were pleasant enough, but Dunigan had nothing in common with them and would have been bored, except the meal was so good. After dinner and a cigar, most of the passengers adjourned to the saloon, where a poker game was going on. Dunigan watched for a few minutes, judged that one of the players was a cheat and resolved not to join in.

The voyage was uneventful and Dunigan spent most of his time in the wheelhouse with Captain Abraham DeCroix, an old timer on the river. Many years ago, he had been all the way upriver to Ft. Union. DeCroix had been on the river all his life, starting as a cabin boy back in the thirties. He told Dunigan tales all the way down river. Quick stops were made at the intermediate landings to offload and onload cargo and passengers.

The crooked gambler stayed all the way to New Orleans, so Dunigan never got in the game, but he observed that few pigeons were plucked who did not deserve it. Outside of the wealth of stories from Captain DeCroix, the trip was profitless, as was the trip from New Orleans to Corpus Christi, which Dunigan caught with only an hour to spare. The Gulf was rough and unpleasant, but the trip was brief and he arrived a day ahead of schedule. Disembarking, he made his way to a livery stable he knew well and got a horse for the ride to his ranch on the Aransas, arriving September 8th.

The first sight of the ranch was a string of red white-faced bulls grazing near the headquarter's buildings, so he knew Pete had beat him back. The bulls were a bit thin, but looked healthy. He counted eighty, so perhaps the death loss hadn't materialized. Pete and the others came out to greet him as he dismounted, and they followed him back in to drink coffee, anxious to hear of his adventures in the big cities.

Pete told him he had dropped off $43,500 at Jim McFaddin's store in Refugio that he had collected for 82 bulls he had sold.

Fifteen had died on the way home and he had turned loose 105 only three days ago. When Dunigan remarked that they didn't look too bad, Pete retorted, "They drove all night, not like longhorns, but once they got lined out, we didn't have much trouble. Lost one at the Red, and I think nine to the fever, but I think most of them have had it by now and gotten over it, so that shouldn't be a problem. The other six had everything happen to them. The first thing was they fought all the time. Joe Campbell got run over and his horse killed, but he was just banged up. We drove them by Goliad and Refugio and there was some interest. I didn't sell any, but I think there'll be several fellers by here in a day or two that'll want to buy some."

"You did real good, Pete, you've got the makin's of a fine cowman. How many of them you think we need for our cows?"

"Oh, about fifty I guess, if you want to do away with all our longhorns."

"I do. You and the boys can cut them out and make steers out of them just as soon as you get around to it."

"I'll take care of that, boss," Pete said, grinning.

Dunigan then told of his travels through Kansas City, St. Louis, down the river and home. All were eager listeners, as San Antonio was the biggest town most had ever seen. They were a bit disappointed that he had not participated in the wilder side that they had heard of, but it was interesting to them and they hung on his every word. One of the hands had taken Dunigan's traps to his house and he designated a man to get the horse back to Corpus Christi the next day. They all ate supper and went off to sleep.

He was waiting for Nick and his crew to show up before he organized the cow hunt, but time was growing short and word was many cow hunters had been active in South Texas that summer. Two days later, Nick showed up and Dunigan, Pete and Nick organized the move and hunt. Pete was to be in charge of gathering and Nick of scouting and security. Dunigan was not going to be around much, as he had to buy steers to fill out his herds for next spring, and would be traveling around to find them. The crew left for the stage station September 19th, which was late, but they felt the cooler weather would help them.

The cow hunt went well, no banditry or accidents, and Pete ended up gathering 2,768 steers. These together with seven hundred steers of Dunigan's own raising meant he would have to buy only sixteen to eighteen hundred steers for spring. They had captured 57 horses, so there were enough mounts, but they would need some mules. Scouting around, Nick and George Harris had journeyed to the spot of last year's outlaw hanging, curious to see if the outlaws had picked up their compadre's remains.

What they found was eerie and both felt uneasy as they surveyed the scene. The hanging rope was still tied to the tree, but rotted off about neck level. There were no signs of the body, but nearby was a small shrine. They surmised the bandit's family had come for the body, but not until the rope had broken, and removed the remains, then built the little shrine to mark the place.

There was no sign of any traffic since the last rains and they guessed the shrine was as good a deterrent as the body, so they didn't worry too much about outlaw incursions.

They had an easy drive back to the Aransas and turned the cattle out for the winter. Dunigan was pleased with the number and condition of the cattle. By then he had bought 1,732 steers for spring delivery and figured he had enough, especially as old man Maille was pleased with what his cattle had returned and wouldn't make any deal except the same as last year. Dunigan told him he would have to charge more, because of his plan to graze the steers all summer on the Osage, but Maille didn't mind and Dunigan acceded, securing two teams of mules in the bargain.

On November 24, 1870, a norther blew in as Dunigan and Michael O'Grady were approaching Refugio to buy supplies. The two were glad to be able to run their wagon into the livery barn and get out of the cold. A young boy in tattered thin clothes and no shoes took hold of the team to take care of it for them. Dunigan eyed him critically. "Boy, you better run home and get on some warm clothes before you freeze. It's cold out there."

It was about 45 degrees with a strong north wind blowing.

"Ain't got no more clothes, Mister Dunigan, and I sleep here in the barn. I ain't got no home, nor any folks," the boy answered.

"What's your name, son?"

"Thad Scott," the boy answered through blue lips.

Dunigan knew the name and had known the family. The boy's father was killed late in the war and his mother had supported herself and the boy doing laundry and sewing around town. Dunigan had even had her do some mending for him.

"Where's your maw, Thad?"

"Maw died two months ago of the fever and Mister Long took the house. I been staying here and workin' and swamping out the saloon some."

"Do you have any money to buy shoes, son? Your feet'll freeze."

"I made a little, but we owed Mister Long some more on the house and I had to pay him," Thad responded.

"Thad, you feed and curry those mules real good and I'll give you four bits when we are ready to leave."

"Yessir, Mister Dunigan, I'll fix 'em up," Thad smiled.

Dunigan and Michael left to get their supplies, mostly staples like flour, beans, rice, and molasses and a few tools, and he directed Michael to see that they were loaded. He left the store and went over to see the sheriff. He wanted to find out more about the orphan boy, Thad Scott.

"He's a good boy, John, but I don't know what can be done. He's sixteen and able bodied, but there ain't a lot of work to be had here, as you know. That skinflint bastard Long threw him out of the house the day after his momma was buried, and I think the saloon feeds him, but I don't think old Smith at the livery pays him much, just gives him a place to stay."

"Would there be any problem if I took him home with me? I can always use a kid around for chores, and he don't have much future here."

"No, John, I don't see any problems. It would even solve some. There may be some church-going busybodies that might object, but I think I can handle them. What does the boy want to do?"

"I haven't asked him, but if he does want to move out there, it is okay with you?"

"Sure, take him along. At least it would keep him out of town and out of the saloon."

The sheriff turned to read handbills and Dunigan walked back to the livery. Michael and Thad Scott had just finished loading the supplies into the wagon and glanced at the mules. They were so well brushed they almost shone.

Dunigan fished in his pocket, pulled out fifty cents and gave it to Thad, who thanked him profusely.

Dunigan shuffled his feet, looked down at them, and then just blurted out, "Michael, take this boy over to the store and get him a pair of boots and some clothes. Also a warm coat. Can't have him freezing on us. Tell them to charge it to me."

"I'll take care of it, Mister Dunigan," Michael said grinning, and started off with the boy.

Before they got to the door Dunigan said, "Thad, would you like to come work for us at the ranch? I'll pay you wages."

Thad beamed from ear to ear. "Yes sir, Mister Dunigan. I'll make you a good hand and I'll pay you back for the clothes."

"See that you do. When you're outfitted and ready to go, come and get me in the saloon."

The two boys fairly ran down the street to get Thad's clothes. Dunigan walked to the saloon for a warm up drink. He had had three drinks and had told the bartender he was taking his swamper with him when the boys came in. Thad was warmly dressed in new clothes and a warm coat, plus a pair of new boots.

Dunigan asked, "Thad, do you have anything you want to take with you? If so, get it and we'll go."

"I don't have nothin', Mister Dunigan. I'm ready."

Dunigan rode in the back of the wagon on the way home. He lay down on some sacks of rice and feigned sleep, listening to the two boys. Although Michael was somewhat older, he had always been the baby of the outfit and was overjoyed to be replaced by Thad. When they got back to the ranch, it was Michael who outlined Thad's job, but he moved Thad in with him.

Chapter 17

The winter was about average and the cattle managed fine. The drive, organized the year before, started on March 18th, after the contract steers were delivered. Five thousand seven hundred steers in two trail herds started up the trail to the Osage, fifty-two hundred of Dunigan's and five hundred of Maille's. Good luck and good weather followed them and they arrived at the Osage village at the end of May.

Dunigan had been in correspondence with Jim Blaylock, who had agreed to handle the cattle sales for him on the Kansas City market, and they estimated that the first steers would be shipped from Newton about midJuly.

The steers fattened nicely on the Osage grass, and five hundred head of fat steers were cut out and trailed to Newton by Dunigan and seven others, arriving there July 12th. Blaylock had made arrangements for rail service and they were boarded for shipment to Kansas City. Dunigan went with them to observe as he had made arrangements with Pete and Nick to cut and drive subsequent herds each week.

The market was good and the cattle were sold by weight, so they brought more money. After freight and commission expenses were paid the cattle averaged out $32.64 per head and Dunigan and Blaylock were well satisfied. This operation continued through that summer, and the weekly numbers rose in August. It kept the crews busy coming and going.

Dunigan divided his time between Kansas City and Newton, and in Newton there had cropped up some talk of Texas fever and quarantine as more farmers moved in to take up the land being offered, but it wasn't too strident that summer. Dunigan could see it would be in subsequent years.

The trail herds would be moved west of the settlement line year by year. That disturbed Dunigan, as his system of fattening steers on the Osage grass was working very well, and a quarantine line would make his drives longer, but he thought he had a few years yet. Kansas was still pretty sparsely populated and the trail herds were bringing in money and activity and were valuable to the state. Still, there was considerable clamor to keep the Texas herds out.

All that summer, Dunigan moved his cattle to market, moving about 250–400 steers to Kansas City each week. Dunigan spent most of his time in Kansas City, overseeing the sales at the stockyards. The cattle market was very good that summer and his cattle fattened well on the Osage grass. He did go down to see the cattle twice, and he was back there when the last fat cattle went to market.

By September, he only had four hundred fifty steers left and they were not fat and probably would not fatten, so he broke camp, sent them all to Kansas City and took what he could get for the tail end. He sold his horses and wagons and sent his crew home on a boat down the Mississippi. He had sent a crew home with Pete Roussel in July, to start gathering steers for the '72 drives, so only a few men were left with Nick to finish up.

After selling his last steers, Dunigan went to St. Louis to see his banker, Gerard Alton. He was pleased to find out he had almost $165,000 on deposit there and determined to leave it, as it was drawing a fair rate of interest. He already had almost $100,000 in banks and depositories along the coast in Texas. He spent five days in St. Louis being entertained by the Altons and their friends and met many attractive young ladies, but they were city girls and not adventurous enough to consider moving to the Gulf Coast wilderness. After four days, Dunigan caught a steamboat to New Orleans and on to Galveston.

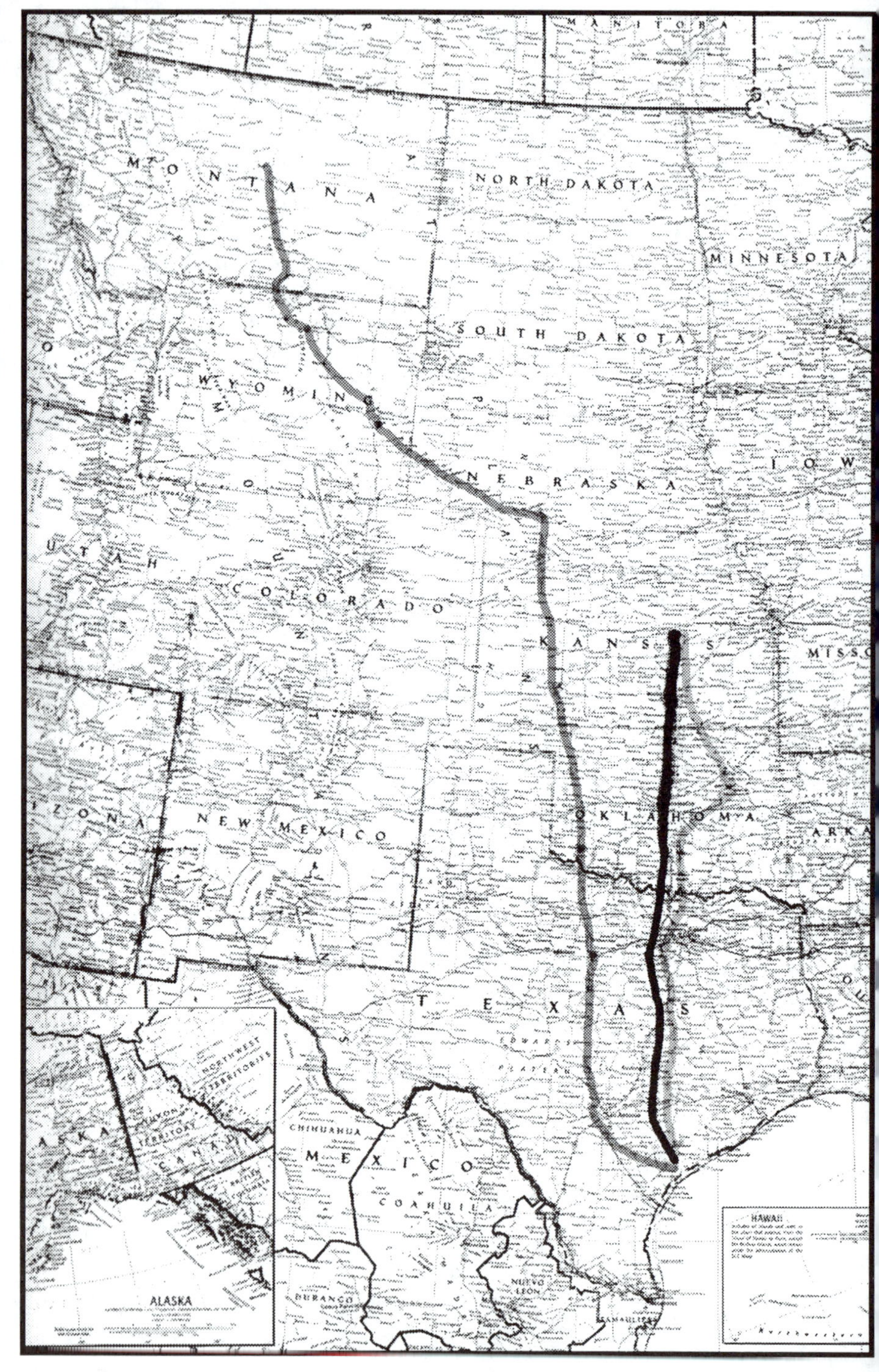

MANITOBA
MONTANA
NORTH DAKOTA
MINNESOTA
SOUTH DAKOTA
WYOMING
NEBRASKA
IOWA
UTAH
COLORADO
KANSAS
MISSO
OKLAHOMA
ARKA
ARIZONA
NEW MEXICO
TEXAS
EDWARDS
PLATEAU
NORTHWEST
TERRITORIES
YUKON
TERRITORY
CANADA
BRITISH
COLUMBIA
ALASKA
CHIHUAHUA
MEXICO
COAHUILA
NUEVO
LEON
DURANGO
TAMAULIPAS
HAWAII

PART II

The Deal

Chapter 18

Dunigan checked in to the Menger Hotel in San Antonio at noon on the 25th of September, 1871, to meet Calvin Block. After securing a room and dropping his traps, he went looking for him. The clerk told him Block had checked in the night before, but Dunigan could not find him.

He left the Menger to find a restaurant and soon assuaged his hunger, then went back to his room to rest.

About 3:30, a knock on the door brought him to his feet. A bellboy had a message from Block, asking Dunigan to meet him in the bar. Dunigan was well acquainted with Block and his activities. The man had come to Texas right after the war, but he wasn't part of the reconstruction regime. He was a staunch Republican, though, and was on good terms with the reconstruction bosses.

Block had come to Texas from southern Illinois, where he had been born in the 1820s. A muscular six-footer with a thick black beard, Block had become involved early in the Texas cattle trade, operating on capital supplied by Illinois corn growers seeking another outlet for their corn by feeding it to cattle.

Block's first deals had involved driving steers north to Baxter Springs and Abilene to the railheads for trans-shipment to Illinois. He was a sharp trader and he quickly acquired a reputation. He was never caught doing anything illegal, but in a place and time in which a man's word was his bond, people learned quickly to deal with Calvin Block only by written instrument.

By 1869, Block was no longer a cattle trader. He had gravitated to land and there was talk of his involvement in East Texas tax foreclosures. He seemed to spend a lot of time in the state land office in Austin and also seemed on good terms with railroad interests, who could always secure vacant land in exchange for construction and acquisition costs. All Block's projects were political in the extreme and he seemed to be deep in the good graces of the E. J. Davis administration in Austin. While Block seemed to be in on every big deal coming to Texas, he was not exactly a carpetbagger, but was doubtless in very tight with the federal administration in the state.

The Yankee's reputation for sharp dealing and his closeness with the reconstructionists forewarned Dunigan against dealing with Block at all. A more timid operator might not have considered any deal with Block, but Dunigan was anything but timid and he knew how to get his trades documented legally. In fact, Dunigan had done a deal with Block in 1867, insisting that Block sign it up. Everything went according to the contract.

Word was, Block was usually personally charming and delightfully at home in society, but if he drank too much, he became bullying and sneeringly arrogant. While Dunigan had never encountered Block in that state, he realized the man could well be obnoxious when drunk. Dunigan had had plenty of warning about Block and was determined to mind his business carefully.

Dunigan put on his coat and went to the bar, entering from a side entrance. He spotted Block seated with another man who was vaguely familiar. Halfway to the table, Dunigan suddenly recalled the other man. At once, Dunigan whirled and left. He was sure the two men hadn't spotted him, but he was badly shaken and needed to calm himself before he went back. In the lobby, Dunigan found a secluded chair behind a potted plant and sat down.

The man with Block was Alan Ewing, the nephew and agent of the Earl of Spey Marnock, who had evicted Dunigan's family from their cottage in Ireland when Dunigan's father died. He had no idea what Block's proposition was, but he knew this man Ewing, knew him as a cheat and thief. Dunigan also knew Ewing had withheld payments from his uncle, Lord Marnock. Dunigan didn't think Ewing would recognize him after twenty-five years, so he wasn't worried about that, but he resolved to be careful dealing with him.

More composed after his initial shock, Dunigan joined the two men in the bar. Block rose and introduced them. "John, I want you to meet Viscount Glencollin, who has a very inte-resting proposition for you," Block said in his cocksure manner.

So he got the old man to make him his heir, Dunigan mused to himself. He was watching for any sign of recognition but there was none. Alan Ewing, Viscount Glencollin, was about 58 or 60, portly, with a flushed face and a supercilious air of superiority.

Dunigan took his hand firmly. "Very glad to meet you, your honor. What is this great proposition you have?"

"First, I think, a drink. What is your pleasure, Mister Dunigan?"

"Bourbon whiskey, your honor, and I thank you. I think all deals are better when preceded by a touch of spirits."

When Ewing laughed his broad belly jiggled. He ordered the drinks and they made small talk and had two more before getting to the business.

Block began. "John, Lord Ewing is agent and manager of a Scottish syndicate out of Dundee, which has acquired a large ranch in Montana. As you know, cows are hard to come by up there, so he wants five thousand next year. I told him you could get them through if anyone could and he wants you to do it. He is willing to pay a fee for the driving or to buy the cows on delivery at an agreed-upon price. Either way, I assure you the money is good."

"Montana is a long way," Dunigan countered. "It is at least fifteen hundred miles from Texas and we couldn't get there before fall. Besides renegades, we would probably have trouble with all sorts of Indians. Off hand, I can think of the Pawnees, Cheyenes, Shoshones, Blackfeet, Crow, and Sioux, that is, if we're lucky. Add some Comanche, Kiowa, Utes, and Arapaho if we're not. I don't think that's been done before, and I don't know the country at all.

"Before I could agree to do it, I would have to see some maps and find out more about the Indians. The Sioux, espe-cially, bother me, because I heard Red Cloud made the army move out of there a couple of years back. Now they are strong enough to stop anything they want to stop in their territory."

Ewing responded. "Mister Dunigan, our ranch is at War Horse Lake, just west of the Musselshell River, beyond the Sioux range to the west—mostly keeping close beyond to the Black Hills in Dakota. The Blackfeet have moved beyond the moun-tains and the other tribes seem quiet and peaceful, really. You would be all right in Montana and Wyoming. About farther south, I know nothing, except the other tribes you mentioned don't venture into Montana. As for your late arrival, we have been and will continue to put up hay for the arrival of the cattle, and at the very least, will have enough for the first winter."

Block spoke up at this point. "Unless you are going a lot farther west than I think, you should miss the Comanche, the Kiowa and Utes. The Arapaho have been quiet since Chivington slaughtered them at Sand Creek and the Pawnees are mostly working as government scouts. The army seems to be patrolling more frequently and farther west in Kansas and Nebraska, so Indians should not cause you much trouble."

Dunigan digested this for a moment. "Even if all you say is true, I will still have to take a good many cattle along for the Indians and that will cost. Cows are a lot more trouble on the trail, too, as we will be traveling during the main calving season. Even though I will try to bring mostly dry cows, many of them will calve and we'll have to care for the calves or deal with a lot of irate mamas. Maybe you ought to think about taking them to Kansas, wintering them there and take them on to Montana in the spring."

"I'm afraid that's quite out of the question, old boy," Ewing retorted. "We have made our arrangements for next fall's delivery—all the feed, finances, personnel, and so on. It is imperative the cattle arrive not later than the end of September."

The conversation was moving ahead much faster than Dunigan wished, so he decided to change the subject. Feigning ignorance of the English system of nobility, which he understood very well indeed, he asked, "By the way, your honor, Calvin introduced you as Viscount Glencollin, then he called you Lord Ewing. I know all that has something to do with titles, but what is your real name, so I will know what to call you?"

Ewing smiled graciously, but somewhat snobbishly. "I know it is sometimes confusing to you Americans, but it is the practice in Britain to call titled persons by their titles, not their given names. Mine is Alan Ewing, but as I am heir to the Earl of Spey Marnock, I am given the title of 'Viscount,' specifically 'Viscount Glencollin.' Glencollin is one of the Earl's properties in Scotland. Normally, a viscount is addressed by 'my Lord,' or 'Milord,' followed either by his name or his title, it matters not. Usually, in my case, it's 'Lord Glencollin' or 'Lord Ewing.'"

Dunigan tried to look suitably impressed, then turned to the Englishman and said, "Well, I'm glad that's cleared up, Alan."

Ewing turned beet red, pursed his perch lips, and bit off what would have been an acid retort. Instead, he coughed.

To himself, Dunigan thought, *I've got your number, Sassenach. You still aren't sure you'll be the old man's heir. That'll be enough to keep you off balance.*

Dunigan rambled on about the dangers of such a drive, with the other two trying their best to assure him of safety. Gradually, a pattern began to take shape in Dunigan's mind. Block and Ewing hadn't walked out on the proposition so far, so he realized they had likely already been turned down by several drovers and that made him one of their last hopes.

He also suspected something was amiss with the whole scheme, when they turned down flatly his suggestion about breaking the drive and wintering over in Kansas. Dunigan's knowledge of Ewing's past and his intense loathing for the man contributed to his feeling of mistrust and uneasiness. He felt almost the same about Calvin Block.

After about three hours, Dunigan said, "If I do this, and I'm not saying yet that I am, I will only do it by sale. I will not drive five thousand cows all the way to Montana on a fee basis. I might under an agreed price on a delivered basis."

He saw the relief creeping into their faces, so he knew that was what they originally intended anyway. Block invited the others to dine with him, arranging a carriage for 7:30. Dunigan went back to his room to dress.

They met again at the carriage and went on to dinner at a restaurant Block had selected. The meal was pleasant and included further discussion about the drive. Ewing probed Dunigan's background, because he had spotted the vestiges of Dunigan's Irish brogue. Dunigan told Ewing he was from Donegal, so as not to betray that he knew Ewing from Cork. Ewing accepted that, then Dunigan told him he had to check the maps and consult the army on the Indian situation if he was to entertain their proposition at all. He agreed to meet them the following afternoon at two.

Dunigan arose early the next morning and rode out to the army post at Ft. Sam Houston, where he contracted Major Frederick Layton, who was an intelligence officer. He asked the major about Indian activity along the route to Montana. Layton was well informed and a good source of information, even providing Dunigan with maps of the area. They were army tactical maps and were excellent. Layton also mentioned some of the army maneuvers in the various Indian Territories and discussed some of the army's plans. Dunigan was so pleased he told Layton he was going to send him a good horse. Cheerfully, Layton accepted the gift in advance.

Dunigan rode back to town, stopping at a lawyer he had used before. He asked about liens and titles on cattle in Montana and got quite a lot of information. He and the lawyer had lunch together and he outlined the operation Block and Ewing wanted him to take on. Dunigan asked the lawyer to draw up a contract based on his knowledge of the deal that would allow Dunigan to retain title to the cattle in Montana until he had been paid. Jesse Singleton, the lawyer, thought he could do that and would have a paper ready early the next day. Dunigan asked him to include some special payment details, but to leave amounts blank. Then he went back to the hotel to meet Ewing and Block.

They met in the Menger bar, had a drink, and Dunigan suggested they move to a room he had arranged on the way in. Soon they were seated in a light and airy room around a large table.

Dunigan made his offer. "I want to make you this proposition. I will deliver no fewer than five thousand cows to your ranch not later than October 15, 1872, for $35 per head plus $5 more for any with calves. The total will be payable at $10 per head now, $15 per head more when I cross the Platte River at Fort McPherson, Nebraska, and the final $10 a head at the destination in Montana. We will agree the cows will not be more than eight years old and in good condition. They will be first class or better longhorn cows. If you agree, I will have a contract drawn up today, then I will get busy planning, because it is already getting late in the year."

Dunigan had caught the plotters by surprise. Both smiled rather queasily, then went into a whispering huddle. Dunigan heard only a few words, but surmised that most of the conversation was by Block, apparently seeking to retain some percentage of the transaction. He did hear distinctly, "Where will mine come from?"

After a few more moments of hissing, the others excused themselves and left the room to have more privacy. After about twenty minutes, they returned slightly more composed.

Block opened. "John, you know your price is way too high. Down here, good cows cost from $4 to $8. Your trail costs to Kansas average about a dollar a head, so double that. This deal you're proposing gives you $25 per head profit. Now that's greedy and it just isn't right."

Dunigan was ready. "Calvin, we might have to fight our way all the way up and back, through all those Indians. I could lose the whole bunch if I am unlucky. Besides, it costs more than twice as much to trail cows as it does steers, and it takes a lot longer. I have a very profitable operation with steers as it is, and I would miss this year. Either I get my price, or I won't do it. It's as simple as that," Dunigan said with finality.

"Dunigan, you're being completely unreasonable," Ewing erupted. "Your price is far too high and your prepayment demand is insulting to an Englishman of the highest character, whom you are dealing with. We cannot, will not agree to this." Ewing was crimson and his voice grew louder as he spoke.

Slowly, but decidedly, Dunigan rose from the table. "Well, I guess that's all we need to say. The drinks are on me." He turned and started for the door. Block stopped him before he had taken two steps.

"Hold on now, John, we can make a trade. Don't go running right off in the middle of things."

"Calvin, you haven't even made me an offer, you have yet to hear all my details, although I doubt you'll like them any better than the basic deal. I'm pretty well set in my terms, so I don't see any wiggle room. Why don't we just forget it and go do something more pleasant. Besides, I'm thirsty."

The others stared at each other for a moment, then got up and followed Dunigan to the bar. He sensed they hadn't given up, but resolved to stand firm. If he couldn't make a lot of money on this drive, he wouldn't do it. It was a huge risk, far too great unless the rewards were commensurate.

Over drinks, Ewing started in. "Dunigan, we don't object to your basic deal, but we will offer you $25 per head total, $10 now and the balance at destination. I really do think that's quite reasonable. Furthermore, there's hardly a place to make payment when you cross the Platte. There's only an army post there."

"I can manage that," Dunigan said. "Of course, you would want someone there to verify we had crossed with the proper number of cows, but that's going to be one of my requirements in any case, because it covers me from a big loss if your tame Indians suddenly turn into murdering savages again."

For the better part of two hours, they argued back and forth. Dunigan did not say much, watching each of the participants carefully. He figured some part of his deal cut out Calvin Block, but he did not yet know how. He felt the same about Ewing, but the only reason he could think of was if they planned to steal the whole bunch. They wouldn't have much margin if they had already paid out $25 per head. It was also clear that they were determined to persuade Dunigan to drive those cows, so he stood his ground and finally, but most reluctantly, they agreed to his terms.

They all adjourned to Jesse Singleton's law office to sign the contract. Again, Ewing objected to the arrangements for payment as insulting to his character as a member of British nobility, but Dunigan won out. Ewing or his agent would wire Ewing's bank in St. Louis to make payment upon the cattle crossing the Platte. The $75,000 would be escrowed in the bank and the wire would trigger payment to Dunigan, acknowledged by return wire to him at Ft. McPherson.

The same arrangements would be in effect for the final payment in Montana. Ewing became more irate, but Dunigan just stared, saying nothing. *You Sassenach bastard,* he thought to himself, *I don't know what you're planning, but I know it won't be good for me, so I ain't gonna budge.*

At last, they all signed the contract, Dunigan got a draft for $50,000, and the deal was done. It had been a hard two days, but Dunigan begged off staying over and left, riding all night and most of the next day until he reached Goliad, where he got a room and slept.

He reached the ranch at noon the next day and immediately called in McCurry, Roussel, Michael O'Grady, George Harris, and Abel Castro. They all sat around the table and ate while Dunigan filled them in on the drive and the fears he had for it. Then he outlined his plan. Nick and Abel Castro would go down to the Rio Grande and contract for twenty-five hundred cows to be delivered at Oakville in Bee County around the first of March.

"I've heard of a Sam Gentry down there at San Ysidro who can get you a lot of cattle. I think he steals most of them in Mexico and in the Brasada, but he is more or less honest. You can probably make a deal with him, but be very careful about quality and age. I told you about my contract and I don't want to have these cows turned back to me in Montana with the snow falling. We will pay up to $8 per head and I will put up 25 percent of the purchase price now, the rest at delivery. I know you will try to get them as cheap as you can and I have enough money on deposit around here to pay for all of them, so I will arrange for both of you to draw drafts for the necessary funds."

Dunigan often used partial or down payments to close transactions. He felt no deal was ever complete unless money changed hands. Cattle bought for later delivery were usually paid for in full at delivery—that was the custom—but Dunigan preferred to pay or to be paid for cattle when the deal was settled. He receipted for the money, with a short explanation of the transaction, which also served as a contract. That way, in his view, it was harder for other people to back out.

He turned to Castro. "Abel, you go with Nick to help out. See if you can find some more men. We will need six or seven more hands who can fight. You might be able to find them around the river."

"Si, patron, lo hago." Castro nodded. Dunigan was satisfied he would.

"Pete, I want you and Michael to do the same thing in the area west of San Antonio, but I want you to perform a chore for me before that. You know that gray gelding of mine, the one I call Ceniza? Take him up to Major Frederick Layton at Fort Sam Houston. After that, look around for cows to buy. Try to do it the same way I told Nick, but we want delivery somewhere around Bandera the first of April. If you can get them from one seller, I'll want George Harris to stay and winter with them. That all right with you, George?"

"Fine with me, boss, I like new places."

George Harris did like new places. As long as Dunigan had known him, Harris had been inquisitive, always wanting to experience new places and new things. A capable hand, he had been Dunigan's segundo for a long time, and he had great confidence in George. His ability to track and read sign impressed the boss, too, and unlike most of the men around him, he was not totally devoid of ambition. Harris's lack of capital was what really separated him from Dunigan, but his ambition was well tempered by loyalty, and in this case, Dunigan felt no threat to himself commercially.

"Try to get two thousand to twenty-five hundred up there. They should be a better class of cows, and put a top on the herd. I'd rather not leave anyone down south, Nick, but if you make a deal, tell the man we will be visiting from time to time."

"John, most of them fellers down there ain't too sociable, and won't take kindly to 'supervision.' I wouldn't recommend that," Nick countered.

"We only want to check on our herd, Nick, to make sure they ain't too trashy. These cows have got to be right. Tell them we'll be down sometime in the winter to help trail brand 'em."

Dunigan continued. "We are going to take about 5,100–5,200 cows with us, and we'll need maybe two hundred steers too, to keep peace with the Indians. We are passing through a lot of different tribes' territories and I hope we can keep them peaceful with 'wo-haw.' If not, we will have to speak with them through Mister Colt and Mister Spencer. Make sure all the men's arms are in good condition. It is damned hard to repair guns in the middle of an Indian fight. By the way, since I expect trouble all along this drive, everyone will draw forty dollars a month, not thirty. That's a fighting wage and I expect everyone to be ready to do just that. The raise will commence in February."

Michael O'Grady spoke up. "Boss, I sure do hate to see Ceniza go. I think he is the best horse we ever had here. Why don't you send that black filly instead? She's a real good horse and dog gentle."

"Michael, Major Layton has been a great help to me already and he will get the army to help us along the trail. I want him to have the best there is. Understand?"

"It's your horse, boss."

"All right. I'm going to leave for St. Louis and Denver to make arrangements for the finances and to find someone who knows that country up there. I have heard those old fur trappers know it best and some of them have settled in around Denver. That whole deal will probably take me a good while, so I most likely won't be back until around Christmas. Nick, you and Pete will have to handle most of the arrangements. We'll organize things just like in the past. Two herds, plus my bunch. Each herd will need one extra wagon to carry calves until they can keep up on their own. Also, we will need extra horses and mules for such a long drive.

"Pete, you and Nick pick your own crews, and have them ready and well equipped. My group this year will be Abner and George, plus Juan Redondo and someone from up there who knows the Montana and Wyoming country. I will leave instructions about drawing drafts for the cattle before I leave or I will send it to them when I get back. If you need any money quick, get it from Jim McFaddin in Refugio. He has plenty to get started on."

"Pete, when you're up around San Antonio, see what you can find out about that new western trail. I heard a couple of herds went that way last year and said it was the best route all the way through Fort Dodge."

Pete nodded.

"Any questions? Because I will be leaving late tomorrow or maybe the day after, and I want everything set by the time I get back."

Everyone seemed to know what to do. Dunigan was always ready to delegate authority and his jefes knew how to shoulder it, so this was nothing new to them. He was sure they would get it all done.

The cow buyers left the next morning and Dunigan looked around his ranch, visiting some of his Hereford-bred calves. He was pleased. He had about 1,400 cows of his own and could make up any shortage from them if he had to. He left the ranch after dinner and rode into Refugio, where he made arrangements with McFaddin to make money available to Nick and Pete. He told him to get more from Sullivan at Indianola, if he ran out. While there, Dunigan bought a pistol and rifle for Thad Scott, who was riding with him. The boy was delighted, taking that as a sign he was heading up the trail next spring.

He and Thad rode out of Refugio headed for Maille's place on Salt Creek, where they planned to spend the night. They arrived about an hour before dark and the old man invited them in for supper and to spend the night, because he and Dunigan needed to talk. Maille was well pleased with how Dunigan had handled the sale of his steers, but was disappointed he would be unable to do that next year. They talked about the weather and markets and other things as cow men are wont to in their leisure moments.

Finally, Maille said, "John, I see you got you another sprout with you. What are you doing, running an orphan's home?"

"Well, these boys are just good help and they pull their weight. As a matter of fact, I want Thad here to pick out some horses and mules for me on his way back from Indianola. Treat him right, will you, just the way you always did with young Michael."

"Sure, John, be glad to. He seems like a good boy. Too bad about his folks, but I guess you and Nick will mother him like you did Michael."

Thad Scott bridled a bit at this conversation, vowing to himself to get the better of Maille in the horse trading. He wasn't a baby anymore. He would show that old man.

They spent a pleasant evening with Maille, and in the morning continued on to Indianola, where Dunigan caught a ship for New Orleans. Before leaving Indianola, he conferred with Sullivan to make sure the money he had there would be transferred to Refugio if needed. Sullivan did not like that, wanting Dunigan to keep all his money with him. He also suspected Dunigan was keeping large amounts in Kansas City, St. Louis, or New Orleans, too, but there wasn't much Sullivan could do about that.

Chapter 19

On October 3rd, Dunigan boarded the little mail packet for New Orleans. The trip was uncomfortable again because the Gulf was stormy and rough. Dunigan spent a lot of time with the underway watch in the wheelhouse, observing their navigation techniques. He thought they might help him to find his way in the sea of grass on the plains. Maybe he'd better secure some stellar charts and a sextant. He re-learned the rudiments on the way to New Orleans, his youthful knowledge coming back bit by bit. When he reached New Orleans, he felt competent again to navigate by the stars.

Dunigan spent only a day in New Orleans before boarding the *Delta Star,* one of the new sidepaddle steamers with fine accommodations. His cabin was roomy and well appointed and the public facilities were purely luxurious. He moved in and unpacked, anticipating at least ten days to St. Louis. He had wired Gerard Alton of his expected arrival and asked him to secure hotel reservations.

The *Delta Star* left the New Orleans docks at four in the afternoon on its way north. A large group of merrymakers was on hand to see passengers off and Dunigan watched them with amusement. Most were cotton planters and traders, but some he couldn't figure out. He supposed the higher fares charged on the newer boat would spare him the company of drummers, so these would probably be bankers and merchants.

They were already well upriver when dinner was announced and Dunigan went to the dining saloon. He had a drink at the bar, then found his placecard at an eight-seat table. Next to him was a woman he classified as mature and attractive. Around thirty and tall for a woman, she was slender with regular features except for a strong aquiline nose. At first, he figured her for someone's wife, but saw no rings on her fingers. He began visiting with her, as dinner partners will do, and found she was indeed unmarried, the daughter of a Kentucky tobacco planter and horse breeder. She had been to New Orleans, personally delivering yearlings to buyers in Louisiana.

They became well acquainted through the dinner hour and she wanted to know all about the western cattle trade and western horses. The orchestra tuned up and they danced, between glasses of champagne, until eleven o'clock, when Dunigan walked her back to her stateroom. He went on to his own, pleased at the promise of seeing more of her during the voyage.

Amanda Green lived with her father, a widower, at the family farm in Washington County, about forty miles west of Lexington, where they raised tobacco and thoroughbred race horses. The Greens had come into Kentucky with John Sevier, so were among the first families, antedating even Daniel Boone.

Amanda was very knowledgeable about horses and, so she said, saw to that end of the family operation. Dunigan did not doubt it. He was impressed by her wide knowledge of bloodlines and the nuances of the business of race horses.

Her hair was black and shiny as a raven's wing, but her eyes were deep blue, and with her aquiline nose, suggested some Indian forebears in the dim past. She was fine looking, too, but not in any girlish, merely pretty way. Rather, Amanda exuded a friendly dignity. She offered very little small talk, being more concerned with serious matters, but she was enthusiastically interested in everything about the west and she hung attentively on Dunigan's stories.

She seemed to be grounded solidly in the subjects she was interested in, not at all flirtatious or flighty, and also warm and sincere.

Dunigan presumed the reason she was unmarried was that she scared potential suitors with her intelligence and her grasp of things that mattered. She could certainly compete with men on their turf and that would make them feel inadequate. Her manner did not deter Dunigan at all. He had always admired self-sufficient people, male or female. He began thinking seriously about this woman, who had so many interests in common with his.

Over the next few days, they spent considerable time together. Amanda knew something of the west and was inclined toward its development. Her family had been politically powerful for many years. She had known Henry Clay as a child and followed his thinking. Her only brother was killed in the war, foresaking Kentucky's neutrality for the lost Southern cause. She had thought him mistaken in his belief, but could not save him.

Dunigan had been of similar beliefs, so they shared deep convictions about the whole matter of the Civil War and reconstruction. Dunigan began to believe they thought alike on just about everything. As the warm autumn days went on, he began to realize he had fallen in love with Amanda, and knew he must reform his life about and around her. For the first three days after leaving New Orleans, they became constant companions, asking and learning all about one another, their histories, ambitions, wants, and desires. Amanda was especially interested in his life on the ranch along the Aransas.

Dunigan began to feel this handsome woman was as interested in him as he was in her. Instead of love or mere lust between them, what seemed to be developing was a deep mutual respect. They could stand at the boat railing for hours without speaking until some particularly beautiful panorama came into view. Most of the time, they enjoyed the vast emptiness west of the river.

Amanda had a sense of the grandeur of the plains, uncommon in most easterners, who generally viewed it with, at best, boredom and, at worst, fear of its space and with utter loathing. To the westerner, the treeless plains were a vast world, seething with life, from the earthworms and grasshoppers to the buffalo and eagle. Though Amanda saw none of these from the boat deck, her imagination placed them all just beyond the horizon, yet not beyond her vision.

In four days, she was scheduled to transfer to an Ohio river boat at Cairo, Illinois, just short of St. Louis. Dunigan was distraught at losing her when he had just found her, so two days before their arrival in Cairo, he confessed to her the depth of his feelings. At the end of this confession, he asked her to marry him and go off with him to the wilds of Texas.

Amanda replied that she loved him deeply and wanted to spend the rest of her life with him, but that she couldn't abruptly leave her responsibilities to her father. She was also enough of a traditional woman to want to be married in her home, amongst family and friends.

All of this Dunigan understood, and he was elated that she would consent to marrying him. They made arrangements for him to come to Kentucky on his way home in a month, but decided to postpone their marriage until after the drive to Montana.

The dangers of the drive were enormous and he didn't wish to leave a young widow alone on the frontier in Texas. Besides, he would be very busy until the drive was over. Having found each other, they would not like being apart, but being mature individuals, they would endure it. She promised to wait until he completed his grand adventure, although she longed to be a part of it.

Their parting at Cairo was bittersweet and loving, but knowing they were committed to each other and would be together in a month eased their pain.

Gerard Alton met Dunigan at the landing in St. Louis and took him to his hotel, informing him that his wife had scheduled a busy round of social activities. At once, Dunigan told Gerard of his engagement to Amanda Green, so matchmaking was out of the question.

"John, I'm sure she has that on her mind, but you are going to have to go through most of the parties anyway. Sounds like you have found yourself quite a woman. I seem to remember a Kentucky family named Green who had some fine thoroughbred stock. Maybe they are the same people."

Dunigan gave in. "All right, Gerard, just so long as these ladies know I am spoken for. I know how women love these social things, but I am a mite busy. I'll tell you all about it, but now I need to talk to a lawyer who knows how title to cattle can be protected in Montana and Wyoming Territory. That is the main reason I came here. There should be someone who knows about that, as much contact as St. Louis has with that area."

Alton acknowledged he might know someone and he would try to arrange a meeting. In the meantime, a carriage would pick up Dunigan at 7:30 that evening for a dinner party at Alton's home.

Dunigan was in front of his hotel when the carriage arrived. Soon, he was greeting Genevieve Alton, most fetching in a green velvet gown. She was genuinely glad to see him. He whispered to her, "Did Gerard tell you I have been removed from the marriage market?"

"Yes, he did, and that has upset all my plans. I had some very fetching tidbits lined up for you, too," she answered impishly. "But my congratulations all the same. Gerard said the family name was Green and that they raise race horses. You know we are originally from Kentucky. There was a fine old family named Green near our old place in Washington County. They raised thoroughbreds."

"Must be the same folks, Genevieve, their place is in Washington County, west of Lexington. Amanda said her folks came in with Sevier, so they have been there a long time."

"Amanda Green! Why, I know her! A beautiful child, last I saw of her during the war. John Dunigan, you have done yourself right proud," she exclaimed, hurrying off to tell her husband.

Dunigan had a good time. Most of the guests were older bankers and merchants, people who had had a lot to do with financing and facilitating the fur trade in the twenties and thirties, so Dunigan was able to secure lots of information about Montana and the Missouri River trade, as well as the northern Indian tribes. The ladies present were pleasant, mostly pretty, but vacuous, mainly concerned with social affairs. Compared to Amanda, they came in a distant fifth. Each time he thought of her, Dunigan had trouble believing his good fortune, and he was already missing her terribly.

The next day, Gerard Alton arranged a meeting with an attorney named Joseph Carter, an older man in his early seventies, who was semiretired. Carter had gained a depth of knowledge from the fur trade, mainly by representing William Ashley and other fur merchants before the federal government. The three men met for an hour and a half, with Dunigan pursuing various avenues to retaining clear and sole title to his herd until he was paid in full.

Carter, who understood how territorial law varied from national and state laws, was most helpful. He felt the best way to retain ownership was simply to mortgage the herd, and not to pay off the lien until the final payment was received. Dunigan thought that was a splendid idea and set about implementing it through Alton's bank.

Although he had $150,000 on deposit in the bank, Dunigan borrowed $100,000, collateralizing it with the herd, listing brands, locations, and so on. The bank would file a lien on the cattle in the Montana territorial capital at Virginia City, so it would be first lien holder on the cattle, effectively blocking any move by Ewing to claim ownership.

A lien would also be filed in Nebraska and the Platte River payment would go to the bank, only Alton's bank would still have first claim on the cattle because $25,000 of the debt would still be outstanding, keeping the lien intact. Alton's bank would take care of the filings and could find out if any other liens had already been filed by Ewing, double checking Dunigan's position.

The plan looked good to everyone and Carter recounted a similar plan having to do with trade goods, but warned that the Montana Stock Growers Association maintained a very powerful position in territorial matters. If they supported Ewing, the deal could become very risky. Everyone agreed they'd have to cross that bridge later, so there was no point worrying about it now.

Joseph Carter was a great help to Dunigan, who now understood something about territorial property laws. There was still some risk to him, but his plan should be iron clad legally. The main danger was that the English and Scottish syndicates were strong and powerful in that area and with the backing of the Montana stock growers, were almost a law unto themselves.

If Ewing took his herd by force, Dunigan had solid grounds for a lawsuit, but he would not have his cattle. More than likely, he suspected, the syndicates owned the judges. If his 'partners' tried to take the herd, Dunigan resolved to fight. He well knew that in Montana, as elsewhere on the sparsely settled frontier, possession was nine-tenths of the law.

The social whirl planned by Genevieve Alton for Dunigan went ahead as planned, but with considerably less fervor, once she had learned of his romance with Amanda Green, but it was still fun and entertaining and Dunigan enjoyed it. He finished his business in St. Louis and was anxious to be on his way to Denver. Alton had given him a few leads to some of the old mountain men around Denver, as well as a letter of introduction to one of his friends who might be able to help Dunigan.

Dunigan caught the train to Kansas City on the morning of October 25th, planning to go through Kansas City to Abilene, then to end of track somewhere near the Colorado line, picking up a horse there to ride to Denver. In fact, he got off at Abilene and was able to buy from the livery there two of his own horses he had sold two years before.

He needed a pack horse for the last leg of the trip, so he also picked up some supplies, loading his horses and supplies onto the train for end-of-track. He left it at a tiny settlement that had sprung up where the track crossed the Smoky Hill River, spending the night there before leaving for Denver.

Dunigan figured it would take him five days to reach Denver, maybe four if he rode hard, but he wasn't in any big rush. The weather was cool and he'd never been in this country before, so he didn't press it. The country was treeless and open and Dunigan checked the sun and the North Star often. He was headed for Big Sandy Creek, which he would follow to Limon, then up to and along the Platte into Denver. Landmarks were few and far between on the plains, with most of the crossing traffic following the Santa Fe Trail. But Dunigan had a good sense of direction and he reached Big Sandy Creek the second day. He had seen only a few settlers' cabins in this immense sea of grass and he thought the country a stockman's heaven, except there was no winter shelter.

Summer pasturage might be all right once the railroad got that far west, which it would in a year or so. The tick problem would be less, too, because this range was considerably higher in elevation. There were certainly not many farmers in the area. He had seen only five soddies since crossing the Smoky Hill. He got to Limon at the end of the third day, took a room and arranged feed and a barn for the horses. Limon was not much of a town, but he found a room over the saloon, where he had a drink and some supper.

Dunigan left the Big Sandy a little ways out of Limon and on the advice of the livery stable owner took up a northwesterly direction toward Denver. About noon of the second day out of Limon, he struck what should be Cherry Creek and followed it north. He had an even better set of landmarks to go by, seeing the Rocky Mountains for about a day. There was snow on most of the peaks. The farther west he went, the colder and higher he got, and soon he had to put on his heavy coat. The horses made better time because of the cooler weather and he rode into Denver about an hour after dark. He stabled his horses and was driven over to the Windsor Hotel on Larimer Street where he checked in for the night.

Dunigan slept late the next morning. His ride had tired him. He rose, bathed and dressed, ate breakfast, then set out to find Robert Latham, the fur merchant to whom Alton had given him a letter of introduction. He found his shop easily, only three blocks down Larimer Street. The stench inside was overpowering and Dunigan's eyes watered.

Latham came out to greet him and told him not to mind the smell, as it was only in the front room. They would go into the back. Dunigan handed him Alton's letter and followed Latham into the rear of the building through the pile of hides of all kinds, but principally buffalo. The odor was less intense but still present in the back, where they sat down to talk.

"Mister Latham, I am driving a herd of cows from Texas to Montana next spring and I need a guide who knows the country from Kansas on north. I need a man familiar with the territory and also the Indians thereabout. I thought through your acquaintance with fur traders from the area, you might be able to put me onto someone."

"I did not catch your name, sir."

"My name is John Dunigan, and I am a drover from South Texas. Please excuse my rudeness."

"No harm done, Mister Dunigan," Latham responded. "I just wanted to know who I was talking to. I do know some people who live close by who know that country and the Indians in it quite well. Most are married to Indian women. Exactly what do you want?" Latham eyed Dunigan suspiciously.

Dunigan figured his best move was complete honesty, so he told the whole story, leaving nothing out, and adding his recent history as a drover to soothe Latham's unease.

The trader seemed reassured by Dunigan's confession. "Mister Dunigan, I can share your fears, for I have had some experience with these syndicates. They are very greedy and they are politically very powerful in Wyoming and Montana."

"Well, I prefer to avoid a fight, if possible, but I mean to keep my herd and I think they want to steal it, so if they try to take it physically, I will fight. I don't think I can count on a fair shake in the Montana territorial courts."

"You're probably right about that, but if there's fighting in the offing, it makes a difference who I recommend to you, if you know what I mean."

Latham paused to reflect. "I know a few of the old mountain men around here, some good, some not so good; we were all in the mountains thirty–forty years ago, trapping and trading beaver mostly. That's all over now. Some of them are still in the mountains and they'll die there. Others have trading posts, some guiding, some hunting buffalo. This store don't make no money, but it used to, and I keep it for a place to do other business. The skins about break even, though."

"They must have been great times back there in the mountains," Dunigan ventured.

"They were that, but it's all done. I could tell you stories about them until next week, but I don't imagine you have that much time."

"I'd like to hear them and I will some day, but you're right, I do have a lot to do and not a whole lot of time to do it in."

"That's what I figured, so I won't keep you. The best man for you is Louis Courrell. He is a real ole hoss. His trading post is up at Fort Lupton, about thirty miles up the Platte from here. He keeps it with his wife, a Blackfoot squaw, and two kids. I saw Louie about six months ago and he had not been back to the high country in about three years and was missing it. He's a little long in the tooth—over sixty—but is as tough as any grizzly. I first met him back in twenty-nine with Ashley's, but he had been out with Hudson's Bay four or five years earlier and he has been all over that country. He knows it as well as anybody and he knows the Indians, too."

"Sounds like he's my man, if he'll agree to go. I'd like to go see him, if that's the thing to do."

"I think it is. Just go on up there to Lupton and look him up. Tell him for me he has $300 credit for the last hides he sent me and ask him to send me word about what to do with it."

"I'll bring word back myself and thanks for all your help, Mister Latham." Dunigan started to go, but Latham wasn't quite finished.

"You're welcome. You know, I kinda think Louie is ready to get away. His squaw has thickened up some and she nags. She was a chief's daughter and pretty as a picture when she was young." Latham waved him out and Dunigan walked on down to the livery, which was close by, to check his horses.

"I'll be leaving at daybreak tomorrow," he told the liveryman, "but I'll only need the grey horse, not the pack animal. I should be back tomorrow night. I'd appreciate it if you'd have him ready for me."

That night, Dunigan visited several local watering spots and met a few Denver residents. Most of them were mixed up in mining somehow and he wasn't really too interested in their conversations. There were some pretty saloon girls, but every time he cozied up to one, he got nasty looks from miners as big as bears. Not being all that interested, he didn't pursue his lust. He had to leave early the next day, so he turned in after eating a good steak in the hotel dining room.

When Dunigan rode out of Denver the next morning, the sun was barely a red glow over the prairie. He followed the Platte River trail north, making good time as the going was easy and the road was fair. He found Courrell's trading post easily; it was one of only seven buildings in Lupton. Inside the dimly lit log house that smelled like Latham's shop were several piles of buffalo robes and fur skins taking up half the space, the rest filled by trade goods.

"Mister Courrell, my name is John Dunigan. I'd like to talk to you about a proposition."

He had spoken to a squat man close to sixty years of age, but who looked as if he could take any man half his age, and twice his size. Swarthy and sinewy, at five and a half feet tall and 160 pounds, with a head of thick, grizzled hair and beard to match, Dunigan knew this had to be Louie Courrell.

The old fellow smiled in greeting. "Mist' Dunigan, you tell me you proposition. I got plenty time. Ain' nothing goin' on here rat now."

"Mister Courrell, why don't we go over to the saloon. I'm thirsty and this might take some time to go over," Dunigan ventured.

"Okay by me."

They walked across the street to the saloon, took a table, and ordered a jug.

"Mister Dunigan," Courrell began, but he was cut off immediately by Dunigan.

"Call me John."

"Okay, if you call me Louie. What is dis proposition you have, John?"

"Louie, I am a drover from Texas. I am driving five thousand cows to Montana next spring to a fella named Ewing, who runs one of those English syndicates at War Horse Lake. I wouldn't do this, except the money is just too good. Neither I nor any of my hands know anything about the country north of Kansas and I need a guide through Nebraska, Wyoming, and Montana. Robert Latham, a friend of a friend, said you were the best. He assured me you know the country and the Indians and that you are the man I need for this job."

Louie Courrell emptied his glass and poured another. He was digesting Dunigan's deal, but finally he spoke. "I know something bout dis Ewing feller and his outfit. I hear from my frens dere he is rough. He run two my frens away from cabins on Box Elder Creek and he got rough hans working for him. You rat to have scare."

Dunigan went on to outline the whole deal, everything that had been done, including the arrangements with Joseph Carter.

Courrell said he knew of Carter from his days with Ashley and Henry and the Missouri Fur Company. "I was mebbe fourteen or fifteen when I first go to de mountain. I go with my uncle after my folks die. He was with 'Odsun's Bay. I leave them in twenty-seven to go to Green River Rendezvous and I sell my furs to Ashley and Henry. I was free trapper after dat. I know all dem fellers, Jed Smeet and Bridger, Bent, St. Vrain, and Hugh Glass. Dey was some gran times in de mountains, but all over now. I trap a little here and buy some furs and robes and my wife, she run de trade. She is Blackfeet princess, you know, an ma boy, he half one. He sixteen now. I live with Blackfeet for five years, but dey move west. Not too many left, not like old days. How much you pay for dis job, John?"

Courrell pronounced 'John' with a soft French accent, reminding Dunigan of his celtic Ireland. He liked this old man of the mountains.

"I will pay you $200 for the job and if we get the cattle delivered for the full price and in one piece, I will pay you $500 more. I will provide food and horses for you and, of course, any expenses having to do with the safety of the herds." Dunigan was sure the scouting this man could provide would make the difference between success and failure.

"Well now, that ain' no bad offer. I tink I can get you troo dat place. I doan know if I can make dat feller pay you, but I will let you take care of dat. I think you know what you are doin. Tell me, do I got to go to Texas for dis job?"

"No, we will not need your scouting until after we leave Dodge, perhaps not until we cross the Platte. We will be in Dodge about June 1st, at Fort McPherson a month later. Why don't you scout around out of McPherson in June and when you know what's about, come south to meet us on the trail."

"Dat soun' like good idea, I meet you on de trail last part of June, an' I will know about Indians north of McPherson by den."

Dunigan fished in his pocket and brought out a purse, counting out $200 in gold.

"I am going to pay you in advance, right now. By the way, Latham told me to ask you what to do with the $300 credit you had with him. I'll see him tomorrow and can tell him then."

"You just tell him 'hold it.' I got some furs to go dere and I take them next week. I see him den."

They shook hands and Dunigan said, "Then I'll see you in Kansas in the spring, Louie. We'll have extra horses for you, but I don't allow whiskey on my drives."

"You won' catch me wid none, John," Louie said, grinning.

They finished the jug and Dunigan headed back to Denver.

On the way in, he dropped by Latham's to deliver Courrell's message. His eyes watered again as soon as he walked into the shop and he moved quickly into the back. When he delivered Courrell's instructions, Latham thanked him.

"You know, Dunigan, that fella Ewing was around here for awhile. I remember him now. Why don't we go get some dinner with some of my old friends who may know more about him?"

"Fine with me. I'll drop off my horse at the livery, or will I need him?"

"No, I have a buggy and it isn't too far. You won't need to clean up, as these are mountain people and they don't stand on ceremony."

Latham picked him up at the livery stable and they drove out to an establishment that looked like a big log council house, called 'Castorville,' after the French word for beaver. Through the windows, they saw dancing and heard accordion music. When they went in, Dunigan was introduced to the landlord, a bear of a man named Vince Ripperdy, who showed them to a table and brought drinks, while they settled back to enjoy the show.

The crowd was different from other bars Dunigan had visited the previous night. There were no miners here; all these people were trappers, dressed in buckskins. They were dancing to an accordion playing old French songs and the dances were almost like Indian war dances with only a few women involved.

All the revelers knew Latham and came around to talk. Latham steered the discussion to Ewing's syndicate. Dunigan picked up a lot of information, such as the fact his hands were all paid fighting wages, but most of the real hard cases didn't like working there and had drifted off. There was general agreement the odds were against bucking the Montana stock growers if they were united against you and that the Sioux were growing restive again after closing the Bozeman Trail.

Dunigan listened, enjoying the tales of the mountain men about the fur trapping days that were gone. Some were sad about the passing of the enterprise and some of them were genuinely lost now that the trade was defunct. Some were nostalgically happy just to have been part of it all. Dunigan realized cattle driving might be like that soon, too. It would be over as soon as the railroads reached into cattle country, but he didn't dwell on that over much. He didn't like to think about setting on the porch, telling young bucks about his wild and wooly days on the Chisholm trail.

He and Latham stayed until eleven, when it looked like things might get out of hand. They retreated to their respective resting places.

Before going to bed, Dunigan wrote a letter to Amanda, telling her he estimated his arrival at Louisville about the 15th of November and that he could stay for five days. She had agreed to meet him in Louisville when they parted and he expected her to arrange their travel to her home. He would stay in Denver another day or two to find out whatever more he could about Ewing.

Next morning, Dunigan wandered about the city, to banks, lawyers, cattle brokers and such. Many had heard of Ewing, but they didn't know much about him. Dunigan could tell that those who had been in contact with Ewing personally had a distaste for him. He heard only one item of interest: Ewing had a standing offer for gunhands and pistoleros, but was getting few takers.

Most of what he heard was repeat stuff, so he decided to leave for St. Louis in the morning, rather than waiting another day. He wasn't all that crazy about Denver, it was just too rowdy for his taste, what with all the miners. Compared with cowboys, miners were a filthy lot. True, neither trade bathed too often, but miners usually had a coating of dirt all over them. And, as with all boom activities, miners were transients, following one strike to another, and just like cowboys, they had few roots. However, Dunigan perceived them to be more inclined to boisterousness. Consequently, he labeled Denver a wide open town, with few rules of conduct enforced. Life was less valued in such places and Dunigan decided he'd better leave. Besides, he might see Amanda a day sooner. He was really missing her.

When the sun peeked over the eastern prairie the following day, Dunigan was already headed down Cherry Creek. He followed the same trail he had arrived on, completing the trip in about the same time. He spotted one small band of Indians the third day out and gave them a wide berth, but there were only seven or eight, and they looked pretty pathetic. All the same, had they noticed him, they might have robbed him for his horses and supplies.

He caught the first train out of end of track, stopped overnight at Abilene to drop off the horses, then went straight through to St. Louis, changing once in Kansas City.

He stayed only one night in St. Louis, having a quiet dinner with Gerard and Genevieve Alton at their home. Genevieve, of course, wanted to know all about his romance with Amanda Green, so Dunigan told them about the boat trip and that he was headed to see her, catching an Ohio river steamer in the morning. He also told her they planned to marry after the spring drive, so she could start planning something social.

Dunigan was very fond of both of them and told Gerard he wanted him to participate in the ceremonies. Gerard was flattered and Genevieve was delighted. When Gerard took Dunigan back to his room after dinner, he reported Joseph Carter had left for Virginia City, Montana Territory, to file the bank's lien on Dunigan's herd and to investigate conditions there. He would write them when he had news.

Dunigan caught the *City of Cincinnati* at ten the next morning. He had a reasonably comfortable cabin and the steamboat was all right, except for the cargo, a deckload of buffalo robes, making the boat smell like most every other place he had been lately. He began to feel that stench was haunting him. He had sent a wire to Amanda confirming his arrival on the 15th on the *City of Cincinnati,* and reaffirming his undying love.

It was only a few days to Louisville and the steamboat arrived on time at three in the afternoon. Dunigan was at the rail when the boat tied up. Glancing over the crowd, at once he saw Amanda wearing a black, fur-lined cloak, accompanied by a distinguished gentlemen with white hair and a mustache, whom he took to be Adrian Green, Amanda's father.

The gangplank was lowered, and Dunigan hurried to the dock, carrying only his battered carpetbag. He had shipped his saddle and traps to New Orleans on another boat. He pushed his way through the crowd and all at once Amanda was in his arms. As they kissed, a warm cloud enveloped him and he held her tightly in his arms. He saw Amanda's father behind her and when they unwound, the men shook hands and went to the Green's carriage and to the hotel, where they would stay the night, going on to the Green's home next morning.

The three had dinner that night at a restaurant called The Paddock, whose owner was evidently dedicated to thoroughbred racing. There were paintings and objets d'art all connected with racing, the centerpiece of all a bronze statue of Eclipse, progenitor of all thoroughbreds.

Dunigan and Amanda talked about horses all through the meal, her father listening politely, but taking little part. Over dessert, he confessed he had never really been very interested in the horses, preferring to raise tobacco. When his children showed an interest in the horses, he turned the operation over to them.

Amanda immediately responded. "Daddy, now you know that's not true. You kept up the quality in our horses for twenty years. Now that I know something about bloodlines, I can see that only very fine breeding was ever done at Sundown Farms. I think you got us interested in the horses to give us something useful to do."

"Amanda, you know I would rather raise plow horses than race horses," he insisted. "John, I want you to see our tobacco and smoke some of it. We produce the finest in Kentucky, and that's saying something. After dinner, I have a cigar for you made from our own tobacco, then you will see for yourself."

Adrian Green did indeed have a home-grown cigar for Dunigan, which he judged superior. There was music in the restaurant and the lovers danced. Dunigan was introduced to some of the Greens' friends, who were quite pleasant. They retired about eleven, to be ready for an early start the next day, as it was a long drive.

Chapter 20

Dunigan thought he had never seen such beautiful countryside. The farms were all neat and clean and well cared for, all the livestock appeared to be purebred, whether equine or bovine. When Dunigan asked his future father-in-law whether it would be possible to purchase breeding stock, he was answered affirmatively. About midafternoon, they arrived at Sundown Farms, the Green family homestead.

It was a lovely place, the main house set back on a hill overlooking white-washed fences, with poplars lining the entry drive. The fields were freshly plowed, and Dunigan could see the stables a quarter mile off. In the distance, a band of mares grazed in a well-manicured paddock, although it was late in the year for grass to be green.

The house was splendid. Of classic design, columned across the front, it reminded Dunigan of some of the fine old homes burned during the late war, when Sherman blazed his way through the rural South.

Dunigan was shown to his room by a liveried Negro servant, who was courteous and helpful, and soon was ensconced in his bedroom. After he put away his things, he decided to stroll down to the stables.

Amanda met him there and showed him the mares and stallions, reciting five or six generations of each. They were fine animals and Dunigan realized why the Green's yearlings brought a premium. The barns and stalls were immaculate and the fresh hay smelled delicious.

Neither of them trusted themselves to touch, but it was unavoidable at times during the tour and Dunigan found himself trembling and sweating, and suspected Amanda was, too.

Inspecting one of the mares, who was near foaling, they both moved to avoid the mare's sudden shifting and came together. They kissed passionately, their bodies straining to enclose each other. The mare nickered behind them, but she could have attacked them for all they cared. Finally, they broke apart, sweat beading Dunigan's brow. He was shaking like a leaf.

Amanda displayed a coquettish smile as she noticed Dunigan's discomfort.

He turned to walk away, muttering, "I want to get a cigar from your father." As he left the barn, he heard Amanda giggling. Back at the house, he lounged on the veranda smoking a cigar until he calmed down, which took some time.

A number of friends and neighbors were invited to dinner that night and Dunigan and Amanda were at the door to greet them. She stood very close to him, trying to rub her hip and thigh against him when no one was watching. She enjoyed herself immensely by making Dunigan squirm. She realized he had probably made some ironclad vow not to make love to her before their marriage, and she loved making him sweat.

"You shameless slattern, now you quit that," he pleaded to no avail. She was heartless in her zeal to break down his stern dignity and soon they both began to giggle quietly.

The visitors had all come to study the barbarian Amanda had chosen, so Dunigan was at his charming best. He would've characterized all the guests as soft and pampered, but they were nice to him, and he liked them. Many raised horses or cattle and he made pleasant small talk with them, as he did with others who were tied in one way or another to tobacco.

Most of all they were curious, but not overly, about the western cattle trade and the trail drives, but more intrigued by Dunigan's home base, way out in the wilds of Texas, amongst all the red savages. Carefully, Dunigan explained that Indians weren't a threat anymore in his part of Texas. The only danger was from Mexican raiders, and they rarely ventured as far north as his place. That the guests were fond of Amanda was apparent. That they were skeptical about whom she was marrying was, too. Dunigan had come to expect that reaction from folks in more settled parts of the country.

Two or three generations back, they were more like Dunigan, but now they were settled and comfortable, incredulous that Amanda was so eager to go to the edge of the frontier. But Dunigan understood, and loved her for it.

Dunigan slept fitfully that night, half expecting Amanda to sneak into his bed. He knew he could not resist that temptation, but he was genuinely afraid she would try. He locked his door, knowing she kept the keys to the house, so if she was of a mind, she could easily get in. His fears were unfounded, but continued to plague him as Amanda teased him with her lithe body the entire rest of his stay.

The next three days, pure hell for Dunigan, were heaven for Amanda. She was a kittenish coquette and Dunigan felt like an incipient volcano. They were caught up in a social whirl, dinner parties, picnics, climaxing with a point-to-point race Saturday, the day before he would board in Louisville a steamboat for New Orleans. Naturally, Dunigan spent some time with Adrian Green, going through the motions of asking for Amanda's hand.

"Yes, John, you can take my little girl off to the wild west. I couldn't stop her if I wanted to. She's made up her mind and she's all-fired stubborn. I just hope you can handle her. She loves you and you love her, that's plain enough to see. I hope you can handle her better than I ever could. But she's from good stock, so she'll do all right out there. You have my blessing and best wishes. I just wish you'd do it sooner. Why do you have to wait a year?"

"Mister Green, this drive I'm making is very dangerous. I could get killed and I don't want to leave Amanda a widow, with perhaps a small child. It's better this way."

"If you say so, John. I know you'll take good care of her, and I'll keep her safe until you return," he said resignedly.

Dunigan caught the *Memphis Beauty* at Louisville on Sunday, November 20th. It was a commonplace journey, punctuated by excellent cuisine. The poker game was rigged by two crooked gamblers, so Dunigan wouldn't play. He stayed one night in New Orleans to purchase an engagement diamond for Amanda, which he sent back by special courier, then he was on his way to Indianola by packet. He had sent a telegraph ahead and Michael O'Grady met him with a wagon on December 10th. They arrived back at the ranch a day later.

Everyone was at the ranch ready to report when Dunigan arrived. He begged off, saying he was tired and would see everyone in the morning. Next day after breakfast they all gathered to report.

Nick was first. He had made contact with Sam Gentry and had bought 2,500 cows for $3.50, Nick had seen some of them and passed them as good. He hadn't seen any local brands, so they shouldn't have any trouble there.

"Boss, Abel did like you said. He found six men down there who are fighting men. They seem to know cattle, but they are the worse-looking cutthroats I have ever seen. Abel vouches for them, though. Says they're from his village."

Abel smiled. "Patron, son hombres brutos, pero anda por su fierro." It was one of the longest speeches Dunigan had ever heard him make.

Dunigan glanced at Pete. "I made contact with a man named George Wilbanks, who headquarters above the Frio. He had eight hundred real good cows on hand and said he should get a total of two thousand. He's going to winter them in the Cañon de Uvalde, and they will cost us $4.50 delivered to Bandera in April. I had to give him $1.50 down, and George will winter with him up there. They seemed to be getting along all right when I left. He will be planning on delivery at Bandera, April 1st."

Michael O'Grady was next. "Mister Dunigan, we got that horse to Major Layton all right and he was right proud. He rode him all over the post and when we left, he was running a saber drill with him. I never saw a man more taken by any mount. Thad, Chito, and I have the horses in good shape. There are a hun-dred forty-five saddle horses, eight teams of good mules, and five teams of Belgian draft horses, and all those teams are first class. We got six teams from old Maille, four back from Kansas, and three from Victoria. I ordered two new wagons and they should be delivered in January from Corpus. Thad has the papers on them. These wagons should do for the calves; they are big and well made. I got them without canvas, but with bows, so we can fix 'em like we want 'em."

Everyone handed in receipts and draw slips to Dunigan for him to sort out. Nick hung behind. "John, about twelve of us went over and hunted cows after we got back. Not much time or effort was expended, but we did pick up five hundred cows and five hundred steers and they are here. Also we got fifteen pretty good horses."

"Good, Nick, that makes our numbers about right for the drive. Now, I want you to go into town and buy ten rifles and ten pistols and four tanned hides, so everything will be in first-class shape. I presume everybody has a good saddle, but we probably ought to have some spares, maybe three, and some spare blankets, too. I don't want anything happening that could be prevented by having the right equipment. You all have done a really good job of getting things ready. By the way, Nick, I forgot to tell you that I'm going to get married after the drive, to a girl from Kentucky that I met."

Nick looked as if he had been shot. "John, you don't mean it, do you? I never figured you to do something like this. Tell me all about it."

Dunigan related the whole story as Nick listened raptly.

He didn't leave anything out and when he finished, Nick said, "You know John, I was born in Washington County, Kentucky, just about three miles from the Green's place. Course, we were dirt pore, and they didn't know me, but I knew them and they wuz quality folks. If any woman might be worthy of you, that gal probably would." Nick walked out kind of smiling to relate the tale to everyone else on the ranch.

Later that day Michael, Pete, Thad, Abel, Pablo, and most of the other hands sought out Dunigan to congratulate him and to ask something about his wife to be. Dunigan was pleased they were so interested in his affairs and felt good all the rest of the day. Loyalty always cheered him.

Chapter 21

Well rested from his trip, Dunigan rode out to inspect his ranch and livestock. He noted with satisfaction the crossbred progeny of his Hereford bulls and the excellent condition of his pasture, largely the result of good fall rains. He had enough money to buy more land, but felt he had better keep it handy in case there were disasters on the big cow drive to Montana.

He was aware he really did not have much hard information about the intentions of Ewing and Block, and that he probably wouldn't in time to do much except defend himself. He itched to take the initiative, but that couldn't be done yet, so for now he would have to react to their action.

Toward the end of the week, mail from Refugio was delivered and Dunigan had four letters, two from Amanda and one each from Joseph Carter and Robert Latham. Although the letters from Carter and Latham were probably more important to the business, he opened Amanda's first and read them eagerly. Besides constant affirmations of love and affection, they were mostly cheerful accounts of happenings in Kentucky, some reports of horse sales, and local gossip.

Dunigan had written her from New Orleans, but had not mentioned the ring he had sent. Evidently, it had not arrived, and he reminded himself to check on that with the New Orleans jeweler.

Latham's letter was interesting, too, with news that Ewing was putting together an operation around Ft. Benton, north of the Great Falls of the Missouri, and also that he had been in contact with a number of Sioux chiefs. This last part gave

Dunigan serious misgivings. If the Sioux were part of the Ewing's plan, that meant hard fighting, because they could muster many warriors, especially since Red Cloud's war along the Bozeman Trail. Latham also reported that Louis Courrell had been up north lately and should have some news when he returned.

Joseph Carter's letter was the most interesting. He confirmed Latham's report about the Ft. Benton operation, adding that the filing had been in Ewing's own name, and not that of the syndicate's. That made it appear Ewing was going into business on his own.

When Carter filed the mortgage on Dunigan's herd, the clerk in the territorial office told him that Ewing was trying to do the same, only his papers weren't in order as Carter's were. Carter surmised Ewing might try again later, then that cat would be clear out of the bag. Carter also reported that the Cameron Ranch Company, Ewing's syndicate, had a large amount of cash on deposit at the Merchants and Planters Bank in St. Louis, so money was handy, not stuck in some bank in Dundee, Scotland.

That was good to know and Dunigan felt that the two letters brought him news that was beginning to clarify what Ewing might be up to. That Ewing would be branching out on his own, perhaps by cheating his uncle at this late date, did not make much sense, but maybe 'once a thief, always a thief' applied.

Dunigan got to thinking about the Sioux business and figured he had better get in touch with Major Layton fairly soon. If Ewing could somehow foul up the Platte River crossing payment, Dunigan could get hurt, especially if the cattle were run off and he didn't have them to sell even for less money. The overall picture was still fuzzy, but he could see more details than before.

For the next few days, Dunigan worked on his accounts and got them into shape. He had bought 4,500 cows and could get 500 or more out of the cows Nick had caught, or from his own, since they were mixed. He would also have plenty of steers for wo-haw, and some left over. He would select the cows from his range soon, so he would have a core of gentle animals to build the herds around. He wrote letters to Joseph Carter, Robert Latham, Gerard Alton, and, of course, to Amanda, and found he could hardly wait until the next mail to hear from her.

All his lieutenants had done such a good job of preparing for the drive Dunigan found he did not have much to do. So he began riding around with the hands in order to get to know them better. He wanted to form judgments as to whether they would stand firm in times of trouble. He took Abner Cottrell with him, because he had come to rely heavily on the man and had a high regard for his views. To Dunigan's surprise, most of the hands passed muster with Abner, even the Confederate veterans, whom he knew Abner did not really care for.

There were two men they both thought were too soft for the expected troubles and when they were eased out and replaced, the whole outfit meshed better. Michael O'Grady and Thad Scott had broken a saddle horse especially for Dunigan and he rode that one most often. A fine looking, big, chestnut sorrel gelding, with a ground-eating saddle gait, Dunigan was justifiably proud of him, naming him 'Sangre.' Both boys were proud they had pleased their boss and wouldn't allow anyone else to get near Sangre.

Dunigan kept trying to figure ways to regain the initiative from Ewing, but couldn't get anywhere. One day, he thought of a way to change the game entirely. That night, he wrote to Jim Blaylock, asking him to find a buyer for the 5,000 cows at anything over $15 per head. What Dunigan wanted was an option to sell the cows to someone else, if Ewing wouldn't pay. If he had an alternate buyer on hand, then he could turn down Ewing and leave with the cattle.

He wrote Blaylock that a buyer anywhere in Montana, Wyoming, or Nebraska would do, but the option had to be exercisable in October. He posted the letter, among the others he had written, and sat back to see what happened. Dunigan was pleased with himself and felt he now had an out, provided he kept the cattle in his possession. He was satisfied with the preparations for holding on to them, too, as his crew was fighting fit. Unless any raiders were desperate, or he was caught unprepared, he knew the crew would exact a heavy toll and that kind of effort usually discouraged hired guns.

Dunigan organized a trip to Galveston, taking Michael, Thad, and Pete Roussel. The purpose of the trip was to secure instruments and maps for celestial navigation and for the boys to see the big town. They all boarded a buggy for the trip, which would take four days, a stay of two, and returning in four more. Some of the hands asked the travelers to buy Christmas presents for them and furnished the money.

The trip was made in fairly easy stages, going by Victoria, Matagorda, and then into Galveston. They saw a lot of cattle, most belonging to Pierce around Matagorda. Dunigan noted that 'Shanghai's Sea Lions' were all in good flesh. They also passed fields of sugar cane and busy sugar mills along the way. Coming into Galveston, they passed many wagons loaded with bales of cotton and sacks of sugar enroute to the docks.

Signs of prosperity were abundant, only somewhat dampened by the presence of so many state police, who were uniformly surly. The black policemen had learned their lesson about harassing heavily armed cattlemen and did not bother the occupants of the buggy. Once into Galveston, they found a hotel and sent the buggy to a livery stable, then got settled.

Freshly bathed and dressed, Dunigan took them all to a good seafood restaurant, to sample the fruits of the coast. They ate shrimp, oysters, and fish with relish, washing it all down with German beer, of which there was a plentiful supply. Dunigan left about ten to go to bed, not inquiring what the others intended. Before retiring, he wrote to Amanda again, because he thought a letter posted in Galveston might reach her sooner.

The next day, they all had an early breakfast and went their various ways, Dunigan to the waterfront, where he found several chandler's shops. He purchased a well-used, but sound sextant and four powerful spy glasses, asking at each shop for a good cartographer. Most recommended a shop named Parker's, only two blocks from his hotel. After a lunch of oysters and crab, he visited it. The shop owner, Parker, did indeed have the celestial maps Dunigan was hunting and he concluded his purchases that afternoon, finding some good maps of the western plains that would come in handy on the drive. Dunigan went back to the hotel at dark, mentally reserving the next day for Christmas shopping.

In the hotel lobby, Dunigan saw Pete and the boys, clean and dressed to go out for dinner. He walked over to them. "I see you are all ready to go out, where you going tonight?"

Michael spoke up. "Boss, we found a Eyetalian place that's real good and we want to take you there tonight, if you don't have any plans?"

"I don't, but give me about fifteen minutes." They all walked down to 'Capriani's,' an Italian restaurant that was clean and well lighted. The food was excellent, and at nine Pete paid the check, after they refused to let Dunigan do it. He warned them about going to some of the rougher spots by the waterfront frequented by a pretty tough lot of sailors off the ships in the harbor. Pete said he would watch out for them, so Dunigan went to bed.

Dunigan bought a cameo for Amanda for Christmas, plus various gifts, belts, jackets, and the like for Nick and Pete and the boys, then he was ready to leave. They all checked out by noon, spent the night at Matagorda and got to the ranch the afternoon of the following day.

Dunigan had several letters at the ranch. Two were from Amanda and he devoured them at once. Her engagement ring had arrived and he was effusively thanked. The rest of her letters were just news of the farm and that one of the colts she had bred had won a big stakes race back East. She ended with pledges of undying love and Christmas greetings. His other letters were from Joseph Carter and Gerard Alton, and were mainly progress reports. But Carter relayed news that there was unrest among the Indians in Wyoming and Montana, and with talk of gold in the Black Hills, there could be some danger.

All of this reminded him he should visit Major Layton soon at Ft. Sam Houston, to get the latest army news and learn the army's intentions for the spring in the area north of Kansas. He thought he could visit right after January 1st, and go on up to the Cañon de Uvalde to see George Harris and the cattle wintering there. February would be soon enough to check the cattle with Sam Gentry at San Ysidro. He wanted to view them as late as possible before delivery.

Dunigan thought about building a nice house for himself and Amanda, either on the ranch or in Refugio and was in a quandary about whether to have it ready when she got to Texas after the wedding.

He decided the present house would do until she got used to the place and they could decide together whether to live in town or on the ranch. He did, however, scout around for a site and found a lovely spot overlooking the river, in a mott of large, beautiful oak trees, only a half mile from headquarters. He knew he could find water there, because the live oaks only grew where there was water they could tap into. Before they left next spring, he would leave orders to dig a well and build a cistern.

There was a small herd of cows close to the mott, among them a big black and red brindle cow, with large gentle brown eyes and long, forward pointed horns. She had probably been raised around people, as she showed no fear of Dunigan coming out to him as if to say, "Do you like my place here, Mister Dunigan? I think it is a nice place to stay." Then she lay down to rest. "I'll be here whenever you want to come visit."

Dunigan was surprised at her gentleness. He waved, hollering, "Glad to meet you, Brindy," as he rode off.

He mentioned the cow to Nick and some of the others, and they all kind of knew her, saying she was indeed very calm and gentle and that when they gathered, she would actually herd her little group by herself to wherever they were going. All the cowboys had to do was to make it known where they wanted them and she would lead them herself.

In his rides around the ranch, Dunigan often went by the place he had chosen to build what he began to think of as Amanda's house. He was anxious to begin planning, but each time he went by, the brindle cow came out to greet him, reminding him of the dangers from the upcoming drive. He and the cow had a speaking relationship by then and he had solidly named her Brindy. The name had been adopted by the other hands on the ranch, and she was known to everybody.

Having almost all preparations completed for the drive, Dunigan spent his time that winter firming up his maneuvering with correspondence to Gerard Alton, Joseph Carter, and through Robert Latham to Louie Courrell. He also spent two days with Major Layton at Ft. Sam Houston, and received a detailed account of the army's dispositions and activities along the trail Dunigan meant to follow, as well as reports of Indian activity in that area.

Layton told him his official information was that the Indians were quiet, but he had detected a note of unease from commanders in Wyoming and western Nebraska, as well as in Dakota.

Dunigan transmitted his own worries about renegade attacks at the crossing of the Platte and Layton said the troop commander at Ft. McPherson was an old friend, so he would write him to be especially watchful, and gave Dunigan a letter of introduction. He also dispatched a copy ahead to the officer, Lt. Col. Charles Archer, the commanding officer of Ft. McPherson.

Dunigan felt his preparations were as good as he could make them, and that the success of the drive was probably in the hands of God, which reminded him he should go to mass next Sunday, and stop worrying about things that were unforeseeable.

Early in February, Dunigan, Nicholas McCurry, Pete Roussel, and Michael O'Grady, along with Abner Cottrell and Abel Castro with a wagon, left for San Ysidro to check out the cattle Sam Gentry had there. Then they would journey on to the Cañon de Uvalde to visit George Wilbanks. They made the ride in easy stages, taking three days, before reaching Sam Gentry's headquarters. He had one fairly large stone house, surrounded by a myriad of jacales.

A few chickens, pigs, and goats were running around loose, but there was a semblance of order to the place, the jacales being built more or less in a circle around the house, and the pens, were in good order. As they rode up, some heads and gun barrels peeked out of the jacales, and a big man dressed in duckin and leather came out on the porch of the stone house. "Hello Nick, I been expecting you. I guess you brought your boss," he said, indicating Dunigan.

"That's right, Sam, thought we'd like to look at the stock some. This here is John Dunigan—Sam Gentry." Nick further introduced everybody around.

"Come in, come in, we got the coffee on, and some tequila, too," Gentry said.

Over coffee, they talked generally about the cattle, weather, and things that interested most cattlemen. Dunigan found himself liking the old pirate, and thought he had a lot of knowledge about cattle, and not just the stealing of them.

Sam Gentry was fifty-eight. He'd come to Texas in 1846 with the river boats supplying Taylor's army along the Rio Grande. He got hold of a tract of land at San Ysidro in 1853, and had traded cattle along the river, slaughtering many in Brownsville. During the Civil War, he was on both sides of the conflict, trying his best to be on the winning side at the end, which he was. Sam was amoral and apolitical, as were many people in that place and time. He hunted cattle in the wild horse desert, as it was called, and stole stock from some of the Mexican ranches near the river. He never stole much stock in Texas, fearing retribution by the Rangers, and generally kept his nose clean on the Texas side.

The wild horse desert was truly wild, not under anyone's control, so Gentry kept a fairly large complement of gunhands. He needed them, too, because not only were there many gringo desperadoes, but the Cortina gangs were active, too.

Dunigan's crew borrowed some of Gentry's horses and rode out to inspect the cattle. Dunigan was surprised the cows were so good and that there were almost no well-known Texas brands on any of them. The only complaint he had was that many of them appeared to be advancing in pregnancy. That would make for trouble on the drive. Gentry said he would do his best to leave the heavier cows behind, as he had access to almost 6,500 to cut them out of.

Dunigan and Gentry agreed John would receive the cattle at Oakville on March 10th. Then Dunigan surprised him by advancing another $2,000 in gold, paying almost half the price in advance without being asked for it. That was taking a chance, but Gentry knew Dunigan was a man of vengeance when crossed, so a little good will might go a long way toward allaying future trouble.

That night, Gentry and Dunigan sat up and talked long after everyone else had gone to bed. Gentry knew about the hanging of the Mexican raider and all the other punishments Dunigan had inflected on outlaws in and around South Texas. He told Dunigan that hanging that man had probably guaranteed his safety for at least ten years. Having been on both sides of that coin, Gentry knew swift, sure retribution was the best way to discourage trouble. Although Sam thought the act somewhat harsh, he had to admire Dunigan's guts.

Dunigan felt more and more comfortable with Gentry. He actually felt he and Gentry had a lot in common. They both took a lot of risks and enjoyed doing it. He was sorry to leave the next morning when they headed north toward Uvalde.

The group saw little in the way of settlement along their route. First Indians, then outlaws and bandits had made this region of Texas a dangerous place for permanent settlers. It was an inhospitable area at best, being a semidesert covered with cactus and thorn brush, but it was good cattle country if properly stocked. A few ranches had established themselves there, but were forted up pretty well.

They camped at a few ranches on the way to Uvalde, and were well received once the ranchers had established they weren't outlaws. Visitors were rare in this isolated part of Texas, and they were welcomed warmly. At each ranch, Dunigan and his party were fed and housed in exchange for news from civilization. During the week that they spent traversing the region, Dunigan and the others were very observant of the character of the country, but each had in mind an enterprise that might prosper there. They were a happy group, spending each night singing or telling tall stories and legends about the locale, dining on fresh game each night.

When they finally arrived at the Cañon de Uvalde and met George Wilbanks and their own representative, George Harris, they were all ready to complete their inspection and return home. The time was upon them to begin the drive.

Dunigan was pleased at the quality of the herd and advanced another portion of the purchase price to Wilbanks. He voiced a warning that the herd contained too many cows with calf, and Wilbanks readily agreed to replace them with dry cows.

Afterward, with Harris and Wilbanks, Dunigan ordered Abner to stay with the herd and to keep their extra horses and the wagon there, so they could make a faster trip back to the ranch. The whole outfit would rejoin them April 1st at Bandera.

Dunigan, Pete, Nick, and Michael loaded their saddle bags and took one pack horse before leaving for the Aransas ranch, arriving on Washington's birthday, February 22, 1872.

They immediately set out to gather Dunigan's cows and cut out some five to six hundred to go with the others to Montana. Work proceeded swiftly and on the fourth day, Brindy brought in her bunch. Working that herd, they cut four or five of her cows to go. Brindy threw up her head and trotted out to join them. She would not be turned back. Dunigan laughed and told the men to let her go, as she wanted to and would probably come anyway.

"She'll probably lead the herd all the way to Montana. She's a better hand than most of us, anyway," he said.

March 1st saw all preparations complete and the herd put together for the drive to Oakville, where they were to meet Sam Gentry. Dunigan sent Nick fifteen men, both remudas, and two wagons to select a delivery site that would be defensible, because even though he liked Sam Gentry, he did not trust him. He instructed Nick to keep out of sight until delivery was made, but to be in a position to reinforce him on call. They left on the second and Dunigan told Nick to expect him on the eighth.

The night of the fourth, Dunigan gathered his initial herd and penned them for an early start. He had 768 cows and 280 steers ready to head for Montana.

PART III

The Drive

Chapter 22

The three-day drive to Oakville was slow and careful, only a training jaunt for the small herd, so it would be ready to form a gentle core for Gentry's cattle. Each morning when they threw the cattle off the bedground, the cow they called Brindy roused her sisters, helped start them, then took her place right behind the lead rider, hooking any others away from her. Brindy seemed to sense where they were headed, urging her sisters along. Nick showed up the afternoon of the eighth to guide them to the bedground he had selected.

Next morning, Dunigan inspected the site and approved it before sending out three men to guide Gentry's herd, warning them to be alert for any sign of trouble. Then he finalized the arrangements: Pete and Abel Castro would do the counting, then the Gentry animals would be counted into Dunigan's small herd. He warned his men against getting separated from their own, as they could be cut off and neutralized. If anything, he told them to move to isolate Gentry's men, if they could do so unnoticed. Dunigan's herd was by no means trailbroken, but it had handled all right and he didn't anticipate trouble from the cattle. Having done all he could to forestall trouble, Dunigan and his crew rested and waited for Gentry to appear.

One of the scouts sent to find Gentry's herd reported next morning that it was about seven or eight miles south and should arrive by midafternoon.

Dunigan rechecked his preparations before riding off, meeting Gentry's bunch about five miles away at Oakville. It was already eleven o'clock and Gentry wanted to drive straight through, so they went without nooning. Dunigan agreed and spent the early afternoon inspecting the herd for culls. He spotted two cripples and two cows so heavy with calf he wanted them cut back. Gentry agreed Dunigan could cut the herd before it was counted. When they arrived at midafternoon, Dunigan, helped by Sam Gentry, cut out twelve cows, which were held apart by three of Gentry's eighteen hands south of the two herds. Then they counted the rest into Dunigan's small herd. Four men counted, three agreeing on 2,491 head, the other counting one cow less. Dunigan accepted the count, as did Gentry, so Dunigan invited him to his wagon to settle up.

Gentry spoke up. "John, I think these cows are too cheap. I didn't know you were going to be so picky, so I think I should have $5 per head, instead of $3.50." When Gentry took off his hat to wipe his brow, Dunigan noticed Gentry's men begin to shift on to higher ground surrounding the herd.

"Sam, we made a deal and we told you we were going to be hard on the quality angle, so I don't think you have anymore coming. I did more than you asked by putting money up voluntarily last month. However, the cows are very good, and I think they are nearly herd broke, and that's worth something to me. I'll give you $4, as I think the cows are good enough to command the extra four bits, so let's get it done," and he turned his horse to ride to the wagon.

"Hold on John, these cows are worth more, and you're going to pay me more, or I'll take them back, and yours too, if you try and fight me." Dunigan glanced at Gentry's men, who had moved halfway up the hill behind the herd. He reached down to untangle his rope from his toe fender, and turned back to face Gentry. He watched as Gentry turned wide-eyed at what he knew was Nick and his fifteen men, all with rifles, coming over the crest of the hill. And he knew because the toe-fender move was his signal to Nick.

"Sam, let's not quarrel about this. We traded in good faith, and I think I've sweetened the offer enough to make it all right, so let's go and settle up."

"I guess you're right, John. I can get plenty of cows around for less to replace them. By the way, I heard about your trade with that Englishman from Calvin Block, so I figured to margin myself a bit more."

"I figured Block was trying to cause trouble, but you just have to stay with people who treat you right, Sam. I don't suppose Nick and his bunch had anything to do with you changing your mind, now did it, Sam?"

"Oh no, John. I just got some bad advice and got greedy is all. It's a failing of mine, don't you know." Sam grinned.

Dunigan and Gentry rode over to the wagon and the rest of the men put their artillery back into leather and drifted in to eat. It was a cool, but cordial supper, Gentry's and Dunigan's hands watching to see that the others did not try to steal an advantage. Dunigan figured out what he owed and counted it out in gold. Gentry was appreciative and complimentary about Dunigan's herd.

Before he left, he asked Dunigan, "John, you sure timed your move just right. How did you do it? I was about ready to start shooting when I saw Nick and his bunch up on the hill. I missed your signal somehow, what was it?"

"I had to untangle my rope from my toe-fenders about then, Sam," Dunigan smiled.

"Well, I'll be damned! I do remember that now. You're plumb slick, John. It's been a pleasure doing business with you." With that he mounted, signaled his men and rode off.

Dunigan called Pete and Abel and told them to follow Gentry to make sure he didn't change his mind again.

They stayed on that pasture for three more days so the cattle could get acquainted, lessening the chance of stampedes, when Pete and Abel reported in that the Gentrys were well away. Dunigan designated Nick boss of the lead herd, most of which would be Gentry's cows; and told Pete to handle the following herd with Dunigan and his group. Abner, George Harris, Thad Scott, Aparicio Medrano, and Chito Guerrico would be go-betweens and scouts for both herds.

They would head due north until passing Ft. Dodge, Kansas, and Dunigan estimated a slow pace of two weeks to reach Bandera and the delivery of Wilbanks' cows. With so many riders, Dunigan wanted to make sure the lead herd was thoroughly trail broke before they reached Bandera, and that goal dictated the slow pace.

Dunigan took Michael O'Grady with him for a final visit with Major Layton to find out what the army was up to and how they might help along the way. He told Nick and Pete to divide the cows equally, but to put a hundred fifty steers in with the first herd and the other fifty with the second.

Chapter 23

Dunigan and Michael checked into the Menger late that afternoon and decided to eat supper and rest before visiting Ft. Sam the following morning. After cleaning up some, Dunigan went to the bar to wait for Michael. He ran into Calvin Block.

"Well, if it isn't John Dunigan. How are you?" Block grinned.

"Tolerable, Calvin, how about yourself?"

"Oh, I'm getting around all right. How about a drink?"

"Sure, Calvin, let's sit here and I'll have some bourbon."

Block asked him about the drive and Dunigan told him it was just underway. He also let him know he was aware of Block's meddling with Sam Gentry.

Block laughed and said he was only trying to improve his position.

"What exactly is your position in this, Calvin? I thought you were just helping the man get some cows and maybe collecting a commission?"

"Why that's all it is, John, just a commission. By the way, which way are you going?" Block asked.

"Well, I think we'll go through Fort Dodge, a bit west of the Chisholm. The railroad has reached there, and there will be some other herds going up that way this year, so we should have some company. But there will probably be some outlaws operating, like they did before they got taken care of along the Chisholm. After Dodge, we'll just have to play it by ear, as we used to on the Chisholm."

"John, aren't you going to send any steers that way this year?" he asked.

"No, I don't want to get too spread out and my steer deal is more complicated than just driving them up the trail. I've been fattening them on Osage grass and shipping them to Kansas City when they are ready."

Block questioned him closely about grazing on Indian grass and how Dunigan went about it. Dunigan answered him off-handedly, imparting little hard information. He didn't want anyone else to horn in on his deal with the Indians, because he meant to make it a return operation, beginning the next year.

Calvin Block was just as secretive, not wanting to let Dunigan know too much about his own deal with Lord Ewing. His reticence served to deepen Dunigan's suspicions of Block, so much so their conversation soon dwindled away. About then, Michael showed up and he and Dunigan went to eat supper, leaving Block in the bar.

Next day, Dunigan visited Ft. Sam to secure the latest information on Indian activities in Kansas, Nebraska, Wyoming, and Montana from Major Layton, who greeted him like a long-lost brother. Dunigan conceded to himself that the loss of his fine grey gelding had been worth the price. The intelligence estimates they examined seemed to point to pacification of most of the tribes Dunigan's herds might encounter, the notable exceptions being the Sioux, Cheyenne, Crow, and Comanche.

By the time Dunigan's herds reached their range, the Comanches should be out on the plains hunting buffalo, so danger from that front could be discounted. The Crow, Sioux, and Cheyenne would likely be directly athwart his path in Wyoming and Montana. The Shoshones had been quite peace-able, Layton said, but Dunigan had to traverse the Wind River Country and they might be troublesome there. If possible, Layton advised a direct approach to Wash-a-Kie, the Shoshone chief.

"I have a guide working for me, Louis Courrell, and his wife is a Blackfoot, who are kin to the Shoshone, and he is an old trapper. He may even know Wash-a-Kie and Louis could talk to him," Dunigan said.

"That sounds good. Also, I know the commanding officer at Fort Fetterman and I'll write you a letter of introduction to him. He may be able to help, too."

"Thanks, major, you have been a great help. I'm beholden."

"John, any debt you may have to me has been more than repaid by your gift of that magnificent gray horse, whom I named 'Windy.' I have never had a mount like him, and I will forever be in your debt."

They talked more about the trail and as Layton went on, Dunigan surmised real trouble was coming from the Sioux, Cheyenne, and maybe Crow, because increasing throngs of settlers, ranchers, and miners were causing friction with those tribes. The army was caught in the middle, forced to irritate the Indians further by reacting to constant demands by whites for protection. Dunigan sympathized with the army, but would howl as loud as anyone for help to get his cattle though.

Layton wrote a letter to his friend, Lt. Col. O. B. Keller at Ft. Fetterman and made a copy for Dunigan.

After Dunigan rode back into town, he got two certified copies of his contract with Ewing, one of which he sent to Joseph Carter in St. Louis, along with a letter telling him to look out for any mention of Calvin Block, because Dunigan had not yet discovered Block's role in the whole scheme. He directed Carter to relay any news to him at Ft. Dodge in midMay, which would be the herd's first stopping place.

He also penned a newsy letter to Amanda, at the end reciting his love. He had missed her more than he could describe, but hoped handling details of the drive might ease his longing.

He and Michael spent two more days in San Antonio, buying supplies, visiting, and tying up loose ends before setting out toward Bandera to intercept the herd south of there. It was an easy two-day ride and everything was going well. The cattle seemed to be going along nicely. There had been adequate rain during the winter, so there was plenty of water and grass. On the 25th, they found a good bedground just west of Bandera. Wilbanks was not due until April 1st, so Dunigan scattered his cows to graze. He organized a relief to go in to Bandera for recreation. Although there wasn't much there to entertain the hands, they all went anyway.

On March 28th, George Harris rode into camp, informing the crew that Wilbanks's herd of two thousand cows would arrive the next afternoon. Dunigan immediately put together the first herd, consisting of twenty-six hundred cows and a hundred fifty steers, turned them over to Nick McCurry, and told him to start north. Nick made sure the cow Brindy was in his herd before he pointed them north. Immediately, she trotted to the lead, setting her horns due north.

"That's quite a cow, Nick. I suppose she'll be there all the way. She sure is a leader."

"John, that cow's been right there since we left the ranch and she'll be right there all the way north. I could let you have three of my hands, cause she replaces them. And you know, she checks the North Star every morning and heads for it all day long. A couple of times, the lead man fell asleep, and his horse started to wander off, but Brindy kept right on straight north. When she got the chance, she would wake that man up and have him get back on the trail. She is shore some cowhand."

Dunigan gazed at her in admiration as she took up the lead. "There goes 'Brindy Polaris,' all the way to Montana." She was his talisman, his good luck charm. He watched Nick's outfit move out, then turned back to camp, unsaddling his horse and grabbing a cup of coffee. He sent a rider into town to fetch the hands to be ready in the morning, giving orders to bunch the cows first thing.

When the herd was gathered and counted, Dunigan had 658 cows and 51 steers. The count was within one on both counts, so he was satisfied. He sent Harris out with Pete Roussel and Chito Guerrico to meet the big bunch from Uvalde.

At noon, they sighted the dust cloud heralding the arrival of the herd and he and his men saddled up and rode out to meet them, leaving four behind to hold the smaller herd they would be counted into. An hour later the herd was stopped and ready for delivery. Dunigan appointed Pete and George Harris counters, and Wilbanks appointed two of his men. The count was agreed on at 2,002 cows, Pete having counted one less, and everyone rode in for lunch at Dunigan's camp. He was effusive in his praise for the cattle and also of Wilbanks's handling of them. The accounts were settled in gold.

"Well, I guess I'd better start on back. If you ever want to do this again, John, you just let me know. This deal worked fine," Wilbanks said.

"Thank you, George. Mostly, I plan to handle steers from here on, but if I do need some cows, I'll sure be in touch."

"Hell, John, I handle steers, too. I'll be right glad to deal with you on them."

"I'll sure keep you in mind, George. Maybe next fall."

Chapter 24

Pete's herd was left on the bedground that night and left at first light, which put them two days behind Nick's. Dunigan's group left right after breakfast and stayed together the first day, trying to keep station about midway between the two.

Dunigan instructed Abner to move at about herd speed for the first few days, before Dunigan and the scouts started sweeping for danger along the route. He sent Medrano south, Chito east, and Thad Scott west. Dunigan and George Harris headed north, past Nick's herd and forty miles farther before turning back. They had found good grass and water all the way, but no sign of anything moving. The area hadn't been raided by Indians since the early forties and it was too far north and east for Mexican bandits, but there were always a few gangs of Anglo stock thieves around. This time though, they found no signs of any, at least not in the northern quadrant.

He and Harris spent the night with Nick at his camp, traded some horses and were getting ready to leave when Nick rode up.

"John, I want you to see this. Follow me." Nick said nothing more. Dunigan and Harris followed him as he roused the herd. It was barely daylight when the three men passed the brindle cow. They watched her stand, look up to check the position of the pole star, and begin prodding her sisters into line with the star. Then she trotted to her spot just behind the lead cowboy.

Dunigan and Harris shook their heads and laughed as Nick smiled triumphantly.

"Nick, I never should have brought her on this drive. She's too valuable ever to have been taken off the ranch. I sure named her correctly, though, when I called her Brindy Polaris."

"I'd sure like a pup out of her, boss," Harris grinned.

"One thing for sure, if she has a calf along the way, we're taking it back to Texas. Hell, we'll raise a whole breed of lead longhorns," Dunigan said as they rode away.

He and Harris worked their scout westward, the more dangerous quarter as the herds moved north. The other scouts moved counterclockwise, too. Two days later they reached Pete's herd, where all was going smoothly and in two more days they were back at Abner's wagon to stay the night. The wagon was close to the lead herd and Dunigan told Abner they would move about two day's drive north and west of Nick's herd, because they were getting closer to Comanche range. With luck, both herds would pass far enough north before the Indians moved below the Cap Rock. Dunigan had been able to avoid fighting by knowing where his enemy was; he intended to keep that up.

All the scouts were at the wagon and no one reported any sign of danger, only plentiful grass and water. There was some sign that two other herds had already passed along the trail they were following, but Dunigan assured them they were steers headed for Dodge along the new route. Moving counterclockwise brought Dunigan into camp at either Nick's or Pete's herd about every three days, so he maintained good contact with them. Movement was good, but slowing as some of the cows were close to calving and could not hold the early pace.

After leaving Bandera, both herds had pointed due north. During the first month they had crossed the Llano, San Saba, Colorado, and Brazos, and were closing on the Red. Dunigan had kept a log like a ship's captain. He reckoned by his astronomical computations that they had traveled about 350 miles that first month, all without much trouble. Now they were within three days of the Red and Dunigan was nervous that his luck had been too good so far. The ground began to get softer and greener, indicating recent heavy rains.

Sure enough, at the Red, one herd of steers was already stopped, waiting for the river to drop before crossing, as it was in full flood. Dunigan sent messages back to the following herds to stop on good grass, but not to let any other herds pass them.

Then he visited the outfit close to the river waiting for it to fall. It belonged to Amos Cooper of Wharton County and he welcomed Dunigan. There were 2,200 steers in his herd and he was headed for the railhead at Ft. Dodge. He was interested that

Dunigan was driving cows to Montana and said he had heard somebody who was planning on it, so now he knew the man.

Cooper's hands were mostly black, so Abner visited with them a bit, and they talked to him freely. It seemed the cattle were owned by A. H. "Shanghai" Pierce and were being driven under contract by Cooper. Dunigan was glad to hear that, because he knew Pierce to be a careful man, who must have investigated the possibilities of this trail thoroughly before committing to it. Pierce did not take many chances.

For two days, everything was stopped waiting for the river to subside. The third day after Dunigan's arrival, Cooper decided he had waited long enough, rafted his wagons across and prepared to swim his herd across the next day. Dunigan, Chito, and Harris offered their help and it was accepted. Cooper drove his herd to the river and finally pushed them in. The downstream riders choused the cattle to make them hold against the current, as the place picked for them to climb out of the river was only a hundred yards downstream. There were some anxious moments when the steers began to drift, but they managed to hit the opposite bank and came out without too much trouble. One man's horse turned turtle and drifted downstream, but he finally made it back to the herd wet but unhurt.

After crossing, Cooper took his herd about two miles north and stopped them, as it was already midafternoon and he had some repairs to make. Dunigan wanted to keep some space between his herds and others, so he didn't move up his cattle until two days later, when the river was almost back to normal.

Nick's herd crossed the same day they got to the river. Two cows and a remuda horse had to be pulled out of quicksand, but the wagons, crossing first, had no trouble, and the herd was driven to the bedground north of the river without incident. George Harris, Medrano, and Thad Scott were sent to fan out to the northwest ahead of Nick's herd, making sure Cooper's bunch was far enough in front.

Dunigan had sent Medrano back to tell Pete to bring his herd forward and they arrived the next day. Dunigan had them cross without stopping, as the river had dropped to a fairly low level. That did not keep them from losing a cow to the quicksand. She was pulled out, but had to be slaughtered when her leg was broken during the rescue. They sent part of the fresh meat to Nick's herd, so there would be no waste, and Dunigan rounded up his outfit to move closer to Nick.

Chapter 25

Three days after Nick's herd crossed the Red River, Lon Castle rode away from his accustomed place just behind the point man, and headed toward the creek bottom about two hundred yards west of the herd. Obeying the call of nature, and being naturally shy and gentlemanly, Lon rode into cover to complete his task. As he rode in amongst the cottonwoods along the creek, he pulled leaves off the branches while he looked for a level spot. When he found one, Lon tied his pony, unbuckled his leggins and britches, and squatted. He was just about through when he heard that most ominous sound, the rattle of a diamondback, too damned close behind him.

Lon's bowels locked tight and with his pants around his ankles like hobbles, Lon tried to leap forward, away from the snake. Just as he launched himself, he felt the snake strike his left buttock. Even as the poison was burning his butt, Lon drew his pistol and shot the snake. He fired twice more, to make sure, and also as a distress signal, lying as still as he could. He still had the leaves in one hand, so he cleaned himself as he waited for his mates to find him.

Abel Castro and Len Bracken were the first to arrive on the scene. They saw a grown man stretched out full length on his belly, his leggins and britches around his ankles, a pile of excrement about a foot behind him. Beyond that was a dead rattlesnake. If it hadn't been so serious, the whole scene would have been hilarious. The two hands jumped from their ponies and Lem held Lon's shoulders while Abel took out a wicked looking knife and sliced an X over both fang punctures.

Both of them could hardly keep from laughing, then Lem

said, "Lon, you're about to find out who your real friends are."

Lon craned his neck to look up at Lem. "What the hell are you babbling about?"

"Well, somebody's got to suck out the poison, you know." Then Lem and Abel burst into laughter. At that point, Nick rode up and took in the scene. He wheeled out of the thicket and signaled the wagon over, then came back.

"I'd surely like to have me a picture of this," he said before he broke out laughing. Straight-faced he asked, "Which one of you is going to suck out the poison?"

"Not me, it's dirty," Lem Bracken giggled.

"Ni yo, tampoco," Abel added.

Lon was exasperated by all the levity, because it was a serious matter, even though the bite was in a funny place.

Shrugging, Nick dismounted and proceeded to suck the poison out of the punctures. Satisfied at last that the wound was bleeding freely, he went to the wagon, got a bottle of whiskey, washed out his mouth, and poured some on the wound, then gave Lon a drink. Nick had Lon strip off his leggins and pants and loaded him in the wagon, where he would have to ride for a few days until his butt healed.

Lon was feverish by noon, but his fever broke before dark. Nick made sure the wound was kept disinfected with whiskey and the next morning Lon felt better, but he rode the wagon for four more days until his cuts healed. When he got back into the routine, the ribbing really started, and he was the object of the outfit's fun for a week or more.

Nick caught some, too, but the hands were wise enough not to rub their trail boss too hard. After a week or so, the new rubbed off, and no more was heard of it.

Dunigan and his scouts had been concentrating on the northwest quadrant because they were closest to the hunting grounds of the Comanche, Kiowa, and Cheyenne. No buffalo were seen, nor were any Indian hunting parties, but a small band of Pawnee were spotted almost directly athwart the trail.

They were a pitiful sight. Three men, five women and eight children, the youngest less than a year old, comprised the band. They had a skinny dog pulling a travois, and the whole group was dirty, thin, and emaciated. When they saw Dunigan, and behind him the dust of the herd, they came forward yelling and pleading for wo-haw, the Indian expression for cattle. Three of the Indians were older than sixty, and presented such a pitiful sight that Dunigan conveyed to them by sign language that they should camp there and he would give them wo-haw when the herd arrived. Smiles broke over all their faces and they moved off the trail to set up camp.

When the herd passed, Dunigan cut out two small steers for the Pawnees. Nick objected to the second, but was overruled by Dunigan, who said one wouldn't get them very far. One steer was killed right off, and given to them to be butchered. The second was roped and tied to a tree for them, but he wasn't much trouble, because he was already lame. As the herd continued by, Dunigan watched the Indians cut up the steer, eating some of the organs raw, they were so hungry. Dunigan sent a rider back to Pete, to tell him not to give them anything more, because they had enough.

Chapter 26

Dunigan's scouting revealed very little sign of Indian danger, but the nearer the herds got to the Canadian, the more sodden the ground was, evidencing recent heavy rains. When he and George Harris finally reached it, the Canadian was in full flood. And it was an awesome sight, fully four hundred yards wide, with logs and even full-grown trees bobbing wildly in the racing torrent.

Surveying the crazed stream, Dunigan turned to Harris, "George, better find us some good bedgrounds and pasture, it looks like we may be here a while."

"Okay, John, I'll try to keep the herds well apart, but we are almost going to have to loose herd them, otherwise they'll trample all the grass."

"See what you can find, even if Pete's herd has to stop several days back."

"On my way, Boss."

Harris rode off and Dunigan looked for a high spot with some trees to make a camp, because it looked like they might need it for some time. While there was no rain, the sky was overcast, especially up the river toward the northwest. Rain there could swell the flow for days. Every draw was running water and the ground was squishy. Dunigan finally found a hill with an oak mott on it that would serve as a campground, and guided Abner to it when he arrived in midafternoon. A little later Thad and Medrano rode up, hobbled their horses, and began gathering firewood for supper.

They ate about dark, George Harris arriving before they had finished, so he got to eat with them, then reported he had found what might be adequate ground for both herds, and they were both stopped. Nick's herd was about fifteen miles south and Pete's about twenty-five. Pete's ground was good, as it wasn't so wet, but Nick's was all right, too. Both herds had put out riders to stop any following herds, and to inform other trail bosses about the state of the Canadian.

That night it rained, not hard, but steady, all night long. In the morning, they rolled out of sodden blankets, and started scouting around for things to make their camp more comfortable. Dunigan sent Harris back to Nick's herd for an extra wagon sheet, and a tent that was not in use there, as well as some extra horses for them. He and Abner took the wagon off for a load of firewood, and he put Thad and Manuel Medrano to building a secure rope corral for the horses, as well as a fire pit for cooking and warmth.

Abner and Dunigan found firewood a mile and a half downstream, and they spent all day chopping, bringing back a heaping wagonful. Harris, Thad, and Medrano had done their chores well, even building sleeping pallets raised off the wet ground. They had also weaved brush arbors from some of the dirt and what few small trees were out of the flooding.

Dunigan was concerned that there was no evidence close to the river of Cooper's herd passing through. Cooper was only three or four days ahead of them, and Dunigan's scouting had not spotted any sign of their being diverted. The rains had obliterated any signs near the Canadian crossing. Cooper could have crossed before the river got so high, but Dunigan thought that unlikely, so he told Harris and Medrano to scout downriver, and send Thad upriver the next day. He told them he intended to swim the swollen river alone, and after some argument, finally agreed they did not have to leave until he had gotten safely across.

That seemed to placate them, but they still did not want him to swim the river alone. At last, they acceded, provided Dunigan trailed a rope behind him, so they could pull him out if he got into trouble. Dunigan accepted, knowing they did not have that much rope with them.

In the morning, the big chestnut gelding, Sangre, was readied for Dunigan, who had stripped down to his drawers for the swim. His clothes were rolled into his slicker and tied to his saddle, along with a little food and other possibles, and he was handed a rope, or rather eight ropes tied together.

Dunigan laughed. "This thing won't reach a third of the way across the river. It'll just be a hindrance."

What Dunigan did not realize was that there was a 1500-foot coil of rope in the wagon to be used for replacement along the trail. Just before he urged Sangre into the Canadian, he saw the men tying it to the collection of lariats he was trailing.

As he eased the big gelding into the river, Dunigan could feel him swimming strongly. After Sangre was into the swim, Dunigan slipped out of the saddle to the downstream side, as this made the horse's swimming easier. When Sangre reached midstream, Dunigan pulled him around to buck the current head first, so they did not drift too far downstream, then slipped behind to hold onto his horses's tail for the rest of the crossing.

About a hundred yards from the far shore, Dunigan felt Sangre's feet touch ground, so he pulled himself back into the saddle and rode out onto the far bank. The first thing he did was tie the safety rope high in a tree, as Harris did on the far bank, then Dunigan stripped and unrolled his slicker to dry everything. There was a fresh breeze, so his clothes were dry in less than an hour, an hour Sangre used for a well-deserved rest.

Dunigan dressed, saddled his horse, and rode north along the trail, which was not too well marked because of the heavy rains. About noon the second day, the country was drier, the trail better marked, but he still did not see any signs of recent passage by a trail herd. He continued for another day to make sure, then turned toward the river and was back in three days.

At the river, he saw it had fallen about five feet, and there appeared to be only about a hundred yards of swimming water, instead of the three hundred when he had crossed.

He signaled Harris on the far bank, then noticed there were five or six more men at their camp, and they were all black. Dunigan surmised they were from Cooper's crew. Maybe they could clear up the mystery.

He stripped and packed his clothes as before, and Sangre crossed the fallen river easily. Coming up on the far bank, Dunigan recognized some of Cooper's hands in the group. He gave his horse to Thad to be turned loose, and dressed in clean clothes from his bag in the wagon. He turned to George Harris. "What happened to Cooper's herd?"

"Boss, they were hit by rustlers just as they were crossing the river. Cooper can tell you better than I, but he was shot twice. We got the slugs out, but he is pretty feverish. I think he'll be all right, no blood poisoning that we can see. We didn't find him until five days after the fight."

"Maybe some of his hands can fill us in; I'll talk to them later. Right now, I am very hungry," Dunigan said, and walked off for Abner's meal.

After eating, Dunigan went to see Cooper. He was flushed and feverish, but there was no evidence of mortification in the wounds, one of which was in the left shoulder, the other in the left thigh.

"They got the whole herd, Cooper?" he asked.

"Yeah, John, except for fifteen or twenty that got across the river. We were starting them into the river when we got hit. They run off the whole bunch downstream. The men in the water never had a chance. There were four of them, and they were all shot off their horses, and we never saw any of them again. I got hit then, too, and again later when we tried to get the herd back, about forty miles downstream. I think I'll probably make it."

"Cooper, you just take it easy and get well. We'll try to do something about your cattle. Do you have any idea who it was?"

"No, John, I don't. I didn't get a good look at any of them, and I recognized no one," Cooper said. "I was too busy dodging lead and cattle."

Dunigan went back to the fire and talked to Cooper's hands. They could add little to what he already knew, except that their wagon had been abandoned, and the cook killed about five miles downstream. Then he talked to Harris, who had tracked the herd farther on, after Cooper's attempt to retake the herd.

"John, I never did catch up to them, but they seem to be making for the Chisholm, maybe to sell the herd in Abilene, or along the trail."

"It'd be my guess that they'll try to sell before they get to Abilene. I think if we can get word to Pierce, he may be able to put something together to salvage the herd. Let me think on it for a minute."

Dunigan went back to talk to Cooper. He was dozing fitfully, and woke up when Dunigan approached.

"How you feeling, old timer?"

"Oh, some better, I guess. Most of the fever's gone. Still pretty weak, though. You find out anything about my herd?"

"No, but I wanted to ask you a few things. For a start, what brand were your steers wearing?"

"John, those steers belong to 'Shanghai' Pierce, and were branded AP. I was just driving them for him, but you probably knew that."

"Yes, but I wasn't sure just how everything was arranged. Do you know where Pierce is? If we could get word to him, he might be able to take the herd back, because it looks like they're headed to the Chisholm, then on to Abilene, if they don't get sold sooner. If Pierce could get those trail detectives out pretty soon, they might get the herd back."

"That might work, John, if we can get word to Pierce. He ought to be in Abilene by now. He had two herds going there aside from mine, and one other that was going to Dodge."

"Harris can ride to Dodge and send a telegram. You aren't strong enough to do anything yet, and I'm too tied up," Dunigan said.

Dunigan went back to the fire and found George Harris and Cooper's hands. He told the black men to get Cooper's wagon in the morning, so it could take Cooper in to Ft. Dodge, because he couldn't ride.

Then he turned to George Harris. "George, I've written a telegram to Pierce. I want you and Thad to take it to Dodge, and send it to him in Abilene, unless you find a closer place to send it from. On your way you can scout the country, and if you spot anything, send Thad back to warn us. The main thing is to get word to Pierce, so he can get his herd back. You and Thad take a pack horse and some extra mounts so you can make good time. You should be there in five or six days unless you run into trouble."

"I understand, boss. Where will you be?"

"I'm going to stay here until we get both herds across, and then I'll be to the west. Rustlers or no, the most danger is still Comanches," Dunigan said.

He sent Medrano to Nick's herd the next day, to tell him to bring his herd on up. The river was down to only twenty or thirty yards of swimming water. Then Medrano was to go on and deliver the same message to Pete. As for Dunigan's crew, they picked up logs, built a raft for the wagons, and moved their camp to the northside of the Canadian. They rafted Cooper and his wagon over first without incident, then the rest of the equipment was ferried over, with the men and horses following. By nightfall, a new camp had been set up to await the arrival of Nick's herd, which would arrive early the next morning.

At dawn, Dunigan sent a couple of riders downstream to stop any cattle that might drift away from the herd, then he stripped for his swim. He saw the herd just as they came in sight of the crossing, Brindy Polaris proudly leading the way. Dunigan stopped the herd and had the hands strip down as he was. They all put their clothes in the wagon, caught their strongest swimming mounts, and drove on to the crossing, the strongest swimmers and most experienced hands moving to the downstream side of the herd.

As the herd splashed through the shallows, Brindy turned back and started poking and prodding her sisters forward into the water. That done, she strolled back to the lead, and jumped in. The cows followed her as they were accustomed to and the whole herd swam across, with the exception of one cow that turned over in the current and narrowly missed the swimming rider next to her. But she was roped and pulled out by the downstream riders Dunigan had set out.

The wagons were then rafted across and camps set up. It was a strange sight to see bootless cowboys, clad only in their longdrawers, holding the herd as others set about drying out their things and dressed in clean clothes. The cattle were loose herded to graze until everyone was fed and reclothed, and after a conference with Nick, the herd started right on toward Ft. Dodge, accompanied by Cooper and his remaining drovers. They would be well clear of the river by the time Pete's herd arrived.

And arrive they did, at almost the precise hour Nick's had the day before. The crossing was as smooth as the first, except the cows did not cross as easily because they had no Brindy Polaris to lead them. Even so, everything went well until two or three cows in mid-herd panicked in the water.

They began to mill and the hands closed on them to break it up. One of the cows lunged at Jim Daniels, goring his horse. Horse, cow, and rider all overturned in a thrashing, bloody whirlpool, and it looked as if Jim was a goner, but he was thrown a rope by one of the downstream riders, and pulled ashore. But the cow and horse disappeared in the current. Jim was shaken but unhurt, recovering well enough to eat a hearty lunch.

Chapter 27

Dunigan and Medrano set off northwest the next morning, Abner following more northerly in the wagon. Nick and Pete had been told to keep the eastern side secure until Harris and Thad returned from Dodge. Two days after they left the Canadian, Medrano and Dunigan met back at the wagon to compare notes.

Neither had seen any Indian signs, nor any other except Medrano in the north quad had seen a great many signs of shod horses traveling two by two in column. They both figured this was the U.S. Cavalry, and that was why the Indians were not around. But that also meant most of the Indians along the route would likely be on the south plains, which would hold until they crossed the Platte. After that, they could expect some Indians to be across the trail.

Nick's herd was within ten days of Ft. Dodge, and Dunigan began to feel more secure. He moved his outfit farther north so he could meet Harris earlier to find out what he had learned at Dodge.

May 22nd found Dunigan camped north of Ft. Supply, and Harris and Thad Scott rejoined them there. Harris had sent a wire to Pierce in Abilene. The army had been informed about the theft and were preparing to send out patrols to search for the herd. He also reported that the army had been pretty aggressive patrolling, though they hadn't been seeing any of the tribes.

"George, did you see many cattle being driven there, and are there buyers?"

"A few herds have been in, and there seem to be buyers, but

I don't know exactly how many, John."

"If I had known the army was going to be so active, you could have stayed and waited for us in Dodge, but, better safe than sorry."

Dunigan had planned a break for the herds at Dodge, but since they had to wait to cross the Canadian, there was no need, because the men and cattle were well rested, but the men could use a break, and Dodge was about the last chance for one. There weren't many towns worthy of the name between Dodge and Montana. Dunigan decided to stop the herds for two or three days so the hands could howl a little. He sent Harris to scout for bedgrounds, one north and one south of Dodge.

On May 26th, Dunigan's scouting crew arrived in the vicinity of Ft. Dodge. After setting up camp on the north bank of the Arkansas River, Dunigan rode over to the fort to find out what he could. After much rigmarole, he was ushered into the office of Col. Charles Archer, the commander. He was offered a drink.

"What can I do for you, Mister Dunigan?"

"Colonel, I wanted to find out what has happened about the Pierce steers that were rustled. I was the man who first found the survivors, and George Harris is my scout."

"Oh, I see. Well, as you know, we wired Mister Pierce in Abilene about it, and have sent patrols out to investigate back easterly."

"Do you know if Mister Pierce received the wire, colonel?"

"I understand he acknowledged receipt of the message, but I can't be sure, as you probably appreciate."

"Yes, colonel. I can understand you wouldn't know for sure, being this far away. Tell me, have there been any other reports of rustling along the trail to Dodge?"

"No, Mister Dunigan, this has been the first, and I hope the last. There have been about half a dozen herds driven here, and we expect more later. I'm glad you brought your cattle to Dodge, as it has been a good market, and we expect to see it grow a lot."

"Colonel, I am driving two herds, but they are cows, destined for Montana for stocking. This trail just looked like the shorter way from Texas."

"Well, I'm sure you'll bring us some cattle some day. Here, let me give you another drink."

"Thank you, I believe I will. I also wanted to ask you what you knew about what the Indians are up to. I am going from here to Fort McPherson, then to Fort Fetterman, and up by the Big Horns into Montana. Any problems reported along that way?"

"Things are quiet here, with the Comanche, Kiowa, and Arapaho, and most of the Pawnees are working for us as scouts. Farther north, the Cheyenne have been unsettled, but the Sioux and Shoshone have been fairly quiet, but that's all from reports I have seen. No first-hand information."

"Well, that's fairly good news. I hope we don't have much trouble. We're drovers, not soldiers." Dunigan accepted another drink and left for his camp.

That night at supper, Dunigan asked George Harris about the state of Dodge City, which was building just west of the fort.

"Ain't nothing much, John, just the usual collection of gamblers, whores, and such. There's a hotel, of course, and there seem to be plenty of cattle buyers here. I have been approached by several, wanting to know about our herds, and they seem to be hunting steers to buy."

"Blaylock's not there, is he?" Dunigan asked.

"I haven't seen him nor any of his firm's people. I guess they're still at Abilene."

Dunigan told Harris he planned to stop for two or three days, and explained his reasons.

"I think that's good, John. There isn't anywhere north of here to let off steam. The rest of the way is pretty barren of civilization. One thing though, I'd sure try to disarm the boys. Everyone here is pretty well armed."

"Thanks George, I'll try."

Nick's herd appeared about midmorning, and by the time they had been driven another four miles north of Dodge and bedded down, it was almost dark. Dunigan took Thad with him to eat supper at their camp. After supper, Dunigan told the hands they could have some time off while they were close to Dodge. He also paid each man a month's wages, which they were all glad to receive. He warned them about going armed into Dodge, but in his usual way, did not make that mandatory. Nick had little to say, except to arrange herd watches, and Dunigan left for the night.

Pete arrived at noon the next day and turned his herd loose south of town. Dunigan went for the noon meal and repeated his speech about going armed. The results were about the same, except Pete reinforced it with a speech of his own. When

Dunigan got back to Abner's wagon, there was a strange pony tied there. He unsaddled his horse, and went to get coffee, and saw the strange pony belonged to Louie Courrell. They greeted one another like long-lost brothers, and sat down to talk over things important to the success of Dunigan's enterprise.

"I fine out dat feller, Ewing, he got a ranch on de Missouri, east of Fort Benton. Now dat place is his; don't belong to de syndicate. Is a Texas feller wiz him, name of Block, but I don't find out much about dis, seems lak big secret. You know, I go see my wife's people later, mebbe the Blackfeets know something."

"Well, I had been hearing about those things, but I didn't know about Calvin Block being in on it, so that's news. I have been in touch with the army and they tell me most of the Indians are quiet, except for the Cheyennes."

"Yeah, dats what I hear, too, an' I hear they gonna be trouble all year. We mebbe try to stay clear of dem Injuns, huh?"

"If we can, Louie, if we can. I'm gonna put you with this boy, Thad Scott, and he will help you find enough horses for yourself. If they're not here, you can get them at one of the herds. We're going to stop here for two or three days, so the hands can get their wild hairs pulled out. You'll have time to get everything arranged."

Dunigan called Thad over and introduced them, instructing Thad to help Louie get settled, and to put together a string of horses for him. Dunigan got some coffee and sat down to rest, then remembered he hadn't checked on mail. Chito was just lazing around the fire, so Dunigan sent him for the mail.

Chito brought back quite a lot of it and Dunigan sorted it, sending some to Nick's herd and Pete's, then turned to his own. He had four letters from Amanda, two from Joseph Carter, one from Jim Blaylock, and one from Gerard Alton. Although he knew Amanda's letters were not as important as the rest, he read them first. They were full of news about Kentucky, the latest race horse sales and tobacco planting, and an aching yearning for his presence. He felt the same, and when he finished reading them, he was emotionally drained.

Then he got down to business with the other letters. Blaylock had good news. He could sell 4,000 cows sight unseen, for $25 a head in Nebraska and Colorado, if they could be delivered by October 1st. He could find pasturage for 2,000 more, if need be.

This was the insurance Dunigan was looking for. If there was any trouble about payment from Ewing at the Platte crossing, Dunigan had an alternate market, so his position was more secure.

Joseph Carter reported that Ewing had indeed tried to file a lien on his cattle, but was prevented by the prior lien filed by Alton's bank. Word was that Ewing's uncle and a bunch of investors were coming to Montana in the fall to see the properties, and perhaps to kill some game, buffalo or elk and such. Carter thought the big augers' visit might coincide with the delivery of the cattle, and if Dunigan was right about Ewing having some scheme to get 1,500 cows for himself, Ewing's scheme would be exposed to his uncle. Carter had heard nothing about Calvin Block's involvement, so that was still a mystery, and that bothered Dunigan.

Alton's letter was mostly questions about Dunigan's marriage, but one piece of news of interest was that the syndicate's bank had inquired about buying Dunigan's note. Ewing was determined to seek an edge with money. When Alton turned them down, they had raised the offer, but he reported that the bank was not inclined to sell notes unless they were in default, and especially not in this case, as Dunigan had over 150 percent of the face value of the note on deposit with the bank. Alton's report meant that Ewing had been busy, trying to gather as much information as he could about Dunigan.

Dunigan answered all the letters, and asked some of the correspondents for specific information. He wrote Gerard Alton that if things went wrong at Ft. McPherson, he would know it as there would be no money forthcoming, so he should get Blaylock in contact with Dunigan immediately, so the cattle could to sold to Blaylock's customers. Dunigan also prompted Joseph Carter to look around for any mention of Calvin Block, and to write him about any action between Ewing and the Montana Stock Growers Association. Then he wrote a long and loving letter to Amanda, telling her all about what was happening.

Dunigan was awakened an hour before dawn, with the news that Billy Parmalee had been shot to death in a saloon in Dodge City. Dunigan crawled out of his blankets, put on his clothes, got some coffee, and tried to collect his thoughts.

"Who shot Billy?" he asked.

"A gambler named Ben Marcus," Pete answered. Billy worked in his crew.

"What was it all about, Pete?"

"As far as I can tell, it was about one of those whores in that saloon. It seems this Marcus had some kind of a claim on her that neither the girl nor Billy acknowledged. They were in her room when Billy was killed, but there were plenty of witnesses."

"Was Billy packing a gun?" Dunigan asked.

"No, John, he wasn't. I saw him go off to town, and his gun was in the wagon. I checked after I got the news, and it was still there, and clean."

"Has this Marcus been arrested, do you know?"

"No, and so far as I know, the marshal has no intention of doing so, or so I've been told."

"Well, I think I'll go talk to this sheriff. I want you and Harris to go with me, Pete, and I want you both armed."

Pete, Harris, and Dunigan strapped on their holsters, saddled their mounts and left for Dodge City. They went straight to the town marshal's office in the jail.

Shug Richter was just rising when they walked in. He looked at Dunigan and his companions as he poured a cup of coffee. Richter was a big, powerful man who was starting to turn to fat. He had been a stage guard and held other odd jobs before being appointed town marshal. His main qualifications seemed to be that he was a saloon fighter and bully boy.

"What can I do for you men?"

"Marshal, I am John Dunigan, and those two herds of cows outside of town are mine. One of my drovers was killed last night and I am here to find out what happened."

"I don't know too much about it. Heard tell it was a fight between him and a gambler over some saloon girl. I ain't gonna worry myself over no gamblers, saddle tramps, or whores. Let 'em kill each other off," Richter said.

"Marshal, my drover was unarmed, and was shot down in cold blood by a gambler named Ben Marcus. If you aren't even going to look into it, then I guess we'll have to take care of it ourselves."

"You do, and I'll come after you. You Texas drovers ain't the law here. This here is Kansas and I'm the law." Richter had raised his voice till he was almost screaming.

Dunigan just stared at him without speaking for a full minute. "Marshal, if you're the law here, then you do your job. Or we will do it for you. Murder is murder, no matter where or who." He paused to let that sink in. "I am going to find out for sure what happened. When I am finished, if you have done nothing, then I will dispense justice as I see fit."

"You son of a bitch, you get out of this town now, or I'll run you out," Richter yelled.

The three drovers looked calmly at the sheriff and made no move to leave. Richter stormed about the office fuming and yelling threats, but the three men still did not move.

"Are you going to leave town or do I have to kill you now?" Richter roared.

"If that's what you mean to do, marshal, I suggest you get on with it, because we are not leaving until this thing is cleared up," Dunigan said, not moving.

Dunigan could feel him back down. Richter stopped his ranting finally. "Okay, I'll look into it, but don't you be putting your nose in my business, or I'll throw you in jail. You understand?"

"I will not bother you if you bring this to a satisfactory conclusion, marshal. Just do your job and you'll have no trouble from me."

When the three went over to the saloon to get Billy's body, they were told it was at the undertaker's across the street. Dunigan questioned the girl and the bartender and they confirmed Pete's account. The girl also told them Marcus and the marshal had an agreement about things, and that was why nothing had been done.

At the undertaker's, they made funeral arrangements for ten o'clock the following morning. Dunigan went back to the marshal's office. Richter was half dressed and still fuming about.

"Richter, we're going to bury Billy Parmalee at ten o'clock tomorrow. I will expect something settled by then, or we will take over."

"I'll do it when I feel like it, you Texas son of a bitch."

"Marshal, that's the second time you have used that name to me. Do not make the mistake of doing it again. I'll be here after the funeral." Dunigan walked out and the three of them rode off to camp.

All the hands that could be spared attended the funeral. Dunigan had found a Methodist preacher to conduct the service and Pete delivered the eulogy. After the service, Dunigan and Pete and four others went over to the saloon. There sat Ben Marcus, playing solitaire.

Dunigan walked over to him. "On your feet, scum."

Marcus did not even look up, apparently secure that his arrangement with Shug Richter would protect him.

Dunigan back-handed the man right out of his chair. When he hit the wall behind him, Marcus pulled out his gun, but Dunigan was faster and the gambler died before he could pull back the hammer.

Pete went to get the marshal, and when Richter saw what had happened, he told Dunigan he was arresting him for murder. Dunigan just stared and Richter made no move. All the witnesses told Richter that Marcus had pulled his gun first, but Dunigan had been faster. Richter backed down and went away to sulk. Dunigan told the bartender the herds were going to move out that day, but that the townspeople had better get themselves a real lawman, or the next Texas herd might burn down the town if something like that happened again.

Chapter 28

With the cattle moving again, Dunigan felt better. He set a more northwesterly course from Dodge, aiming to cross the Platte at Ft. McPherson. Brindy Polaris still wanted to go straight north, but after a half day on the new course, she settled down and led the way.

Before he left Dodge, Dunigan had talked to Amos Cooper, who was going over to Abilene as Pierce had sent word that he had a line on his missing cattle. Cooper thanked him for all his help and said Pierce appreciated it, too.

They had been in the true plains country for over a month, but Dunigan had kept his log current, and knew exactly where they were by his star sightings. He kept his wagon close to the lead herd's eastern flank, and his patrols were mainly northwesterly, but with one eye to the east, as well. He figured to arrive at Ft. McPherson in about three weeks. The danger on this leg was mainly from the Cheyenne, but could come from bands of other tribes, too. Western Kansas was sparsely populated, but they did glimpse farmsteads from time to time, although it was still pretty dangerous out there, unless you kept moving.

They sighted some buffalo, but they were small herds, unlikely to attract the attention of major tribal hunts. Dunigan hoped the bigger herds were farther west and that the Indians were after them. George Harris killed one occasionally, as the hands had acquired a taste for buffalo meat, and George kept the men supplied.

Calves were dropping and becoming something of a problem. There were only five on the ground when they got to Dodge, but now there were over a hundred, and the calf wagons had plenty of passengers. Usually, the cows would drop them on the bedground, and in the morning the babies were roped out and put in the wagon, the mothers naturally following their offspring to the wagon, where they would tag along all day. When they bedded the herd, the calves were put on the ground, and the mothers would take them off to suckle.

That procedure was repeated every morning until the calves could walk well enough to keep up with the herd, usually at three to five days of age. From then on, the calves stayed with the herd, but at times it seemed for every calf walking, two rode in the wagon. It was a time-consuming process, but necessary. Any calf born weak or deformed was killed, but they yielded pitifully little meat. Needless to say, the calves' mothers did not take kindly to this system, and that provided some amusement for the trail hands.

There was little evidence of a trail along their route, so Dunigan found his celestial navigation essential. Scouting for watering places and river and creek fords assumed more importance, and took time away from scouting for hostile activity. Since the cattle were well trail broke, Dunigan felt he could afford to recruit two men from the herds to help look for Indians and cow thieves. He picked Lon Castle from Nick's herd and from Pete's, Chano Gomez, one of the men Abel had brought from Mexico. George Harris had seen a couple of small bands, but nothing large enough to cause concern. Still, they were getting close to Cheyenne country, and Dunigan wanted to be doubly vigilant.

The land in western Kansas was short grass prairie, and the herds were improving as they marched northward. The country looked like paradise for cattle, but Dunigan had heard enough about the winters there to realize there'd be real problems keeping cattle alive through the cold weather. He figured his future lay on the Aransas River, not the Arkansas or Platte, so he kept his imagination in check. Still, this sea of virgin grass gave a thinking man pause to consider its potential.

He had not seen Louie Courrell in almost a week, but Louie was pretty much of a loner, and he had Thad Scott with him, teaching him the ways of this country. Dunigan knew that when Louie returned he would have some real news. He was probably sitting in an Indian lodge somewhere, enjoying boiled dog and young squaw, and gleaning every bit of talk for news of hostiles.

George Harris came back that day to report seeing tracks of three small bands, all with travois tracks, indicating women and children, which meant just movement and not raiding. The next day a small band of Arapahoes appeared, asking for wo-haw and were given three steers. They were on the eastern edge of their range, and consequently, their claim for toll steers was weak, but Dunigan gave them the three steers anyway, not wanting any trouble. The Arapahoes seemed to be a conquered people, and this was not surprising, for they had already made peace when Colonel Chivington and the Colorado militia had hit them on Sand Creek in 1864, perpetrating an uncalled for bloody massacre on a camp of Indians genuinely at peace with the whites. That massacre had taken all the pride the tribe had left, turning them into beggars and drunks.

Louie and Thad showed up five days later reporting very little Indian activity. They had seen signs of a few small parties, but only two that could be said possibly to be dangerous, and these were too small to attack the herds, but might try to steal some horses or cattle. He and Thad had stayed with some Pawnee and also some Arapahoes that weren't in a hostile mood, but they were also worried about the Cheyenne, who seemed to be thinking about going on the warpath. The other Indians said the Cheyenne were upset about the buffalo slaughter going on, but were short of horses for a major campaign. They were farther west for the most part, and should be busy hunting until fall.

They had crossed the Smoky Hill River, and were fording fairly large creeks about every other day. There had been bountiful rains earlier, and all the creeks were still flowing, but there had been no tough crossings since the Cimarron. A cow or two had bogged and had to be pulled out, and a calf was lost, but no real trouble developed. Another few days would see them out of Kansas and into Nebraska, and they still hadn't seen any Cheyenne.

About the only diversion for the cowboys was the morning roundup of calves, for each morning there would be some kind of wreck that would amuse the hands. Otherwise, it was dust and boredom from dawn till dusk. The drag riders were all trying to help with the calves, because their stations were the dustiest and most boring. Getting out of the irate mother cow's path of destruction was considerably more interesting than following 2,500 docile bovines in a cloud of choking dust all day.

There were a few instances of fist and mouth fights among the hands, but not anything unexpected. As long as knives and pistols were kept holstered, Dunigan felt things would go all right.

They were still making good time on the trail and at this rate, could reach their final destination by early September, but there were more calves every day. Dunigan estimated that there were no fewer than four hundred calves per herd, with more dropping every morning. In another two weeks, Dunigan estimated, the pace of the herd would slow perceptibly. He was glad the early drive had been quick.

Dunigan had been urging his own party on and was now about even with the leading edge of Nick's herd, and a little to the east. Each day brought reports of more Indian signs, but still most were of small family groups. They were almost to the Nebraska line when Louie Courrell and Thad returned one evening reporting signs of a group of eight Cheyennes without women or children. Louie figured they were young bucks looking for trouble. They had tracked them west and realizing they were close to Dunigan's camp, had come in to report, eat, and stay the night.

"I'll get back on the trail first thing in de mornin. Dese Injuns might be trouble."

"That's right, Louie. Just you and Thad be careful. I'm going to have George on the west side tomorrow. If you have trouble, skedaddle back to the herd. There should be enough guns here to handle it."

"I think they mebbe two or three days ahead of us, so we may not catch up, but we see tomorrer."

Thad nodded. Dunigan had noticed he followed Louie all the time, even copying his mannerisms, so Thad had a new hero. Dunigan was glad. He knew the old man liked Thad, and would teach him a world of lore he had learned in a lifetime in the wilderness.

George Harris checked back at noon the next day, having found no sign. He had seen Louie and Thad earlier, but not since. Dunigan was still pushing his little group, so he was now north of Nick's herd, in order to be as close to the danger point as possible. After Harris and Chito ate dinner, he was going to send them out to overtake Louie and Thad, but the two rode in before Harris was even ready to leave.

They came in at a long lope, their horses pretty well lathered up, and came direct to Dunigan.

"Boss, we found them injuns, or where they were. They raided a farm about fifteen miles north, killed the man, but the woman drove them off, and three of them were killed. Near as I can tell, they went off west and won't be back, but what's left there is in bad shape," said Louie.

"George," he said to Harris, "you and Chito go with Louie back to that place and take a pack horse with what they need; food and such, and look after them. Abner and I will be there tomorrow. If you see any of the other scouts, take them along, and find out where those Indians went."

The four rode off to help the survivors. Dunigan told Abner that they would leave in two hours to follow them, and for him to pack some food for supper, as they would go straight through to that farm. Louie said the farm was on the south bank of the Republican River, and Dunigan estimated from his morning position sighting that it was between 20 and 25 miles away, rather than 15. The horses were well rested though and they could go through the night. By the time they got everything packed it was almost five o'clock. Lon Castle and his partner Chano Gomez had come in by then, and he sent them back to their respective herds with news of the raid, and to watch to the west for this particular group of Indians. Dunigan would be back in touch with them at the Republican River crossing.

When he and Abner set out they were able to follow the scouts' trail very easily. It veered west of their general line of march, but not much. There was probably a better crossing along this line, so the herds might come by this way anyhow. There was daylight until after eight, so they had come a ways by then, but they slowed a little after dark, because the trail was not as clear. Dunigan rode ahead to show the way and Abner followed with the wagon. About eleven they stopped, fixed some coffee, and ate a cold supper, then continued all night, arriving just at daybreak.

The farmstead was a wreck. There had been a house, but it was burned, as were the barn and corrals. The only thing left was a sod root cellar, and it was there the woman and her two children had stood off the Cheyennes. The husband and older son, age eleven, had been hitching up a team when the Indians were seen out on the plain. He had sent his wife, Lutie, and a son age seven and their four-year-old daughter to the root cellar, along with a rifle and a pistol. The man got his Sharps and determined to drive the Indians off. He was trying to pick a sniping spot when he saw his older son out in the open by the corral.

He ran to him, but the Indians had closed on them. The farmer shot one off his horse, but he and his son were lanced while he was reloading.

They were scalped and the Indians looted the house and barn, setting them afire. Then the raiders looked around for other people, because the house indicated more than just a man and his son. They began to beat on the root cellar door. Lutie crammed her pistol into an air hole in the door and fired. She heard something hit the ground outside, and peeked through the opening. She saw the Indians dragging off a body and fired again, hearing a yelp of pain when she did.

The Indians gave up direct attacks after that, but a few minutes later got on top of the root cellar, which had a small roof projecting out of the earth, and began chopping at it with their hatchets. Lutie fired her pistol through the roof and heard another cry of pain. After that, the Indians rode around the farm yard, yelling and shaking their lances in defiance. They galloped up and down, daring one another to attack again. Finally, one got up his nerve enough to charge and he was shot dead for his foolhardiness. Lutie knew how to use firearms.

The Indians then gathered up everything usable and all the livestock and rode off. Lutie and the two kids stayed in the root cellar for another three hours before they came out.

This was all related to Dunigan by Louie Courrell as they ate breakfast. Abner set up a tent for the woman and her kids and fed them.

Lutie Grimes was a typical farmer's wife. Born on a farm herself in Indiana in 1840, she had married a neighbor boy, Mason Grimes, when she was seventeen. Three years later, he had marched off to war, leaving her pregnant. He was away four years, but came home to move them to new lands in Missouri, impregnating her again on the way. He found land in western Missouri and farmed three years there before going broke. Again, they moved west, this time to Nebraska, where they had stayed for over two years. Mason was a good husband, but not a good provider and his family had lived in intermittent poverty ever since the war. Lutie had suffered from it.

She had been a pretty girl, but the years of toil had aged her. She was still slender, even a mite thin, with washed-out blond hair. A quiet, patient woman, she had tolerated her husband's failures with resignation, but now that he was dead, she felt relief more than anything. The loss of her eldest son still grieved her, and so did the loss of all her possessions except for the clothes on her and her children's backs. That condition made her very fearful for the future. She said little, moved little, and seemed to be in a trance. Dunigan classified her as a lost soul.

On the second day, George Harris rode in, exhausted from tracking the raiding party.

"Boss, I tracked them over forty miles, and I never caught up to them. I did find a grave, so one of the wounded must have died, which puts them down to four, and one of them is wounded. But they are moving out of here pretty fast. I ran across a cavalry patrol and told them of the raid, so they took out after them. Maybe they can get something back, but I doubt it. Those Indians don't want to be caught up with and the cavalry would be satisfied if they just kept moving. They don't much like people living out here where they can't protect them."

"Well, at least we're here, and the herds are safe for the time being," Dunigan said.

The scouts had been at the farm three days when the herds caught up. Pete and Nick came over after the cattle were bedded down, to find out what was going on, as they had had only sketchy reports and wanted to know how serious it was. They were also tired of their cook's meals, and knew Abner put out the best grub in the whole outfit.

After the raid story had been explained, Nick and Pete ate their supper and just sat around the fire drinking coffee. Lutie Grimes had been sitting in the same spot for two days, saying nothing. When Nick asked her if she'd like some coffee, she said yes. He got her a cup, and sat beside her, and asked her some questions. She answered yes and no, but that was more than anyone else had been able to get out of her. Nick was a kindly old bear, so she began to talk some. They carried on a conversation until bedtime. In the morning, Lutie was more animated and helped Abner with breakfast. She began to come out of her shell of grief and that made everyone feel better. No one knew what to do with the Grimes, except they couldn't be left where they were and they had no money and no place to go.

Nick suggested a solution. "John, we can't leave these folks here. Let me take them along with me. Miz Grimes can help with the cooking, and all my boys need a lot of washing done.

The kids could help with the calves and they could earn a little money, at least until we get to Fort McPherson. Then we can decide what to do. I feel like I can get Lutie out of her funk by then and maybe we can send 'em back to her folks in Indiana. At least we'll be able to get some messages back so they will be able to tell their folks what happened, and maybe get some help."

"I think that is our best shot, Nick. Maybe the army has some way to help, too. It should be you to take them on, because they seem to cotton to you. You ain't gettin' sweet on them are you?" Dunigan winked.

"No, John, I just am able to talk to them because they seem to trust me."

"We'll take 'em along to the Platte, and we can drop them off there," Dunigan said, ending the discussion.

The Grimes family moved to Nick's herd and Dunigan watched as the herd started out to the Platte the next morning. Brindy Polaris was leading the way as usual, but now she had a fine-looking bull calf by her side. Dunigan made up his mind to take that calf home with him. The whole outfit got started that day, with Dunigan's scouts ranging to the east and west, as the north was crisscrossed by army patrols out of Ft. McPherson, so Dunigan expected no trouble from any sector, until they were considerably north of the fort.

Seven days after leaving the Grimes farm, Dunigan's wagon was in sight of Ft. McPherson, the cavalry post just east of the junction of the North and South Platte Rivers. The date was July 1, 1872, and Dunigan was on schedule. It was there he was to meet Viscount Glencollin, to receive his $15 a head payment. This payment was integral to his plan, but Dunigan had hedged his bets with Jim Blaylock if Ewing failed to pay.

Chapter 29

Dunigan had gone ahead to the fort to talk to the commander, Lt. Col. Charles Archer. He was ushered into his office and offered a drink.

"I got a letter about you from Major Layton down in Texas, and he asked me to extend what courtesies I could to you when you passed through."

"Well, I thank you, colonel. This glass of whiskey is sure fine courtesy, if I do say so. Other than that I need information about what the Indians are doing around here, and I have one more problem, that of a sod buster's family."

Dunigan then proceeded to relate the dismal history of the Grimes family, and the fact that they were utterly destitute.

The colonel responded. "Yes, I had heard of them from one of my patrols who pursued the Indians, but could never catch up. I believe some of your men informed the patrol about this matter. There is very little I can do about these settlers' plight, as they have no legal status here. We can help them get back to their families, but that is about all."

"She may not have any family left, I just don't know. It is a pitiful situation, but we'll do all we can to help her," Dunigan replied.

"We can telegraph her kinfolks, if we know who and where they are, Mister Dunigan, and will be glad to do so," the colonel said.

"I'll try to get that information to you as soon as possible. On another matter, colonel, I am supposed to meet my buyers here, and they must make a payment on the cattle if we are to continue to Montana. I wondered if you had heard anything from them? The principal is a man named Allan Ewing, but he is a titled Britisher, who likes to be called Viscount Glencollin. He is manager of an outfit called 'Cameron Ranch Company,' a British syndicate in Montana. Have you heard anything?"

"No, I haven't, Mister Dunigan," Colonel Archer replied. "But our patrols to the northwest are not due in until day after tomorrow. They might have seen somebody headed this way."

Dunigan was satisfied that Ewing was not around, and went back across the river to his camp. Once there, he instructed George Harris to scout for bedgrounds for the two herds, both north and south of the river, as it looked like they might have to wait on Ewing, and Dunigan would go no farther without the $15-a-head payment. Harris took Aparicio Medrano with him to look for suitable grass and water. The herds were slated to be at the river in two days, so he didn't have much time. Dunigan saddled a fresh horse to ride to Nick's herd, scouting for trail to the east flank. He noted nothing but cavalry tracks and arrived at the herd in time for supper that night, the herd being only a bit more than a day's drive from the Platte.

After eating supper and visiting with Nick's crew, Dunigan and Nick moved away to talk. Dunigan told him they might have a delay at the Platte, and that George Harris was out looking for grass and water for the herds. Nick nodded. Dunigan changed the subject to the question of the Grimes family.

"Nick, I want you to take the nesters into Fort McPherson tomorrow. I will take over the herd until we get there. There's a telegraph there, and the army can find out about any family they might have back in Indiana, and what they can do. The army can handle it from here on out. Take one of the wagons if you need to. I see you don't have but about three small calves to haul, and we can handle that with one of the other wagons, and we'll be going slow enough for them to keep up. You can leave in the morning."

"All right, John, I'll take 'em in, and try to sort everything out. They sure have been handy, as you can see by the way the hands is all spruced up, and Lutie sure makes good pies. I'll be sorry to see them go," McCurry said. "You be careful with my cows, and don't wilden them up none."

"I'll try not to have any wrecks, Nick, I surely will, and I hope you can find something for these folks. I'll see you at the fort after I get these cows settled."

They discussed details of the herd, who stood the night hawk, and various things, mainly about the hands' pecking order, and Nick went to get everything ready for tomorrow.

Next morning, Nick and the Grimes family left before all the hands had finished breakfast. Dunigan noticed that all the hands made a point of saying goodbye to them, and all the well wishes were heartfelt and genuine. The nesters had made many friends in the crew, and all were sorry to see them go.

Turning the herd off the bedground, Dunigan went to the lead to observe his old friend, Brindy Polaris. She seemed to recognize him, and made a circle to show off her bull calf to him. The calf was red with a white face, surely an offspring of one of the Hereford bulls from Abilene, and half again as big as the pure longhorn calves. Satisfied that he was pleased, she helped get her sisters up and moving, taking the lead as always. She headed unerringly north and strode out strongly. Dunigan circled the herd a couple of times in the morning to check the herd's general condition and was pleased. The cattle were strong and in reasonable flesh and health. The calves were coming along fine and keeping up with their mothers. Dunigan would have to give Nick a rating of excellent so far. Dunigan felt good to be driving a herd again, and forgot all his other troubles, at least for that day.

That evening, George rode into camp. He reported he had found two areas for the herds, one about five miles northeast of the fort, and the other on the south side of the river, eight or nine miles upriver from the fort. The river could be used as a boundary as it had no ford there, but the cattle could get to it to water. Harris suggested that Dunigan take Nick's herd to the ground to the north. He could pick up Chito at the Platte crossing to guide him, as he had helped George guide it. Then he could go on to Pete's herd, and take them to the upriver site.

Dunigan agreed, and Harris left the next morning for Pete's herd. Harris told Dunigan enough about the location that he felt he could find it himself, but since Chito was at the crossing, he could serve as guide. The herd arrived at the Platte about ten, and they crossed without stopping, as it was not swimming and the bottom was good. They crossed without incident, then stopped for nooning, before resuming the drive to the holding grounds. Pablo Mendoza had crossed the chuck wagon first, and had dinner ready when the herd was across and settled.

The herd was again on the move that afternoon. He sent Chito ahead to guide Pablo and the wagons ahead, so they could find a good campsite. The herd arrived about six thirty and they bedded the cattle loosely and came in for supper, at which time Dunigan set out the night hawk schedule, and told the hands they would likely stay there for four or five days. Since there wasn't much in the way of recreation, they may as well spend their time in repairs and curing galls. He also told them in the morning he would send out any mail that was at the fort.

He and Chito spent the night, and in the morning went back to the fort, taking with them any horses that were too badly galled to be of any use in the next month. Since there were plenty of horses at both herds, Dunigan felt that the horses might get better treatment with his remuda, as Chito, Michael O'Grady, and Abner were all known as good horse doctors.

Arriving back at Abner's wagon, Dunigan turned in the horses to his remuda, instructed Chito and Abner to start treatment, and to have Thad help when he got back from scouting with Louie Courell. He then rode to the fort for mail and news. He found Nick, who related that messages had been sent to the Grimes's relatives, but no replies had been received. Dunigan picked up the mail and sorted it. There were three letters from Amanda, one each from Gerard Alton and Jim Blaylock for him, and various and sundry others for the hands. He dropped by Colonel Keller's office to check on whether his patrols had reported in and was told they hadn't.

Once in Abner's camp, Dunigan sorted the mail and sent it out to Nick's herd with Chito. He determined to deliver Pete's himself. He needed to visit Pete's herd, as he hadn't been there in a while, and this was a good excuse. Then he read Amanda's letters. They were the same as always, newsy and loving. Alton's conveyed some information. The syndicate had indeed tried to buy his note, but had been turned down, and the note had been renewed. Also there was information that the transfer funds were in place, as was the mechanism for transferring them.

All of that led Dunigan to believe that Ewing would show up. The letter from Blaylock said his alternate buyers were still on the line, but wanted to get the cows earlier, and additionally, there was word of an outfit at Ft. Benton that wanted 1,500 cows, which was too much coincidence for Dunigan. This had to be Ewing and Block, and Dunigan would write to Blaylock to stay away from this deal.

Dunigan gathered up the mail and set out for Pete's range, figuring to pick up Harris there or on the way back. He crossed the river and turned upstream. On the ride, Dunigan could see how rich the Platte Valley was, and how many people it would support once the Indians were settled. He thought that even the Indians might farm it instead of hunting buffalo, but dismissed that as wishful thinking. He arrived at Pete's camp about the end of the day, turned in his horse to the remuda, and got some coffee. He could see the herd in the distance being bedded down, and knew Pete and the others would be in for supper soon.

Dunigan passed out the mail when the crew came in, then after supper went off with Pete to discuss everything that was happening with his herds. After filling Pete in, Dunigan asked how the cattle were holding up. "Pretty good, John, I think two or three days' rest will help, but they are putting on flesh and generally getting stronger. I think most of the calves have dropped, and they can keep up now. I reckon we got about seven hundred calves now."

"Pete, I think you got more prolific cows in your herd. Nick's only got about five hundred. I'm going to spend the night so I can get a good look at the herd in the morning, but everything seems to be going fine. I want to take any horses that are badly galled back with me. My bunch will cure them up faster, and it looks like you won't miss them. You have plenty of mounts."

The next day, Dunigan had a good look at the herd. The cows were dead level with Nick's, perhaps a bit more flesh on the average, but the difference between the herds was not apparent. He said so to Pete before he went back to the fort, and that pleased them both. The approval of a cowman means more to another cowman than that of a buyer or butcher or anyone else.

Back at the fort, Dunigan went to visit Colonel Archer to check on various things. After a drink the two men then started into matters that Dunigan wanted to know about. First, Archer told him that there was a party on the way to the fort, seven riders, a wagon and a buggy, as reported by one of the cavalry patrols.

"That sounds like the Sassenach bastard. I guess he's coming, but he'll probably be trying to reopen the trade again," mused Dunigan.

"I haven't been able to find any family to take on the Grimes people. We were unable to find her kinfolks anywhere. We could send them back to Kansas City, Omaha, or St. Louis, but then they are on their own, or they could stay around here, down on suds row, to do washing and such. It's not a very good option," Colonel Archer said.

"Well, that doesn't sound too good. I'll talk to Nick. He may have an idea. Colonel, what can you tell me about Indian activities in Wyoming and Montana?"

"Mister Dunigan, " he began, "I can tell you a lot, but not specific locations or bands and such. The Cheyennes are on the prowl because of encroachment on the buffalo range, and that mainly west of here, a hundred miles or more. All the Indians will kill any buffalo hunters they catch, and none too pleasantly, either. The Sioux, northeast of here are not hostile right now, but it won't be long, because they have found gold in the Black Hills, which is Sioux sacred ground.

"We are trying to keep the whites out of their way, but we can't control everyone, and when the Indians catch them, they get killed. With more gold prospectors and buffalo hunters coming out west all the time, trouble is going to be major out here in the next couple of years. There are a lot of Indians on the plains, and we haven't enough troops to handle them. I don't know when, but it'll be sometime soon, and there will be a real war."

"That doesn't sound too good, colonel, but I would like some information that's more specific. To start with, I intend to spend the winter in Texas, so anything after October doesn't interest me. Also, I am turning northwest from here. I intend to follow the river to Fort Fetterman, then turn north and either go along the east side of the Big Horns, or up the west side, and on into Montana to War Horse Lake. What can you tell me about Indians that I might run into?"

"John, you shouldn't run into too much trouble that way. You are going to miss the Sioux to the east. If you go up the west side of the Big Horns, you will be in the country of Wash-a-kie's Wind River Band of the Shoshone. They are friendly, but it will cost you some cattle for passage. If you go up the east side, you could run into some small bands of Sioux, but you have a big enough outfit to handle them, unless you get surprised.

"Farther north, there will be Crows, but they are not hostile, but will require a few head for a passage toll. I think the west side of the Big Horns is rougher but safer, especially if you can make some arrangements with Wash-a-kie. He doesn't want war and will do all he can to avoid conflict on his range.

"Colonel, what you've told me helps a lot. My lead scout, Louie Courrell, has a wife who is a Blackfoot squaw, and I think some of her people are with the Wash-a-kie band, so we can probably make some good medicine with the old chief. My worry is that the way there may be pretty tough for cattle, but I don't know. The east side is shorter, and easy going, but maybe the west side is best, if that way can be traveled. I'll have to get Louie out pretty soon to scout it out."

They had another drink and then parted, Dunigan going back to Abner's wagon for supper. Since they had not had to move in a few days, Abner's meals had been excellent, and they had quite a few visitors of late. This evening was no exception, with Nick and the Grimes and all of Dunigan's scout group. Dunigan decided he had best tackle the Grimes problem head on, and he took Nick aside after supper.

"Nick, what can we do with this nester family? The colonel tells me they don't have any folks anywhere, and we can't keep taking them with us. That just moves them in the wrong direction. Do you have any ideas?"

"John, it's a poser. We can't send them back to some town like Omaha. We all know what will happen to them there, and taking 'em along with us is not helpful to them, and we will end up dumping them out in Montana, with no way to survive. They have been helpful to us, cooking and washing, but it's not a necessity, it's really charity. But I really like them, and me and the boys feel like they're kinda family now."

"I know you have become fond of them, but we are heading into the most dangerous part of this drive, and it's not fair to subject them to that," Dunigan said.

"You know, John, everything you've said is true, but that doesn't help. I've even been thinking about settling down somewhere with them, so you know I've been thinking about it pretty hard. She's a good woman, and the sprouts are very nice, but who would have an old codger like me?"

"Nick, any real woman would be lucky to catch you, but you better think long and hard about getting married. It's a big step, and you'd have a ready-made family. Your prospects are not too bad, as you have quite a credit built up with me, $5,000 about, I figure, and you'd have a place there on the ranch."

Dunigan continued. "Thinking about it, Nick, the ranch is getting to be a fair sized deal and probably needs someone full time in charge. Besides, this gypsy life of cow hunts and trail drives is getting kinda old, if you know what I mean?"

"Uh-huh, John. I don't know whether I want to do this yet, however, would you think we could take her along as far as Fetterman while I make up my mind?"

"Sure, Nick, it's up to you anyway, but Fetterman is farther away, you know."

"Yeah, but I might decide to do something there. This is might good looking country around here, and I hear it can be had pretty easy. I may just stay around here."

Dunigan laughed. "Nick, remember, this is midsummer. I wouldn't know what to do when the snow started covering everything up. Besides, I hear the country east of the mountains is awful good. Keep your eyes open on the way, and you may find something you like better, if migration is on your mind."

"John, I'm just daydreaming, thinking about things. I'm really not too serious about moving from Texas, but you have to admit, it's tempting when you look at all this good country that's unoccupied," Nick countered.

"This country ain't unoccupied, or unclaimed, Nick. It really belongs to a lot of Indians, who might contest your title, like they did the Grimes's. You better think hard before you put that family in the way of hostiles again."

"I am, John, and like I said, I ain't real serious about it but it is tempting."

Late that night, Louie and Thad arrived, but did not confer with Dunigan. They went straight to bed as they were worn out. Straight off at breakfast, Dunigan questioned them about what they had found.

"Louie, what can we expect between here and Fetterman?"

"I don find anything to look dangerous, an' de Sioux are way east, and de Cheyenne have gone sout'west to Colorado after de buffalo, so we should get troo okay."

"Louie, is there anything else on the way that might affect us, like grass or water?"

"Well, we follow de river, so dere plenty water, and seems to be plenty grass, but it is dry along dat way, but dat is about normal this time of year," Louie explained.

"Louie, it looks like we're going on, as I have heard that the Englishmen is on his way. When we leave here, I want you to go on past Fetterman, and find out what is the best way to our delivery point. Mainly, I want to know whether we should go up the east or west side of the Big Horns into Montana. Also, I want you to make contact with Wash-a-kie and his Wind River Band, and perhaps get some help from them. We'll give 'em some beef for it. I think the closer we get to our final destination, the more danger we're in, and the Shoshone may be able to help there. After all, it's their country we'll be going through, particularly if we go west of the Big Horns."

"You know, I know dat ol' man. He is a good feller. My wife from dat bunch of Injuns, and yo right, he can help us get troo." He continued. "I think you right 'bout dat English. I see a buggy wit some riders 'bout two days back. Dey be in tonight late, mebbe. Them men with him look tough, but dey is kinda young. Mebbe he look for trouble."

"Maybe he'll find it here if he's looking. Along that line, I want you to have Pete and Nick each to send me two of their toughest and steadiest hands. Tell them to be here by tonight, and to bring their arms. I want you to leave Thad with Nick, just to keep him out of this trouble."

Louie nodded, told Thad to get his bedroll, that he would be staying with Nick for a few days, and the two of them left.

Lord Ewing and his entourage arrived at noon the next day, he riding in a covered buggy, with four riders and a cook wagon.

"It's good to see you, Lord Ewing, come in and eat dinner, you and your men, and we can talk," Dunigan greeted him.

"I'm damn glad to be here, Dunigan. That trip was most uncomfortable and my chef cannot put out a decent repast with the foods you have in this god-forsaken country. I hope you have something better, but I doubt it," Ewing sneered.

"It ain't fancy, but it's filling, and you can do a day's work on it," Dunigan replied.

Dunigan eyed the five men with Ewing. One was obviously a cowman, as his clothes and accouterments were neat but worn, and he looked like any man who'd been around cattle. The wagon driver was well dressed and looked like what Dunigan thought an English butler transplanted to Nebraska should look like.

The other three were more interesting. They were all young, nattily dressed mostly in black and had their guns tied down. Two of them even wore two pistols and all were carrying a lot of silver buckles and conchos. They all appeared to be gunfighters with limited experience, but they could be dangerous.

Everyone went over to Abner's fire and got a plate full of

beef, beans, and rice, found a sitting place and started to eat. Dunigan watched Ewing as he ate, sort of mincing around the plate, looking disgusted. Dunigan saw that the rest were eating heartily, so he didn't worry. Ewing quit eating and threw his plate away, mumbling something about filth. This seemed to be a signal to the three gunfighters who flung their plates in the dirt. One got up and stormed up to Abner, calling him a 'nigger son of a bitch.' Abner knocked him flat. There was a blur of movement at Dunigan's side and another of the gunfighter's shirts was pinned to the wagon he was leaning on by a knife thrown by Regino Herrera, one of the reinforcements sent over from Pete's crew. By this time, Dunigan's men had Ewing's bunch covered, and Dunigan sought to restore order.

"You men get rid of your arms. You are guests in my camp, so make no more trouble."

"As for you, Ewing, make sure your hands mind their manners around my outfit, if they want to keep on living. This outfit don't back down to nobody!"

Dunigan turned to Ewing. "Milord, I hope we can smooth over this little fracas and get on with our business. I take it from your presence here that you have come to count the cattle and approve the second payment of $15 per head, I know the arrangements are pending. The cattle are in two herds, one on this side of the river and one below the river. You could count one herd today and one tomorrow, or both tomorrow, if you prefer."

Ewing rose to his feet, sucked in his little pot belly as best he could, and said, "Dunigan, I don't propose to pay any more money for these cattle until they arrive at my ranch at War House Lake, so there is no need to count them here. My word as a member of the British ruling class is sufficient for you to be on your way, and you will be paid in full in Montana, if and when you get there."

"Ewing, you will pay as agreed or forfeit the $50,000 you have already paid in. We have a contract that stipulates it and Colonel Archer here at the fort can adjudicate it as the army has authority here," Dunigan replied quietly but with authority.

"I have no intention of submitting my affairs to the dubious judgment of some frontier army subaltern, and I demand that you drive the cattle on to Montana at once!" Ewing roared, becoming red faced and cutting glances at his three gunhands.

Things got very quiet then, but the silence was broken by the click of cocking hammers. One of the fighters glanced to his left and he saw that Abner was standing over that way, enfilading all three with a double-barrelled shotgun, whose hammers were the source of the clicking. Each of them relaxed his hands away from his pistols, making sure the movement was interpreted as nonviolent.

Dunigan spoke evenly and quietly. "Ewing, you have three choices: count the cows and pay the $15, call off the deal and ride away, or see what Colonel Archer says about the contract. Take your pick."

"I have no intention of doing anything of the kind, Dunigan. I may cut out two thousand cows here and drive them home, as I have paid for that many already," Ewing blustered.

"You may take what you got coming here if you want, but it ain't two thousand. It's less than fifteen hundred at $35 per head, according to the contract, and in this deal the contract rules," Dunigan answered quietly. "You think it over and give me your answer by tomorrow morning because I can make other arrangements. But if I haven't heard anything by eight o'clock tomorrow morning I will assume you mean to forfeit your down payment and I will dispose of the cattle elsewhere."

Ewing was beet red and trembling so much he was unable to speak. It was hot at that time of the day and Dunigan thought the man might collapse from apoplexy. He didn't want him to die that way because it would complicate his plans.

Ewing regained a portion of his composure, turned on his gunfighters and screamed, "Du-du-doooo something!"

The three men looked at Dunigan and the six men around him, but made no move. There was a pregnant silence that was finally broken by one of them. "I didn't sign on for these kinds of odds, Ewing, I don't want nuthin' to do with this deal."

He turned and walked to his horse, followed by the other two. They mounted and rode out to the east.

"Well, milord, what's it going to be? Because it looks like there's not going to be any gunplay. Please let me know by eight in the morning, as I said before."

Ewing did not answer, as he had already turned and walked away, followed by his cowboss. Dunigan felt he would know soon enough and worried no more about it.

At six the next morning, as they were eating breakfast, Ewing's cowboss showed up. He introduced himself as Joe Hansen, and was invited to eat. As he ate, Hansen related that

Ewing had left the afternoon before, but had wired instructions to his bank to pay the $15, and authorized Hansen to tell the bank to do so after counting and ascertaining that the numbers were right.

"Mister Dunigan," he said, "I want you to know that I work for Lord Ewing as his ranch foreman, and I'm a cowhand not a gunhand so I'm not hunting trouble. I will count the cattle and wire the bank to pay the money and I'll be at the ranch to receive the cows, but I don't know nothin' about this deal and really don't want to. I just do my job and draw my wages."

"That's fine with me," Dunigan responded. "If you want, we can count both bunches pretty quick and you can leave tonight or tomorrow. We can get started right away."

"Fine with me, let's do it."

Dunigan dispatched the four drovers back to the two herds with instructions to have the cattle ready to count. Dunigan's group saddled up and rode off with Hansen to Nick's herd. They were bunched and ready to count when they got there and the count was completed by ten o'clock. Dunigan and Hansen rode off to Pete's herd and arrived just before dinner. After they ate, they chose fresh mounts and counted the herd—5,108 cows when all the counts were reconciled. Dunigan, Hansen, and Dunigan's group loped back to the telegraph station at Ft. McPherson.

Once there, Hansen wired the Ewing bank to transfer the money to Gerard Alton at the Bank of St. Louis. About two hours later a wire came back to Dunigan from Alton confirming the transaction. By then it was nearly six o'clock and Dunigan invited Hansen to eat supper with them before leaving in the morning. Hansen accepted, but with some trepidation as the events of the day before were still fresh in his mind. Counting the herds with Dunigan and seeing his outfit had convinced him that it was a professional outfit and not a bunch of gunhands. Abner put on a good spread of steak, rice and beans, and Hansen put away his share.

After supper, he and Louie Courrell and Dunigan drank coffee and talked of the trail ahead. Of particular interest was Hansen's opinion of the trails east and west of the Big Horns. Hansen had been both ways and thought the eastern trail was the easiest and fastest, but said the west side was passable, had good water and the Indians were friendlier.

Dunigan felt Hansen had spoken truthfully, but gave no

indication which way he was going. He did not want Ewing to know that in advance, in case he decided to try to steal the cattle. Hansen said his goodbyes and everyone turned in.

In the morning, Dunigan sent word to Nick to throw his herd on the trail and move out. He sent word for Pete to do the same, then had a powwow with Louie, telling him to scout the trail to Fetterman and beyond and to meet him there. The herds would follow the old Mormon trail paralleling the Platte to Fetterman and as it was well marked, Louie and Thad would not have to be too diligent until they passed Fetterman. Also, the army was actively patrolling between Forts McPherson and Fetterman and any hostiles stayed pretty well clear. Dunigan thought the passage would be pretty quiet and would take about two weeks.

Dunigan told Louie they would have to make a decision at Fetterman whether to go to east or west of the Big Horns and information on what they could expect from the Indians would be the determining factor, so he should concentrate on that aspect. He told Louie they probably had at least a hundred cattle to use for payments for safe passage.

Louie took Thad Scott with him and set out. George Harris was to scout directly north of the trail as far as he could, but that he would be careful as the area was the traditional range of the Sioux, who, while not overly hostile, were not especially friendly, either.

The drive to Ft. Fetterman was quiet. Everyone was rested, the trail was well marked and had plenty of grass. Most of the calving was over and there was plenty of water as the trail paralleled the Platte. The only incident occurred when Dunigan arrived at Nick's herd to spend the night and found the Grimes family with the herd.

Dunigan had completely forgotten about them in the press of getting paid by Ewing, and Nick had decided just to keep them with him. Dunigan watched them that night, and figured Nick had just about decided to settle down in the near future with a ready-made family. Dunigan was still wary of trouble from Ewing and really didn't want the nester family to be put in the middle of a shooting war, but he couldn't do much about it now.

July 19th brought them to Ft. Fetterman, and Dunigan rode in to get acquainted with Lt. Col. O. B. Keller and to give him the letters he carried from Major Layton in San Antonio.

Colonel Keller was cordial to Dunigan, having already received Major Layton's letter. A hearty, bluff Irishman, young for a frontier officer, Keller shared current scouting reports, Indian movements and attitudes, and other topics of interest to Dunigan. He invited him to dinner at his quarters that night.

Dunigan arrived at Colonel Keller's quarters at precisely seven, and was met by the Colonel and Mrs. Keller, a petite blonde lady from Frankfort, Kentucky. This naturally brought up the subject of Dunigan's engagement to Amanda Green. Mrs. Keller had heard of the family, but did not know them personally. However, she did know some of the Kentuckians Dunigan had met in his visit the fall before. It was a pleasant meal, well suited to the frontier environment in which they all lived. Dunigan made his goodbyes about ten.

About ten the next morning, both scouting groups, Courrell's and Harris's, rode in about ten minutes apart. They all sat down together to discuss what was happening.

Louie led off. "John, I made a deal wit Wash-a-kie and de Wind River Band. Dey take the eighty cattle and dey will guarantee passage up to the Crows around Yellowtail. Dey make sure no Indian bother you tru de whole Big Horn basin, and if anybody attack, dey help you fight. I want you meet dat chief. He is good man, and he does what he says. I got some bad news, too, but I save it coz it ain't too bad, and I want to hear what George find out east of de Big Horns."

George Harris's report was that the Sioux were in their hunting range, not bothering anybody, letting the wagons through and pretty much in a peaceful mode, but that there had been some fights with buffalo hunters and miners in Montana. He said he had picked up a rumor about a shipment of rifles off loaded at Ft. Union on the Missouri, by the Cameron Ranch Co., and taken west by wagon and that Gall's band had met the wagons somewhere below Ft. Peck. Gall was reported to have around forty warriors with him. George said the Crow were quiet and most of the other Indians were giving the Sioux a fairly wide berth.

Louie Courrell broke in at that point. "I hear dat from the Shoshone, dats my bad news. Dey say Gall and his band got new Winchester repeaters, 'yellow boys,' and dey git dem from the English, so I guess dey make deal, no?"

Dunigan took all this in, thought a minute, then said, "Looks like it, Louie. From what you all have said, it appears that Ewing wants to get Gall and his Sioux to raid us and take the cattle. For that reason I have decided to go west of the Big Horns, but they'll probably come after us there, too."

"Louie, I want you and Thad to spy out canyons and ravines where we can fort up to keep the cattle safe and fight off the Indians between here and War Horse Lake. I'm going to give you two extra men, so we will always know what to do. Also, that'll leave you free to stay in touch with Wash-a-kie for support.

"George, I'm going to do the same for you, but your main job is to locate and keep an eye on Gall's band, because that is Ewing's attack force. We must have advance warning of the attack."

Dunigan caught his breath and was silent for a while. George Harris was contemplating his job and didn't like it. Finally, he spoke. "Boss, it ain't gonna be easy to do. These Sioux bands are touchy, and if we get in their way, they'll just take us out. You know how they are when they're hunting, and any stranger they see is in line for a close hair cut."

"George, I know what you're up against, but we now know what we are looking for—Gall's band. You can probably get a good idea where they are from wagon scouts, miners, army patrols, and the like. If they hit us in the mountains, we're probably all right unless we get surprised. What can be really bad is if they wait for us out on the prairie where we won't be able to protect the cattle and ourselves at the same time. Our only help there would be the army, and that's a long way out for them. I think if you approach the scout from the point of finding where Gall is, and where it looks like the attack will come we may be able to handle it. George, if you can do that, leave one man to keep an eye out and get back to me quick.

"Louie, maybe the Shoshone can scout for us above Big Horn Basin. It's Crow country isn't it? Maybe the Crows are peaceful enough or we can trade beeves for scouting with them. I don't think the Sioux care if they make any other tribes mad, but they usually stay out of any ranges they don't claim as their own. Think it's worth a try?"

"Yeah, John, I work on it."

"Louie, how long did you stay with the Shoshone?"

"We stay dere bout four days. We have a big time dere. Dey have big celebration, plenty elk meat and some dog, too. Thad, he don't like dog too good but he like other things there."

"Louie, you didn't get that boy mixed up with any Indian girl, did you?"

"Well, John, you know how young boys are. The Shoshone women are pretty, you know, and very hospitable to travelers. They gave us our own teepee and dat first night a young girl, bout fifteen I guess, came in Thad's buffalo robes with him. I don' think he knew what to do, and he was scared, but that girl she calmed him down and show him what he suppose to do. Then everything all right. She came back every night and Thad, he don' want to leave that camp but he came on when I made him. He kinda drawed down, though."

"That girl, she Wash-a-kie's granddaughter and de old man, he took a shine to dat boy. He didn't want to see him go."

"What was the girl's name, Louie?"

"They call her, 'Berry Finder,' in English, John. I don' know how you say it in Shoshone, but mebbe Thad know?"

"Berry Finder, huh, I'll ask Thad about her," Dunigan said smiling.

"Don' be too hard on him. I think he like her pretty good."

Dunigan asked George to drop by the herds on his way out and tell Pete and Nick and their segundos to come in that afternoon late. "I want to make medicine with them for the rest of the drive."

That afternoon, Dunigan went to see Colonel Keller in the fort, as he had arranged over dinner the night before. Dunigan questioned him exhaustively about the Indians' attitude toward trail herds, but found out little he didn't already know, except that the army patrols were active all the way into the Big Horn Basin. He told Colonel Keller everything his scouts had reported, which was of interest to the colonel.

Dunigan then broached the subject of horses, and Colonel Keller said he would be in the market for quite a few as his stock was somewhat depleted.

"Colonel Keller, I'll have about 150 to 175 horses when I get back in and I'll sell about all of them. There are about thirty first-class horses that would do for officer's mounts, real good ones. Over a hundred that would be good remount horses and the balance not so good. Might make pack horses or something. Anyway, if you're interested, I suggest we take a ride in the morning and you can inspect them."

"Yes, John, I'd like that. I want to be prepared if we have to take the field, and it looks like we might."

Dunigan went back to his wagon to meet with his herd bosses, Pete and Nick, who had ridden in.

"What's up boss?" Pete asked.

Dunigan explained what he knew and assumed about Ewing and Galls's band of Sioux. Then he delineated his plan to complete the drive.

"First off, I want the herds closer now, three to five miles apart. The cattle are going well so that shouldn't be a problem. I want to make the rest of the drive, which is about three hundred miles, on a pretty lean basis. We are going to leave any equipment we don't need right here. I think each herd can go with one wagon and I'm going to leave my outfit here. Anything anybody needs to buy or do, do it now because we will have no more stops until the finish.

"Also, Nick's crew will be responsible for continuous contact with Louie Courrell and Pete will do the same with George Harris. We have to have contact because we are pretty sure we will be hit. If it's in the Big Horn Basin we will probably run both herds into a canyon and fight them off at its mouth. If we get hit out in the open, we'll just have to do the best we can to protect the cattle, but from all indications it's going to be around the mountains and not on the prairie."

"When we left Fort McPherson, I kind of forgot about Lutie Grimes and her children and I understand she is still with your herd, Nick. We will leave our extra wagons and gear here and they can stay with it and watch it, because I sure don't want them anywhere near another Indian fight. That suit you, Nick?"

"Yeah, John, as I assume we'll all retrace the trail at least through here, and we owe them some money for cookin' and washin'. They'll be all right."

"Nick, we'll leave enough grub for them in our wagon, and I'll pay them $50 just to watch the stuff, and care for the extra wagon horses. I'll pick out a site tomorrow, and clear the whole deal with Colonel Keller.

"We'll be on our way day after tomorrow. Any questions?"

That night he told Abner his plans and to transfer their possibles to Nick's wagon and that Abner would be working directly with him on their scouts. This suited Abner fine as he was tired of cooking. He told Abner what he knew of everything that lay ahead of them on the trail as he had instructed Pete and Nick to do with their crews.

Dunigan met Colonel Keller precisely at eight the following

morning, and they rode to both herds to look at the remudas. By dinner they had seen them all, and stopped for dinner at Nick's camp. Riding back to the fort, they settled on $78 a head as Dunigan explained he would be using some for transportation from the fort to the nearest railhead. He also explained to Colonel Keller about the Grimes, and his wish to leave extra stock and equipment there. Colonel Keller said it would be all right and took him to a place about half a mile from the fort that had an old corral for the horses and would be generally suitable. When they reached the fort they had gone through everything and Dunigan bade him goodbye, saying he should be back in five or six weeks to deliver the horses.

The wagons were delivered to their storage spot that afternoon and some of the hands came along and helped fix up a good shelter for the Grimes family and repaired the old corral for them. Dunigan and Abner moved to Nick's camp along with Chito, and all preparations were complete for the final phase of the drive, which got underway at daylight on July 22, 1872.

Leaving Ft. Fetterman, the herds headed northwest, gradually leaving the Platte valley and heading to the Powder River crossing. There was good grass, but water was scarce as they moved away from the Platte, but there were only a couple of days when the cattle were not well watered. All went quietly the first week and Dunigan was feeling less apprehensive.

Chapter 30

About sixty miles out of Fetterman, Dunigan was shaken awake about 2:30 in the morning. It was Nick, in stocking feet, who woke him.

"Wake up, John, we got a bad problem."

Dunigan rolled out and pulled on his boots. "What's wrong, Nick?"

"John, the two-to-six nighthawks couldn't find the earlier pair when they went to take over. They looked good and found Tom Rankin with his throat cut and Manuel Garcia out cold, their horses gone and maybe some cattle, although we won't be able to tell until daylight."

"Was the remuda hit?"

"No, John, just the two horses."

"Is Garcia conscious yet?"

"Yeah, but he doesn't know anything, except he thinks it was about midnight when it happened. He's all right except for a bump on his head, but Tom's dead."

Dunigan took a moment to formulate his plans. "Nick, Louie and Thad got in last night. Wake 'em up. I'll need them for tracking. Also, I'll need three of your men to go with us, I'll get Abner and Chito ready, but we can't do much before daylight, which is less than three hours away. If they've taken cattle we should be able to catch up with them pretty quick. I'll want Abel Castro in this bunch, and have the cook make us something to eat. I want to start at first light."

Dunigan woke Abner and Chito, told them to catch their best horses and one for him and to be ready to move right after they ate.

After breakfast and saddling up, Dunigan gathered the seven others.

"You all know by now what happened. When we can see we will spread out around the herd to pick up the trail, and we will follow it to recapture our property and punish whoever did this. Whoever finds the trail first, stop and signal, as Louie and I want to find out just what they've gotten off with, and how many of them there are. It should be light enough to see in about fifteen minutes, so be ready."

They mounted and rode out at daylight, circling the herd to pick up the rustlers' trail. Dunigan was closest to the herd, and rode past Brindy Polaris. She was looking around as if she was missing something and sort of glared at Dunigan as if were his fault. From her attitude, Dunigan was sure the outlaws had driven off some cattle. He was quickly proved right as Louie Courrell picked up the trail, estimating it at about fifty head. They set off following the trail at a fast pace as the rustlers had about six hours' head start, Dunigan figured. The trail was easily followed as it was dry and the dust and broken grass stems were plainly visible on the open prairie, as it led off to the southwest.

Louie and Thad got a mile or so ahead so they could spot the dust of the outlaws' herd before they spotted the pursuit. About ten o'clock, Dunigan stopped on seeing Louie and Thad coming back. They rode up and Louie said, "John, I spot de dust bout three to four miles ahead. Dey been goin' fast and a wagon join them 'bout where I see the dust."

"How many of them are there, Louie?"

"Tree, mebbe four men wid de cattle, I don' know in de wagon. I don' tink too many for us to handle. Look like a buffalo hunter's party to me."

"I'd sure like to get around 'em. Them buffalo hunters can do some damage out in the open," Dunigan mused.

"I think mebbe they stop at de next creek to rest and eat. If we go sout'west we hit another creek that joins the one they should stop at, den we can go up dose creeks and mebbe they not see us."

"You think they'll see us if we light a shuck to the creeks and then come up on them through the bottoms?"

"I think dat work good, Jean, let's do it."

They set a fast pace off to the southwest, and hit a creek bottom nearly a mile out. They turned up the creek for another two miles until they ran into the confluence of another creek that ran due north. They felt safe as the trees and general humidity had masked any dust they might have raised.

"Louie, how far up this creek do you figure they are?"

"Not more dan one mile," he answered.

"Okay, men, no talking now, and no noise. Anything that is clinking or squeaking, fix it and tie it down. We will ride quietly as we can from here on. Stop on signal from me or Louie."

The eight men wound their way through the creek bottom for nearly a mile when they heard the clang of a pan, perhaps 150 yards to the north. They all stopped instantly, dismounted, discarding spurs and anything else that might betray them. Thad Scott was left in charge of the horses, much to his chagrin.

The men slipped quietly through the trees, staying well back in the shadows until they could see the outlaw camp clearly. There were three men dressed in hides and a woman with two children. There was another man mounted out by the herd they had stolen, tending to them. Dunigan told Louie to watch that man and if he tried to fight or run away, to kill him.

Getting as close as they could, Dunigan and five men then broke cover and strode to the cooking fire. One of the men, a big rawboned man in greasy buckskins, jumped up to grab for his rifle, but was quickly shot down by Chito. The others, seeing they were outnumbered badly, raised their hands as did the mounted man by the herd. The big man was holding his thigh, glaring daggers, blood seeping between his fingers. Dunigan's men disarmed everyone, tied their hands and tended the big man's wound, which was not serious as Chito's bullet had passed through the fleshy part of his thigh.

A wagon was loaded mainly with buffalo hides, and was carrying a fat blonde woman and two children dressed like the others in dirty buckskin. Over a cook fire, meat was roasting; a cow carcass hung in a nearby tree with one hind quarter gone: the meat being cooked. The cowhide had been skinned off and was lying under the carcass. Dunigan picked up the hide to make sure it was branded DG, it was, then turned to them.

He said to the woman, "You married to any of these men?"

The big man answered for her. "She's my woman and the little boy is mine, if it's any notion o' yours."

"You hunting buffalo out here?" asked Dunigan.

"Yep."

"You should have kept at it and not gone to stealing my cows. You'll find that Indians would have been less dangerous,"

Dunigan said.

"We found them cows about five miles east o' here. We jist figgered em to be strays, finders keepers. Kin you prove them's yours?"

"We tracked you from our herd to here, after one of my hands was murdered and another pretty badly damaged. I can prove all I need to prove, like those two horses were ridden by my men last night. You haven't even unsaddled them, and all those cows bear my brand. You are guilty of murder, horse and cow stealing, but since there ain't no law out here, I reckon we'll just settle this on our own."

Dunigan turned to the woman. "Pack up your things, hitch up a team, and you and the sprouts get ready to move. We'll give you a rifle when you're ready to go, but make it fast and take all that meat with you. These men won't be able to choke it down."

Things became pretty clear to the captured men about this time and the lad who had been holding the herd blurted out, "I don't have nuthin' to do with all this. I was at the camp all the time with Rosie and the kids."

The boy didn't look to be more than seventeen and had not been armed when captured. Dunigan looked at the woman and the other men for confirmation and they nodded, except for the wounded man, who continued a malevolent glare at Dunigan.

"All right son, you can go with them, but be quick about it. I want you out of here in ten minutes." He was cut loose.

The two young men began trying to explain away their guilt, and blame it all on the big man, obviously the leader and brains of the pathetic outfit. Dunigan listened a bit, but had already made up his mind. "Chito, make two nooses, and set them in that cottonwood tree over there. Thad, bring up Manuel and Tom's horses. These two can take a ride on them."

"Abel, you and Abner cut some rawhide strips off that cow-hide and get something to sew them with."

The speed of decision on punishment took most of Dunigan's men by surprise. Hanging cow thieves was common enough, but wrapping a man in a green hide to be squeezed to death when it dried in the sun was not often done, and made all them feel a bit uneasy, but the big man had been identified as Tom's killer, so they felt the punishment was just.

The wagon group was ready, and Dunigan saw them off to the south, and told Louie to follow them for at least five miles before catching up.

The two young men did not face hanging bravely. They protested their youth and innocence and said they had learned their lesson, but Dunigan was unmoved. Abner and Abel bound the big man tightly in the fresh hide and dragged him to where there would be no shade.

"Damn you to hell, you son of a bitch, damn you and yours for all eternity. I curse your soul forever," he said and spat at Dunigan, who paid no attention.

They put the two men on the horses, nooses set on their necks. Dunigan looked at them and said, "Ask forgiveness from your Lord."

They stared blankly back and the horses were led out from under them. Both necks were broken instantly, as they struggled not at all.

Dunigan said, "Thad, get some canvas or bark, and print 'Cow Thief' on two squares, and 'Cow Thief and Murderer' on the other and pin them on."

They put out the fire then and headed the cattle back toward the herd. Dunigan rode over to look at the ringleader before he left. He was flushed and gasping as the hide was shrinking quickly in the hot sun.

"You won't have too long, hider, to contemplate your ruined life." He rode away to join the others.

There was little talk on the way back.

Louie Courrell caught up with them about midafternoon and they got to the main herd about seven. Brindy Polaris trotted out to greet her sisters, but she knew one was missing and ran about bawling for a while, then settled down as the stolen cattle moved into the herd.

Supper that night was a sober affair, not much talking or joking. Like all cattlemen, Dunigan's crew disliked doing these things they had done that day, but the lack of law in the west made it necessary, and they all realized that. It didn't make it any easier. Dunigan and Louie Courrell conferred that night. Louie telling him he had contacted Wash-a-kie, who would help in return for the eighty steers. According to Louie, Wash-a-kie's warriors were already roaming over the Big Horn Basin in search of hostile activity.

The herds resumed their normal pace the next morning. It was about the same as before, but the herd bosses had to watch closely for signs of the cattle getting hot. Both herds were stopping a long time for dinner, but driving earlier and later. The weather had been hot, but not oppressively so, and water was still fairly abundant. If the cattle could be watered often, overheating was not troublesome, but Nick and Pete were very watchful. The Powder River was crossed without trouble, its flow down to only about two feet above the ford bottom. One of Pete's calves floated off downstream, and had to be roped and pulled out, but that was the only incident.

A couple of days after crossing the Powder, the Big Horn range was seen to the northeast. The herds were generally heading northwest for the Nowood River, following it to the Big Horn, through a pass in the mountains that Louie had scouted. Following along, the Big Horns loomed before them in all of their splendor, but lacking a white cap. Dunigan felt they would have one when the outfit returned, however.

Thad met them to guide them through the pass and stayed with the herd until they were well into the basin. He reported that the Shoshone had seen no evidence of the Sioux around, but were still hearing rumors of Gall's band, well armed and mounted, but still east of the Big Horns.

North of Gooseberry Creek, as they came in close to the Big Horn River, Louie rejoined them with some Indians. Dunigan stopped early, made a camp between the herds, slaughtered a fat calf, and generally made preparations for a banquet, for one of the Indians was Wash-a-kie, chief of the Wind River Shoshone, and a great man.

Abner cooked a feast, which was attended by Pete, Nick, Abel Castro, Lem Bracken, and all the Indians, and as luck would have it, George Harris and Chito Guerrico, who rode in from their scouting east of the Big Horns.

Dunigan broke out some whiskey, guitars and fiddles were sent for, and a general celebration was held. Dunigan spent most of his time with the chief. They got along well, as Wash-a-kie spoke some English, and Louie had given both men a big build-up to one another. Dunigan, Louie, Wash-a-kie, and George Harris got into a huddle to pool their information.

Wash-a-kie was a great chief among the Shoshone. He had made peace with the whites by that time but was renowned as a great warrior. It was told that once when confronted by a band of Crow, he and the Crow chief met and decided only the two of them would fight and settle the matter between them, to save some of their warriors' lives.

They had a battle-royal, taking most of the day, but at the end, Wash-a-kie won and killed the Crow chief. He then honored him as a brave warrior by cutting out his heart and eating it.

He had led the Wind River Band for many years, keeping the peace with the whites, but also with the Sioux and Crow, which also bordered him. His band had dwindled, but prospered, unlike the unlucky Arapahoe. Dunigan talked with him most of that night, enchanted with his story, and in the end, thought maybe the difference between the Shoshone and the Arapahoes might just be the leadership of Wash-a-kie.

The consensus from all the sources was that they would be attacked while in the Big Horn Basin, as the Sioux wouldn't be encroaching too much on other tribes, although the Shoshone considered it their range, but didn't get there often. George Harris confirmed that, as he had seen Gall's band crossing the mountains about opposite the north fork of the Big Horn River. They all agreed there was a good defensible position up a canyon off the Nowood Valley, with room enough for both herds, but narrow and high for defense. Louie said they could be in position a day before the Sioux could reach them.

Wash-a-kie ventured, "That good place, Shoshone fight, too. Gall bad injun, Shoshone no want in valley."

"Chief, we can hold him out of the canyon. It would be better if you ran off Gall's horses, and threatened his rear," Dunigan said and Louie took up the chant.

"You can steal Gall's ponies, get scalps, run 'em off out your land."

Wash-a-kie nodded assent.

"We catchem Sioux ponies, we keep watch on Gall. We tell Louie where, when, come Sioux. Gall bad injun. We fix."

Dunigan was satisfied with those arrangements.

"Louie, you and the chief work to make sure we don't get surprised, so stay on this side where you can get to us. We're leaving in the morning for Nowood Valley."

"George, I want you to go into the mountains to watch our rear. I'll make provisions for an attack on us from behind, but I need to know if they're coming that way. Louie can probably tell if they decide to hit us from the mountains, but I want you there to tell us exactly where they are coming from. We will want you to keep in touch with us in the canyon, as we will have information from Louie about their movements, and if you see them trying to get in behind us we may be able to ambush them on their way up the mountains."

"Boss, we will leave first thing in the morning, and by the time this is over, don't shoot any mountain goats 'cause it might be me," Harris answered.

Next morning, the herds were off the bedground at daylight, hurrying along. Dunigan and Abner set a fast pace in order to find the canyon before sunset. About three in the afternoon, they crossed the Big Horn above its confluence with the Nowood at a shallow ford, continuing east to the second canyon, which was steep and narrow. About a mile in, the canyon widened a bit around a spring and there was about three hundred acres of grass between the spring and a bluff, which closed the canyon on the north. Behind the bluff, Black Butte rose to nearly 10,000 feet, according to Dunigan's maps.

"Abner, this couldn't be better. Our crew could hold off the whole Sioux nation here and with plenty of water it would take them a month to root us out of here."

"It sho is fine, boss. Them Indians gonna play hell getting our cows," Abner answered solemnly.

"Let's make camp by the spring, and we'll meet them and bring them in in the morning." Abner nodded and went about making camp. Dunigan went up on the canyon rim to pick defensive positions along it as it rose.

Dunigan planned to man both sides of the canyon, the better shots with the Sharps .50s higher and farther back, and the repeaters lower down. He found a couple of gullies leading into the canyon walls that were about the right size to hold the horses. The only thing wrong was that there wasn't an abundance of trees about with which to make barricades and he wanted two, about two hundred feet apart. If he had time he could find enough timber, so it didn't bother him much and there were some trees on the canyon rim.

Exploring, Dunigan found game trails along the rim, and even a foot track up the bluff at the back of the canyon.

Dunigan met Nick's herd about a mile south of the ford at eight the next morning and guided them into the canyon. He drove the first herd all the way to the bluff end and tentatively set up a dead line between the two herds at the spring, not that he thought they wouldn't mix, but left some drovers to keep them apart for the time being. The rest of the men went to felling trees for barricades.

By the time Pete's herd got into the canyon, it was a beehive of activity, trees falling off the rim of the cliff and horsemen dragging them into place, with ax men trimming them for barricades. Pete stopped his herd across the spring from Nick's and left a couple of riders to keep the herds from mingling, as Nick had done, but Brindy Polaris had taken over the job from the riders, and was moving her strays back to the herd by herself. While the riders were still there, she turned back several cows from Pete's herd and was loping back and forth. So far, the cattle hadn't mixed.

Pete's men joined Nick in building two log barricades, one at the mouth of the canyon, about four feet high and a second one about 150 yards farther into the canyon. The second barricade was bigger and taller, in order to stop any attack that would penetrate the first barricade and limit the mobility of the attackers. Neither was to be manned, as the defenders were to be placed on the rim of the canyon, but if the Indians got caught between the barricades, they would be subject to a murderous crossfire.

There were soon enough logs for both barricades, so Dunigan put most of the men to preparing rifle pits along the canyon rim. He arranged a defense in depth, aimed at defending the entry to the canyon, but that could also repulse a flank attack. He envisioned putting men armed with Sharps .50s higher up, as he wanted the men with repeaters closest to the barricades, where their increased firepower would be more effective at closer range. Besides, the men who carried Sharps were usually better shots, and more effective at longer ranges. They would be better able to protect the flanks as they were higher up.

Dunigan had the remudas put in the gully he had found, but had each man keep his best horse picketed by the spring, and they would be saddled before the battle as a means of escape or attack, depending how the fight went.

By midafternoon, most all preparations were complete. Louie Courrell and Thad Scott rode in and went to the camp established by the spring to see if there was anything left over as they hadn't eaten. Dunigan met them there.

"What're the Sioux doing, Louie?" he asked.

"They have crossed de mountains, Jean, and dey are 'bout thirty miles north of here. Dey be here tomorrow mornin," Louie reported.

"How many?"

"Oh, 'bout de same, like forty, and dey got some repeaters, some one shot, and some old musket. Dey well arm' for Injuns."

"What about the Shoshone?" asked Dunigan.

"Shoshone back to west, but dey keep a good eye on de Sioux. Dey plan to steal all horses tomorrow night. Shoshone watch to see if Sioux go back up in de mountains to attack, and dey tell me in plenty time."

"That's good, Louie. I don't think they can get in here, but if they do all bets are off, but we should hurt them pretty bad when they rush us, and if the Shoshone put 'em afoot, it should just about end it. We don't want to wipe them out and we won't pursue them if they leave, but we're gonna hurt them hard, and if they leave, you and Thad follow them to make sure they don't come back. Once we get word from you or George, we'll move out the cattle."

Thad and Louie left not long after that, covering their tracks. Dunigan put out picket scouts to give early warning in case the Sioux were swifter than Louie had predicted, but arranged a relief so the guards stayed out until the Indians appeared. George Harris and Chito Guerrico appeared at the bluff about supper time, tied their mounts, and scrambled down the bluff. As he watched them, he picked out a place where one rifleman, protected by a rock fall, could cover the trail down and deny the Indians entry to the canyon by the foot trail.

Back at the camp, he detailed Abel Castro to that post, knowing that he would do plenty damage if the Indians tried that way. Dunigan also instructed Abner to take cover behind the second barricade, to take down any Indians that might get through. Pete's cook was given that job, also. Dunigan had already told his crews of the whole plan at supper and every man knew what was to happen, where his post was, and what he was suppose to do. Dunigan felt he was prepared to do battle and slept well that night.

The next morning, the picket scout came in to report the Indians had been sighted about three miles north of the canyon. Every one of the hands was in place and all Dunigan could do was hope his preparations were right. He figured his men would acquit themselves well and the rest was in God's hands. He could do no more to control the situation, so he took a position on the canyon rim, just in front of the second barricade.

From ten o'clock on, the men began seeing glimpses of Indians, but remained still and hidden from them. Dunigan felt they were trying to reconnoiter his position, and work up their nerve to attack. No Indian had been seen on the flanks, and Dunigan did not expect attacks from those directions, as the mountainsides were impossibly rugged, but could be traversed with difficulty, so he couldn't be entirely sure.

About one, the cooks circulated with meat sandwiches and coffee. No Indians had been seen for over an hour, but some noises had been heard beyond the river.

When the attack came, it came slowly, and from an unexpected direction.

It began with six Indians racing north to south, parallel to the mountains toward the canyon mouth. This put the Indians in range of the Sharps riflemen for a longer time than coming straight in from the river, and as a consequence, three never reached the canyon mouth, but the three that did began trying to tear down the barricade.

The Sharps shooters could still see them from higher up, and killed one and wounded another before they partially pulled down a section of the logs. They had ripped a couple of logs down so that about a ten-foot section was only two and a half or three feet high. As the survivors retreated, the main band broke out over the river to attack straight in.

Dunigan heard the boom of the Sharps again, and two more Indians dropped from their ponies, as well as one horse and rider. Several horsemen jumped the lowered barricade, others left their ponies and climbed over to fight afoot. Then the Winchesters, Spencers, and Henrys came into action with devastating fire. Indians and ponies were going down everywhere between the barricades. One Indian climbed the second barricade, only to be blown backward, Dunigan guessed, by Abner's shotgun. The Indians quickly saw it was a murderous death trap and hurriedly retreated from the crossfire.

Dunigan and his men waited some time for a second attack, but after half an hour, Dunigan decided it wouldn't come for a while. He got up and checked his men. There were no casualties except for one cowboy who had a scratch on his upper arm, probably caused by rock fragments from a bullet strike. Dunigan sent him back to the springs, where Abel and Abner could disinfect and bandage him.

Dunigan watched Jacko Easton come down from the canyon to be bandaged. He was laughing and joking with the hands and showing his wound. Dunigan thought, "Isn't that the way. The most experienced soldier gets wounded and wears it as a badge of honor."

Jacko was one of the strangest stories in a whole area of strange stories. He was in his midforties, the third son of a British peer. His father had bought Jacko a commission in the army in India, and there he had been cashiered over some irregularities in mess funds. He told Dunigan that another officer had stolen the money and he had been framed, mostly because he had a reputation for wildness, so it was relatively easy to do. Jacko then got a commission in the Confederate army and served with Jeb Stuart's forces throughout the war, emerging as only a captain.

That seemed strange to Dunigan, as most officers who served throughout the war came out as colonels or generals, but in light of what Dunigan found out later it was not surprising. An absolutely fearless horseman and a crack shot, Jacko was the embodiment of a cavalier. He had been observed more than once killing a coyote with a pistol from a running horse at a range of almost two hundred yards. He could have been the chief instructor at any cavalry school in the world, so great were his mounted proficiencies.

Dunigan had recognized those abilities when Jacko first came to work two years before and had tried to get him to take more responsibilities, but had failed. Puzzled, Dunigan had a talk with him about it, and that's when he learned about the deal in the Indian army. Jacko had told him, "Never again. If I'm not responsible, I can never again be blamed." So it had had an effect.

Jacko Easton was one of those early cowboys who lived by the creed of "Any work, any job, just as long as I can do it on horseback. If the work is on the ground, you can forget me."

That was the attitude of all the early cowboys, and one had to be careful because as long as there were plenty of riding jobs, most good hands would quit before they would work afoot. Jacko was one of those.

Chapter 31

From the rim of the canyon, Dunigan counted fourteen bodies between the barricades, and six Indian ponies down. He signaled for three men to follow him and they all went down to the canyon floor and checked the bodies. Only two Indians and four horses were still alive and these were quickly dispatched with a bullet to the brain. They scaled the canyon wall again to wait for another rush. Dunigan figured at least eighteen dead, so the Indian force had been at least halved and possibly worse, counting braves who were either dead now or dying, and the badly wounded.

Dunigan checked his watch. It was 4:30 in the afternoon. A lot of time had passed, but only about ten minutes of that had been actual fighting. He was proud of his outfit and thought that as savagely as the Indians had been mauled, that it was all over with. At least he hoped so.

About suppertime, Dunigan sent his men down to eat by threes and fours. He told them to bring back blankets as they would be spending the night in their rifle pits. Just before dark, the dead Indians were dragged out of the canyon and left where their brothers could get the bodies without getting shot at much. Nick, Pete, and Dunigan didn't get any sleep that night. One man in three was supposed to be awake at all times, but it had been an eventful day and the order wasn't always observed. Nevertheless, there was a lot of traffic between the canyon rim and the camp all night long, and there was always a pot of coffee on the fire. Abner kept one eye cocked at the bluff, but no intruders showed up.

All night there was wailing and yowling from across the

river, but about 4:00 A.M., there was a great uproar and a flurry of shots from the same direction, then more wailing. Dunigan supposed that was Wash-a-kie's band running off the Sioux ponies, and he warned his men to be on the lookout for Louie, as he might come in and Dunigan didn't want him shot accidentally.

Louie and Thad did come in, but it wasn't until two hours after daylight. Dunigan scrambled down to the canyon floor for whatever Louie might know.

"Well, Louie, tell me what's going on. You been by the Sioux camp this morning?"

"Jean, you don' have no mo' trouble. Dem Sioux got no mo' fight in dem. Wit what you kill yesterday and de Shoshone last night dere ain't no more dan ten left, and dey got about six ponies. De Shoshone get over thirty horses last night and kill another three or four Sioux. Even Gall is hurt, so dey gonna move out. Give 'em till after noon and dey be out de way."

"They better go south or we'll meet up again from what you say. Keep an eye on them till dinner, Louie, then come on back so we can get started."

"Okay, Jean, we be back for dinner."

Leaving only a couple of men up high, Dunigan brought the rest of the men off the canyon rim to get ready to move out. They dismantled enough of the big barricade to move Pete's herd behind it and it didn't look like the herds had mixed. Brindy Polaris looked a little peaked as she and a couple of her sisters had kept the herds from mixing for the better part of two days. Dunigan rode by and gave her his thanks, which she acknowledged by a shake of her massive head.

Louie and Thad rode in about dark, preceded by George Harris and Chito by half an hour. Both reported the Sioux were preceding south out of Big Horn Basin, to get back east of the Big Horns into their home range. Both reported that the party was badly mauled and dispirited. Dunigan ordered everyone to be ready to continue the drive the next day, with Pete's herd in the lead. Louie would scout ahead and arrange to meet Wash-a-kie at the head of the basin, where he would receive the eighty steers Dunigan had promised him for his help.

George Harris would cross back over the Big Horns to make sure no more attacks would come from there.

The cattle were moving at daylight and Nick let Pete get about three miles ahead before he started. Brindy Polaris was trolling back and forth, irked not to be leading everything, but eventually settling down to an even pace. Four days later, the herds stopped as they came out of the Big Horn Basin and met the Shoshone's under Wash-a-kie. Pete, Nick, Dunigan, and others cut out the eighty steers.

After the exchange, the old chief wanted to trade some of the horses the Shoshones had stolen from Gall's band for some colored horses Dunigan had. Wash-a-kie showed up with two bays and a black, and Dunigan wasted the rest of the day trading for a paint and a white-maned sorrel the old chief particularly admired.

Wash-a-kie had brought a couple of Crow chiefs with him and Dunigan gave them twenty steers to ease his further passage. In consultation with Louie Courrell, Dunigan kept the herds going straight up the Big Horn River, but meant to cut west to cross the Yellowstone at Pompey's Pillar, a landmark on the river where there was a good ford.

On September 1st, Dunigan first glimpsed Pompey's Pillar, expecting to meet George Harris and Chito there as he had instructed them to be there. When the herd arrived, only Chito was there and he informed Dunigan George had sent him on to get some wagon horses. The scouts had come upon a hunting party on the Tongue River that had had all their horses run off by a band of Sioux, but had fought them off. Two men were killed and the rest were immobilized without horses.

Chito gave Dunigan a note from Harris and Dunigan read it. The message was that they needed two teams to get moving again and that Harris was not sure, but thought one of the men in the party was Ewing's uncle, as he was English and they were headed to War Horse Lake. Chito said it would take about five days to pack them up and get back, so Dunigan detailed Abner to go with Chito and take two teams to pull the wagons.

Dunigan felt he had run into a bit of luck, for if the man was the old Earl, there might not be any more trouble with Ewing, as the old man would be grateful for being rescued. It was worth a trip anyway. He crossed the herds and put them on good feed to fill up for final delivery, and settled in to wait for the wagons. Louie and Thad rode in the next day and after reporting, Dunigan sent them out to find out as much as they could about what was afoot at Ewing's headquarters. Dunigan told them about the hunting party, warning Louie not to let on if he met Ewing.

On the fourth day, Dunigan could stand the inactivity no

longer so he saddled his horse, and taking Michael O'Grady with him, rode out to meet Harris and the wagon. He found them about a day's drive from the ford, fell in with them and introduced himself to the Englishman.

They shook hands and the Earl said, "Mister Dunigan, you don't know how grateful I am to you and your men. I am Arthur Coniston, Earl of Spey Marnock. My guides were killed by the red Indians, and Herbert, my valet, was wounded along with one of the teamsters. Your man Harris was a godsend. We were without horses and really didn't know where we were, as our guides were gone. I was on my way to my ranch at War Horse Lake and was engaging in a bit of sport on the way, shooting a few buffalo. Your man Abner has been very helpful with the wounded and we are all most grateful."

"Lord Coniston, I am driving two herds of cows to War Horse Lake so you can certainly travel along with us. These cows are going to Alan Ewing, who I think is your nephew and manager, so we will be glad to assist you in any way. By the way, I grew up on one of your properties in Ireland, near Fermoy."

"Well, isn't it a small world." Coniston then introduced Dunigan to the other members of his party, mostly servants and teamsters and a doctor, Thomas Hughes, an old friend and shooting companion.

Dunigan did what he could to hurry them along, eager to get back to the herds. They crossed the Yellowstone at twilight and camped with the herds that night. Dunigan told Pete and Nick to be ready to move at daylight. With Doctor Hughes and the Earl, Dunigan had a pleasant supper before turning in.

In his blankets that night, Dunigan mused over the day's events. He liked the two Englishmen. Coniston, about 72 or 73, seemed to be a kindly, unflappable gentleman who took the world as it came to him. Hughes, on the other hand, although Coniston's age, seemed more vigorous and more interested in the world around him. Later Dunigan learned that Hughes was an accomplished botanist who had collected a number of species of plants on his trip and would later catalogue them in a small volume that would prove helpful to botanists of a later age. Because of his animosity toward Ewing, Dunigan was probably drawn to the older man, because he felt Ewing was stealing more from his uncle than he was from the people he was doing business with in his uncle's name.

When they resumed the drive the following day, Dunigan

estimated by celestial navigation they were about a week from War Horse Lake. He told George Harris to stay with the herds and detailed another cowboy to scout the east side with Chito Guerrico. He had in mind letting Harris act as a hunting guide to Lord Coniston and Doctor Hughes, and he lent them horses for their forays, but suggested they hunt well out from the herds. By helping their rescuers, the two Englishmen felt they were doing something constructive.

About two days from War Horse Lake, Louie Courrell returned. Dunigan took him aside to remind him again about the party of Englishmen to make sure Louie said nothing about what was going on at the ranch headquarters. Dunigan was toying with the idea of sending the hunting party on ahead with Louie, but thought the older gentlemen were having a lot of fun and would rather stay with the herd. Louie reported that Ewing had hired a fresh supply of gunhands, but there didn't seem to be much preparation for a fight. Ewing had not even sent out scouts out to locate the herd. Dunigan ordered Louie to leave after he had eaten, to keep close watch on the ranch until the herds were delivered.

For the next two days, Lord Coniston and Doctor Hughes stayed around the herd as they had provided plenty of meat, and Dunigan was able to spend considerable time with them. They questioned him about Texas and the trail north, and in turn Dunigan asked about their home territory in Scotland. The older men entertained the idea of returning back down the trail with Dunigan, but discarded it, as Lord Coniston had to tend to the business of his ranch. As easily as he could, Dunigan informed them there had been some trouble with Ewing, but tried not to put the whole blame on him.

Lord Coniston said very little, but listened intently. "Mister Dunigan, one of the reasons I am here is that after Alan came over, I had my accountants go over the books in Ireland and in London, where he had managed things. There were a good many discrepancies that could not be explained. You told me once that your family were tenants on my Irish properties. Would you have any knowledge of anything there?"

Well, Dunigan thought, *the cat is out of the bag. I might as well tell him.*

"Lord Coniston, there were certain payments we had to make that had to be paid in produce, over and above the crop rental. I don't know if these went on the books or not, but I suspect not, in that they were sold at places other than where we sold the crop. There was also cottage and barn rent that most tenants in Ireland weren't forced to pay."

Lord Coniston seemed taken aback. "It is not now, nor has it ever been my policy to charge tenants for buildings that were used by them on my properties. You are sure of this?"

"It has been a long time, sir, but that is my recollection."

Then Lord Coniston wanted to know all about the cow deal, and Dunigan told him the whole story, including the fact that he had found out that Ewing and Calvin Block had acquired a ranch around Great Falls, that would run about 1,500 cows.

"Who, pray tell, is Calvin Block?" asked the old gentleman.

"Oh, Calvin is an old cattleman, who now just seems to do all kinds of things. I don't really know what all he does," Dunigan said. "But I think he is mainly in land speculation."

When they started next morning they were about five hours' drive from the ranch headquarters. Louie and Thad were back in from watching the ranch, so Dunigan sent Thad back to tell Nick to send up an additional five of his toughest drovers, and to keep Thad there. He sent Louie out about a mile from the herd to give warning, if necessary. Dunigan had twenty men with the lead herd, not counting the Englishmen, and he arranged them to react quickly in case of trouble. Dunigan was out front far enough so that he could see Louie Courrell up ahead.

About half past ten, Dunigan saw Louie stop atop a ridge and gaze downward. Louie turned and gave a prearranged signal to Pete, which meant their destination was in sight and to send the English party ahead and to loosen up in the saddle in case there was trouble. Dunigan touched his spurs to Sangre, the big sorrel, and loped forward to catch up with Louie.

He stopped beside Louie and sure enough, they were overlooking the Cameron Ranch Co. headquarters. It appeared about the same as all ranch headquarters: bunk house, barns, cook shack, pens. The only thing different was that the owner's house was some grander than most. There seemed to be quite a few people scurrying around saddling horses and getting ready for something. Dunigan counted twenty men at the ranch, so he expected about fifteen of them to be fighters.

He had them outnumbered already, and his main weapon, Lord Coniston, was nearing the spot where he and Louie sat watching. When the wagons drew abreast, Dunigan sent Louie back to tell Nick what was going on, then he rode down the ridge toward the headquarters with the wagons. Dunigan saw four riders detach from the group and start out to meet them, one of whom looked like Ewing. He thought he recognized Hansen, Ewing's cow boss, too. The other two he thought would be a couple of pistoleros. Dunigan looked up to see a cloud of dust leaving the ranch from the far side. The rider looked like an Indian.

Dunigan said to himself, *No wonder they were surprised. The Indians just reported their failure.*

Dunigan, with the two elderly Englishmen on horseback, rode on toward him, followed by their wagons. Dunigan could see Ewing clearly now, his red face shining in the sun. Dunigan kept his eyes on Ewing, watching for him to recognize his uncle. When the two groups were about sixty yards apart, Ewing's face turned from beet red to ghostly white. He stopped short, staring at the approaching riders. The other men with him stopped and turned to see what he was doing.

Ewing said something, and one of the riders detached himself, loping back to the big group at the ranch house. Then the remaining three continued toward Dunigan, whom they passed by for the Englishmen's horses.

"Uncle!" Ewing exclaimed. "I had no idea you were this close to the ranch, or I would have sent an escort for you. Your last letter was from Baltimore, when you landed."

"Don't trouble yourself, Alan, we have been in the excellent hands of Mister Dunigan and his cowboys these last few days, and they have been extremely kind to me and Doctor Hughes. We have had great adventures with which I shall entertain you later," Lord Coniston responded.

"Uncle, let us get you settled in at the ranch house. I'm sure you're tired after your ordeal."

"Thank you. We would like to get unpacked and settled, Alan, but we are quite fresh."

"Hansen, take Lord Coniston and his party to the house and unload them, and turn out their horses," Ewing said.

"No Alan, these horses belong to Mister Dunigan. Feed them, and take them back to him," Lord Coniston instructed.

As Hansen led the wagons off toward the ranch house, Dunigan spoke up. "Do you want to receive the cattle now, Ewing? We are ready to get 'em off our hands. We have given away all our steers, but I think we have about five thousand a hundred and fifty cows and thirteen hundred calves. Just tell me how you want to handle it."

Ewing pulled himself up to his full height, about five-seven. "I must see to my uncle's needs first, if you please, Dunigan. Then I will deal with you." He turned his horse and loped off toward the ranch house. Dunigan signaled his herds to stop and sent word to fix dinner.

Dunigan's crews ate and took naps waiting for Ewing. At three in the afternoon, with no sign of Ewing or his men, Dunigan rode to the ranch house to find out what the plans were. He knocked and entered the house, finding Lord Coniston, Doctor Hughes, Ewing and not so surprisingly, Calvin Block. Coniston and Hughes rose to greet Dunigan, but Ewing and Block kept their seats.

"Mister Dunigan, we were just talking about you. I'm hearing some very disturbing things about this sale, and I'm glad you're here," Lord Coniston said.

"I have a copy of the contract if you'd like to see it, milord."

"By all means, if I may."

Dunigan produced a copy of the contract. Lord Coniston took it to a desk in the corner to read it, which took a good thirty minutes, as he read it several times.

Dunigan spoke to Calvin Block and he answered in a strained but casual manner, saying he was only present to see if the drive had turned out all right. Ewing said nothing. It was obviously his plan to ignore Dunigan's presence, and to treat him as he would an inferior, which was why he never offered Dunigan a seat. Dunigan thought about walking out, but figured he might get fair treatment from Lord Coniston if he waited for him to become informed.

Just then the old man arose from his corner and walked to the center of the room. He looked at Dunigan, then around the room and said, "Mister Dunigan, please do sit down. I have some questions for you."

Dunigan found a chair.

"This contract seems to be quite specific covering the whole transaction in detail."

Ewing was on his feet. "It is a forgery, uncle, I told you. Dunigan wrote that himself after we made the deal, didn't he, Calvin."

"Calm down, Alan. I see this document is all properly notarized, even down to its registration in the County of Bexar, Texas. This document is certified as a true copy by the county clerk of that place, so if the document is a forgery, a great many people are in conspiracy to defraud me. If you didn't sign this document, whoever signed for you is a very accomplished forger, indeed."

He looked intently at Ewing, who turned his head away, muttering, "That was not the proposition we agreed to, and Calvin here will attest to that, won't you Calvin?"

Block got up slowly. He knew that if he called Dunigan a bald-faced liar and cheat, that he would have to answer to him, and he wasn't looking forward to that. "Well, you see, your Lordship, the deal was some different."

"In what way specifically, Mister Block?"

"Well, the price of the cattle, for instance, it wasn't supposed to be but $25, not $35, and they were supposed to be paid for in total when they got here. And there were supposed to be only thirty-five hundred not five thousand. You know that this ranch will only carry thirty-five hundred, so that makes sense. Another thing, we were not suppose to pay extra for calves, it's standard for calves to go with their mommas at the same price," Block finished explaining.

"So you say the whole contract was written after the agreement, and the signatures and validations were forged. Is that right?"

"Yes, uncle, that is exactly right. Dunigan made the whole thing up after we left with an agreement, and it is entirely forged," Ewing said, rising from his chair, having gained courage from Block's statement.

"Mister Dunigan, what do you say to this?" asked Lord Coniston.

Dunigan was barely holding on to his temper, but determined not to give way to the insults. "Milord, you see all the drafts and expenditures for this place, do you not?" Dunigan asked.

"I see everything over a certain amount."

"Did you see a draft to me for fifty thousand dollars dated the 27th of September, the same date as the contract, in the amount specified in the contract to close it?"

"Now that you mention it, Mister Dunigan, I remember it, but not the exact date, but around that time, and I remember it was specifically approved for payment by my nephew, and it was for cattle. If that is so, and it is, according to my recollection, why was that payment made, Alan?"

Ewing was crestfallen again, and did not rise out of his chair. He said nothing for a while, but eventually he reluctantly explained.

"Uncle, what we told you was the way we thought the deal should be done. Dunigan would not agree, so we were coerced into doing it his way, but it was not the proper way."

Block was nodding in agreement, glad to be off the hook for implying Dunigan was a liar.

"So the contract is a valid instrument?"

Both Block and Ewing reluctantly agreed by nodding.

"Then the only question I have is why five thousand cattle instead of the thirty-five hundred I have been told is all this land will carry? Did Mister Dunigan force you to take the extra fifteen hundred?"

Both Block and Ewing remained silent, trying to think of some way to explain that.

Dunigan decided to press his advantage. "I believe I can answer that, Lord Coniston. I have it on good authority that your nephew and Calvin Block have secured a ranch over near Great Falls, about a hundred and fifty to a hundred and eighty miles west of here and I am told it will run about fifteen hundred head. The numbers fit, but I don't know how that fits into the deal."

"That's a lie! You don't know that. You have no way of knowing anything like that!" Ewing screeched, leaping to his feet.

Dunigan's face was dark. "Ewing, you're an outlander, so I won't kill you, but don't ever call any man a liar unless you intend to back it up. As for the truth of the matter, I can produce a letter from Joseph Carter of St. Louis, my attorney, who examined the deed records before he informed me of that fact."

Lord Coniston stepped between Dunigan and his antagonists.

"Dear me, gentlemen, let's have none of this. Now, Alan, we will go into this later, but I am satisfied that the Cameron Ranch Company owes Mister Dunigan whatever the contract calls for, and I want those cattle received and paid for the first thing in the morning. In the meantime, I say we adjourn until 7:30 when we will meet for dinner. Mister Dunigan, please bring Mister McCurry and Mister Roussel with you. Alan, have Mister Hansen attend also."

Dunigan left and sent word to Pete and Nick about dinner

and that delivery would take place in the morning. He also included a warning to be especially watchful this night, because he wasn't sure Ewing and Block were through.

Nick and Pete met Dunigan a little after seven o'clock. They were reasonably clean, shaven, and wearing fresh but rough clothes, as was Dunigan. He had considered dressing in his good clothes, but thought he should be on a par with his herd bosses. They rode down to the ranch house and were let in by Lord Coniston's valet, much improved in health from his Indian wound.

Everyone was there when they entered and after one drink, they sat down for dinner, which was roast beef, with vegetables and all the trimmings. It turned out to be a very pleasant evening, as everyone was on their good behavior. When coffee was served, Lord Coniston opened the conversation.

"Mister Dunigan, after due consideration, I have decided the Cameron Ranch Company will honor your contract fully. I trust Mister Hansen can settle the delivery details with Mister McCurry and Mister Roussel. Does that meet with your approval?"

"Yes, sir, it does. There may be a few cows and some steers over the agreed number. If you want them I will sell them to you. If not, I'll drive them back and sell them somewhere else, probably at Fort Fetterman, as I have contracted to sell my horses there."

"I would like to buy a few of those horses if I might, Mister Dunigan, specifically two wagon teams, and the horses you lent Doctor Hughes and myself for hunting, if that is agreeable," countered Lord Coniston.

"Certainly, milord, I'll have plenty of horses left for the army."

"Yes, and we will buy the overage of cattle, too, if it's not too many."

"Well, we would like to count the cattle to you in the morning, but Mister Hansen and my men can work out the details now." Dunigan nodded to Pete and Nick, who left the room with Hansen.

"Lord Coniston, I want to give you a gift. There is a cow in the herd that led the way up here who is almost human. She is a fine animal, and will help settle the other cows. I would take her back to Texas with me if I could, but I can't, so I want you to have her. Her name is Brindy Polaris."

"Is that the beast I saw leading Mister McCurry's herd? Sort of brindle with wide horns?"

"Yes, sir, the same."

"Well, she is a fine beast and I shall treasure her, Mister Dunigan, and I do thank you. By the way, how do you want to be paid?"

"Your draft will be quite satisfactory, milord."

Coniston nodded. There was nothing to be done, so Dunigan said his goodbyes, picked up Pete and Nick, who had finished their delivery arrangements and went back to camp.

By eleven the next morning all the cattle had been delivered: 5,034 cows, 16 steers, and 1,378 calves in all, with Brindy Polaris taken off the count as a gift with the two teams and the horses. The draft came to just over $60,000. Lord Coniston himself drove off Brindy Polaris, put her in one of the pens, and hand-fed her hay and brushed her for an hour, delighted with the animal. Ewing and Block looked pretty sullen the whole morning, saying nothing. Dunigan ordered his men to pack up and be ready to leave after dinner. Then he rode down to where Lord Coniston was playing with Brindy to say goodbye.

"Mister Dunigan, this is a delightful animal, I shall treasure her and her calf as long as they live. I thank you again," he said.

"You are very welcome, sir. I just came down to say goodbye to you, and to wish you well."

"I wanted to talk to you, John, if I may call you that. I am going to take Alan back to England with me and I will need someone I can trust here. Mister Hansen seems a good sort, but I'm not sure he can do without supervision. I'm taking over the ranch at Great Falls, and he should be able to handle that, but I need a man qualified to operate both ranches. What I am asking is, would you do it?"

"I am very flattered, milord, but no, my future is in Texas, not Montana. I am to be married soon in Kentucky, and I have my own ranch in Texas, so it would be out of the question for me."

"I'm very sorry about that, for I know you are capable and trustworthy, but I do understand."

"You know, both my trail bosses are quite capable, and I would hate to lose them, but if you would like, I'll ask them if they would consider the job and if either of them would, I'll let him talk to you. One of them, McCurry, is considering taking on a family that we saved from the Indians down in Nebraska, but the other is single, and as far as I know, not tied down. What do you think?"

"From what I have seen, John, I think either man is quite well qualified. I would appreciate your talking to them for me."

"Lord Coniston, I probably need to know what you want to pay these people, and also whether you would need any of my other hands. As you know, cowboys are wanderers, but many of mine are Mexicans, and probably don't want to get too far away from their homeland. The others are mostly Confederate veterans, uprooted by the war, and are free to live where they choose."

"John, I would pay a manager here $500 a month and provide him with a home and food. The hands I would pay $60 per month, plus room and board. I think these wages are generous, from what I hear, but I demand loyalty from my employees, and I would like you to approve of any man who wants to stay."

"Those terms are quite generous, milord, and I will not recommend anyone who is not trustworthy or who would not do a good job. Give me about an hour to talk to them and I'll bring back any volunteers."

Dunigan rode back to the wagons and motioned for Nick and Pete to join him. "Coniston is going to take over the country Block and Ewing had at Great Falls and he is sending Hansen over to run it. He wants a man to oversee both places. Ewing is going back to England with him, where Coniston can watch him closer. He asked me, and I told him I would ask you if either of you wants the job at $500 a month, a house and groceries. He also will hire up to seven of our men at $60 a month, room and board. I wanted to go to you first to see if either of you wants to do it, and if one of you did, you could pick what men you want out of the outfit. I won't be hurt if either of you decides to stay, and nothing will be changed between us, but if one or both of you wants it, it's a hell of a good opportunity."

"Can we think about this a little bit, John?" Nick asked.

"I told him I would bring the volunteers back in an hour, but if it takes longer, one day's delay won't matter."

The two trail bosses moved away, talking together. After Dunigan got a cup of coffee and began to sip it, some of the cowboys drifted up and began idle chatter with him, asking when and where they would be paid, and how they would get back to Texas, and such. Dunigan told them he planned to pick up the train at McPherson and go to St. Louis. They would be paid there, and could take boats back to Texas or the train, as they saw fit. He was going to Kentucky to be married, as they all knew. He asked Abner to accompany him to Kentucky, and Abner agreed. He said he would need his regular hands at the ranch and would probably be taking cattle back up the trail in the spring, so he would need most all of them then.

Dunigan saw Pete and Nick approaching, so he got up and joined them, out of earshot of the rest. Nick started the conversation.

"John, you know I have been trying to make up my mind about Lutie and the kids, and this would be a great deal for us to start married life on, but I have been with you so long, and I have liked it plenty, and I have a little something going with you, and I would just as soon stay with you for the rest of my time, but I don't know how Lutie fits into that. Pete doesn't want to do it, he says it's too cold up here for cows. So, if you agree, I'd kinda like to take a crack at this deal up here."

"Nick, I think you made the right decision. It's a good deal, and you get to see new country. You're a mountain man, anyway, and you'll have brand new country to start a brand new life. I owe you your part of the cattle in Texas, and I'll send it up when I get it figured. You two go talk to the men and pick who you want, and we'll leave here at about two. I'll leave you a draft for wages that I owe those who are staying here, unless I have enough cash to cover it. If any of them want to keep some special horse, I'll take that off their wages, if it's all right with Lord Coniston for them to have their own horse, but only one per man, okay?"

"Right, John, I'll get this sorted out right now." Nick went over to the men to find out what they wanted to do.

"Pete, I'm glad it turned out this way. I think Nick wants to settle in with his new family, and I'll need you real bad back in Texas."

"Well boss, I'm a flatlander, and I don't like the cold. I'd be a fish out of water up here, so if you don't mind, I'll go back to Texas where I belong."

Nick and five men joined Dunigan, and they rode over to meet Coniston. Dunigan was surprised that Jacko Easton was not one of them. After all, this was new country and a new deal.

On the way back to Fetterman he asked Jacko why he didn't stay.

"I saw a big pile of wire rolls out by the barn, and you know how I feel about fences," Jacko replied.

Dunigan arranged for Lord Coniston to deduct what he owed the men joining him, and to issue him a new draft, which he happily did. He also bought the five horses from Dunigan for the men he hired. Nick explained that he had to go to Ft. Fetterman to marry Lutie and would be back in a week to take over. Coniston was delighted with all of this, as was Hansen, who had been very unhappy about the tension and potential gunplay, and was quite content to be working for a cowman again.

Dunigan bade Lord Coniston and Doctor Hughes farewell, and invited them to his wedding, which he figured would be in a month, if they would be in the vicinity. They thanked him, and said they would try.

The men were packed and saddled when he got back and they got on the trail immediately. They returned the same way they had come, figuring it was safer, for the Sioux might be a bit touchy about the beating they had taken at his hands. At the campfire that night the mood was sober and subdued, some of them missing their friends that had stayed behind, all of them somewhat awed by the realization that they had driven five thousand cattle 1,500 miles, and had come through safely. They were not home yet, but they were on the downhill slope.

They reached Ft. Fetterman on September 15th, and delivered the horses to Colonel Keller. Keller also paid Dunigan for the horses he was to ride to Ft. McPherson to catch the train, saying he had talked to Colonel Archer, and he needed them, and they would settle amongst themselves for what they got. Nick had gone to propose marriage to Lutie Grimes, and received permission to be married in the post chapel that evening.

Dunigan used the army telegraph to send word to Amanda to expect him in twelve to fifteen days in Washington County, and to make wedding arrangements post haste. He also wired Gerard Alton that he would be in St. Louis about September 25th, and that he would then go to Kentucky for the wedding, if they wanted to go along.

Colonel Keller paid Dunigan over ten thousand dollars in cash for the horses and mules, so Dunigan had enough to pay wages to his hands.

The wedding that night filled the chapel, social occasions

being well attended at frontier army posts. Dunigan threw a party for the couple afterwards, kissed the bride and the children, and wished them all luck. He gave them the wagon and team that had stayed in at Fetterman to take to Montana, and said his goodbyes that night.

That same night, Louie Courrell came to Dunigan to tell him goodbye, that he would go directly home from here. Dunigan paid him what he owed him, and thanked him overly much, but Louie said that he hadn't had as much fun in twenty years, and ought to pay Dunigan for it.

They laughed and Louie said, "Jean, you a good man, and I like you, an' you take good care of dat boy, Thad. He's gone grow up to be a real man, an' you see to it that he turn out all right. You come see Louie in Denver, now."

"You can bank on it, Louie." They shook hands warmly.

The trip from Ft. Fetterman to Ft. McPherson was as fast as Dunigan could push it, and there was no trouble along the way. It took only eight days and the horses and teams were well jaded by the time they were turned over to Colonel Archer. Dunigan explained the haste, and the reasons for the condition of the horseflesh, and Colonel Archer understood, but was disappointed because he needed the animals right away.

Dunigan and his men had only a short wait, catching an east-bound train at nightfall. Their train trip took them to Grand Island, then south and east of Kansas City, where they caught another to St. Louis, arriving on September 26th. He took his men down to the riverfront and arranged boat transport for them through New Orleans to Indianola, then paid them off.

The boat was not to leave until the 28th, so everyone repaired to a nearby saloon for a few farewell drinks, after which Dunigan sent Abner to get hotel rooms for himself and Dunigan for the night, as he had arranged to catch the boat to Louisville the next evening. Thad Scott had begged Dunigan to take him to Kentucky. He was so persistent and so persuasive Dunigan told him to come along. After heartfelt farewells, Dunigan caught a carriage to the Alton residence, arriving unannounced at about six.

He was warmly greeted by Gerard and Genevieve, who wanted a full account of the long drive and also of his plans for marriage to Amanda. Dunigan accepted a glass of whiskey and related a synopsis of his adventures. Gerard Alton already knew a great deal of the story since he had handled the financial end for Dunigan, but Genevieve was fascinated. But soon she wanted to know all about his wedding, as these things are much more of interest to ladies. Dunigan told them he was leaving the following day for Washington County, and expected to be married within a week. He asked them if they would accompany him, as he wanted Gerard to stand up with him as best man.

"I would be most honored, John, but I'm afraid we can't leave so soon. I have a lot of business to take care of, but we could follow in two or three days, which should be plenty of time. By the way, most of that business is winding up your affairs, John," Alton said, smiling.

Genevieve was a bit disappointed at not going right away, but conceded they needed to make arrangements and that they could not leave for at least two days. Dunigan then proceeded to talk over his finances with Alton, asking him to clear all of his indebtedness at various places, pay a fee to Joseph Carter, and to bring $10,000 in gold for him to Kentucky, for he planned an extensive honeymoon. Alton agreed to take care of these matters for Dunigan, and assured him he would be in Kentucky with the money in plenty of time for the wedding.

About that time, a servant appeared and announced dinner, so they repaired to the dining room and enjoyed a delicious meal. Afterwards, over brandy and cigars, Dunigan felt relaxed and happy.

"Gerard, I guess I am a rich man, and I've been twice blessed, working with good men at a hard game, and winning, and not only in wealth, but finding a wonderful woman to be my wife and mistress of the ranch I am going to build. But also in the people I have met and the friends I have made along the way. I have come a long way for a bog-Irish orphan boy from Cork."

"Yes," Alton said," but I don't know anyone who deserves it more, or who has worked harder for it."

"I do," Dunigan countered, "hundreds of them, but they didn't have my lucky star."

"Let's drink to your star and its continued shining," Alton said, elevating his glass.

"To its shining on," Dunigan echoed.

Dunigan was up bright and early the next morning, buying clothes for himself, Abner, and Thad Scott. He purchased mainly evening clothes, but did pay a visit to a jeweler, where he bought a sapphire necklace for his bride. They went by the Bank of St. Louis after lunch, to sign papers and so Dunigan could get some cash, as he was running low. He also asked Alton to bring to Kentucky some of the clothes Dunigan had ordered, which would not be ready until the next day. Alton agreed, and Dunigan's troop left, stopping to buy some luggage and to check out of their hotel. They boarded the steamboat at five o'clock. Dunigan had wired Amanda his arrival time the day before, so he felt confident they would be met at Louisville.

Dunigan and Thad shared a stateroom and Abner repaired to quarters on the lower deck. Abner didn't mind, and Dunigan nor Abner wanted to make an issue of his color.

Dunigan took Thad along to the dining saloon for dinner. The young man was dressed in his brand new hand-me-down suit, grinning proudly in his new finery. They had a sumptuous meal, complete with wine. Thad got a bit tipsy, so Dunigan sent him along to bed, then looked around for some action, as the tables has been cleared from dinner, and the card games were beginning. Lounging about, he watched one table in particular.

There were four men seated. One appeared to be a Louisiana planter or sportsman, but who could tell, things being what they had been were since the war. The other three appeared to be Yankees, probably manufacturers, maybe from Ohio. They all seemed wealthy, but were not playing for particularly high stakes. Dunigan saw no evidence of cheating after watching for thirty minutes, so he walked over, and asked if he might sit in. They agreed, and he introduced himself.

The others introduced themselves and Dunigan found out he was pretty close. They were Al Carney, an ironmonger from Cincinnati; Bill Phelps, who owned a coal mine in West Virginia; and Jim Cronin, who made wagon fittings in Maysville, Ohio. The other was Etienne DuLac, a sugar planter from New Orleans. Dunigan enjoyed himself and won about $75.

After about an hour and a half, Dunigan noticed the stakes were getting higher and one of the players, Jim Cronin, had lost some money and was becoming unpleasant. He and DuLac were pushing the stakes higher, and Dunigan decided he would get out when he could. He watched DuLac closely as he dealt the next hand, and spotted cards being second dealt. When he picked up his hand and saw he had three queens, he was immediately suspicious.

Cronin opened and was raised by Phelps, then Carney. The bet came to him for $250 and Dunigan threw in his hand, sensing a trap. DuLac was disturbed, but raised the pot by $250. Watching closely, Dunigan saw DuLac get rid of Dunigan's draw before dealing himself two cards. The betting became heated, and there was over $7,000 in the pot when Cronin called the last bet.

DuLac turned over a straight flush over Cronin's four jacks, and a full house each for Phelps and Carney. Dunigan cashed out and went on deck, not wanting to get involved in what looked like trouble brewing.

On deck, he was finishing his cigar before going to bed when a shot rang out. He went to the door, and saw DuLac holding a derringer on Carney and Phelps. Cronin was slumped over the table, moaning. Dunigan walked over and stuck his .44 Colt in DuLac's ear, telling him to drop the gun. He did, and Dunigan put his away. The captain was called and a doctor who was present came over to examine Cronin. Seeing that his wound was in the upper chest, he had him taken to his stateroom to be treated. Leaving, the doctor said that from the location of the wound, he thought he might not die, and he would send word when he knew.

The captain had arrived by then, and started asking questions. Both Phelps and Carney told him Cronin had slapped DuLac, who demanded an apology and retraction from Cronin, but Cronin jumped at him and was shot. The captain asked if they knew if DuLac was cheating and they said no, but he was winning most of the money. It was established that Dunigan had left the game before all of this happened, so finally the captain came to him. At Dunigan's suggestion, they walked off together out of earshot and Dunigan explained.

"Captain, I am to be married in a very short time and will be met in Louisville by my intended, and I don't want to get hung up in any proceedings, so I will just tell you what I know. The man DuLac was cheating. I saw him dealing seconds, and he had stacked the deck. He had just started it, but I know he was doing it so it is really a matter for you to handle unless Cronin dies, but please do not get me involved, as my life is complicated enough as it is."

"Mister Dunigan, I appreciate your position, and unless Mister Cronin dies, I'll not bother you anymore. You have my thanks," the captain said.

Next morning, a steward knocked on Dunigan's cabin door, and told him Cronin was better and was expected to live.

Dunigan breathed a sigh of relief, but then had to answer all Thad's questions concerning the night's activities, which he had slept through.

At midmorning, when the steamboat docked at Cape Girardeau, Dunigan was on the upper deck, watching the loading and unloading of freight, and he saw the debarkation of Etienne DuLac. It was quiet and without any trouble, but the captain saw him off and DuLac gave Dunigan the blackest of looks. Dunigan joined no poker games that night, and they disembarked at Louisville the next morning, Friday, the last day of September 1872.

PART IV

Epilogue

Chapter 32

Dunigan spotted Amanda and her father on the pier as the boat was docking. They waved and he waved as the boat was being tied up. When Dunigan stepped onto the dock, Amanda flew into his arms and gave him a long and lingering kiss. His head was swimming as he kissed her back and he felt peculiar stirrings from head to toes. When she finally drew away, they looked at each other for an interval, savoring each other like rare wine.

Amanda said simply, "I have missed you."

Dunigan introduced Thad and Abner. After the men brought his baggage he and the Greens got in the carriage for the ride to Bardstown, where they would turn for Fredericktown and the Green family homestead. Amanda's father had already assured Dunigan that he had adequate quarters for Abner and Thad. Dunigan also told him about the Altons, but they would probably be staying with Genevieve's family, so Mister Green needn't worry about accommodating them.

The presence of Mister Green kept Amanda's and Dunigan's amorousness in check, but only outwardly. They devoured each other with their eyes so greedily that Adrian Green was embarrassed. Amanda had set the date of the wedding for the following Saturday, which was fine with Dunigan, and the invitations had already been posted for a week, so there was no turning back. The couple discussed the arrangements for the wedding and Dunigan was told when and where to be and who was throwing the parties and all those other things a groom had to do. Dunigan asked Amanda if she would like to spend their honeymoon in New Orleans and she was delighted.

The trip to the Greens took most all day and half the night, but they arrived in good order and were bedded down by midnight. Nothing began the next day until almost 10 o'clock, as everyone was exhausted by the trip and slept late. Abner and Thad had been up for a while, wandering around and admiring the horseflesh and the farm. They were mighty impressed by the facilities and by the beauty of the horses. The manicured quality of the countryside impressed them, too, but they missed the open spaces and big sky of the plains. They also noticed that the air already had a nip in it, although it was only October 1st.

Abner had had some experience with tobacco as a child, but only experimentally. Both he and Thad were much more familiar with and interested in the fine thoroughbred horses that lived such a pampered life at the farm. Both of them even gained some knowledge of the lineage and breaking of the animals there, and would talk glibly to Dunigan about Eclipse, Matchem, and Herod.

"You boys learn about the bloodlines," Dunigan directed them, "and find out what is thought about them, and how they cross one another, for I feel like Amanda is going to want to have some good horses down home one of these days, and you'll probably be taking care of them. Spend some time learning how they care for these horses, because they take lots better care of them than we do. We depend on keeping a lot of horses, so that if one can't be used, there are plenty more to pick from, so we don't really take much care of them. That'll change if we ever have some good horses, and you'll need to know how to keep them in shape." The two horsemen agreed.

Each night that week was consumed by parties, balls, and other get-togethers. Amanda was very much the belle of all this socializing, although the "proper" Kentuckians treated Dunigan more or less like an impoverished, ignorant, country bumpkin. Dunigan didn't mind because he didn't have to pay too much court to anyone, and he wasn't jealous, either, when all the gay blades danced with Amanda and tried to squire her around the parties and dinners. A couple of young ladies paid some attention to Dunigan, as he cut a very handsome sight in his dress clothes, but he was having none of that.

As it was her last fling in polite society before moving to the wilds of Texas, Dunigan did not restrain Amanda at these parties, but she guessed he was not enjoying himself and she felt somewhat ashamed, but not enough to slow down. Dunigan did make some friends with some of the larger property owners, enjoying his time with them. Almost to a man they had courted Amanda, but failed to land her, and they deferred to the man who had.

Thursday morning after breakfast, Adrian Green commanded Amanda and John to follow him to the stables, where they were surprised to find Thad and Abner and two of the Green's grooms, each holding a haltered mare, except Thad, who held a magnificent stallion.

Adrian spoke. "This is my wedding present to you both. Amanda may prefer some of the other stock, and if so, she may trade them, but I would hope that she would not destroy our breeding here, and I think she probably agrees with my choice. These mares are all safe in foal to other studs, so that you would start with protection from inbreeding. They are yours to do with what you will, and my best wishes go with you."

Dunigan looked at the horses for a minute, then glanced at Amanda, who appeared to be about to say something. He spoke up. "Adrian, this is a magnificent present. There are probably some mares in your stables that Amanda might like better, but I think I am a better judge of what animals will be able to thrive in our not-so-salubrious climate, and I accept with gratitude and our heartfelt thanks."

Amanda had been aced. There was a mare in the stables that she loved and had raised as an orphan with her own hands, but the mare was fragile. Dunigan knew that, as did Adrian Green, and neither wanted the mare to leave her home, although Dunigan was sure Amanda wanted to take her out of love.

Amanda gazed over to the stables, then went to her father and embraced and kissed him.

"They're wonderful, daddy, the best of all your stock. We cannot thank you enough."

It was done and done well. When Dunigan looked at Thad and Abner they grinned broadly.

"I guess you know who is going to take these horses home, don't you?" They both nodded. "Well, you better get familiar with them, because they can't go any farther than Baton Rouge by boat, and you'll have to ride them from there," Dunigan said.

Abner spoke. "We been ridin' and feedin 'em, and we're real friendly with 'em, and we all gets along good. We won't have no trouble with 'em all the way to the Aransas River, no sir."

Dunigan hugged Amanda and she melted into him, glowing.

He said, "We can go as far as Baton Rouge with them, darling, as I had planned for us to spend some time in New Orleans, kind of like a honeymoon, if you would like that?"

"That suits me just fine, John. I love New Orleans, especially if I can be there with my husband, and I can see to it that your two roughnecks treat our bloodstock properly, at least as far as Baton Rouge."

All of them laughed and petted the horses for a while. Amanda then took Thad and Abner to the stables to pick out tack and equipment for the trip. She fussed over the stuff for a long time, and gave all sorts of instructions to them.

By Saturday morning, Dunigan had had all the socializing he could stand, and wanted to be married and away. His loins ached constantly and he felt he would burst from being so close to Amanda for so long without making love to her. He felt she was in the same shape, but did not show it. Gerard and Genevieve Alton had arrived for the ball on Thursday night, bringing Lord Coniston and Doctor Hughes. The Altons had met them on the boat from St. Louis, and persuaded them to come along, putting them up at Genevieve's family home.

Gerard told Dunigan they had wanted to come and hadn't needed much encouragement. The two Englishmen had captivated and been captivated in turn by the Kentuckians. Of course, the Altons were back home and knew everyone, and all of them were having a wonderful time. Lord Coniston was even having a romance with one of the unattached ladies, and was playing it to the hilt. Doctor Hughes was an interested spectator to all these goings-on, and was highly amused, but also very protective of the Earl, making sure none of it got too serious. He was genuinely fond of Lord Coniston, who he recalled, had been a consummate ladies' man in his middle years. The good doctor did not want to see his friend get involved in any foreign amorous entanglements.

The wedding was scheduled for three o'clock in the afternoon, and Dunigan had bridegroom's nerves all day, wondering if he should call it off. This being a chronic state in all bridegrooms, he finally decided as most all do, to go through with the nuptials. His only attendant, Gerard Alton, with the help of Thad and Abner, took care of all the details and everything went off on schedule. Amanda had several bridal attendants, who cared for all of her needs and one of them had her eye on Lord Coniston. Amanda and Doctor Hughes conspired to derail that romance and everyone but the disappointed lady breathed a sign of relief.

At the appointed hour, Dunigan and Amanda left the reception, dressed, and departed in a buggy driven by Adrian Green's driver. Followed by Thad and Abner with the wedding presents, they left for Louisville, arriving at their hotel in the wee hours of the morning.

It was a joyous night for them, as it was the first deep personal commitment for both of them, and as they were both very wary of their independence, it was all the more moving. Awaking in the morning found them both so satisfied and loving they almost missed the boat scheduled for a one o'clock departure.

Chapter 33

Abner and Thad had seen the horses aboard and secured, and were waiting to help the couple board. Dunigan had reserved the best stateroom for his bride and himself, and most of the luggage had already been brought on by Abner and Thad. The steamboat left only ten minutes late.

As they entered the Mississippi, there were more bright leaves on the trees than along the Ohio. The vista became more and more colorful as they traveled south, and the Dunigans spent a lot of time on deck just admiring the scenery. They were a popular couple and had invitations for dinner every night. Amanda knew distantly some of the people they dined with, and all were curious about the barbarian she had wed, but Dunigan enjoyed himself and the trip went quickly. They would visit the horses from time to time, taking tidbits of carrot or apple. The animals seemed to enjoy their trip and had been brushed to a high gloss by their traveling grooms.

Dunigan and Amanda, although sociable with the other passengers, spent most of their time alone, quietly exploring one another. The other passengers remarked at their seeming so much in love at an age when love becomes complacent, but the couple seemed more like they were just past teenage puppy love, rather than approaching maturity. Both Dunigan and Amanda were sure each had found their own true and ordained life partner, and bliss followed them like an aura.

The trip passed so quickly that almost before they realized it, Thad and Abner were unloading the horses at West Baton Rouge, with both Amanda and Dunigan fussing over their care. Thad and Abner allowed that they were well versed in horse care, and left almost before the steamboat cast off for the last leg to New Orleans.

It took less than a day from Baton Rouge to New Orleans, where they checked into a hotel in the French Quarter. Amanda had taken care of the rooms, as she had spent a lot of time there. Dunigan joined her after he had seen to further passage home. Luckily, there was a boat going directly to St. Mary's on October 17, and Dunigan booked passage, arranging to have the four crates of wedding presents, mostly silver, china and household goods they had brought from Kentucky, delivered to the boat for St. Mary's from the riverboat. On his way to the hotel, he sent a wire to Pete, telling him to have a buggy and a wagon for him at St. Mary's on October 21st.

Arriving at the hotel, he was shown a lovely suite of rooms overlooking the 'Vieux Carré.' Amanda was waiting for him with a stack of invitations from friends of hers in town who had learned of her marriage. Dunigan looked mournful when she told him the first one was a dinner party that evening.

"Amanda, I know you like all this party stuff, but I am about done in by it. If I don't have to look at those dinner clothes before next June it will be soon enough."

"John, you have had the boat trip to recover from the wedding parties and these are dear friends of mine and I simply can't refuse them. I am tired of all this, too, but we have to do it. Besides, they are all customers for our horses."

"All right, Amanda, but I warn you, my society manners are wearing a bit thin, and I might revert to barbarism any minute."

"John, I know you will do just fine." She reached up and kissed him, which led to tickling and giggling, which led to more.

That night at seven, they took a carriage to the home of Etienne LaRoche, a beautiful, old four-story house. The home was blazing with candlelight. They entered the house on what seemed to Dunigan the second floor. All the guests seemed to know Amanda and were very cordial to Dunigan, the ladies especially. All the men were connected somehow with cotton or banking, and almost all were of French extraction. They were interested in Texas, mostly from the point of view of raising cotton, but were somewhat curious about the cattle business. Some of the bankers had handled cattle financing and Dunigan related the story of how he and Alton had kept the cattle mortgaged, to keep them from being stolen. They were very pleasant, cordial people, and Dunigan liked them, but they were what he thought of as "soft" people.

There was plenty of champagne and Dunigan enjoyed meeting the upper crust of New Orleans. Amanda, of course, was the belle of the party. One couple, the Armand DuPards, were horse people and invited the Dunigans to the races the next day, so they had another social engagement to fulfill.

Next day at the New Orleans race course, Amanda and Dunigan had won the first two races, mainly because of Amanda's knowledge. In the third race they decided on a $100 bet on a long-odds horse and Dunigan went to place it with the oddsmakers in the infield. As he approached the bookmaker he had been betting with, an argument between the bookmaker and another man became loud and abusive. As always, Dunigan was cautious, and when he was near, he saw that the man abusing the bookmaker was none other than Calvin Block.

Dunigan had already decided to back away when Block turned and recognized him.

"Dunigan!" he yelled.

Dunigan guessed he had to face Block sooner or later, so he stopped and held out his hand.

"Good to see you again, Calvin."

"You ain't gettin' off that easy, you son of a bitch," Block snarled. "I had a chance to make a real fortune, and you made a mess of it. I'm gonna kill you if I get a chance."

"You have used that name on me before Calvin, and I have warned you about it. Don't do it again," Dunigan said quietly, trying to calm the situation.

"You know what you did? I had that land at Great Falls, two railroads, maybe three, were coming together there and I could sell it for a fortune. All I had to do was to get the cattle there to prove it up, and I stood to make hundreds of thousands. You made a mess of it and you're gonna pay."

So that's what it was, thought Dunigan. *He must have found out about the railroad junctions from some politician, gone to Ewing, and they did it together.* Dunigan knew there must have been substantial acreage involved to pasture 1,500 cows, but two or three incoming rights of way and the junction itself would use a lot of land, too. Moreover, the rest could be sold at reasonably high prices because of its proximity to the junction. He had indeed messed up a very profitable transaction.

What Dunigan could not and probably never would understand was why Ewing and Block couldn't have paid for the cattle they needed. It would have cost them less than fifty thousand in all likelihood, but perhaps neither could come up with the money, and perhaps Ewing was afraid to pull a fifty-thousand-dollar trick on his uncle. As far as Dunigan knew, Block would have trouble getting that much from banks in Texas and Kansas, but there were always individuals who would invest. And if they knew the whole picture, they would buy in, instead of financing.

Maybe it was the oldest reason of all, greed, and the pair's unwillingness to share the profits, even though there would be plenty of money to go around for everybody. That, Dunigan decided, was the real reason, because he knew both his adversaries were avaricious in the extreme. Greed had led them to overestimate their ability to get his cattle with any of their schemes and to underestimate Dunigan's ability to defend his herds.

Dunigan noticed Block was well on his way to being drunk, so he decided to end the encounter. Turning on his heels, he started away, only to be knocked to the ground by a blow from Block's cane. When he got up, he found himself surrounded by Louisiana gentlemen, as was Block. The Creoles sensed an opportunity to foment a duel, the standard method for resolving differences in New Orleans society.

Armand DuPard immediately became Dunigan's second, and Block picked a gambler to be his. The two of them went into a huddle as Dunigan rubbed a big knot on his skull. Block was yelling that he didn't care about any duel, he would kill Dunigan right now, if someone would find him a gun. The Creoles were careful not to let that happen, as they enjoyed the socializing connected with duels, and soon DuPard and Block's second were at Dunigan's elbow.

"M'sieur Dunigan, as your second, M'sieur Allard and I have arranged that the duel shall be at dawn tomorrow at Bayou d'Arc. Does that suit you?"

"If I have to, that suits me. But I had just as soon forget the whole thing."

"Non, m'sieur. You are the aggrieved party, so you have the choice of weapons. What will you use?" DuPard asked.

Dunigan glared at Block, who averted his eyes, then to no one's surprise, he chose pistols.

"Et bien, Monseiur Dunigan, I have a fine set of pistols for your use, or you may provide your own."

"I would be most grateful, M'sieur DuPard, for your

weapons, as I have only my personal revolver with me and I understand the code allows only one shot," Dunigan said.

"That is just so. I will arrange for a carriage at four o'clock to take us to Bayou d'Arc, and I will bring the weapons."

"My thanks, M'sieur DuPard."

Dunigan saw the bookmaker at the edge of the crowd and walked over to place his bet. The man looked at him somberly as he took it, but said nothing.

He went back to the stands to tell Amanda, but she had already been informed. There were tears in her eyes.

"John Dunigan, are you going to widow me before I am really married?" With that she broke into tears and hugged him.

"Amanda, the only way Block is going to kill me is to back shoot me before I get out to the dueling ground. Don't worry about me dying, I'm gonna live for a long time yet." Dunigan held her until she quit weeping, reassuring her all the time.

Amanda wiped her eyes in time to see the horses off and they watched to see their horse win, driving by a neck over the favorite. Their horse had gone off at twelve to one, so they were $1,200 richer, but more important, Dunigan saw it as a sign that his luck still held.

As he collected his money from the bookmaker, the man said, "I hope your luck holds, Mister Dunigan, for I do not like this Mister Block, and I would be careful with him."

Dunigan nodded, made his way back to the stand to collect Amanda, and they went back to their hotel, as he did not feel like being among people anymore that day.

They had a quiet supper in their room and Dunigan tried hard to reassure Amanda of his ability to survive the duel.

They made love that night. Amanda approached it with quiet desperation and Dunigan held her in his arms until finally she slept. Awakened by the hotel staff at three, he drank some coffee, meeting Armand DuPard's carriage precisely at four.

The ride to Bayou d'Arc took over an hour, during which time Dunigan examined the lovely matched dueling pistols. They were an engraved pair made twenty years before in Liège, Belgium, for Armand's father. A precisely balanced set, they had been lovingly cared for and were cased with their accessories in a polished mahogany chest, with powder, shot and caps. They were single-shot percussion pistols, of .36 caliber. For the balance of the ride, DuPard instructed him on the fine points of the dueling code as practiced in Louisiana.

They arrived at Bayou d'Arc just as the sun's red ball was showing in the east. Block and his second had just arrived, too, as well as other spectators. One, Justin LeClerc, seemed to be in charge and called the duelists over to instruct them. Dunigan tried to get the whole thing called off, and Block seemed to want to as well, but the Creoles said Block would have to apologize abjectly to do that, so that ended it.

LeClerc was very precise in his instructions. He told them to stand back to back with cocked pistols. He would count ten for ten steps each. On the count of ten they would both turn and fire. Any premature fire would result in both seconds and himself shooting to kill the offending party.

LeClerc supervised the loading of the pistols, whereupon Dunigan and Block each selected one. They stood back to back and LeClerc began to count, Dunigan and Block taking one step at each count. After the count of eight, Dunigan heard a shot and instinct took over. He whirled and fired, and a small red spot appeared a half-inch above the plane of Block's eyes. Two more shots rang out as the seconds missed, for Block was falling backward. Calvin Block was dead before he hit the ground.

Dunigan had felt a tug at his coat with the first shot and found a hole where his coat was pulled out by his upraised arm. He breathed a sigh of relief and retraced his steps to Block's body. He shuddered at the waste of a life for no good reason, and asked Armand to take him back as soon as possible.

They left soon after, Armand talking the whole way about Block's shameful behavior, but Dunigan added nothing to the conversation. He thought he might have let Block live if instinct hadn't taken over so completely, but decided it was probably for the best, as he would eventually have had to deal with Block.

He thanked DuPard for all his help, and leapt out at his hotel, running to his room, where he found his red-eyed bride. He held her in his arms for a long time as she finished crying and was silent.

She stepped back and looking into his eyes said, "John, don't you ever bring me back to this town."

By midafternoon, Amanda had recovered and was her gay self again. They had another dinner party that night and though Dunigan was in no mood for any of it, he had become the current lion of Crescent City society because of the duel.

It was like that for the next few days. Parties every night and sporting events by day. Dunigan was worn ragged. The night before they were to leave, a couple took them to the opera. Amanda was in her finest dress and jewels and Dunigan in his evening clothes, as they were ushered to a box at the opera house. Dunigan fell asleep during the second act, and didn't awaken until the fat lady finished singing.

On the way back to the hotel that night, Amanda looked at him tenderly. "Cowboy, it's a good thing we're leaving tomorrow, cause you're all used up."

Tired as he was, Dunigan could not fall asleep. A nagging thought that he had killed Calvin Block from vengeance and not necessity kept him awake for hours. Maybe he hadn't tried hard enough to settle it without gunplay, but the more he thought about it, the more he concluded that there would be a bone of contention between them always, and it would have to come to the same conclusion some day. He never doubted the outcome, but he wished it had been Ewing rather than Block.

Dunigan just made it to the boat in time the next morning. Amanda found their cabin and moved in. She was the *Crescent Queen*, powered by steam and sail. It would take about four days to St. Mary's, and she was taking a load of lumber and hardware there, picking up hides and glue at Rockport. The ship was rarely out of sight of land, sailing not far out in the Gulf.

Amanda studied the land most of every day, wanting to know more about her new home. Dunigan told her it was all flat and featureless and uninteresting, but she looked at him with the same expression she had on their first boat trip. She was sure she could see far beyond the coastline to the eagle's nest and the panther's lair. He felt a surge of pride. Amanda was a woman who could ride his lucky star by his side.

Dunigan missed having his navigation instruments, but knew his position from constantly checking the charts on the bridge. He could see from the course that they were probably going inside the barrier island from the Gulf at Aransas Pass, then beat north to Copano Bay and St. Mary's. Once inside, Amanda would be able to judge the land more accurately, but Dunigan already knew it had been a wet fall from the amount of grass on the islands, and that there had been no early frost, so the grass was green everywhere.

Chapter 34

The boat lay outside the pass all night on October 20th, the captain not wanting to navigate the shallow water in darkness, but by breakfast time, the *Crescent Queen,* was through and headed north for the passage to St. Mary's. They could see the wharves and buildings at Rockport as they passed and Amanda inquired about the town. Dunigan told her what little he knew, relating some of his adventures sailing in his youth. The boat docked at St. Mary's at five o'clock, and Dunigan could see about five men with horses and a wagon.

Pete Roussel, Michael O'Grady, Lem Bracken, and Abel Castro were there to welcome the new Patrona and Dunigan. He introduced Amanda all round and each man had something nice to say. Michael O'Grady was last as he was holding the reins of a fine-looking blood bay mare.

In a clearly rehearsed speech he said, "Mrs. Dunigan, we have heard that you are a fine horsewoman, and we have a present for you from all the hands. Of course, the mare belongs to Mister Dunigan, but we all had a hand in breaking and training her for you, and if he'll let us, we will buy her for you. We did buy the saddle and tack, and it is our wedding present to you with our best wishes."

Amanda took the horse's reins and started to examine her. Dunigan took Pete aside to say, "Gimme five bucks, Pete, and the deal's done, okay?"

"That pony's worth more 'n five bucks, John. It wouldn't be right."

"Okay, ten will do it, but that's my last offer."

Pete put a ten-dollar gold piece in Dunigan's hand and they

all turned back to Amanda and the horse.

Abel Castro gave her a leg up onto the sidesaddle and she started walking the mare around. She was calm and gentle and responded to every signal Amanda made.

Dunigan spoke. "Amanda, I think you'll want to ride her to the ranch, as it will be more comfortable than the wagon. Pete paid me for her so she's all yours. I may have to charge you for feed and care, but as of now you own her lock, stock, and side-saddle. We might as well be going, if we're going to make the ranch by dark." Dunigan mounted the wagon and they were on the way.

Abel Castro was driving the wagon, and as usual, silent as a tomb. Dunigan watched the mounted group as they moved ahead. It reminded him of bees gathering honey as they jostled for position to talk to Amanda.

She was enjoying all the attention she was getting, plus checking out her mount. They even had a race, which Amanda won. Dunigan could not tell if they let her win, but suspected they did. She was at her most charming and quickly all three fell in love with her. Dunigan tried to get some information out of Abel, but all he could get out of him was that rainfall had been adequate and that there was plenty of grass for the winter. Dunigan finally gave up and just watched the countryside.

Pete Roussel finally gave up the contest for Amanda's attention and came to ride beside Dunigan.

"Boss, everything at the ranch is in good shape, and I have been over to our old camp below the Nueces, just in case you want to trap some steers for next year. Surprisingly, there are still quite a few steers and it didn't show much activity over there," he paused and then continued. "You didn't tell me to, but we are having a party tonight. We invited everyone around. I guess there'll be maybe two hundred people there, probably about the time we get in. Pablo Mendoza is barbecuing two steers and there will be plenty to drink. We all talked it over and it seemed the thing to do. I hope you don't mind."

"Did you tell Amanda?" Dunigan asked.

"No, it's supposed to be a surprise, but I thought I better tell you."

"Don't tell her, Pete. We'll let it surprise her."

"Pablo's wife and the rest of the ranch women have the place spic and span and the screens are all on, and everything is working in the house. They got that well dug out by the oak mott where you wanted it. You know where you're thinking of building a house?"

"That's good news. By the way, Pete, I am going to take some cattle up the trail next year, so you better figure on trapping steers this year in the Nueces country. How soon can you start?"

"Next Monday, boss."

"Okay, Pete, see to it. It looks like I'm going to be tied up about a week or more being newly married. By the by, have Thad and Abner showed up?"

"Haven't seen 'em yet, Boss."

"Amanda's father gave us three mares and a stud for a wedding present. Thad and Abner are bringing them from Baton Rouge. They are really fine horses, probably the best out of one of the best thoroughbred stables in Kentucky. I kinda figured they would beat us back, but not by much."

"I imagine they still might. They'll sure miss one hell of a party if they don't."

"They got all the partying they could manage up in Kentucky, same as I did!" Dunigan laughed.

Pete then filled him in on what had happened at the ranch, all of which seemed favorable. Good rains, plenty of grass, and a good number of steers on which to build a herd for Kansas. He reported a quiet trip home and that he had plenty of good hands to gather wild stock below the Nueces. Michael and the others at the ranch had all the horses they would need in a fit and gentle condition.

Dunigan was well pleased, as Pete had only been back for two weeks and seemed to have everything in hand, even thinking ahead for next year. He was also proud of the men who had been left behind, who seemed to have done everything that needed doing. He determined he would give them some kind of a bonus in line with what he gave the Montana drovers.

Pete went on to tell Dunigan about what had been done at the ranch. They had cut and put up post and rail fences and corrals, painted the barns and sheds and put in a garden that grew things other than pinto beans. The miles fell behind them swiftly as they talked and watched Amanda and the others. About two miles from the ranch house, Dunigan began to smell beef barbecuing.

A little later, Amanda dropped back. "John, what is that marvelous aroma?"

"That, my dear, is our welcome home party. The entire population may be eating and drinking on me tonight, but to answer your question, it is the aroma of beef being barbecued by a most excellent cook, Pablo Mendoza."

"A party, you say. What are you thinking of, John Dunigan? My clothes are filthy and so am I. I don't suppose I could have a bath. This is most inexcusable, John. Why did you even think of it?"

"I had nothing to do with it, Amanda. All of the young men you have been busily enchanting put it together. You can brush off the dust and wash your face when we arrive and everything will be fine, my darling."

Amanda stared at him imperiously, turned and galloped back to her slaves, tongue lashing them for their parts. From a distance, they all appeared properly contrite.

When the little group breasted the hill overlooking the ranch, it appeared half the country was there already and more buggies were coming in from the east all the time. Dunigan yelled to Michael to come to the wagon.

"Michael, let me borrow your horse, as I should ride in at Amanda's side, don't you think?"

"Yes, sir, I do." Quickly, they changed places.

Taking his place beside Amanda, Dunigan felt a surge of pride that was all-encompassing. She sat her horse like a centaur, as if she were growing out of the saddle. The horse was calm but alert, doing exactly the right things at the right times. He had no doubt that if she ever decided to sit astride, she would soon be breaking horses.

As they neared the ranch, they saw that most of the guests were surrounding one of the corrals that had been built while Dunigan was away. They could see four horses in the corral, so they supposed that Thad and Abner had arrived with the bloodstock. It was just starting to get dark, but there were lanterns all over the place, and Dunigan could hear some music, so they had even hired a band. He and Amanda rode directly to the new corral and dismounted, handing over their horses to the other riders, who would unsaddle them and care for them. They were surrounded on every side by well wishers, but quickly checked to see that the Kentucky horses were in good condition. Amanda disappeared to freshen up, accompanied by Pablo Mendoza's wife and daughter, both of whom quickly assumed a proprietary interest in her.

Dunigan was engulfed around the corral by the horse fanciers, as almost all cowmen were. Everyone commented that three mares were not enough to keep the stallion busy, and most offered to provide dams to expend the stallion's excess capacity. Dunigan replied he would sell some service, but only if he approved of the mares. This went back and forth until Dunigan because exasperated.

Dunigan cried out to all, "Please, gentlemen, I just got home with a new bride. You all know me and know I will try to accommodate you, but I have only one new stud. I can't breed all the mares in Texas with him. Give me a little time to work it all out, will you?"

Most of his friends quit pushing, but a few persevered. When Dunigan ended by refusing to talk of it even these left him alone. He finally got a drink for himself, and the questions turned to the drive and what he had found on the northern ranges. As he was explaining, a hush came over the crowd. Looking toward the house, Dunigan saw it was caused by the reappearance of Amanda, seemingly fresh, in changed clothes, looking radiantly beautiful.

The whole crowd left Dunigan and moved toward her. Dunigan raced to her side, kissed her, and began the laborious process of introducing her to, seemingly, the whole population of Refugio County and its neighbors. Amanda was at her most charming, and even some of the wives went away enraptured. This lasted for almost an hour and the lanterns had all been lit. Dunigan and his bride got to eat before the dancing started, and then Amanda was in constant demand.

When Dunigan rescued her after an hour or so, she had dark sweat stains on her dress. She sat down panting and Dunigan refused to let anyone else take her away. After that, the people started drifting home and by midnight almost everyone was gone. John and Amanda walked over to spend their first night together in Texas, and those who were still upright left them alone.

The house was in proper order for the newlyweds and they both fell into bed and to sleep. The inauguration of the home would wait until morning.

Chapter 35

unigan, always an early riser, tiptoed to the kitchen before six to tell the Mendoza ladies to let them sleep a while longer. He crept back in to bed, but Amanda stirred a bit and murmured to him. He rolled to her and they kissed, moulding their bodies to one another. A bit later they arose to the delicious aroma of bacon frying and coffee boiling. Evidently, the ladies had surmised that breakfast would be wanted soon.

After eating a big breakfast, John and Amanda enjoyed one more cup of good boiled coffee. Amanda was not looking forward to unpacking all the household goods they had brought from Kentucky. She was eager to see the country around her.

"John, I don't want to unpack now. I want to look at this country of wide open spaces and that sea of grass I saw some of yesterday."

"Amanda, you must organize the house, Pablo's women will take care of it for you, but they want to know what you want done. I want to show you the country myself, anyway. I will be back here at noon to eat, and then we will go looking around, okay?"

She seemed satisfied and Dunigan followed her into the kitchen to help her around the language barrier. Being a well-educated young lady, she had studied Latin and French and could limp about in Spanish. Dunigan soon left to confer with Pete and Michael.

"Pete, send a couple of men over to the house to help with the heavy stuff, will you? Michael, tell me about our horse population and the cattle, too."

Dunigan found that he had over eight hundred steers to start his herd with and enough horses and mules for the drive north in the spring. Michael had already tried to horn in on the new Kentucky horses, but had been held off by Thad. However, Michael had already picked fifteen mares to be bred to the thoroughbred stud. Dunigan was sure he was going to have to do some refereeing, but it was a two-man job anyway. Michael showed Dunigan the new horse he had trained for him: a blue roan that was a brother to the filly he had sent to Major Layton the spring before. Dunigan rode him a bit and put his stamp of approval on him, telling Michael to have him and the mare they had trained for Amanda ready after lunch.

"By the way, what did she name that filly?"

"She named her Concondin, Mister Dunigan. I don't know what it means, but the mare seems to cotton to it."

"Pete, would you ask Pablo to let Rosa and Elena help at the big house for awhile, till Amanda gets settled and we decide what we want to do. We may want to build a house over at that oak mott on the river."

"I don't think we have anything to say about it, boss. They have taken over and we couldn't move 'em with blasting powder. Neither can Pablo, so we're all stuck with it."

"It'd be nice if everything could be settled as easy, wouldn't it, Pete?"

"Yeah, it's nice that some things turn out right, whatever we do. I just hope it don't make Pablo mad. Good camp cooks are scarce and hard to keep happy."

"Well, figure to take him over to cook for the cow hunt, maybe that'll settle everything down."

"Okay, boss, I was kinda figuring on it anyway."

They talked about all the things happening, how the carpetbaggers seemed to be leaving Texas, grass, the cow herd on the home ranch, pens to be built. Pete had heard of a couple of blocks of land bordering Dunigan's that were on the market, but Dunigan had been given the same word at the party the night before and resolved to complete the transaction soon. Satisfied that everything seemed to be in good shape, Dunigan dismissed them and walked back to the house, as it was nearing dinner time.

The house was in an uproar, crates being opened, linen, silver, and crockery being carried back and forth. Amanda was standing in the front hall ordering everybody around and everybody scurried to do her bidding.

"Oh, John, I don't know what I should do. We need so many things, but we have so much to do with. I'll have to go to town to get material for curtains, and some rugs. Oh, I guess I better be making a list."

"Is my dinner ready?" he asked.

Rosa answered quickly. "Momentito, patron. No más que diez minutos."

"Bueno." He sat down in the one chair that wasn't piled high with things from Kentucky.

"John Dunigan, what do you mean, coming in here and disrupting everything, calling for your dinner. Can't you eat in the ranch kitchen? We have a thousand things to do, the least of which is to feed you," she bridled.

"Amanda, my love, I have promised you a look at the ranch this afternoon and I have made arrangements to do so, but I am hungry and you could give these people time to do the chores you have already outlined, so let's have something to eat and then ride out. I have some very important things to talk to you about."

Mollified, Amanda told everyone to break for dinner, but to be back to get everything unpacked and stored. They went into the dining room and ate leftover barbecue hash for dinner.

"What was it you wanted to talk to me about that was so important?" Amanda asked.

"Later, darling, when we are riding," Dunigan said with finality, and they finished their meal.

Michael and Thad had their horses saddled and ready when they left the house after eating. Michael assisted Amanda up, and both boys started to mount their own ponies. Dunigan stopped them. "Boys, Mrs. Dunigan and I want to ride alone. You take care of your other chores this afternoon. There is plenty to do with the outfit leaving Monday."

Riding off toward the river, Dunigan talked about his ambitions for the ranch and the two of them, then turned to a more specific subject.

"Amanda, the old ranch house is solid and sound and you have seen enough of it to know what we need to do if we are going to live and raise a family there. We will have to add some rooms and enlarge it if we stay. Of course, it is good to be close to where everything else is, so that is a plus. If we want to build a house for ourselves, then we can relocate. I have plenty of money to do this, and also to provide quarters for servants and such, but it would be our place, rather than the business head-quarters. What do you prefer?"

"First of all, John, I can make a home where we are now, without wasting a lot of money on a grand mansion, at least until we have children, which may not be far off." Dunigan looked at her sharply, and thought he saw a glow to her that hadn't been there before. *It's too early to tell,* he said to himself, but the glow was still there.

Amanda continued. "I would like us to be separated more, because even though I love all these people, there are a lot of them, and I have had experience with this at the farm. I know we'll get involved in all their problems and such, but I think it would be good if we were separated from them, even if it's only a mile or two. I would like to see the places where we could build before I make up my mind."

"I have found only one place, Amanda, but I think it is the most beautiful spot on the ranch. I even had a well dug there last summer, and they tell me the water is plentiful and sweet. It's only about a half mile from headquarters, so it is plenty close for me and for your security when I'm gone. However, we will have at least one family out there with us, so that will be company for you. It is also closer to Refugio, but I'll let you look at it before you decide. If you don't like it, you can look for some other place."

"I'm sure the place will be perfect, John. You know your ranch better than anyone and I'm sure you have scouted it thoroughly. I'll just wait till we get there."

They rode on, not saying anything, Amanda absorbed in handling her filly. John was studying her more closely, seeing if he was imaging the emanations that seem to come from women when they approach motherhood. He was not sure, but he felt that before another month passed, she would be pronounced pregnant. His spirits soared.

He saw the mott long before they could really see the site. He could tell she had spotted it, too. They rode round and round the site, and finally stopped in front of the mott of large old live oaks.

"John, it is perfect. It is so beautiful here, and I do want to build here, but I don't want a house from Kentucky, I want one that is native to right here. A one story with a gallery all round, just like all the houses at headquarters."

Dunigan was sure now. The glow she gave off had to be impending motherhood.

As they rested, sitting on their horses, she talked about how the house should face, how the rooms were to be arranged, and so forth. Dunigan noticed a small bunch of young cows off about a hundred yards. They appeared to be some of the first offspring from his Herefords, showing their first pregnancy. As he watched, one detached herself from the group and walked toward them. She was a two-year-old heifer getting ready to calve for the first time, red with a white spotted face and just a trace of brindle on her body. Her horns were wide, and just starting to curve inward, but she showed plenty of the blocky, meaty body characteristics of her Hereford sire. She walked up to within twenty feet of them, as if to say, "This is my place, I hope you like it here, come whenever you want."

Dunigan whooped with delight. Brindy Polaris's daughter started, but did not run off, and Amanda looked at him in surprise.

"Amanda, that's Brindy Polaris's calf. You know, the cow I told you about, the one that led us all the way to Montana!"

Amanda dismounted and walked out toward the heifer, stopping short, so as not to spook her. "You and I, we shall be friends. We are going to build a house here, and we want you to visit anytime you can."

The cow looked at Amanda with her gentle liquid eyes, nodded, and walked back to her little herd.

Dunigan's star was still in the heavens. Brindy Polaris had left her mark, as would John Dunigan. He was sure now.